EVERYTHING CORGI

WIT AND WISDOM FOR LOVERS OF CARDIS AND PEMS

A BOOK TO BENEFIT CORGIAID

Financial Support for Cardigan and Pembroke Welsh Corgi Rescue

Second Printing: March, 2003

Credits

Editor: Cindy Read

Design and Typesetting: Nancy Matzke Moncrieff

Cover: Illustration: Chris Vrba; Layout and Typesetting: Robert Hartman

Concept and Distribution: Peggy Neumeier

ISBN: 0-615-12183-7

http://www.corgiaid.org

CONTENTS

INTRODUCTION

Welcome to *Everything Corgi: Wit and Wisdom for Lovers of Cardis and Pems*, a book created to celebrate two enchanting and thoroughly endearing dog breeds and to benefit CorgiAid, a nonprofit organization that helps with extraordinary expenses and medical treatment for corgi and corgi-mix rescue.

Most of the contributors to this book met on Corgi-L, the Internet's largest e-mail list and Web site devoted to these magic big dogs in little dog bodies. On Corgi-L, we ask questions. We answer each other—at length—sometimes out of professional knowledge, sometimes out of our own experiences, always out of love for our corgis. We share triumphs, funny stories, and tragedies, from arrival of a puppy or litter to the last journey home to the Rainbow Bridge. We write stories in corgis' own special language, corgese. We plan picnics and parties and get-togethers at shows, and when we finally meet in person, we happily recognize each other as family. For each of us, the very best corgi in the world, whether a champion show dog or a corgi-mix rescue, is the one who fills our house, our heart, and our life with joy.

For the past three years, we have been creating ways to raise money for CorgiAid, sometimes as simple as a jar for contributions at a picnic, other times as complex as the twice-yearly online auction, our first collaborative quilt, and now this book. Many of the book's authors are experienced dog trainers, breeders, veterinarians, or competitors. Others are simply fortunate to share their lives with one or more of what we sometimes call "bunny butts" and "swishy tails." In writing, each drew on her own experience and knowledge, as well as on the wealth of information on the Corgi-L Web site (http://

corgi.ncn.com) and in the list archives. This book would not have been possible without the dedication of all the contributors and the collective wisdom of everyone on Corgi-L for the past eight years.

We all hope that *Everything Corgi* brings you information to think about and use, pleasurable reading—and perhaps even a tear or two. The corgis and corgi mixes whom CorgiAid will help because of your generosity join in a collective aroooo of thanks.

Cindy Read, Editor

Nancy Matzke Moncrieff, Designer

Peggy Neumeier, Concept and Distribution

August 2002

To be born Welsh
is to be born privileged...
Not with a silver spoon in your mouth,
But with music in your heart
and poetry in your soul.

Cathy Santarsiero

ALL ABOUT CORGIAID

by Nancy Matzke Moncrieff

The CorgiAid Mission: CorgiAid exists to provide a framework for support of rescue efforts for Cardigan and Pembroke Welsh corgis, and corgi mixes, for the enhancement of animal welfare and the betterment of mankind.

Financial Support for Cardigan and Pembroke Welsh Corgi Rescue

CorgiAid is a non-profit organization that helps fund medical and other extraordinary expenses of those who rescue corgis and corgi mixes. If a rescuer rescues a dog that needs veterinary care for heartworm, bad teeth, or other problems, CorgiAid pays the bills. The dog gets the treatment it requires to regain health and be placed in a loving home without requiring the rescuer to pay from his or her own funds. Without CorgiAid, the hardship of a continuing financial drain on the rescuer would cause many to stop their much-needed work.

CorgiAid is a 501(c)(3) non-profit organization run by volunteers from their own homes or workplaces. The low-overhead operation allows almost all of the donated funds to be distributed to cover the expenses of the rescuers. The organization has a board of directors, operating officers, fund-raising operations, and a grant committee that reviews applications for funds.

CorgiAid doesn't do direct rescue; it neither has dogs in its care nor directly helps those looking to adopt or place dogs. Instead, CorgiAid supports those individuals or organizations that provide this service. When people in search of a dog or who need to place a dog approach Corgi-Aid, we refer them to the CorgiRescue mailing list or organizations that can directly help them.

Accomplishing this mission requires the help of many others. Let's take a look at how CorgiAid works.

How CorgiAid Works

Corgi lovers fund CorgiAid through their tax-deductible donations. Each year, many people donate corgi-related items to auctions benefiting CorgiAid. Breed clubs and other organizations run raffles, pass the hat at gatherings, or donate some proceeds of their own fund-raisers. Vendors donate portions of the sales of corgi or dog-related products. Individual families donate as a memorial to a deceased pet, or often "just because." The sum of these small, heartfelt donations allow CorgiAid's existence.

Rescuers of eligible dogs submit an application that includes a picture of the dog and an itemized list of anticipated or actual expenses. The grant committee, upon ensuring the request is within CorgiAid guidelines, authorizes the treasurer to send the needed funds to the rescuer.

As CorgiAid does not have sufficient funds to care for all dogs, it requires that the dog be in rescue and be predominantly or entirely a corgi. Applicants to CorgiAid must be rescuers, not permanent owners, of the dog. A dog in rescue has no permanent home. It is in foster care, by either an individual or an organization, possibly because it was turned over by an owner who no longer could care for it, had been found as a stray, or was rescued from a puppy mill or other detrimental conditions. How ever it got to the rescuer, when the dog is healthy enough, it will be placed in a permanent home; the rescuer's job is to take care of the dog and locate that home. A picture of the dog allows CorgiAid to ensure the dog is a Cardigan Welsh corgi, a Pembroke Welsh corgi, or a dog of mixed breeding that shows predominant characteristics of one or both of these breeds.

CorgiAid currently limits the reimbursable expenses to medical and extraordinary expenses. All medical expenses, such as inoculations, spay/neuter operations, orthopedic or skin care, heartworm preventative, tests, treatments, dental care, and so on, are reimbursable. Any other expense is up to the judgment of the committee. Relatively routine expenses, such as shelter fees, boarding, food, identification tags or chips, collars, and crates, are generally not reimbursed. An exceptional expense, for example a high transportation cost required for rescue, may be reimbursed. Please see the CorgiAid Web site for the most current grant guidelines.

Behind the scenes of these transactions, the officers of CorgiAid keep the organization operating efficiently and legally, and the board of CorgiAid meet through a mailing list, conference calls, and Internet meetings to set the policies of CorgiAid, meet all state and federal requirements of a non-profit corporation, and keep the business healthy.

It took an effort to move from a great idea to a viable organization. Here's what happened to bring CorgiAid into existence.

CorgiAid's History

CorgiAid started with a pup that paddled instead of walked. In the summer of 1998, a friend contacted Caroline Leibich, a reputable Arkansas breeder of corgis, to tell her that she had come across a purebred Pembroke Welsh corgi pup that would not stand or walk. The questionable breeder of this pup was willing to give her to the friend with the understanding that if she was healed and bred, they would split the profit. With no intentions of breeding, the friend rescued the eight-week old female pup, and began, with Caroline, to determine what needed to be done.

Caroline wrote to Corgi-L, an e-mail mailing list for corgi fans, and let them know of the pup's progress. A Little Rock vet referred her to Louisiana State University, where x-rays revealed both hips and patellae were fully luxated; Heidi would need expensive femur surgery to be able to walk.

Heidi's plight touched the hearts of many of the Corgi-L subscribers, and Tori Warden, a co-administrator of the list, volunteered to start a fund to pay for Heidi's expenses. She set up a "raffle" that gave donators a chance to win corgi-related prizes. This effort and the generosity of many raised more than $2,000 to help Heidi. Heidi had her surgery, gained the ability to walk, and was placed in a loving home. And there was more than $1,000 left over!

Pleased with the success, the administrators of Corgi-L formed a panel chartered with the task of establishing a permanent "Heidi Braveheart" fund to help corgis. This panel struggled to define the use of the funds, the administration of the fund, and all the other business obstacles that seem to get in the way of charitable wishes. One final obstacle caused them to fail: they could find no way to incorporate legally and leave the funds under the control of a mailing list with variable membership.

In July, 1999, members of CorgiRescue, an e-mail list run by Millie Williams for those who rescue corgis and corgi mixes, raised a question: whatever happened to those funds? Caroline Leibich said that they remained with her, and she would like to distribute them. A group of volunteers started the effort again and incorporated as a business, using the leftover funds as starting capital, while maintaining close informal ties to the Corgi-L mailing list. CorgiAid, Inc., was incorporated in January 2000 and received IRS permission to operate as a 501(c)(3) non-profit organization. Heidi, as mascot, proudly appears on the logo.

Heidi becomes a logo

Since then CorgiAid has received and distributed thousands of dollars to aid many dogs in need of medical help. It's amazing what one pup, and the hearts and efforts of many generous folks, can do. If you'd like to join this effort, please read on to see what you can do to help.

HOW TO HELP CORGIAID

The easiest way to help CorgiAid is to send money. Please send your check or money order to:

CorgiAid
c/o Joyce Trittipo, Treasurer
4038 Cherokee Dr.,
Madison, WI 53711
USA

Although you should check with your tax professional for your individual situation, CorgiAid is a recognized 501(c)(3) charity and your donation should be tax-deductible on your U.S. income tax.

You can help CorgiAid while shopping, too. Many merchants donate some of their proceeds to CorgiAid. Check out the shopping pages on the CorgiAid Web site, www.corgiaid.org, or on the Corgi-L shopping page, http://corgi.ncn.com.

While you're at the CorgiAid Web site, read about upcoming CorgiAid auctions. Peggy Neumeier, the CorgiAid fund raising chair, runs periodic auctions whose proceeds benefit the company. You can help by donating items to be auctioned, or by bidding on them!

You can be a fund-raiser for CorgiAid. Many donations come from other organizations that include CorgiAid as part of their fund raising by donating some of the funds raised by their efforts, or requesting direct donations to CorgiAid from their members. The next time you are with a group of corgi lovers, pass the hat!

You may wish to establish a memorial for a beloved pet. CorgiAid will post a picture on their Web site as a reminder of those loved ones who have departed.

If you'd like to help the CorgiAid staff, please contact them at yourfriends@corgi-aid.org. The volunteer effort that runs this organization always needs help! Thanks.

HOW TO GET HELP FROM CORGIAID

If you have rescued a corgi or corgi mix with intent to re-home the dog to a permanent home, you may be able to get financial grants from CorgiAid to help cover the medical expenses, or other extraordinary expenses, associated with the rescue. You can find an application at the CorgiAid Web site, www.corgiaid.org, or by requesting one through e-mail at yourfriends@corgiaid.org. Be prepared to send receipts or estimates, and a picture of the dog. Don't hesitate to apply: CorgiAid exists to help rescuers.

MORE INFORMATION ON CORGIAID

If you have other questions about CorgiAid, please check the Web site at http://www.corgiaid.org, or contact them at yourfriends@corgiaid.org.

The Moncrieff's Banshee

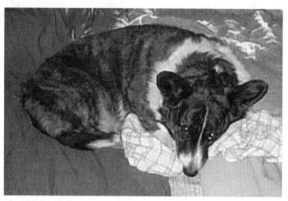

"Mom, I'm bored...get off the computer!"

FINDING YOUR CORGI

ASK THE BREEDER ABOUT CORGIS

by Millie Williams

Tailed and detailed…

What do you ask when you are choosing your dog from a breeder? Millie Williams, a breeder of Pembroke Welsh corgis, tells us here.

Why should I ask the breeder specialist? What's this whole thing about pet shops, puppy mills, and backyard breeders anyhow?

Breeder specialists are unique people who have devoted a great deal of time to the promotion and protection of their chosen breed. This means that they strive to produce the best dogs that they can. They make sure the physical, mental, and genetic health of the puppies they produce are as good as they can make it. Great care and thought goes into each breeding, not just "put Sally in with Bob over there so they can make puppies." They are proud enough of their dogs that they get out and compete at dog shows with their dogs on a regular basis, to show other breeders what they have produced.

Pet shops are not a good way to go. Usually they are staffed by minimum wage workers who "love animals" but don't have a clue as to how to match you up with the correct dog. You wish to buy a corgi? Fine, we have one right back here. What if the corgi breeds are totally wrong for you and your family? The bottom line is all that matters, how much the shop will make off the sale of the puppy. These dogs are produced by commercial breeders, that is, breeders who are out to make a profit. No time is spent searching for the right stud dog, he always lives right there or over at a neighbor's, who also produces puppies for sale. Although there are "puppy farmers" out there who take good care of their "stock" (and it is considered livestock by both the farmers and the USDA), they still do not do the genetic tests and learn about each dog as an individual, to say nothing of the general conformation of the parent dogs. Most dogs produced this way somewhat resemble a corgi to the untrained eye, but in reality have as little to do with a well-bred corgi as a labrador does to a golden retriever.

Roger Caras said it best at the Westminster Kennel Club dog show a few years back:

"The dogs you see lined up here are not from a puppy mill. Not a one of them. They are produced by breeders who specialize in their breed. Not one of these dogs you see competing today came from a pet store."

On the surface, pet shops do appear to care about their livestock. If there is a problem, you can bring the puppy back. They offer "guarantees," but this is of little use if you must return the puppy and take another possibly defective puppy in its place. The puppy that is returned is nearly always destroyed—after you have fallen in love with it.

There are more classes of breeder. "Backyard breeders" refers to kindly folks who raise a litter or even several litters a year. They love their dogs and take good care of them. But they will tell you that hip dysplasia is not a concern in their line; they do not test the eyes annually. You are expected to sign your check for the puppy and leave, and if there is a problem, please don't call. They are also considered puppy producers. They also charge nearly as much as a breeder specialist does. I have seen families who specifically bought a dog to breed to put money in the bank to pay for their child's college education. Do you think that much care or concern was placed into the production of puppies from these breedings?

What is the difference between Pembrokes and Cardigans?

These are totally separate breeds, developed apart. It is thought that the Pembroke, which is the "de-tailed" type, came from southwest Wales. They are more spitz looking in type, more likely to bark, more sound sensitive, just as many spitz type breeds are. They bear a remarkable resemblance to a breed called the Swedish Vallhund, which, in turn, bears a resemblance to the Norwegian Elkhound. It is believed that there is some terrier influence in the breed, due to some early photos showing a dog that looks somewhat like a solid red Jack Russell Terrier type with prick ears.

As a general rule, Pembrokes are generally more active and bouncy than Cardigans, and they've never met anyone they don't like. As with all breeds, there is a general tendency to some traits, but the Pembroke personalities run from a very sweet and laid back dog to a very tough terrier attitude, with every shade of personality in between. It's best that you tell your breeder exactly what you expect from your new dog.

The Cardigan corgi is a more ancient breed, having its roots with the Teckel type of dogs, from the European continent. They are longer and heavier dogs and have quite a twist to their front legs, which you also see in dachshunds, another Teckel type breed. They tend to bark less but are still sight-oriented, as are many herding breeds. The personality of the Cardigan also has many shades of gray, from a calm yet interested easy going Labrador type of personality, to a very shy and retiring individual.

Both breeds are easy to train. One must, however, be smarter than the dog. Sometimes this is difficult. Both have a well-developed sense of humor and love to play. Most individuals of both breeds do best with a job of some kind, even if it is nothing more than accompanying its people about their daily routine. Both breeds will sulk and hold a grudge if scolded, particularly if it is about something that the dog does not understand.

Both breeds make excellent pets.

What health issues should I be concerned with?

Pembrokes have three main problems for which there are tests, with several others for which there are not yet tests. The health problems for which there are tests are hip dysplasia, a variety of eye problems, and von Willebrand's disease.

Hip dysplasia is a potentially crippling disease that currently affects about 20% of the Pembroke population. The good news is that it can be managed successfully in this breed, for the most part. You would want to keep your dog trim, keep toenails short, and make sure exercise is moderate. If the degree of hip dysplasia is very severe, then hip replacement surgery could be considered. The best thing to do is to be sure that both parents have an OFA (Orthopedic Foundation for Animals) number; the breeder should be able to provide you with copies of these reports. This does not mean your pup will never be affected with this problem, but knowing the parents are sound will stack your bets that the pup will have less of a chance of getting it.

There are a number of eye problems in Pembrokes, including persistent pupillary membranes, retinal folds, and cataracts, as well as progressive retinal atrophy. Every dog of breeding quality should have an exam by a veterinary ophthalmologist once a year, to be sure it is free from these problems. Again, copies of the actual eye exams (not just a CERF registration) should be provided to the new prospective owners. In addition, a breeder specialist will usually provide an eye check on the puppy you are interested in.

Von Willebrand's disease is a clotting disorder, much like hemophilia in humans. There is a simple DNA test that can be done to the parents on a one-time basis. The three degrees are Clear (does not have the disease), Carrier (has the ability to produce the disease), and Affected (has the disease and will produce the disease). Parents should be clear/clear or clear/carrier. Carrier bred to Carrier will produce 25% affected puppies. Carrier to Affected will produce 75% affected puppies. I cannot think of a single breeder anywhere who would use an Affected dog in a breeding program.

Cardigans are prone to some of these problems, too. In spite of what some may tell you, according to the OFA site (www.offa.org) Cardigans do get hip dysplasia. Many breeders seem to feel this is not true and will tell unsuspecting puppy buyers this. Both parents should be checked and cleared. Also be sure to see the actual eye exams on both the sire and dam of your prospective Cardigan puppy. Cardigans are also prone to progressive retinal atrophy (PRA), as well as other eye diseases. PRA can now be tested for in this breed by a DNA test that works like the von Willebrand's test for Pembrokes. They also have Clear, Carrier, and Affected status. PRA is carried through the bloodline in the same way described for von Willebrand's in Pembrokes.

Do not buy a puppy from a breeder who is unwilling to do these tests, tells you that their line is "free" from these problems, or has no idea what you are talking about.

What are the good points and the bad points about this breed for my family?

Any breeder specialist that you contact should be able to go on quite a lecture about these points. Every breed is not perfect for every person. As much as I love my breed, I do realize that trying to send a corgi home with someone who really is more suited for another breed is a big mistake. I talk with people for quite a while to be sure that this breed fits their situation and family and that they are not in love with just the "look" of the breed, but the total breed.

Is there a contract? What are the terms? Will you take a puppy or an adult back?

Good breeders protect their puppies, their new owners, and themselves by giving a contract with a clearly written out warranty. The terms may vary. The contract should clearly point out the names of the parent dogs, their AKC numbers, and the birth date of the puppy. There should be a clause insisting on spaying and neutering and a time frame in which to do so. If a breeder wants to include "Breeder's terms," meaning that they want you to breed the pup at some point and they will get all or part of the litter back, be aware that this is a risky and unprofitable venture and may even result in the life of your puppy being forfeited. If a breeder likes this dog well enough to breed it, then they should keep it themselves. Many people think they will be getting a "free" dog, but that never seems to be how it works out. If a breeder wants to use a male pup at some point as a stud, then be aware that some of the benefits of neutering a male dog are that they will not mark in the house or display other hormonal-related problems, such as dominance, fighting, and humping on guest's legs. You would have to deal with these problems; the breeder would have your money and the use of your dogs. It can also be inconvenient to have your pet leave you to be bred.

Any breeder should take back a dog of his or her breeding at any time in the animal's life. This should be clearly spelled out in the contract. If taken back within a few weeks of purchase, all or some of the money should be refunded. If the dog is given up by you and returned to the breeder at a later date, then don't expect a refund, but do expect to pay the shipping costs. The breeder will make every effort to find this dog a new home that is suitable for it. If the dog has a problem that is covered in the contract and the breeder offers a refund or replacement puppy, you should be allowed to keep the original dog unless there is some reason that you don't want to. Then it should be returned to the breeder. You will have grown attached to the original dog, and if you are willing to care for it, then you should be allowed to do so.

Do you exhibit your dogs at dog shows? How often? May I see some photos of you showing your dogs?

There is a class of breeders out there who "regularly" attend a dog show—once or twice a year. This allows them to tell people, "we proudly show our dogs at shows." A breeder specialist, however, will attend many shows throughout the year to try and earn championships on their dogs. "How often?" is a very important question in this case. Any breeder specialist will be glad to drag out dozens of photos of them showing their dogs, to the point you may become bored of looking at them! If they cannot document that they exhibit their dogs, then be wary.

But I just want a pet, not a show dog. Why do I have to ask these questions?

There is a world of difference between a "pure bred dog" and a "well-bred dog." A well-bred dog is carefully produced by a breeder specialist. Much time is spent looking at prospective sires at many dog shows and specialties (a type of show where only that breed of dog is exhibited.). The breeder specialist will have scrutinized the pedigree and will know many of the dogs as individuals, not just a cute name on a piece of paper. They will know who has had their hips cleared for hip dysplasia and who has clear eyes. They will know the temperaments of these individuals. They will know the genetic background of these animals and will be breeding the very best dog that they can. As a consequence, there will be several other pups in the litter. Just breeding a show dog to a show dog does not yield all show dogs. There will be pets, very correct, very pretty, that will resemble the parents closely. These pups will be offered to people who desire a wonderful companion. This way you will get exactly what the breeder was striving for to improve their line, with the added bonus of having a well-bred pup. This contrasts sharply with the so-called breeder who has

two or three dogs and has a litter "to make some extra money" or "so the kids can see the miracle of birth," two reasons that should make you run in the opposite direction.

How are the puppies raised? How do you socialize them? Where are they raised?

Most breeder specialists raise their pups in the home, although I know a few who raise them in a kennel building for various reasons. I prefer to send people to someone who raises them in the home. The reason is obvious. A pup raised in the home has many opportunities to see normal household activities, such as the dishwasher making noise, the TV, the heater kicking on and off. They are taught at a young age that chewing on furniture or carpeting is probably not a good idea.

Socializing is the single most important thing your pup can experience. He or she should have been started on short rides in the car, being petted by strangers (to them), and seeing new and different things in the world every day. This takes dedication on a breeder's part, to take the time and effort involved in getting the pups out to new situations. The more new things a pup sees, the more he can deal with when he gets older. Many pups never go anywhere at all, and when it is time for a change in their lives (going to a new home, going to obedience class, going on a family vacation), the dog cannot deal with this and is very unhappy.

How old are the puppies' parents? Are the mother of the pups and some other relatives available for me to see?

When you go to view a litter, these are important things to ask. A dog cannot have a permanent OFA (hip) reading before he is are two years old. Ideally, this should be the youngest age that you should see being bred. Some breeders will breed a couple of

14

months earlier when a youngster has finished its championship, but this does not happen often. If a breeder has not shown a dog, ask why. The answers should make good sense to you. Sometimes you may hear the excuse that dog shows are political or some other nonsense. This is not true, or I would never win! Older females, over age eight, should never be bred, in spite of whatever rationale you are offered. This is also against many breed clubs' code of ethics.

If a breeder is happy with her dogs, there should be some close relatives running about. This will give you a good idea of what your future pup will turn out to look like, as well as their temperament and personality. Often a breeder will tell you that this pup will look just like Aunt Micah over there, or that her Grandma Panda was just like that at her age.

At what age do you allow your puppies to leave home?

Although many codes of ethics say that eight weeks is the youngest that a pup should go home, in my opinion as a dog trainer, ten weeks is the minimum and twelve weeks is even better. Dogs learn an incredible amount of social skills, both canine and human, during this time with their littermates, mother, and other adult dogs and people. These skills are difficult to learn at an older age. Nearly every dog I see in my obedience classes who was taken at a very young age has problems in social skills that we have to work around in training.

What clubs do you belong to?

It is desirable for the breeder to belong to clubs that promote the particular breed that they breed. This is so they may stay in contact with others who are like-minded and so that all can work together to promote and preserve their breed. There are

regional clubs and national clubs. When you ask a breeder this question, follow up with a letter or phone call to the club involved. Ask if they are indeed a member and if there is a code of ethics for this club that the breeder is expected to follow. Ask for a copy of this code, and read it carefully. Then be sure and ask about points in the code when you speak to the breeder again.

Casual pet breeders and commercial breeders do not bother joining these clubs, although they might lie about belonging to them.

What do you think will be the general temperament and activity level of this pup?

All pups within a certain litter will have differences in their personality, temperament, and activity level. If you have a quiet home and want a dog that will sit nicely with you while you study or read, then do not take home a super lively and wired puppy. You also would not want to take a very quiet pup to a home with lots of activity going on. Your breeder will know which pups would be more suitable for your situation, and they will spend a long time getting to know you and what your life is like so that they may choose the best pup for your family. A good breeder sits and watches their pups and knows which is the busy pup, which is the cuddly pup, which is the Einstein of the litter. This takes much interaction on the part of the breeder. Trust their judgement on which pup will be the best match for you.

Do you raise other breeds?

Oftentimes, this can be a warning sign. People who raise multiple breeds will find it impossible to display excellence in raising one particular breed. If there were numerous breeds at the home, my advice would be to keep looking for another breeder.

When you go to view a litter or a particular dog, keep your eyes open.

Are there things that don't sit right with you? Are there answers to questions that don't make sense? Do you feel you are not seeing everything? Use your eyes and your nose to see and smell cleanliness. The yard should be picked up, as well as the runs if the dogs are kept in runs. Puppies should be spotless. It is okay for a puppy to smell like a puppy, but they should not smell bad. Eyes should be bright and clear; there should be no discharges from the nose. Pups should be lively and friendly, coming happily up to you for attention. Resist the urge to take the little shy one in the corner. Look for pups that look you in the eyes when you pick them up and that allow you to hold them. Pups may be a bit tired if they have just eaten or laid down for a nap, but when company comes, they will make an effort to say hello and be friendly.

Don't ever buy a pup just because you "feel sorry for it" or "had to get it out of there." The breeder of this pup won't care. They will just breed the poor parents again to make a cash crop, hoping for more suckers just like you to stop by.

Will you provide me with references, including your veterinarian?

If they will, then one of the most important questions to ask a reference is "Would you buy another dog from this breeder?" You would be surprised how often the answer is no. The owners do not want to be disloyal to their dog; they love their dog and would never give it up. But did they have health problems with the dog or other problems with the breeder? Did they see things at the breeder's home that they did not like? Was the breeder helpful when there was a problem?

The veterinarian will also be a good person to talk to. Has he seen problems in the line that he is concerned about? Does this person have a good reputation in the community? Would he feel comfortable buying a dog himself from this breeder?

Where do I start to look for a breeder specialist?

You can check on the Internet at www.pembrokecorgi.org for a list of national club breeders and also for a list of regional clubs in your area that will have lists of breeders. For Cardigan corgis, check at www.cardigancorgis.com.

Questionable "breeders" have built a number of Web sites on the Internet. Be very wary of buying a dog from one of these sites. Some are legitimate, and some really sound good but are nothing more than fronts for casual breeders or commercial breeders.

I hope that the above questions and answers will be of help to many of you in your search for the perfect corgi, tailed or de-tailed!

Millie Williams and Barney Anne

CARDIS AND PEMS

by Cindi Nicotera and Chris Vrba

In "The Tell-Tale Tail of Two Corgis," Cindi Nicotera outlines the history and differences between the two breeds of corgi. Chris Vrba, in "If Corgis Were…," characterizes the breeds by an insightful set of analogies.

THE TELL-TALE TAIL OF TWO CORGIS

To get a tail or not to get a tail, that is the question. If you think the only difference between a Cardigan Welsh corgi (Cardi) and a Pembroke Welsh corgi (Pem) is the tail, read on! If you are interested in making the commitment to being owned by a corgi, the following information should help you understand a little more about the origins of the breeds, the breed standards, their temperaments, diseases they may be prone to, and so on.

History

The Cardigan is the older of the two breeds and is descended from the Teckel family of dogs (the Teckel family also produced the Dachshund). The Cardi is believed to have been brought to Wales by the Celts around 1200 B.C. The Pembroke is descended from the spitz group of dogs, who were brought to Wales by the Flemish weavers. The spitz were crossed with the Cardigans to produce the Pembroke.

From 1925 until 1934, the British Kennel Club exhibited both the Cardi and the Pem as a single breed. After a great deal of dissatisfaction among the dog owners, the Kennel Club separated them into two distinct breeds in 1934. They are both members of the herding group.

The Cardigan came to America in 1931, when Mrs. Roberta Bole imported a pair for breeding. Mrs. Roesler brought a breeding pair of Pembrokes to America in 1934.

To Tail or Not to Tail

Most people assume the only difference in the two breeds is the tail. So what are the major differences in the breeds? The Breed Standards for both the Cardigan and the Pembroke can be found at the American Kennel Club Web site, www.akc.org. The following is a brief synopsis of the differences in the breed standard.

The Cardigan, at 10.5 to 12.5 inches, is slightly taller at the shoulder and heavier (30 to 38 pounds) than the Pembroke, at 10 to 12 inches (30 pounds.). The heads of the two corgis are very similar in their foxy appearance, but the Cardigan head is wider and more muscular with a more prominent nose. The Cardigan ears are large in proportion to its head, where the Pembroke has medium size ears. As might be expected, the Cardigan is longer and heavier-boned than the Pembroke, and the forearm of the Cardigan is curved more than the Pembroke's in order to fit around its rib cage.

Ah—the tail…The Pembroke tail is docked as short as possible without causing it to be indented. The Cardigan shows its tail in full glory and should have a fox-like brush that reaches below the hock.

Colors provide another area for differences in the two breeds. The Cardigan has a wider range of acceptable color, as it can have all shades of red, sable, brindle, and blue merle. Pembroke colors are red, sable, fawn, black, and tan, with or without white markings.

The characters of the two dogs are similar in that they are intelligent, hard working, highly trainable, and extremely dedicated to their beloved humans. The differences tend to lie in their temperament. The Pembroke is considered to be bolder and more outgoing than the Cardigan, who is reported to be more "laid back" and wary of strangers. Of course, talk to corgi owners and you will probably get as many stories as there are dogs! Just as we are all individuals, so are our fur kids. For an interesting look at previous discussions on Pems vs. Cardis search the archives on Corgi-L (list members only: listserv.tamu.edu/archives/corgi-l.html; enter Pembroke and Cardigan in the subject search box). There isn't a great deal of information, but there are some amusing anecdotes. Both breeds are happiest when they have a job to do and are involved in some activity, such as obedience, herding, or agility.

Hereditary Diseases

Hip dysplasia (HD) is a developmental disease of the hip joint that can appear in corgis. It may affect one or both of the hip joints. The symptoms can vary from mild to crippling in extreme cases; treatment may require surgery. The best way to protect yourself and your potential puppy is to go to a reputable breeder and ask if they have done hip testing.

Several eye conditions appear in both corgi breeds. Again, a reputable breeder will have their breeding stock tested and not use these animals for breeding. Progressive retinal atrophy (PRA) is the most common of the eye diseases in corgis. It is a degenerative disease and will eventually cause blindness in the dog. PRA typically shows up in dogs over two years old. There is currently no treatment available for PRA. Secondary glaucoma is also seen in corgis. It is also congenital and usually does not show up until the dog has fully matured.

Von Willebrand's disease is an inherited bleeding disorder, similar to hemophilia but less severe, that can appear in corgis. It is important to know if your dog has it in case surgery is required. The good news is that it is seldom fatal.

There are other conditions that affect corgis. You can learn more from the Pembroke and Cardigan FAQs written by Corgi-L cofounder Perrine Crampton, which are on the Corgi-L site, corgi.ncn.com.

The average life span of the Cardigan is an average of 12-15 years; the Pembroke average is 11-13 years. Take good care of your corgi, and you will have a faithful and loving companion, Cardigan or Pembroke, for a very long time

Cindi Nicotera with Fletcher

...and now, for a slightly different look at the topic

IF CORGIS WERE...

The difference depends on the dog, of course; it's hard to make generalizations. Folks seem to agree that Cardis are more reserved and Pems more outgoing—and then you meet the bouncy, pouncy, "HEY-I'm-a-Cardi-glad-ta-meetcha-canI-lickyourface" and the Pem who eyes you from a respectful distance and says, "SO pleased to meet you, old chum." But here's what I'd say. Keep in mind, I'm thinking mature corgis, not pups.

If corgis were...

CARS...

- a Cardi would be a stable late-model sedan, much loved for its steady reliability.
- a Pem would be a peppy little economy model, ready to vrrrrroooom.

BIRDS...

- a Cardi would be an owl, ever watchful, wise, and observant.
- a Pem would be a magpie, flitting here and there and storing away bright, interesting objects.

HOUSES...

- a Cardi would be a ranch-style dwelling in an established neighborhood, with a wide expanse of lawn and a charming deck (with a bar-b-que, of course).
- a Pem would be a loft apartment in the city, decorated in an eclectic blend of traditional and Bohemian styles.

VACATION DESTINATIONS...

- a Cardi would be a national park like the Grand Canyon, or a Rocky Mountain ski resort.
- a Pem would be Walt Disney World or Las Vegas.

CITIES...

- a Cardi would be Seattle, Madison, WI, or Washington, DC
- a Pem would be San Francisco, New York City, or Miami Beach.

ISLANDS...

- a Cardi would be Martha's Vineyard or Nantucket.
- a Pem would be Key West.

STORES...

- a Cardi would be Sears: plenty for the workman, but with a softer side, too.
- a Pem would be Wal-Mart: a bit more hype, a bit more busy, but carrying pretty much the same stuff.

COLORS...

- a Cardi would be rich, constant earth-toned shades of brown, forest greens, and royal blues that speak of depth and thought.
- a Pem would be the color of springtime: fresh greens, sky blues or the colors of autumn foliage.

SHAPES...

- a Cardi would be a rectangle: solid, useful, and ever present.
- a Pem would be the bouncing ball you follow in karaoke.

MUSICAL INSTRUMENTS...

- a Cardi would be a deeper woodwind: maybe a sax, maybe a clarinet.
- a Pem would be a bright, brassy trumpet.

MUSIC...

- a Cardi would be classical or new age, with perhaps a touch of oldies pop in playful moments.
- a Pem would be jazz and show tunes.

FAMOUS MUSICIANS...

- a Cardi would be Louis Armstrong or Barbara Streisand.
- a Pem would be Elton John or Cyndi Lauper.

ACTORS...

- a Cardi would be Gregory Peck or Katherine Hepburn.

- a Pem would be Tom Hanks or Sally Field.

TALK SHOW HOSTS...

- a Cardi would be Oprah
- .a Pem would be Rosie

Chris Vrba
with Quentin and Riley

SPECIAL DOGS, SPECIAL PEOPLE: THE WORLD OF RESCUE

by Pat Pearce

Homeless dogs need special help to find their way to a new life. Pat Pearce, a breeder and long-time rescuer of corgis and other dogs, tells about special dogs that have found help and informs us about what is involved in rescue.

I am involved in corgi, corgi mix, and French bulldog rescue. I am a part of For-Paws Corgi Rescue, and I am also a breeder of Pembroke Welsh corgis and French bulldogs. Rescue is something that I am very committed to and I get a big kick out of finding these homeless "kids" a super forever home.

I have always done rescue. In the beginning, it would be the stray pup along the road or the dog that came up to the house and wouldn't leave. My mom kept saying, "No more dogs!" but she always let us keep the next one. And now there's the stray pup at Wal-Mart, or the call from a neighbor asking, "Can you take this dog?"

SOME RESCUE STORIES

Starr

My first formal corgi rescue was a pretty red-headed tricolor Pem that we named Starr. She came to us just before Christmas and was a rare jewel. She was overweight, heartworm positive, and as sweet as could be. She stayed with me a while, was treated for heartworm and lost weight, and then went to a lovely forever home in North Carolina. I hear from her mom every so often, and she tells me how well Starr is doing and about the nice long walks she and Starr take.

Toby

Toby came to me one day when the shelter called. Could I please come get this dog? He was a bit older, had been abandoned by his owner and was **terribly** unhappy in the shelter. When I got to the shelter, I found a small black and tan guy who looked like he was a chihuahua/corgi mix. He had hot spots and long nails, and was not a very happy camper. After a few days here in a somewhat calmer atmosphere, he began to come around. The hot spots went away, and he regained his confidence. He went to a new home with another small dog. I got a card at Christmas with Toby in a Christmas hat looking very dapper, and a note from his mom about how loved he is.

Midnight

Midnight came to us from Tennessee. A friend was driving through to Oklahoma and brought her to us. Midnight was a flat-coated retriever/corgi mix. A wonderful dog, but she was black and acted like a retriever. We eventually placed her through a rescue group in New York. We had people going to that area who took her with them. But Midnight never made it to the New York foster home. She was adopted on the spot by pre-approved people who think she is just darling. She is a lap-sized Lab type, at 35 pounds. We hear from her, and she is the delight of her family.

Genie

Genie came to us in a most unusual way. A Golden/Lab rescue group contacted us. They had found this funny-looking dog running in traffic in Manhattan. They had worked with her and decided that she was part corgi. All of their people really liked her, but she had these **very** strange behaviors. Could we take her? They had someone coming this way, so she got to ride as extra baggage in an airplane to Oklahoma. I brought her home and watched her for several days trying to determine what sort of bizarre behavior she had. Then it dawned on me. She was acting just like a corgi! She did the alligator thing with her teeth and herded the other dogs. I had a big laugh, then wrote the Golden people and explained typical corgi behavior. She was adopted by a nice family when her new doggy brother-to-be wrote out the application for adoption (too cute!), and went to live near Houston.

These stories are about the "easy" ones. The dogs had neither real health concerns nor major temperament problems. Thus, they were fairly easy to place, and we didn't have any real issues to deal with.

But then there are the true, hard-core rescues.

The Story of Buddy, Now Cisco

One of our problem dogs came to us named Buddy. Buddy's mom called rescue and asked if we could take him. She had a new job, was moving out-of-state, and felt it would be better if Buddy had a new home. She didn't want to take him with her. Buddy had been purchased as a five-week-old puppy. He had lived with his family, a single woman and two teen-aged boys, since then. Buddy was six and a half years old.

As the rescuer talked more with the woman, she discovered that the owner was really afraid of the dog, as were her children. Buddy was not happy, spending most of his days in the utility room by his own choice. When the rescuer went to get Buddy, she learned more of his story: that he had been purchased very early, that he would only walk on this leash, eat out of that bowl, and so on. The owner gave the rescuer all of Buddy's stuff, his toys, bowls, food, treats, leashes and collars, and even his doghouse. And this is where it really went sour.

The rescuer put Buddy in a wire crate in her van, loaded all his stuff, and listened to the owner. This was the only home Buddy had known since he was a tiny puppy. When the rescuer got to the vet clinic where Buddy was to stay overnight, he threw a fit, and not just a little fit. He pitched a **big**, bouncing-off-the-walls **fit**! In fact, they could not even get him out of the crate. They finally fastened leashes to the crate so they could carry it inside without

getting bitten. The rescuer called me and asked what to do.

Now, mind you, this is an experienced rescuer who has rescued big dogs, and she had never before seen anything like this. When she told me the whole thing, it came to me that this dog was scared out of his mind. His owner had given him and all his possessions away, had felt anxious and guilty about doing it, and our Buddy had picked up on all that. He didn't know what was happening, but he was very sure it wasn't good; so, he did the only thing he could. He threw a fit.

After much discussion, I told the rescuer just to leave him in the crate, as I would be taking him the next day anyway. I would give him a chance, knowing that if worse came to worst I could always put him down, but I felt I needed to give him that chance. We transferred him to my van the next day, again using leashes attached to the crate. I had thoroughly cleaned a run for him before I left to pick him up, knowing that I might not be able to get back in that run for a long time.

When I got him home, I carefully carried the crate into his run, closed the gate behind me, and said, "Well, I wonder what I do now?" Buddy had been in that crate for over 24 hours with no food or water, and no potty breaks either, so I put the crate door next to the water bowl, and slowly opened the crate door. He still had his Flexi lead attached to his collar, so I told him, "Wait while I get your leash." He stopped and I unhooked the leash and put it in my pocket. He stepped out of the crate. I closed the door behind him, picked up the crate and walked out the gate with it while he was getting a drink. Whew! I'm thinking, "That wasn't so bad."

He had calmed down a lot from the day before. I had talked to him all the way home, two hours, in a soft voice, just telling him about what he would find when we got home. And maybe, since I was calm, it helped him to be calmer too.

I feel that this boy had been terribly afraid the day before, much like any of us would be if some strange person took us away from the only home we had ever known, and away from the only people we had known, and then put us in a strange cage in a strange place, with no explanation. No doubt we would have panicked too.

Buddy immediately got a new name, Cisco. It was something completely different from the one he had in his unhappy former existence. Cisco, a beautiful red headed tri, was in an indoor/outdoor run by himself. There were other dogs in runs on either side of him. For several days, as I fed Cisco twice a day, I made a point to talk with him and to praise him. I also made a big point of playing with and petting the dogs around him, and talking in a happy voice to them, and, of course, they were all happy to see mom. And I just sat in his run at different times, and talked to him. He would come close to me, and allowed me to pet him. He was in no way aggressive toward me—not sure of me, but not aggressive.

It became evident pretty early that he was a beta-type dog and not alpha at all. So when his former family had let this mild-mannered dog take over the household—of course, no one else was in charge—the corgi in him made him be the one in charge. It was totally against his innate submissive nature. No wonder he was so unhappy there!

The other big problem was that he had **no** idea of how to interact with other dogs. So I made sure that he got to watch the dogs around him. You could see that he was interested in them, but wary too. I eventually put a sort of dominant bitch in with him, one that was big enough to defend herself if need be, a little dominant to keep him in his place, but not a super-alpha. The first experiment was not very successful.

He tolerated it for a couple of days and then became very upset and growly; so, I took her out and allowed him to watch the other dogs interact some more.

A couple of weeks later, I put the same bitch back in with him. He greeted her nicely and slowly learned how to get along with her. She was a gentle but firm teacher, and he was a quick study once he learned he needn't be afraid of her. Then, after a time, I put another mild-mannered bitch in with the two. So now Cisco got to learn more about pack order and, yes, he was low man on the totem pole. Both girls got along very well, and were gentle but firm with Cisco, and he learned to play with them and wrestle and act like a regular dog.

While all this dog interaction was going on, I was also working with him a little every day. He learned that I was going to be in charge, that I would pet him when I wanted to, that I would give him pills if he needed them, trim his nails, comb his coat. He learned that I was gentle and wouldn't hurt him. And I was definitely in charge; he was very happy with that, because **he** didn't have to make the decisions anymore.

Well, after some time Cisco became his true self, a very nice, sweet, loving boy who just wanted a little attention and some love. At that point we began actively to look for a home for him. It happened that very soon we had applicant that met our criteria. They were a couple, mid-thirties, who had no children and no intentions to have any. In addition she worked with horses a lot, and understood how to be an alpha and not let an animal take advantage of her. They were familiar with corgis and were looking for a dog they could love and that needed them.

So, after much discussion, and many cautions, and long explanations about Cisco and his behavior in the past, what they might expect and how to handle it, and promises of obedience classes, we agreed to allow this lovely couple to adopt Cisco.

I talked to Cisco about where he was going, and all I knew about his new people. And then came the day when I put him on a plane for California. I worried all day. I knew he would be fine, but still I worried. What if he acted out? What if they didn't like him? What if? And then came an e-mail. It was very short. They said how perfect he is, and loving, and to cap it off, there was a wonderful photo attached of Cisco in her lap. Glory, Glory! Cisco had lost the worry lines on his forehead! For the first time, I saw the **real** Cisco. He was totally and completely happy and secure, and it showed.

We have heard from the new parents often. They were careful to make sure that he knows his place and have showered him with love. They have taken him to classes. He goes with her to the barn when she goes to ride, and behaves like a gentleman. They took him with them at Christmas for a family gathering, and he was a real treat for everyone. He loved all the little kids, and his new parents are so pleased with him. They think he is the greatest dog ever. And they are so glad they decided on an older dog rather than a puppy. This is the true reward of rescue. Cisco literally came within minutes of losing his life, and here he is now, blissful, at his real home, and loved.

Saving Gina

The other dog I want to tell about is Gina, a red Pem. Gina came to me via another rescuer from a commercial breeder. The former owners had stopped caring for her when she didn't conceive. She arrived late one evening. She had an appointment at the vet early the next morning; so, I walked her, fed and watered her, and left her in the van. The weather was very nice, so she was comfortable, and, to be honest, she stank.

In the light of morning I checked her out. Oh, my! This poor little girl of about 21 pounds was in terrible condition. She reeked to high heaven, her eyes were matted shut, her coat was just nasty: dry and brittle and oily too—yucky. Her nails were so long that she was forced to walk on the sides of her toes. She had a mass in one of her breasts (oh, please, let it not be cancer), and, of course, she needed to be spayed, and she needed all of her shots.

I took her to the vet and explained where she came from. Could they please do whatever they could for her? They asked me to leave her overnight. They bathed her, clipped her nails (three times), spayed her, and fixed the inguinal hernia (thank goodness only a hernia—not cancer!). They cleaned her teeth. They told me she had a staph infection on her skin (baths and antibiotics), eye infections (eye ointment), a nasty mouth (more antibiotics). And through this entire ordeal this little nine-year-old girl was as sweet, pleasant, and happy a dog as you could hope to find.

Gina came home, and over the next several weeks, with the antibiotics, routine care, and good food, she turned into a very pretty red/gold girl. She always had a sunny smile, and she learned to walk on the bottoms of her toes. And her coat—my goodness—all that old coarse hair was gone, and in its place was a wonderful red-gold coat that shone with health. She just glowed.

There was an ongoing problem with her eyes. We decided that she had a fungal infection, and we treated that. We finally took her to the vet ophthalmologist, who thankfully gave us a rescue discount. He declared her eyes perfectly normal for a dog of her age—in fact, in great shape for a dog of her age. So we were free to finish up her treatment. The vet had to go back in and repair the hernia again. It was such a big hole that the first procedure hadn't worked. When she recovered from this surgery, we were ready to find her a forever home.

During this time another Pem girl had come into our rescue. She was only three, but very shy and mild-mannered. She and Gina were roommates and developed a real affinity for each other. We wanted to place them together, but knew that would be hard, so we offered first one then the other to various people, and for all kinds of reasons no one took either of them. Then one day a wonderful adoption application came to us. When I read it, I immediately wrote to my partner and said, "This is the one for the girls!" So we contacted the applicant and told her about the girls and asked her to call me. Then I waited and waited for her to call. Nothing. Oh, the disappointment...

Then one Monday morning, three weeks later, the phone rang. A woman at the other end told me her name. It sounded familiar, but I couldn't place it. Then she said that she had called to ask about the girls! Did we still have them? She had a family crisis right after she applied and had been away. She was so afraid that the girls were gone.

They had lost their Pem several months before and had finally decided they were ready for another. They hadn't planned to get two, but since these girls came as a package, they would take them both. The woman told me that she had dreamed of the girls the night before, a dream of contentment and homecoming.

Well, after some confusion about flights, we finally got the girls to their new parents after a long, ten-hour flight. The girls settled in pretty well, but Gina was sad. Her new mom was worried about her. I have always deliberately kept my rescues at a bit of a distance. I want them to know I love them and care about them, but I don't want them to bond to me; they know that I am a temporary caregiver, and that they will soon have their forever homes.

But Gina was different. I was the first person who had ever been truly kind to her in all her nine years. I had to handle her a lot: daily meds, and then weeks and weeks of twice-daily applications of eye ointments, and making sure that her nails were kept short, combing her coat, and so on. And although I hadn't realized it, she had bonded to me. So her new mom and I talked, and we decided that she should tell Gina how much I loved her, but since I had other dogs here to care for, I had given her care to her new mom who had only Lulu and Gina to care for and love. Well, from that moment she started to acclimate to her new home. She has continued to blossom and thrive, and is getting younger and younger as time goes on. Both her mom and dad feel so blessed with these girls. Lulu is the outgoing, knock-you-over type (she has come out of her shyness!). And Gina, in her very calm, sweet, sunny way, adds a soft loving tenor to their home.

I heard from the family just before Christmas. The girls have been there a year-and-a-half, and they are in better health and condition that ever. They are thoroughly and beautifully loved and cherished.

Gina is a CorgiAid kid; CorgiAid picked up the expenses for her extra treatments. Gina is a true rescue. If she hadn't come to us soon, she wouldn't have made it. And now, through her sweet, sunny disposition, she is adding a whole new dimension to a couple who had no idea how much Gina and Lulu would bring to their lives.

TOUGH SITUATIONS

Cisco's and Gina's stories, while rather involved, are still not terribly complicated to handle. But we occasionally have a dog come into our rescue that has had a terrible time: there has been neglect or abuse, or the dog has simply been allowed to take over the family, and in some cases has been rewarded for inappropriate behavior. These dogs need the special talents and patience of special rescue people who can help the dog work through the problems and become a more nearly normal dog. These cases take time to reverse the damage, and, at a point determined by the person doing the "rehab," we find a very special family for that dog, a family who understands his problems and has the ability to continue the rehabilitation. We stay in very close contact with such families, to help with any rough spots.

There is another condition that occasionally faces dog owners and rescuers, called "Rage Syndrome." Unfortunately there is not a lot of concrete knowledge about this syndrome. Typically the dog is acting fairly normal, then suddenly, with no warning, gets very aggressive and violent. Sometimes the dog bites other dogs or humans. If rage syndrome is suspected, the dog should be carefully handled so that no harm can come to anyone. First the dog should have a **very** thorough exam by a knowledgeable veterinarian, to rule out any medical problem such an ulcer, an abscess, infection, or other unsuspected problem that could be causing unresolved pain. If no medical problem is found, then there might be a chemical imbalance causing the dog to have bad reactions. This is a very difficult, frightening problem, and often, for the safety of all involved with the afflicted dog, the dog must be put down. The risks to the owner, the owner's children, and other animals are just too great, and the hard decision must be made.

Rescue is very rewarding, but can be heartbreaking too. Sometimes we are unable to get to a dog that needs help, and sometimes the dog is in such poor condition that there is nothing we can do to help except ease him to the Rainbow Bridge. And sometimes a dog has been so terribly abused that only very special rescuers can help, and then there is the search for a **very** special home for that dog. Most rescuers have found others to work with for transportation, and have found wonderful vets that will work on rescues for small fees.

The Internet has made communication between rescuers a simple and quick way to get information from one group to another. We can send a photo to a potential adopter or rescuer in just a few seconds, and that sure helps with identifying dogs of a particular breed and with allowing a potential adopter to see the rescue immediately! Web sites are set up that showcase rescue dogs. Transportation, in particular, has become easier with the Internet. Transportation groups can be contacted to set up a run. Airline schedules are available 24/7.

BASICS OF RESCUE

I try to keep in mind a couple of things whenever I am working with rescues. I am never going to take unnecessary risks to my well-being—or that of those close to me—for a "stray." I remind myself that it will take a rescue ten days to two weeks to settle in, and for the true dog to emerge. And I make it a practice **never** to do anything that will hurt a dog during the first couple of weeks he is with me. If there is a life-threatening condition, like a tick infestation, I take him to the vet's office and have them bathe him. If he is horribly matted, or if the nails are really long, I leave it until the dog knows me better. If there is a real problem, we go to the vet for help. My own dogs will take a lot from me, because they trust me and understand that there is a reason I am doing some hurtful thing, even if they don't like it. But a new rescue is frightened, in completely unfamiliar surroundings, and a stranger is hurting him. He may have been badly hurt by a human in his previous life, and, expecting the worst, will snap or bite out of fear. In a short time, when he trusts you, he won't react so violently.

The other thing I do is to talk with the dogs. I explain what is happening when I pick them up, when we are going to the vet, when I am doing routine things to them, and most especially when they are going to their new homes. I tell them all I can about their new people, about their new doggy brothers and/or sisters, about other animals in their new home, about the process of getting there, and what they can expect when they're finally there. I know it sounds silly, but I am completely persuaded that they understand the essence of what I am saying. I think we don't give dogs enough credit. They certainly seem to have an easier time of adapting since I have started talking with them. One comment we hear over and over: "He acts like he has always been here."

One more thing that is very important. Follow your instincts. I am a very "black and white" sort of person, and I try to be logical. However, I have found that regardless of how perfect a placement may seem to my head, if my gut, heart, instinct, whatever you call it, is uneasy, I had better listen. The times that I haven't, have not been good. We all have instincts, some of them are buried pretty deep, but if you mess with dogs enough they will begin to emerge. When they do—**listen**. If you get bad vibes—don't go there.

WHAT IS INVOLVED IN RESCUE

The basics of rescue are:

1. Identifying the rescue
2. Acquiring and getting the rescue into a foster home
3. Doing necessary vet work
4. Evaluating the rescue
5. Matching the rescue to the perfect home for that dog
6. Obtaining transportation

7. Providing education.

Identifying the rescue

There are a number of ways we learn about potential corgi rescues. Several people scour the Internet postings for shelters and alert the corgi rescue community when they spot a corgi. Other breed rescue groups sometimes have a corgi or corgi mix come into their rescue programs, and they in turn notify a corgi rescuer they know. Rescue-friendly shelters usually call local breed rescue groups if they have a corgi in their facilities. And then we get those phone calls from an owner who, for some reason, feels the need to give up a dog. Or sometimes it is a family member or neighbor who makes the call. We try to make sure that the dog is what is it claimed to be, a corgi or corgi mix, either by a personal visit by a corgi-knowledgeable person or by looking at several photos.

There is another issue that faces rescuers, the pet store puppy. The puppies in pet stores come either from commercial breeders through brokers or from local "backyard breeders." Typically, these pups are not as carefully bred as they might be. The commercial breeder may not do health checks on adults, and may not know that their dogs are passing on bad temperament traits or physical problems. In addition, people will often go to a pet store, see a cute pup, and purchase it without any knowledge of the breed. Often that pup is abandoned, put on the street, or turned into the pound because of health or temperament problems, or because the dog is not appropriate for that family. Also, commercial breeders will sometimes give their retired dogs to rescue. Many times these dogs have problems: lack of socialization, lack of handling, and possibly physical problems as well. To find out more about commercial breeders go to: www.nopuppymills.com.

Acquiring and getting the rescue into a foster home

Once a dog has been identified as a corgi or corgi mix, a rescuer volunteers to take the dog. If it is local, (i.e., within a few hours), that rescuer will either go to get the dog or ask other local rescuers to help get the dog to her. If it is a distance away, volunteers will form a transport "run," each person taking a portion of the run, then handing the dog off to the next person, and thus get the dog to the rescuer, who will house and feed the dog, get vet work done, and evaluate the dog. Please note that there may be adoption fees from shelters or pounds at this level, although these are sometimes waived for bona fide rescue groups.

Doing necessary vet work

When a rescue dog comes in, the preliminary thing is just to observe the animal to see if it appears to be okay. One of the very first priorities is to get the dog to the vet for a health check. Sometimes it has come from someone who has had the vet work done, and those records are with the dog. But most dogs have received little or no vet care, or there are no records of any. My vet is very helpful with the rescues. He gives us a big discount on rescue work and helps any way he can, and he is worth his weight (and then some!) in gold; in fact, this makes my rescue feasible.

Rescuers are usually very dog-knowledgeable, and will observe the dog and point out anything that seems a bit odd so the vet can check that out while the dog is at the clinic. The vet checks heart and lung function, ears, eyes, weight, and so forth. We try to determine how old the dog is from its teeth, if the age is unknown. Then we always do a heartworm test, spay or neuter the dog (if necessary), and get a rabies shot. If the dog is heartworm positive, we treat the dog. If there are other problems, we address each one and do the best we can to give the dog a long, happy life. I have vaccines on hand and give each dog his booster and bordetella vaccines. We generally come out okay on normal expenses: (spay/neuter, heartworm test, vaccinations, heartworm preventative, food and transportation) with our minimal adoption fees. But if there are conditions above the routine, we can apply to CorgiAid for assistance with extraordinary expenses.

Evaluating the rescue

This is the fun part of rescue. When a dog comes to my home, she is very carefully introduced to my "herd" of existing dogs. Depending on the particular dog, I will put her in a pen in my living room for a few days until she feels more comfortable about mixing with the others; some will mix with the herd immediately. I watch the interactions with the other dogs to determine if she is an alpha dog, or a beta, or other temperament. I watch how she responds to other temperaments, how she acts with the pups, older dogs, very soft dogs, and so on. Then there are the ongoing household things. Is she housetrained; is she crate trained, leash trained? Does she understand ordinary household goings on, or is she freaked out by everything? Is she tractable, stubborn, scared, defiant, or just completely out of her element? What kind of manners does she have? Is she hand or foot shy, afraid of sudden noises?

You just watch everything the dog does, both with humans and with other dogs, always with the thought in mind, "What kind of family situation does this dog need?" (And you often get a feel for what kind of experiences the dog may have had before rescue.) Would she be better with an older family, or a single person, or with children, with other dogs, or as an only dog? What about cats? Does the dog need a lot of activity, or a calmer home? This is an ongoing process that is refined as the dog settles in and becomes more at home.

Matching the rescue to the perfect home for that dog

Once the evaluation is done, we try to match the dog with a perfect home from applications we have on hand or receive once the dog is posted on our rescue site. When we think we have an applicant that might be a good match for the dog, we do e-mail interviews with the person or family. Then follows a phone interview, during which the person is told all we know about the dog, and we find out all we can about the family and how the dog might fit into their household. If the interviews are positive and it seems like a match, then we do follow up things, such as checking references.

If all is favorable and the adoption is a go, then we have an agreement for the adopters to sign. One provision of the agreement specifies that the dog be returned to us if the adopters cannot keep her. There is an adoption fee to cover expenses, and the adopter pays for transportation and for a crate, if one is needed.

Obtaining transportation

Once the adoption is a done deal, the adoption agreement signed, and the adoption fees paid, transportation must be arranged. Sometimes the adopter is within driving range and will come to the foster home to get the dog. or they will meet us at a mutually convenient place. Sometimes the adopter is a distance away, but not too far. Then a "local" run can be organized. The rescuer probably knows other rescuers in the area who will help set up a short run of 200 or 300 miles. If the distance to the adopter is greater than about 300 miles, there are options: a long distance run, a special courier service, or shipping the dog by air.

If a long distance relay run is the choice, there are several ways to make this happen. We post to the corgi lists, other rescue lists, or local rescue lists. There are people out there who set up rescue runs time after time. They are the experts: "Transport Goddesses." There are many groups that do these. A Web site has been set up that lists some of them, and it would be a good place to start if you don't know anyone personally. DogsNeedingPeopleNeeding-Dogs is a very useful site for anyone doing rescue

* http://dogsneedingpeopleneeding-dogs.org/index.html

Transportation groups are listed at:

* http://dogsneedingpeopleneeding-dogs.org/transportation.html

There are also commercial services that transport animals by van. Some of them give rescues a discount. They are usually run by caring, knowledgeable people, but since they are usually small businesses, you definitely want to check references and make sure you understand exactly what their service consists of and how long the trip will be, and to make sure that they have insurance and any necessary licenses.

Note that a long road trip can be very stressful, and the dog's system can be all out of sorts by having his routine completely upset. Dogs may not eat or potty while on a long road trip. This is something to consider with a dog that might not be accustomed to being crated for long periods or to riding in a vehicle for long distances.

For the longer distances, I personally prefer shipping by air, priority cargo. It is usually cheaper than ground transportation services (if you have to pay full fare), and the dog gets there in 4 to 6 hours for most trips and is rested and ready to adapt to his new home. There are things you have to do to make the air transportation safe, but most of it is common sense, and the cargo people at the airlines will help too. If you want to ship a dog by air, I would be happy to help you with the details. Contact Pat Pearce: ppearce@brightok.net.

Providing education

Education is part and parcel of rescue. The first question to answer is "Rescue? What's that?" Rescuers constantly help dog owners with ordinary things like housetraining and basic obedience, as well as more intense problems like interaction between dogs or dogs with children. We are committed to helping dogs and the people who own them with the myriad of problems that can present themselves. We answer questions and offer suggestions, and we refer people to helpful sites on the Internet, to local trainers, classes, and kennel clubs, or perhaps to a helpful dog owner to join for walks. In addition, we help owners identify their problem, and make suggestions so they can work through the problem. We also help people decide what dog breed is best for them and help them find sources for that dog. Basically any type of doggy thing is our thing.

BEGINNING TO HELP WITH RESCUE

If you would like to help with rescue, I suggest that you subscribe to a breed e-mail list like Corgi-L (sign up at: corgi.ncn.com/~corgi/) and a breed rescue mailing list like CorgiRescue (CorgiRescue@yahoogroups.com). I also suggest that you find a mentor, either locally in your breed or a compatible person with another breed, or someone who will take you under her or his wing via phone or the Internet. It is always nice to have someone who knows the ropes to ask those little questions you never thought about—and there are lots of things that come up! Every rescue is different.

There are organized rescue groups and individual rescuers all over the United States and Canada. The primary corgi groups are:

- Affiliate Regional Clubs of the Pembroke Welsh Corgi Club of America (Pem rescue groups)

  http://www.pembrokeCorgi.org/affiliate-clubs.htm

- Cardigan Welsh Corgi Club of America (Cardi rescue groups)

  http://www.cardiganCorgis.com/clubsFrames.htm

- ForPaws Corgi Rescue (independent Corgi & Corgi Mix Rescue)

  http://www.ForPaws.org

Thanks for the help of: Pam Miller, Transportation, TX; Barb Chen, Transportation, PA; Lynn Stoltzmann, Rescue group info, MN; All the lovely dogs who have "trained" me; And a BIG sloppy corgi kiss to John Klaus, IA, my editor.

Pat Pearce and a Rescue Corgi

INTERLUDE

PENNI

It was the day after Thanksgiving. The table, countertops, and refrigerator were all stuffed with the leftovers from a feast for 20 people. I was exhausted from cooking and cleaning and serving. A relaxing, hot shower would do me good. Usually Penni accompanies me into the bathroom, but that day she decided not to follow me. I should have realized that she was planning something; corgis never do things without a reason.

I let the hot water run for quite a while and took my time drying my hair. When I left the bathroom, I walked into the kitchen and immediately sensed that something was amiss. The scrumptious Dutch apple pie from a posh bakery in New York City was gone. A clean pie plate stared at me. Also missing was the half of pumpkin chiffon pie, my signature dish, that I had labored over two days before. Not even the plastic wrap remained; only the disposable pie plate was left. How could this have happened? I have two teenage sons with the appetites of longshoremen, but they weren't even awake yet. And then I spied the culprit. Licking the crumbs from her whiskers was Penni. She looked very pleased with herself, as if she was saying, "Well, you taught me agility and 'table' is a command in agility. So I gave myself the command and rewarded myself." Then her middle started to expand and her expression changed from smug self satisfaction to one of extreme discomfort. "Oh, oh, maybe this wasn't such a good idea," her brown eyes seemed to say.

I quickly called my vet, who, after he stopped laughing, said I should bring her in right away so that they could induce vomiting and prevent pancreatitis. I dropped her off at the vet and later picked up a much slimmer but not repentant corgi.

The moral of the story? Never underestimate the determination of a corgi in search of a snack. *~Florence Scarinci*

MOLLY

Last year, our rescued corgi, Molly, was in the den with us while we were watching Animal Planet. There was a program about polar bears on and, for some reason, Molly was mesmerized by them and watched the TV screen in rapt attention. Our TV happened to be sitting on an entertainment center, which we had placed inside an empty closet in the den. When the TV was not in use, we just closed the doors. Well, as the polar bears walked to the right side of the screen and disappeared off camera, Molly started barking and ran into the bathroom, which is directly behind the den, looking for the bears. She was sure they had left the TV and must have been in the bathroom. She continued to look for them for several minutes. Pretty astute corgi! ~*Sue Cowan*

RYLIE

We brought our boy Rylie home when he was 12 weeks old. Potty training was initiated, and we were making some headway. One morning, my husband went into the bathroom and proceeded to take care of business. Rylie was intrigued by the sound of water hitting water and followed him in. He stood on his hind legs, put his two front paws up on the bowl to watch, caught the scent and promptly let go with a stream of his own. That kind of potty training was not exactly what we were aiming for. ~*Kat Connor-Litchman*

GRETA AND MAX

They play so well together. I marvel at the easy relationship between these two. Greta is my mother's Weimaraner, a huge grey ghostly dog with human eyes and a sedate nature. She was rescued from a shelter, having been abused and neglected her whole life, then tagged for euthanasia. A Weimaraner owner picked her up and my mother got her from him, the beginning of a unique and friendly relationship.

Max is my dog. He's a Pembroke Welsh corgi, a little steam engine of a dog, deep brown typical puppy dog eyes, fiercely protective and playful. He considers his herd his domain, and any intruders are regarded suspiciously for days, weeks sometimes. He has not known a day of want or neglect in his whole life, and, as a dog will do, he knows which side his bread is buttered on.

I watch them interact, Max initiating play, Greta too tired and hot to follow. She feels bad though and licks Max's muzzle. He joyfully kisses her back and allows her to lie down. He lays a short distance from her, head on paws, and regards her with his liquid eyes with fascination and adoration. Greta looks at him with half-lidded eyes and a smile on her face; they have the ideal relationship. Max rolls over on his back and Greta nuzzles his chest affectionately. No pressure there, no expectations. They just love and enjoy each other.

Greta and Max are filled with joy and rediscovery at every new meeting. Familiar companions, joyously sniffing each other, recalling past play times, never regretting the time they are apart, simply loving the opportunity to spend more time together. They circle each other, Max short enough to walk under Greta's legs, Greta bowing her head to meet his. Greta pounces forward catlike, front paws outstretched on the ground to get Max to play.

He runs to her and tugs at her ear carefully, prompting her to roll onto the ground in front of him. She leaps up and pounces at him again, and he takes off at a full run around the house like a tiny locomotive. She barks at him, not menacingly but teasingly, and places herself in his path forcing him to either weave or stop. Sometimes he simply drops onto the floor in front of her and exposes his tummy, conceding to her size and strength. Sometimes she rolls over in front of him, in respect for his friendship and trust for his kindness.

I have seen Max and Greta play together countless times. Greta is older and so more sedate, but if she is in the right mood it is quite a romp. She seldom initiates play, but when she does, the delight in Max is palpable. Greta is twice his size easily, but she treats Max as an equal, and he appreciates it. They roll on the floor together, Greta nipping at Max's furry chest in a grooming fashion, Max's head back and tongue lolling out in delight, then back up for another few dozen laps around the dining room table.

I often wonder why people cannot get along more like Greta and Max do. Tolerant, understanding, loving. Is it a function of their lower brain capacity that they argue less and love more? Or is it that our brains are too complex to simply enjoy each other without demand or suspicion? I watch the dogs together and try to emulate their generosity of spirit. The joy in their eyes as they play and the contentment as they rest is so very desirable.

Greta looks at me with her human eyes and her innocent smile, face drawn up in such a perfect imitation of a human smile, like a child. She shows her age and her character in her eyes, but her bad past

experiences are nowhere to be found. She trusts me entirely and loves with all her canine heart. I respect her trust and wouldn't dream of betraying it. Her stub of tail wiggles enthusiastically whenever she sees me, putting her paws on my shoulders to give me kisses in greeting. I pat her head and call her "my sister Greta," looking into her grey eyes with appreciation for her love.

Max is my child. No less than that. He has a place in my heart second only to my children, and he earns it daily. He shows utter devotion in his eyes, his happiness at my return and his indignation at my departures. Fiercely protective, his herding nature keeps us in his constant watch, but he is never overbearing. He lies in my arms like a baby sometimes, all 30 pounds of stocky little dog, looking up at me with adoration. It's so fulfilling to have a living being regard you that way.

Max and Greta have different natures, but their natures mesh with each other perfectly. They trust, they play, and they tolerate. When the time comes, they go separately without tears and simply appreciate the time together. This is truly something we can aspire to. To not want knowledge of the future, to not worry about what tomorrow brings, but just to rejoice in the time we have together.

Greta and Max teach us all a valuable lesson if we watch and pay attention to their interaction. Tolerate, love, and give space where needed. That is the best possible definition of "a dog's life."
~ *Jamie L. Longstreth*

TAKING CARE OF YOUR CORGI

TEN HEALTH AND BASIC CARE QUESTIONS TO ASK YOUR VET

by Barbara Bronczyk

Barbara Bronczyk offers some help on finding a good vet, and asking the right questions at that first visit with your new corgi.

This chapter provides an overview of some questions that you should discuss with your vet when you get a new corgi, either a puppy or an adult. Remember, though, that each dog, even a purebred, is an individual and has individual preferences and needs. Your family is also unique. So while this section provides general guidelines, it is important to go over the specifics of your situation with your veterinarian.

1: How do I find a good vet?

The first thing you need, before you ask any questions, is someone to ask. If you already have animals in your household, this will not be a problem. However, if you are a first-time pet owner, you will need to find a vet to take care of your new addition. Even if you have existing pets, you may need to find a new vet if you move, your vet retires, or you become dissatisfied with your current vet.

The best way to find a vet is by word of mouth. Ask your friends, neighbors, fellow workers, or any other pet owners you know what vets they use and if they are happy with them. Ask what they like and don't like about the clinic. Obviously, some things that may be important to you, such as prices, location, hours, and so on, can be found out about without ever visiting the clinic.

Make an appointment to talk to the vet. When you speak with the vet, it is a good idea to have a list of questions with you so that you don't forget to ask something important. During this first appointment, you may want to leave your pet(s) at home. If you are looking for a new vet for your existing pets, bring medical records for them so that you can discuss any special medical conditions your pets have. At this time, you can discuss the vet's treatment philosophy for these conditions. The new vet may have some new ideas, so keep an open mind.

Ask about making appointments and whether clients are allowed to restrain their own pets during exams, along with any other concerns you may have about handling pets. If you have an aggressive or fearful dog, this is the time to find out how the vet handles these types of behavior. This is also the time to find out their opinion about corgis in general. There are some vets who have had bad experiences with the breed and don't like them and others who love corgis. You can also find out if they have a lot of corgis in their practice to see how familiar they are with the breed.

Make sure to find out about emergency procedures. You need to be able to reach someone 24 hours a day in case an emergency develops. Many vets now use after-hours emergency clinics rather than have someone on call all the time. If you prefer for your pet to see one of his regular vets during an emergency, you will want to find a clinic that has a vet on call rather than someone who uses an emergency clinic. If you are willing to go to the emergency clinic, find out which clinic they use and where it is located so you can check it out also.

Another thing to be sure to check is whether someone is there to monitor the animals after hours. This is important to know if your pet needs to stay overnight following a surgery or because of an illness. Many owners will not leave a pet overnight unless someone is there to monitor the pet's condition after the clinic is closed.

Depending on your concerns, this is the time to ask about prescriptions for heartworm preventatives from warehouses, multi-pet discounts, payment plans, and so on. Do they take credit cards, allow payment plans for large bills, accept pet insurance?

If you don't bring your pet along on the initial visit, you'll want to arrange a visit with the pet later. This should be just a well-check appointment, not for something critical; it's your chance to see how the staff and vet handle your pet. Do they greet the pet, give scritches behind the ears, or just grab him, put him on the table, and start poking? My personal number-one item to notice on this visit is how they interact with the animal. I kept my vet when I moved because he and all of his staff obviously love animals and treat the pets in their practice accordingly.

The bottom line is that you want to find a vet you can talk to, who will listen to your concerns, and with whom you and your pets feel comfortable. If you cannot establish good lines of communication and don't feel comfortable with the vet and staff, it really doesn't matter how great they are at the medical or surgical stuff. It's all a very individual choice, just like choosing a doctor. Pick someone you feel fits the personalities of you and your pets.

2: What vaccinations does my corgi need?

The following information was provided to me by Lois Kay, breeder of Pembroke Welsh corgis:

> Your puppy's litter was given DHP-P shots at approximately 8-9 weeks of age, with boosters at 4 week intervals. You must continue the series of shots for your puppy on a schedule recommended by your vet. I give DHP-P (distemper, hepatitis, parainfluenza, and parvovirus) boosters every four weeks until the puppy is at least 14 weeks old and continue with a parvo booster at 20 weeks. Rabies vaccinations are given as early as three months to as late as six months, depending on state law.
>
> Bordetella (commonly called Kennel Cough) vaccinations are recommended only for those dogs boarded, groomed, taken to dog shows, or for any reason housed where exposed to a lot of dogs. The intranasal vaccine provides more complete and more rapid onset of

immunity with less chance of reaction. Immunity requires 72 hours and does not protect from every cause of kennel cough. Immunity is of short duration (4 to 6 months).

> You may want to discuss with the vet the frequency of vaccinations that he or she recommends. My vet, for example, does not vaccinate old dogs for anything except for state required rabies. I know of several other vet specialists who quit vaccinating their own dogs at the age of six or seven. The reasoning is that they believe that immunity lasts longer than previously thought and that continuing to challenge the immune system in the older dogs may be counterproductive. Other people do titer tests for each disease to check the immunity level and see if vaccination is needed.

It is important to note that many states require rabies vaccinations. Check with your vet for requirements in your state. Also, many kennels require the Bordetella vaccination or they will not board your dog. Check with the kennel ahead of time to avoid surprises.

Vaccinations that are NOT generally recommended are Leptospirosis, Giardia, and Lyme. All three have a high incidence of adverse reactions in dogs. Your vet may recommend the vaccinations for Lyme and/or Giardia if you live in an area that is high risk for these diseases, but they are not recommended as a matter of routine care.

3: Will my corgi get along with my current pets?

Corgis are friendly and social dogs and generally get along with other dogs and cats. However, it is good to ask the vet and/ or the breeder about your particular situation. Depending on the type and ages of your existing pets, the vet or breeder may recommend a corgi of a particular gender or may recommend an adult dog versus a puppy (or vice versa).

4: What type of routine care does my corgi require?

Corgis need to be brushed and groomed about once a week. They shed quite a lot for a shorthaired dog, since they have a double coat; so grooming will remove a lot of hair. If you have a fluffy corgi, more frequent brushing may be required. The following information was provided to me by Lois Kay:

> Nails need to be cut frequently, and corgis hate it. Be prepared for a struggle, but remain calm and persist. Nails need attention about every two weeks. I like the Black and Decker Wizard nail grinder the best. It is rechargeable, battery operated, very quiet, has plenty of power, and has two speeds. Nails are lots less likely to bleed using grinders than they are if you use clippers.
>
> Teeth start building tartar when corgis are about a year old and it seems to form on this breed more quickly than it does on some others. Have your vet clean your dog's teeth once or twice a year so they will still be there when your pet gets old. Do keep alert for tartar buildup.
>
> Teething puppies will especially appreciate the Frosty Paws treats. A good thing for pups to chew on is a damp washcloth tied in a knot and put in the freezer. It feels good on those irritated gums.
>
> Ears should be checked to see if they are clean and smell normal. Very dirty or smelly ears usually indicate a problem such as ear mites or an infection and would warrant a trip to the vet. Normal light dirt can be cleaned with a cotton ball and a little baby oil. Do not try and clean down into the ear canal.

Now a note from the author: If the thought of taking a power tool (nail grinder) to your struggling puppy's toes gives you the willies, most groomers and vets will cut nails for you for a reasonable price. The doggie day care where I take my dog charges $7.50, and I am in a high price area. I have them do it every two weeks.

5: What are good chew toys for my corgi?

Corgis, especially puppies, need to chew and you want to give them some options other then your shoes and furniture. There are many different types of chew toy and a variety of opinions on each one. There does not, however, seem to be a 100% safe chew toy! Your corgi's chewing habits will determine what types of products are safe for him and what products are not; many corgis are "power chewers." The most important thing is to supervise your corgi anytime you give him a new type of chew toy to make sure it is not posing any danger. If your corgi can pull off large pieces of a chew toy, it is a danger as far as choking and/or digestive blocking. Hard chews such as nylabones and cow hooves can cause tooth breakage in some dogs. Also, some dogs' digestive systems are sensitive to certain types of chews, so watch for any vomiting and diarrhea after giving a new kind of chew.

Some of the common types of chew toy are:

1. Rawhide, which is basically dried cow skin.
2. Nylabones, which are synthetic hard bones, often with flavoring.
3. Cow hooves (self-explanatory)
4. Pig ears (ditto)
5. Kongs, which are a hard rubber beehive shaped toy that can be filled with treats

6: When should I spay or neuter my corgi puppy?

Both male and female puppies should be altered at around six months of age. There are advantages to spaying and neutering in addition to the obvious one of eliminating unwanted puppies. For neutered males, there is zero risk of testicular cancer and a reduced likelihood of prostate cancer and enlarged prostate. Also, if a male is neutered early (at six months) there are less undesirable behaviors like marking territory and "humping" household objects. For spayed females, there is zero risk of uterine cancer and a reduced risk of mammary cancer. A female does not need to go through one heat season before she is spayed.

7: What is the best way to housetrain my corgi?

Crate training is the easiest and most recommended way to housetrain a puppy or dog. This is because it is an animal's natural instinct not to soil its sleeping area. If you have a puppy, make sure the crate is small enough that the puppy cannot sleep in one part and "do its business" in another. If you have an enclosure that turns out to be too big, part of it can be blocked off until the puppy is trained.

Use the crate to confine your dog when you are not supervising him. Take him outside immediately after he wakes up in the morning, when he wakes up after a nap, right after meals, and after play sessions. In addition, take him out every two to three hours while you are around and last thing at night before you go to bed. When the dog is outside and "does his business" praise him. Since corgis tend to be very food-motivated, you may also want to reward him with a treat.

A general rule of thumb with puppies is that they can "hold it" for the number of months they are old plus one. This means that a four-month old puppy can "hold it" for about five hours. Do not leave the puppy in the crate for longer than that amount of time, or he may have no choice but to go in the crate. If you are at work during the day and cannot come home at lunch to let the puppy out there are a

couple of options. You can ask a trusted neighbor to walk the puppy or hire a professional dog walker. You can also provide a larger area to confine your puppy during the day, keeping in mind that it will be soiled when you get home. If you use the latter method, it may take longer to housebreak your puppy, as he will have to go in the house sometimes.

8: How much and what type of exercise does my corgi need?

It certainly seems that corgis vary greatly in the amount of daily exercise they need. When I was researching the breed, I found many statements like "happy to sit by the fire," "likes to curl up with you while you read a book," "needs only 15 minutes of exercise twice a day," and so on. The people who wrote these things have quite obviously not met my corgi, Malcolm. Malcolm's exercise needs are measured in hours, not minutes, a day, and his response to book reading is to jump up and lick your face until you play with him! So obviously even among purebred corgis there is a lot of variation. You will need to observe your dog to determine the amount of exercise that is right for him.

Some types of exercise that are appropriate for corgis are walks, playing fetch, learning tricks, obedience training (such as heel and recall), playing with other dogs, and agility. Other things that are not recommended are anything involving a lot of jumping on and off of things (bad for their backs), running up and down stairs (too much stress on the front leg joints), and vigorous games of tug (can make the corgi aggressive). Also, putting the corgi out in a pen or fenced yard by himself does not necessarily count as exercise; corgis are social animals and will not necessarily "play" in this situation. When I put Malcolm in his "exercise" pen, he usually lies down in the sun and takes a nap! Interactive exercise is best and will help keep you in shape, too.

9: How do I tell if my corgi is overweight?

It is generally acknowledged by vets and breeders, as well as owners, that it is hard to keep a corgi slim and trim. Most corgis live to eat, and some can be quite good at training their "owners" to give them just about any treat they ask for. Corgis are prone to obesity and the health problems that go along with it, making weight monitoring all the more important.

It is a good idea to weigh your dog—and not just once a year at his annual vet checkup. The AKC standard for the Pembroke Welsh corgi states "Weight is in proportion to size, not exceeding 30 pounds for dogs and 28 pounds for bitches. In show condition, the preferred medium-sized dog of correct bone and substance will weigh approximately 27 pounds, with bitches approximately 25 pounds." For the Cardigan Welsh corgi, the standard states that "Ideally, dogs should be from 30 to 38 pounds; bitches from 25 to 34 pounds." That said, just weighing and comparing against the standard probably isn't going to work for everyone, because even purebred corgis come in a variety of different sizes and shapes. In addition to weighing, all corgi owners should objectively look at their corgis and feel them. You should be able to feel your corgi's ribs without having to dig for them. Your corgi should have a waistline, looking both from the side and from above.

A couple of additional things to remember: Don't necessarily be content if your vet tells you that your corgi is "just fine." Many vets are so used to seeing patients who are grossly obese that they often ignore the dog that is only slightly overweight. Also, a good weight for a pet that hangs out on the couch is not the same as a good weight for a dog that competes in an athletic sport, such as agility. It is much more important for the "athlete" to be at her ideal weight to reduce the risk of injuries while competing.

10: Is it true that corgi puppies should not go up and down stairs?

Although most everyone agrees that corgi puppies can handle a couple of steps out to the yard or into the den, many corgi breeders recommend that puppies stay away from full flights of stairs. The reason is that stairs can be a stress on forming joints and going down the stairs is more of a stress than going up. They recommend that a puppy not be allowed to go up a flight of stairs until at least six months of age, and not allowed to go down a flight of stairs until seven or eight months of age. Some breeders recommend minimal stairs for corgis at any age because of their short legs and long backs.

On the other hand, some vets say that, as long as the puppies are prevented from inappropriate racing and playing on the stairs, there is no reason to keep them away from them. They say that it is important for young dogs to learn to negotiate stairs, so they can go up and down them safely, and that it is much easier to do this when they are younger, rather than waiting until they are a year of age, and seeing steps for the first time. There is also the question of the owner carrying the dog up and down the stairs, and whether there is more risk of the owner having a problem (say if he or she has arthritis) or dropping the puppy than there is of the puppy injuring itself.

Barbara Bronczyk's Malcolm Gets His Yearly Exam

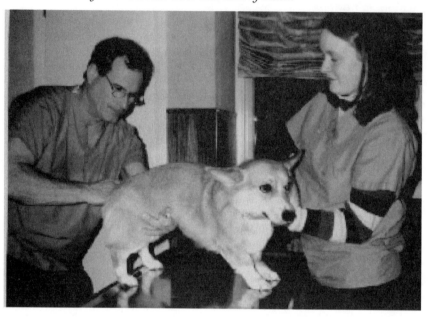

THE THINKING PERSON'S GUIDE TO DOG FOOD

by Florence Scarinci

Florence Scarinci provides a thorough guide to understanding and analyzing the contents of dog food.

You have just brought home that adorable corgi puppy you have wanted for years, or taken that older dog who wound up in rescue. You have prepared yourself for the dog's arrival. You have a leash and collar, a comb, some squeaky toys, a ball, the indispensable hedgie, a crate, a bed, and food and water bowls. But when it comes time for meals, which food will fill that shiny new bowl? You have heard about the raw diets but you are not convinced of their efficacy or safety, and you don't have the time or expertise to prepare a home cooked diet. So how do you select from among the thousands of dog foods that are commercially available?

In this chapter I will provide you with some facts that should help you make an informed decision. Under the heading, "Reading the Lines," we will discuss how to read a dog food label, how to decipher the ingredients, how much and when to feed. In the section entitled "Reading Between the Lines," we will answer such questions as how to switch from one brand or one life stage of food to another; whether or not to supplement with vitamins or enzymes; how to get the most nutrition for your money; whether or not to give treats; how to evaluate your dog food's efficacy—in other words, the kind of information not found on a label. There's a list of references at the end if you want to investigate further, as well as a chart with contact information for most major dog food manufacturers.

READING THE LINES

When you pick up your dog from the breeder or rescue contact, that person will probably have suggestions for feeding. She will probably send you home with a supply of the food that the dog was being fed while in his/her care. But perhaps that food is not readily available in your area, or you feel that the dog is not thriving on it, or you just cannot tolerate the smell, so you want to switch. You take a trip to your local pet shop, specialty pet food store, or supermarket and find yourself facing many brands attractively packaged to appeal to you, the consumer. You pick up a bag or a can of one of the 300 brands of dog food, put on your glasses, and attempt to decipher the label. What information is contained on the label and what must you know to make a selection? This information may get a bit technical and unless you are carrying a calculator, you may not be able to evaluate the information while you are standing in the aisle. But what follows is almost everything you will want to know to read the label.

The information printed on the label is federally mandated. The regulations are printed in the *Code of Federal Regulations*, Title 21, Part 501. The *Code* specifies that the package list the brand, name and address of the manufacturer, life stage, ingredients including preservatives, expiration date, AAFCO statement or nutritional adequacy statement, guaranteed analysis, feeding instructions, and weight. Here's what those terms mean.

TERMINOLOGY

Brand

The name of the party responsible for the quality and safety of the product must appear on the label (Bren). You might be surprised to learn that several of the major commercial dog foods are manufactured by subsidiaries of major multinational companies: Alpo, Friskies, Mighty Dog, Dog Chow, ProPlan, and Purina One are Nestle Purina products. Heinz manufactures Cycle, Gravy Train, Kibbles-n-Bits, and Nature's Recipe. Colgate-Palmolive is the parent company of Hill's Science Diet. Proctor and Gamble owns Eukanuba and Iams. Kal Kan, Mealtime, Pedigree, and Waltham are Mars' products. There are also numerous smaller companies and companies whose distribution is limited to one region of the country. Supermarket chains distribute some of the food manufactured by big name producers under their store label.

Much money is spent by both the large and small companies on marketing research in the naming of these products and in the design of the packages—all to appeal to the person who makes the purchasing decisions. Names like "Science Diet", "Sensible Choice," "Solid Gold," "Nature's Recipe," and "Beneful" conjure up images of good health, excellent quality, scientific foundations, and intelligent selection. But no matter which brand name or store name appears on the package, the name of the manufacturer or the responsible party must also appear on the label. Ideally, the street address and phone number of the responsible party should also appear. But the law indicates that this information need not be included if it is readily available in a city phone book. Many companies include 800 numbers on their label in case the consumer needs to contact the responsible party with a complaint or question.

Life Stage

AAFCO, the Association of American Feed Control Officials, specifies only four life stages: Growth or Puppy, Gestation/Lactation, Maintenance, All Life Stages. Pet food manufacturers have created variations on these stages, such as their formulas for large breed puppies, senior maintenance, performance, or weight reduction. But AAFCO recognizes only the four stages specified. Manufacturers also make variations such as small tidbits or large chunk, but these are variations in the size of the kibble and not in the formula itself. AAFCO does not recognize any of these distinctions.

The newest trend is custom tailoring dog food to create "breed specific" food.

Nature's Recipe has begun to produce food specific for toy dogs and terriers. Dr. William D. Cusick has written a book entitled, *Meeting the Nutritional Needs of Your Breed of Dog,* with the premise that different breeds with different origins and different purposes have different nutritional requirements. However, there is little research to prove the different dietary needs of the diverse breeds and no rules govern these statements about breed-specific appropriateness.

Ingredients

The *Code of Federal Regulations* specifies that the ingredients must be listed in descending order by weight. You might assume that if chicken or lamb is the first ingredient that it is, therefore, the major component of the food. However, read further down the ingredient list. You might see that the food also contains wheat flour, wheat germ, wheat middlings. It is possible that if you could add up all the quantities of ingredients having the word "wheat" in them, that wheat would constitute most of the food by weight. The label does not specify the quantities, and is not required to do so, since quantities are part of the proprietary formula and the exact formulation is protected by law. However, you can assume the quantities of ingredients by studying the descriptive name. If the product says "Liver for Dogs," 95% of the product must be the named ingredient. "Liver for Dogs" should be a can of liver with possibly vitamins and minerals added. If the can says "Liver and Beef for Dogs," the combination must total 95% of the finished product, with the amount of liver being greater than the amount of beef since liver is listed first.

Other Terms

The use of the words, "dinner," "recipe," "formula," "with," and "flavor" are defined by AAFCO regulations PF3 (b) and (c), and give the consumer an idea of the proportion of ingredients contained in the food. The terms "dinner," "recipe," or "formula" means that an ingredient or combination of ingredients constitutes least 25% of the weight of the product (excluding water sufficient for processing) but less than 95%, for example, "Beef Dinner." A combination of ingredients is permitted, as long as each ingredient comprises at least 3% of the product weight and total at least 25% and the names appear in descending order by weight. If the term "with" is used, each ingredient must constitute at least 3% of the food by weight, excluding water sufficient for processing. "Dog Food with Liver," for example, must contain at least 3% liver.

The word "flavor" may be used if a certain flavoring is added in quantities sufficient to impart a distinctive flavor, for instance, "Bacon Flavored Dog Food" (Dzanis).

The term "natural" has no mandated definition. Consumers may interpret it in any number of ways, e.g. having no preservatives. Be aware that "natural" is not synonymous with "organic." The term "organic" refers to condition under which plants were grown and animals raised and suggests the absence of certain pesticides, fertilizers and hormones in the growth and production of food (Dzanis).

The terms "premium, "super-premium," and even "ultra-premium" might also appear as a descriptor of the food. There are no regulations concerning the use of these terms. Some companies produce several product lines. Calling one product "premium" may indicate that the ingredient sources in that product are of higher quality. It is best to read the ingredient list and decide for yourself if MNO Dog Food has "premium" ingredients when compared to FGH Dog Food produced by the same parent company. There are also no regulations covering the phrase, "Recommended by Veterinarians." However, the label cannot make health claims. Manufacturers walk a fine line when it comes to this; for example, they can say, "Helps maintain joint health," but they cannot say that their food "Treats arthritis" (Freeman 22).

NUTRITION

Now that you can tell how a name reveals quantity and, possibly, quality, how can you tell if serving the food to your dog will provide complete and balanced nutrition? A nutritionally balanced food must contain protein, carbohydrates, fats, fiber, vitamins, and minerals (Palika 25).

Protein

Proteins are the building blocks for hair, muscle, skin, cartilage. Protein is broken down into amino acids, which are necessary for neurological responses and immune system functioning. While the dog's body can synthesize some amino acids, called nonessential amino acids, essential amino acids must be supplied by food. Sources of protein may be animal or plant. Animal sources of protein include chicken, chicken by-products, chicken by-product meal, chicken liver meal, chicken meal, beef, lamb, lamb meal, turkey, poultry by-product meal, poultry digest, liver, organ meat, glandular meat, animal digest, milk and milk products, eggs, fish, and fish meal. Vegetable sources of protein are alfalfa meal, brewers dried yeast, corn gluten meal, soy flour, soybean meal, soy protein concentrate, soy protein isolate, and wheat germ (*Understanding Ingredients*). Animal sources of protein are of higher quality than plant sources. Dog food that provides a blend of protein sources provides the best mix of amino acids (*Frequently Asked Questions About Dog Nutrition*).

Carbohydrates

Carbohydrates are sources of energy and bulk. Carbohydrates may be simple, such as sugars, or complex, such as starch and cellulose. Although the dog does not digest some complex carbohydrates, these ingredients serve as roughage for good intestinal health. Sources of carbohydrates include corn, corn meal, corn grits, ground yellow corn, dried whey, brewers rice, brown rice, ground rice, rice flour, oats, oat groats, sorghum, lactose, molasses, pearled barley, peas, potatoes, sugar, wheat, wheat flour, ground wheat, and wheat bran (*Understanding Ingredients*). Since different carbohydrates are metabolized at different rates, it is desirable to include several different kinds to provide quick sources of energy throughout the day.

Fats

For the dog, fat is the primary source of energy. Fats provide more than twice the number of calories (energy) per gram than do carbohydrates. Fats also are the source of the fat-soluble vitamins, A, D, E, and K. Besides providing energy, fats help maintain body temperature, control inflammation, and are important for proper blood clotting and promoting healthy skin and coat (*Palika 31*). One additional very important function of fats is to add palatability to food (*Frequently Asked Questions About Dog Nutrition*). There are both animal and plant sources of fat. On the dog food label, you might see listed animal fat, beef tallow, chicken fat, poultry fat, fish oil as animal sources and borage oil, corn oil, safflower oil, sunflower oil, vegetable oil, and flax meal as plant sources. (*Understanding Ingredients*).

Fiber

For good intestinal health, fiber is necessary. Fiber promotes water absorption and slows the passage of food through the intestine so that nutrients can be absorbed and a healthy stool can be formed. (*Palika 32*) Beet pulp, rice bran, wheat middlings, corn bran, and cellulose are sources of fiber (*Frequently Asked Questions About Dog Nutrition*). Apple pomace, carrageenan, cellulose, citrus pulp, guar gum, peanut hulls, pea fiber, rice bran, soybean hulls, tomato pomace, vegetable gum, and xanthan gum are also fiber sources (Understanding Ingredients).

Vitamins

These organic compounds are necessary for proper metabolism of food. The dog's body can synthesize vitamins A, C, D, K, and niacin. But food must supply the B complex vitamins: thiamin, riboflavin, pantothenic acid, pyridoxine, biotin, folic acid, cobalamin, choline and vitamin E (*Palika 40-45*). There are both animal and plant sources for vitamins.

Minerals

These inorganic compounds are catalysts for biochemical reactions necessary for proper growth and functioning. Dogs need calcium, phosphorus, magnesium, sulfur, iron, copper, zinc, manganese, iodine, selenium, cholide, and potassium (Palika 45-48) Meats, vegetables, and grains are sources of minerals.

In addition to the nutritive ingredients, a label must also list any other additives such as preservatives, artificial coloring, and ingredients added to aid in the manufacture of the food.

Preservatives

Fats must be preserved. When an ingredient is added as a preservative, its function must be specified, for example "citric acid-a preservative." The *Whole Dog Journal* recommends the use of natural preservatives such as vitamin E (mixed tocopherols) and vitamin C, ascorbic acid (Whole Dog Journal's Top Ten Dry Dog Foods). Rosemary, an herb that adds some flavor, and citric acid are also natural preservatives. Natural preservatives do not provide as long a shelf life as artificial preservatives. However, the artificial preservatives, BHA (butylated hydroxyanisole), BHT (butylated hydroxytoluene), and Ethoxiquin have been alleged to be implicated in the development of diseases, and the *Whole Dog Journal* as well as other authors advise against their use in dog food (*Pitcairn* 17-18).

Artificial Coloring

Dogs do not see color in the same way that humans do. Color adds nothing to the palatability of food for a dog. Adding coloring to food so that it more closely resembles beef chunks, chicken pieces, and so on is done to appeal to the human purchasers of the food.

Other Additives

These ingredients add nothing to the nutritive value of the dog food. They are added to improve taste, stability or appearance of food. They usually have long chemical sounding names, and their purpose should be identified. They may be emulsifiers, anticaking agents, antimicrobial agents, ph control agents. The law requires toxicity studies of these ingredients (*What's Really In Pet Food*).

Before we look at an actual label, let's define the terms: meal, by-product, digest, tallow. These definitions were established by AAFCO and specify what parts of an animal may be included in pet food:

- "Meat" is the clean flesh of slaughtered cattle, pigs, sheep, or goats. Flesh can mean muscle, tongue, diaphragm, heart, esophagus, fat, skin, sinews, nerves, and blood vessels normally found in the flesh.

- "Meat By-Products" are the clean, non-rendered parts of slaughtered animals listed above not including meat. These can be organs such as the lungs, spleen, kidneys, brain, liver, and bones and blood, stomach, and intestines emptied of their contents. It does not include hair, horns, teeth, or hooves. Those pig ears people like to give as treats are defined as by-products.

- "Meat Meal" is ground, rendered meal made from animal tissue. Rendering means that food is heat-processed to remove the fat and water from the product. Meat meal cannot contain blood, hair, hoof, horn, manure, or stomach contents and cannot contain more than 14% indigestible materials.

- "Meat and Bone Meal" is rendered from meat and includes the bone. The same rule about percentage of indigestible material applies.

- "Poultry By-Products" are the clean parts of slaughtered poultry: chicken, turkey, duck. These parts may be heads, feet, and internal organs such as the heart, kidneys, lungs, liver, abdomen, or intestines and must not contain feces or foreign matter except in unavoidable trace amounts.

- "Poultry By-Product Meal" is the ground, rendered, clean parts such as necks, feet, undeveloped eggs, and intestines of slaughtered poultry. It does not contain feathers, except those that are unavoidably included during processing.

- "Animal By-Product Meal" is meal made by rendering animal tissues that do not fit any of the other ingredient categories. It still cannot contain hair, hoof, and so on.

- "Animal Digest" is a powder or liquid made by taking clean, undecomposed animal tissue and breaking it down using chemical and or enzymatic hydrolysis. Digest is "predigested." Animal digest does not contain hair, horn, teeth, hooves, or feathers, except in unavoidable trace amounts. Digest names must be descriptive of their source: chicken digest must be from chicken, beef from beef.

- "Fish Meal" is clean, dried, ground tissue of undecomposed whole fish or fish cuttings, with or without the oil extracted.
- "Beef tallow" is fat derived from beef. (*Palika* 56-57).

Notice that AAFCO specifies that the animals used in dog food must be slaughtered: not road kill, nor animals that died from diseases. There has been discussion in the literature about how stringently inspectors are able to enforce this regulation. Allegations have been made that rendering plants accept the bodies of euthanized animals and turn them in to meal and then sell that product to some of the large pet food manufacturers. However, a discussion of such disreputable practices in selecting animals for inclusion in dog food is beyond the scope of this chapter.

Also notice that some of the parts allowed in dog food would not be consumed by humans. It is important to remember that animals in the wild eat almost the entire beast that they have hunted and killed: entrails, hearts, and bones, in addition to the muscle meat. Indeed, when the ancestor of the dog stepped out of the forest and into a human encampment, he was tolerated because he cleaned up the garbage that humans refused to eat. In fact, wolves get their vegetables by eating their herbivore prey's intestines, which contain the leaves and seeds that their prey had recently been consumed. According to William Burkholder, D.V.M., Ph.D., the pet food specialist at the Food and Drug Administration's Center for Veterinary Medicine, the protein quality of these by-products is sometimes better than that of muscle meat (*Bren*). By-products as ingredients can be sources of good nutrition.

Some pet food manufacturers make the claim that their foods contain only human grade ingredients. Before assuming that the chicken in Great Brand Dog Food is Tyson chicken breasts or Perdue chicken thighs, contact the manufacturer and press the customer service representative to be specific. (A list of contact numbers and URLs appears at the end of this chapter.) If the label says human grade, it should be muscle meat, not a part of the animal that we would not eat. I called the customer service department of a company manufacturing "natural" food that uses "human grade" meat, and I was pleasantly surprised to hear the answers to my questions about their definitions of "natural" and "human grade." I asked the representative if their food was "organic," and she answered honestly that it was not, but that the food sources were pesticide- and hormone-free and not genetically altered. You must be the consumer advocate for your dog. When selecting a new food for your new best friend, it is wise to take the advice of the ancient Romans: "Let the buyer beware" and, I might add, "nosey."

Now that we have the theoretical knowledge to interpret the information on a label, let's see what an ingredient list actually looks like. The table Figure 1, "Ingredients of Premium Food," on page 57, is an example taken from a bag of "premium" adult maintenance dog food. We have added the nutrient supplied after the ingredient. Remember that the ingredients are listed by weight.

When reading ingredients, you should observe that the protein and fat sources are specified. Specific protein sources, such as chicken, chicken by-products, lamb, lamb meal, or beef, are preferred to generic sources, such as "meat meal" or "animal digest." The same principle is true for fat. "Beef tallow" is preferable to "animal tallow." Selecting foods with specific protein and fat sources will mitigate the suspicion and fear that the sources were one of the

"4 D" sources: dead, dying, diseased, and disabled animals (*Pitcairn* 16) that are sent to rendering plants and turned into animal meal.

TABLE 1. Ingredients of Premium Food

Ingredient	Nutrient	Ingredient	Nutrient
Chicken	protein	Vitamin E supplement	vitamin
Corn Meal	carbohydrate	Zinc Oxide	mineral
Chicken By-Product Meal	protein	Ascorbic acid	vitamin and natural preservative
Ground Whole Grain Sorghum	carbohydrate	Manganese Sulfate	mineral
Ground Whole Grain Barley	carbohydrate	Copper Sulfate	mineral
Fish Meal	fat and protein	Manganous Oxide	mineral
Chicken Fat (preserved with mixed tocopherols and citric acid)	fat	Vitamin A acetate	vitamin
Brewers Rice	carbohydrate	Calcium Pantothenate	mineral
Natural Chicken Flavor	flavoring	Biotin	B vitamin
Dried Beet Pulp (sugar removed)	fiber	Rosemary Extract	flavoring and natural preservative
Dried Egg Product	protein	Vitamin B12 supplement	vitamin
Brewers Dried Yeast	protein	Thiamine Mononitrate	B1 vitamin
Salt	preservative	Niacin	B vitamin
Potassium Chloride	mineral	Riboflavin	B2 vitamin
Sodium Hexametaphosphate	mineral	Pyridoxine Hydrochloride	B6 vitamin
Flax Meal	fat	Beta-carotene	A vitamin
Choline Chloride	B vitamin	Potassium Iodide	mineral
Calcium Carbonate	mineral	Folic Acid	vitamin
Ferrous Sulfate	mineral	Cobalt Carbonate	mineral
DL-Methionine	amino acid (protein)		

We have completed looking at the chemical components of the label. It is now time to study the mathematical portions of the label.

LABEL NUMBERS

Weight

Packaging can be deceiving. The net quantity statement tells you how much product is in the container. Cans holding 14 ounces may be the same size as those holding 16 ounces. Bags of "reduced calorie" dog food weighing 12 pounds can have the same proportions as bags of maintenance food holding 15 pounds because of the density of the product. FDA regulations do not specify that a bag of 12 pound food should be smaller than a bag of 15 pound food; they only specify the size and placement of the net quantity statement on the bag (*Dzanis*).

Expiration Date

The package should contain a statement that reads "use before....(month, day, year)." Generally speaking, a dry dog food that has not been opened is usable up to one year from the date of manufacture. Canned dog food is good for two years. It is always wise to select a bag or can with the most distant expiration date. After the expiration date, some ingredients begin to break down. Feeding such food, at best, may result in poor nutrition, unpalatability, and a bad smell, and, at worst, could actually make your dog sick. (*Frequently Asked Questions About Dog Nutrition*). After canned food is opened, it must be refrigerated so that it will not become a medium for the growth of deleterious bacteria and should be used within three days. It is not a healthy practice to leave canned food in a dog's dish all day long. Dry dog food, provided that it has not been moistened, may remain in the dog's dish all day. If dry dog food has been moistened, it should be removed after 20 minutes because it, too, will become a medium for the growth of bacteria.

Once a bag of dry dog food has been opened, it should be kept in an airtight container to prevent the absorption of moisture leading to spoilage and also to deter any bugs from invading the package. The airtight container also makes it difficult for the dog to also help herself to a midday snack. Several years ago my Labrador Retriever, Rocky, opened the kitchen cabinets and helped himself to an eight pound bag of cat food. A drastic change in diet can result in severe intestinal upset. Rocky spent the night in the vet with intravenous tubing and medication to help him overcome what was diagnosed as "dietary indiscretion," and I had a huge vet bill to help me learn a lesson in proper storage.

When you have used all the food in the airtight container, it should be washed and dried before refilling it with new dry food. Fats from the old food may be present in the container and may be spoiling. The rancid fat could contaminate the new food.

You will notice that also stamped on the package is a series of numbers and letters. This is a code for the lot. If something should be found wrong with food from that lot, the manufacturer can issue a recall of those bags or cans bearing that code only.

Guaranteed Analysis

This statement is required on labels. It states the minimum or maximum nutrient values of four nutrients. Values that must be listed on the label are minimum percent of crude protein, minimum percent of crude fat, maximum percent of crude fiber, and maximum percent of moisture. (*Zezula* 9). Some manufacturers include other values but crude protein, crude fat, crude fiber, and moisture are the only values mandated. "Crude" refers to the total content, but not necessarily to the amount that is actually digestible. Digestibility depends on many factors including the quality of the ingredients and the metabolism of the individual dog. (*Palika* 54). The minimum daily requirements and the formulae to compute the actual amounts of nutrients in dry and canned food will be discussed further on.

AAFCO Statement or Statement of Nutritional Adequacy

AAFCO, the Association of American Feed Control Officials, was founded to establish uniform standards for feed industry. AAFCO is not a governmental agency and lacks enforcement capabilities; it makes recommendations that the Food and Drug Administration and the United States Department of Agriculture administer.

The AAFCO statement of nutritional adequacy or purpose, which is also referred to as the "nutrition claim" or the "complete and balanced statement," identifies the life stage for which the product has been approved: growth or puppy, gestation/lactation, maintenance, all life stages. There are three methods AAFCO recognizes for substantiating the claim of nutritional adequacy.

The first method is laboratory analysis. Using this method food is analyzed in the laboratory and the results compared to the minimum nutritional values established in AAFCO profiles. If the method of substantiating nutritional adequacy is laboratory analysis, the label will read "XYZ Dog Food is formulated to meet the nutritional levels established by the AAFCO Dog Food Nutrient Profiles for…(appropriate life stage. e.g. growth, adult, all life stages)."

The second method of substantiating the nutritional claim is feeding trials. In this method, a specified number of dogs are fed the food being tested for 26 weeks. The test group of dogs is examined by veterinarians at regular intervals, and weights and blood tests are performed. If feeding trials are the method of substantiation, the label will read: "Animal feeding tests using AAFCO

procedures substantiate that ABC Dog Food provides complete and balanced nutrition for (appropriate life stage)."

The third method is comparable analysis. Using this method, laboratory analysis of the food in question is compared with nutritional values from a similar product fed to dogs according to AAFCO procedures. If comparable analysis is used, the label will read: "LMN Dog Food provides complete and balanced nutrition for (appropriate life stage) and is comparable in nutritional adequacy to a product which has been substantiated using AAFCO feeding tests." (*AAFCO Statements Explained*)

The use of feeding trials as a method of substantiating the nutritional adequacy claim is preferable. A food may meet theoretical standards, but unless and until it is actually tested on dogs, its nutrition claims are just that, theoretical. It is important to remember that AAFCO sets minimum standards, not optimum ones. Nevertheless, having a minimum standard is preferable to having no standard at all or having individual states or individual manufacturers establish separate standards.

Feeding Instructions

The manufacturer supplies a chart on the label with suggestions for the appropriate amounts to be fed depending on the dog's weight. These amounts are only suggestions. Amounts will need to be varied based upon the dog's activity level and individual metabolism. The manufacturer of the food Penni eats recommends that a dog of her weight eat a total of 1 to 1 ½ cups a day. When Penni is practicing agility every day in preparation for a trial, I will feed her a total of 1 ½ cups, so that she will run like the wind on the agility course. When she is laying around in the off season, I feed her about one cup in order to keep her weight around 22 pounds so she can soar over the triple jump. An important point to remember is that the label makes a recommendation for *total daily* consumption. If you feed your dog twice a day, the amount fed at each meal should be half of the recommended daily amount

If you are feeding the recommended amount and your dog is getting fat even with adequate exercise, then reduce the amount being fed or switch to a reduced calorie dog food. Conversely, if you are feeding the recommended amount and your dog is too thin, increase the amount or consider one of the performance formulas. If your dog is neither too fat nor too thin, she will have a waist, when viewed from above. You should also be able to feel your dog's ribs, but not count them (*Fogle* 45). If your dog has a waist, palpable ribs, and a normal energy level for the breed (no one would expect a Basset Hound to bounce around like a Jack Russell Terrier), then you are feeding the correct amount.

Now that you have learned to read the information that the label provides—brand name, responsible party together with contact information, ingredients: type and quantity, expiration date, guaranteed analysis, AAFCO statement, and feeding instructions—you might have some questions about the kinds of information that are NOT on the label. This is the section called "Reading Between the Lines"

READING BETWEEN THE LINES

The first thing the label does not tell you is how the lamb, chicken gizzards, hulls, middlings, dried eggs, rice, niacin, and iodine became dry dog food. The process by which meat and dry grains become kibble is called extrusion. The ingredients are mixed and combined with moisture and then heated. The mixture is pushed through a plate shaped like the finished product and then sliced. When the kibble hits the air, it expands accounting for the holes in the kibble (*Palika* 4-5).

Another fact the label does not tell you how many calories are in a cup of food. In fact, it does not tell you how many calories your dog should eat each day. Granted the manufacturers have made these calculations and have translated them into their recommendations for the amount to be fed each day. But you would like to know how many calories your dog is consuming or should be consuming. The table "National Research Council: Calories Required Per Day," on page 60, which is based on the National Research Council's recommendations explained in *Nutrient Requirements for Dogs*, 1985, should answer your questions. Another way to calculate

TABLE 2. National Research Council: Calories Required Per Day

Size of Dog	Weight	Calories Per Day
Small	5-20 pounds	240-690
Medium	20-50 pounds	690-1370
Large	50-100 pounds	1370-2310
Extra Large	100-150 pounds	2310-3130

the total number of calories can be found in the following chart from Dr. Russell A. Hansen's WhiskerWatch Web site.

TABLE 3. Caloric Needs by Weight

Weight	Caloric Needs Per Pound
1-2 lbs.	60
5-10 lbs.	45
15-30lbs.	35
30-45lbs.	30
75-110lbs.	23

Using the first chart, I will need to feed Penni, who weighs 22 pounds, between 690 and 1370 calories a day. Using the second chart, I would feed Penni 770 calories a day (22 lbs X 35 calories), which is within the range that the National Research Council specifies. Manufacturers are not required to list caloric content on the label, although they have counted the calories and translated them into the amounts recommended to be fed daily. While different brands vary in caloric content, it can be estimated that dry foods for adult maintenance contain about 1500 calories per pound. Canned foods for the same life stage contain about 500 calories per pound (*Hansen*). Penni eats about 1 cup of dry food a day, as recommended on the dry dog food she is fed. One cup weighs 8 ounces, which equals about 750 calories. I deduce that she is receiving a proper caloric intake, which falls within the recommended range, no matter which chart I use.

Also not listed on the label are the minimum daily requirements for each nutrient. From reading the label you know what the guaranteed analysis for protein and fat are, but what is the recommended daily requirement these nutrients. You would like to compare foods based upon how well they supply the minimum daily requirements (MDR), but these requirements are not listed on the label. AAFCO has established the minimum

requirement for protein for adult maintenance foods at 18% and the minimum requirement for fat at 5%. For growth foods the percentages for protein and fat are 22% and 8% respectively. (*Palika* 10). Now take out your calculator.

By knowing the guaranteed analysis, you can calculate the percentages in the food under consideration and compare them to MDR. These percentages are expressed on a dry matter basis. To arrive at the percentage of food that is dry matter, deduct the guaranteed analysis amount for moisture from 100%. The remainder is the amount of dry solids. Next take the guaranteed analysis amount for protein and divide it by the amount of dry solids. For a bag of adult maintenance dry food that has a guaranteed analysis of not less than 25% for protein and a guaranteed analysis of not more than 10% for moisture, subtract 10 from 100. The result is 90, meaning that 90% of the food is dry matter. Then divide 25 (the percentage of protein) by 90 (the amount of dry matter). The answer is 27, which exceeds the minimum requirement for protein.

Perhaps you want to compare a dry food to a canned food. The same formula applies. A can of adult maintenance food lists the guaranteed analysis for protein as 9% and the guaranteed analysis for moisture as 78%. Subtract 78 from 100. Then divide the remainder, 22 into 9. The answer is 40, which also exceeds the minimum requirement of 18% and also exceeds the amount of protein in the dry food. Remember AAFCO has set a **minimum** standard but not a maximum standard, and not an optimum one. You must judge if the food is meeting your dog's protein requirement by her energy level, her rate of growth if a puppy, and so on.

The same formula can be applied to fats. Again the standard is a minimum one. Look at your dog's coat, energy level, weight, and decide if the fat content in the food meets your dog's requirement.

If you want to figure out how much of the food is carbohydrates, add the crude protein, crude fat, crude fiber, ash, and moisture and subtract that total from 100. The remainder is carbohydrates. For example, if the label indicates that crude protein is 25%, crude fat is 16%, crude fiber is 5%, and moisture is 10%, add 25, 16, 5, and 10. The sum is 56. Subtracting 56 from 100, gives the remainder of 44. Carbohydrates constitute 44% of this food. (*Zezula* 12)

While AAFCO has set minimum standards for vitamins and minerals, you will not find these percentages listed on the label. You must assume that if the food has the nutritional adequacy statement, then it meets the minimum standards.

Realistically, you cannot stand in the aisle of the supermarket and perform all these calculations. There is an easier way to compare foods. The PetsMart Web site has a Dog Food Comparison feature that allows you to compare four foods at one time. You select the foods you want to compare, and within a few seconds you will see a chart that will provide you with the top ten ingredients, the guaranteed analysis, the weights of the packages, and the prices of those packages.

VALUE AND PRICE

Speaking of price, how do you determine if you are getting the most value for your money? Some of the least expensive foods use lower quality ingredients, necessitating feeding more of the food to provide adequate nutrition. Some of the premium foods, made with higher quality ingredients, actually require you to feed less. The price per bag is not the figure to be considered. The price per feeding is the important figure. Take out the calculator again. Divide the total cost by the number of days the food lasts (*Choosing a Pet Food*). A 20 pound bag of premium dog food that costs $20.99 and lasts 30 days costs $.69 a day to

feed. A 20 pound bag of supermarket brand dog food that costs $17.49 and lasts 20 days costs $.87 a day to feed. It seems more economical to feed the premium dog food.

PUTTING IT ALL IN PRACTICE

The chemistry and mathematical lessons are over. But you probably still have questions about feeding. When should you switch your puppy to adult food and your adult dog to a senior formula? How should a switch be effected to avoid digestive upset? How many times a day you should feed your new companion animal, or should you put a bowl of food down in the morning and let her nibble all day. Is dry kibble or canned food better? Should you add supplements to the food you purchase and may you give treats? Will a dog become bored with the same diet day after day? Since you want to provide the exercise and stimulation for your dog, you want to know how soon after eating you should take your dog for a romp. We will now address these issues.

While the puppy was at the breeder's house, she was gradually introduced to solid food. The breeder either fed a "Growth/Puppy" formula or one that was suited for "All Life Stages" as AAFCO specifies. The pup should be fed 3 or 4 times a day until she reaches 40 to 50 percent of her adult weight. Some of the larger breeds may take longer to arrive at 50 percent of adult weight and will consequently eat puppy food for a longer period of time (*Cusick* 41). At 12 weeks, Penni weighed 12 pounds (the recommended maximum weight for an adult corgi bitch according to the standards is about 25 pounds). Since she had reached 50% of her adult weight at 12 weeks, I was advised to put her on an adult maintenance food. If you have adopted a dog of uncertain origin, the so called, "All American," "Designer," or "Generic" dog, and you have no idea what the ideal adult weight should be, your veterinarian will advise you of the appropriate time to switch foods and reduce feeding. Once feeding is reduced to twice a day, that schedule should remain for the rest of your dog's life. Veterinarians believe that feeding twice a day helps prevent bloat, a life threatening gastric disorder (*Thompson* 168). Feeding twice a day insures that there is some food in the stomach, thus preventing vomiting caused by an empty stomach. Finally, feeding twice a day also insures a more constant level of nutrients in the dog's body. Some even assert that feeding twice a day cuts down on begging. (*Palika,* 94)

I have a corgi and two retrievers. Food is number one on their priority list. From my experience with these dogs, I would have to say that nothing cuts down on begging. Ignore the sad-eyed look if you can, teach the dog to remain on a down stay when you are seated at the dinner table so that you do not see the look, but don't think that a steady stream of nutrients in her blood stream will make the dog stop asking for tasty tidbits. Remember that if you feed twice a day, you cut the recommended amount recommended on the label in half and give that amount at each meal.

Be consistent. Try to feed at approximately the same time every day and in the same place. Dogs are creatures of habit. Also it is a good idea to feed your dog **after** you have eaten. This practice establishes your dominance over the dog. In the wild, the alpha wolf eats first and the rest of the pack eats what is left. By having your dog eat after you do, she learns her place in your household "pack." (*Palika* 92) When the dog is finished, take the food bowl away. Do not permit the dog to growl at you when you do (see recommendations for taking away treats).

It is not a good idea to put a bowl of kibble down in the morning and leave it all day. This practice can result in the dog overeating and irregular bowel function (*Thompson* 168). However, water should be available to the dog at all times. Water, which is the most important nutrient, essential for certain biochemical reactions, provides the conduit for the other nutrients to enter the bloodstream.

FEEDING SENIORS

When does your adult dog become a senior? Veterinarians define dogs as geriatric when they have reached the last 25% of their expected life span (*Feeding Dogs for Life Stages*). So the answer varies depending on breed and size. Large breed dogs, who take longer to mature, also age faster. Manufacturers of senior formulas have suggestions for the appropriate age to switch to the senior formulation. Purina suggests that small dogs are geriatric after age 12, medium dogs after age 10, large dogs after age 9, and giant dogs after age 7. You should look for signs of aging, which include weight gain, difficulty moving, hearing, and seeing, and changes in bowel and bladder habits (*Feeding Dogs for Life Stages*), using the manufacturer's definitions as guidelines only. I started feeding my Golden Retriever, Honey, senior formula when she was 7. By Purina's definition, I should have waited until she was 9. But she has hip dysplasia and she seemed to be having trouble getting into a standing position. The vet thought that the glucosamine and chondroitin in the senior formula of the brand I use would help her, and because she gets up easier now and enjoys a daily game of fetch, I believe that it has. I don't anticipate putting Penni, who is 6, on senior food until she is 10 or 11. But I will make that decision based upon her activity level and her ease of movement and with the advice of my trusted veterinarian.

There is controversy in the literature about the content of senior food. Some studies show that seniors need reduced protein and more carbohydrates. (*Cusick* 46) Other studies show that older dogs benefit from increased protein. A friend of mine found that putting her "All American" retriever mix on a high protein diet actually improved his coat and his energy level. Other older dogs with medical problems such as failing kidneys, cannot handle high protein and need a diet lower in protein or even a prescription diet. Decisions on what to feed the older dog and when to convert to senior food cannot be made in the pet food aisle. They must be made in consultation with your veterinarian.

SWITCHING FOODS

If you have made the decision to switch foods, either because your dog has advanced to another life stage, or is overweight, or because you are not satisfied with the present brand your dog is eating, the changeover must be gradual so that the dog's digestive tract can readjust gradually to a different balance.

Do you remember the story of my Lab, Rocky, and the results of his gluttonous consumption of 8 pounds of cat food? Intestinal upset is the only polite way I can describe it. I will spare you the details. If you have ever changed a dog's food abruptly, you know what I mean; there is no need for me to paint a vivid picture. To avoid diarrhea and other attendant symptoms, the 75/25 rule for changeover should be followed. On days 1 to 3 of the changeover, serve a mixture of 25% new food and 75% old food. On days 4 to 6 serve 50% new food and 50% old food. On days 7-9 serve 75% new food and 25% old food. On day 10 serve 100% new food. (*Frequently Asked Questions About Dog Nutrition*). During the switch, observe the dog for any untoward effects. If diarrhea develops, slow down the rate of change. If diarrhea persists, consider returning to the old food or selecting a different new food.

In considering a switch in foods, you might also be trying to decide between canned and dry. Since manufacturers create complete and balanced nutrition in both forms, the choice should really be based on cost and the dog's preference and tolerance. In general, dry kibble is less expensive to feed and has the added benefit of helping to scrape tartar off teeth. The cost to feed Penni dry food alone would be about $.70 a day. The cost to feed her canned food alone would be $1.09 a day. If I were basing the choice on cost alone, I would select the dry kibble. However, I like the appearance of canned food. Although it is really a combination of meats, grains, and so on, it looks like meat and it makes me feel that I am giving her real meat, which would be her diet in the wild. So I mix the dry and the canned, and I add fresh vegetables, fruits, and sometimes home cooked meat suitable for human consumption to her already complete and balanced super-premium dog food.

SUPPLEMENTS

My practice of supplementation brings us to the question of whether or not to add vitamins or other foods when feeding a commercial dog food that is complete and balanced. There are passionately held beliefs on each side of this argument. Manufacturers and some veterinarians claim that to add to a diet that was selected for its completeness unbalances the diet and perhaps even makes it unsafe depending on the degree of unbalance. They advise that if a particular brand of dog food is not meeting your dog's needs, then change to another complete and balanced variety rather than play amateur chemist/nutritionist. Others argue that a complete and balanced diet meets only minimum standards and that every breed and possibly every dog is unique and may require more of one nutrient. Furthermore, they argue that nutrients may begin to be lost the longer a food remains on the shelf, despite its expiration date, and that certain pollutants or stresses in a dog's life warrant higher doses of vitamins, minerals (*Mindell* 172). You must weigh the arguments and decide for yourself.

I began to supplement my Golden Retriever's food with a fatty acid supplement. No matter what premium food I fed Honey, what should have been a lovely golden coat lacked luster. She shed a great deal all year long. After a few months on the supplement, her coat glistened and the shedding decreased. Also, poor Honey had an ongoing anal gland problem, which was heading for surgical resolution because it could not be resolved just by periodic emptying. I added some fiber, specially formulated for dogs, to her daily rations and the problem has disappeared, thus eliminating the necessity for surgery.

On occasion I have added string beans to Rocky's and Penni's diets. Filling up on a nutritious and low calorie vegetables helped them to lose weight in a seemingly painless manner.

I have even supplemented my cat's diet on the advice of my vet, who suggested adding canned pumpkin for bulk to help ward off the blockages that can be life-threatening to cats. You will have to decide if you want to supplement based upon your dog's condition. Supplements can be anything from fresh fruits and vegetables, to vitamins, minerals, probiotics, and enzymes. But there is a great deal of difference between adding a few vegetables and adding megadoses of vitamins. Remember that vitamins work in concert with each other. Too much of one can throw off the amount of another. It is wise to check with your veterinarian before starting a supplementation regimen and educate yourself about the pros and cons so that you can make an informed decision.

Although I like the idea of giving my dog meat, you may be a vegetarian and may want your dog to be one as well. Dogs are omnivores. While they eat meat, they can thrive on an all-vegetable diet. You do not have to prepare this diet yourself. There are several companies that make a complete and balanced vegetarian diet.

TREATS AND CHEWS

Since we are on the subject of adding to a diet, you might want to know if giving treats is allowable. Treats can certainly be given during the day but unfortunately—just like human snack food—treats have calories and, for the most part, are not part of a complete and balanced diet. Treats should not constitute more than 10% of the total daily caloric intake. Furthermore, anything labeled as a treat is exempt from the requirement of the AAFCO nutritional adequacy statement and feeding directions (*Freeman*). So limit the amount of treats, and make an adjustment in the total amount of food consumed daily to make allowance for their inclusion.

Avoid the temptation to give a treat "just because"—just because your dog is the best, cutest, smartest, most lovable animal in the world, just because you missed her, just because you need to show her you love her. The statement "There is no free lunch" should be your motto. Make her work for every treat. Even if she is begging and you want to give in, at least make her sit or give paw. By making the dog earn the treat, you reinforce your position as the pack leader.

Treats can be biscuits, rawhides, and what I call "body parts": pig and lamb ears, hooves, pig snouts, and so on. According to FDA regulations, these treats must indicate their content, but they do not have to list the same information such as guaranteed analysis that appears on a bag of pet food. Also, don't ignore fresh fruits and vegetables as treats. These fresh foods are much lower in calories than store bought treats. All my dogs relish apple slices, carrot sticks, orange slices.

Rawhides, which have been touted as having tartar removal properties, and also help keep jaws strong and gums healthy while preventing boredom (*Mindell* 169), may also be given as occasional treats. They can be in natural form, pressed, or granulated. Natural are sheets that are formed into knots, circles, and braids and may be flavored. Pressed rawhide is formed by pressing the sheets together. The process results in a product that is dense and hard and that tends to last longer. Granulated bones are made of ground rawhide that are molded into shapes. Granulated chews break apart easily. Rawhide is a by-product. It is made from the inner layer of cow hide. The hides are cleaned by placing them in large drums filled with water and, usually, hydrogen peroxide and agitating them. After cleaning, the hides are rinsed for a minimum of an hour and then dried, cut, and shaped. (*Rawhide Rules*). Select rawhide is made in the United States from U.S. raised beef. Since the outbreak of "Mad Cow Disease," (BSE, bovine spongiform encephalopathy), pet food products made from meat raised in countries whose herds are infected may not be imported into the United States. If you have any questions about which nations are on the prohibited list, you can call the FDA's Center for Veterinary Medicine at 301-594-1755 (*Bren*).

There are safety considerations when giving your dog a rawhide. Never leave a dog unsupervised when she is enjoying a rawhide. Aggressive chewers can break off and swallow large chunks of rawhide, which can cause choking or blockage. Rocky, my voracious, gluttonous Lab, can consume a rawhide in no time, and then he and I suffer the consequences for days. He gets diarrhea, and I get to clean it up.

Also, for the very same reasons, follow the same guideline of not leaving a dog alone with a hoof. I used to give both Rocky and Penni hooves, especially during the puppy stage when they were teething and needed something acceptable to chew on. But both

of them, despite the great disparity in their sizes, were able to crunch the hooves and swallow large pieces. Hooves are brittle and can have sharp edges. I was very lucky that they did not suffer any stomach or bowel perforations, and I decided to substitute other treats.

Should you give your dog bones as treats? This topic is hotly debated. I still adhere to the long-held opinion that chicken, lamb chop, and steak bones should not be given because of the danger of splintering and gut perforation. The proponents of the raw diet might take issue with my stance. Veterinarians themselves are divided on the issue. They do agree that if you are going to give a bone, give beef tails or ribs which are too large for your dog to swallow whole. The bones should have some meat attached and as much fat as possible removed. Raw bones or those cooked in water are preferred to baked, broiled or barbecued bones because bones cooked with a dry heat method are harder to digest and are more brittle. If you give a raw bone, take it away and throw it out after two days since it will spoil quickly (*Morn* 18). Again, read the opinions of experts on each side of the argument and decide for yourself.

Some pet owners allow their dogs to enjoy marrow bones, both raw and cooked. Penni had a very bad experience with a marrow bone. When she was a puppy, but after her adult teeth had come in, I used to give her a sterilized marrow bone filled with cheese or peanut butter to enjoy. In the blink of an eye, she would devour the filling and would proceed to gnaw on the bone. It occupied her for quite a long time, as nothing else did. However, one day she was munching on the bone and cracked a tooth. The slab fracture was treated with a root canal. Unfortunately that tooth began to disintegrate and had to be extracted. After the slab fracture, I removed marrow bones from my list of acceptable treats and never gave them again.

When giving a treat for the first time, observe any ensuing digestive problems and consider an alternate treat if your dog experiences any upset.

If you limit the time your dog is allowed to enjoy the rawhide, pig ear, or marrow bone, and you wish to take the remainder of the treat away to save for another day, or if the rawhide or bone has reached the stage where it can be swallowed whole, and you wish to take it away, do not tolerate any possessiveness on the dog's part. Growling, snapping, and guarding can be avoided if you first teach the dog the command "trade." Have a piece of carrot or kibble or other tasty tidbit and offer it to the dog using the word "trade." When she drops the chew, take the treat away and give the carrot, apple slice, or other treat. The dog will learn that by giving up one good thing she gets another good thing, and you avoid inappropriate behavior (*Thompson* 82). Remember you are the Alpha. Your motto should be, "The Alpha gives and the Alpha takes away."

Since we are talking about giving foods such as carrots, apples, and sweet potatoes, you might wonder if all foods that humans eat can be eaten by dogs. The answer is no. The ASPCA lists the following foods, which are safe for humans, as unsafe for dogs: alcoholic beverages, apple seeds, apricot pits, cherry pits, chewing tobacco, chocolate (baker's, semi-sweet, milk, dark), cigarettes, cigars, coffee, hops (used for home brewing), macadamia nuts, moldy foods, mushroom plants, mustard seeds, onions and onion powder, peach pits, potato leaves and stems (green parts), rhubarb leaves, salt, snuff, tea, tomato leaves and stems (green parts), walnuts, and yeast dough (*Pet Poison Prevention Tips*). Individual dogs may have reactions to certain foods not on the list. Rocky gets itchy when he eats zucchini. Observe your dog when giving a food for the first time and limit the number of new foods you introduce to one at a time. If a reaction occurs, you will be able to identify the offending food. Reactions can be anything from excessive gas, to vomiting, diarrhea, constipation, excessive scratching.

While we are on the subject of bowel habits, you might be concerned about the frequency or consistency of your dog's stool. It is not unusual for a dog to have two bowel movements for every meal when she is young. As a dog gets older, her intestinal tract slows down and the number of bowel movements a day will decrease. Also observe the type of stool. Too large, too hard, too loose? Consider changing the food. I fed Rocky a well-known premium brand. It was recommended to improve his coat and it did live up to its claim. But his stools were too large and too loose and he had a lot of gas, so I gradually switched him to another premium brand and achieved a good coat and acceptable stools and clean air. As you know, each dog may differ in ability to metabolize certain ingredients, and ingredients in even the best dog foods differ. If one dog food does not meet all your requirements, choose another from the more than 3000 varieties that are available commercially.

THE QUESTION OF VARIETY

If you and I ate the same food every day, we would become bored in no time. Even a daily dose of McDonald's fries would lose its appeal in a matter of days. For the most part, though, dogs do not become bored. In fact, being creatures of habit, they seem to prefer the same food day in and day out (*Answers to Common Questions About Feeding Dogs & Cats*).

However, there are those animal nutritionists who argue that food should be changed periodically. They maintain that over time, a healthy diet should contain a variety of sources of protein, carbohydrates, fats, and other nutrients. Dr. William Burkholder, the Center for Veterinary Medicine's pet food specialist, says, "Doing so helps ensure that a deficiency doesn't develop for some as yet unknown nutrient required for good health" (*Bren*).

On the other hand the argument can be made that picky eaters are made, not born, and that constant changes can result in a finicky eater (*Answers to Common Questions About Feeding Dogs & Cats*). If you wish to rotate the brand of food your dog eats every few months, remember to effect the changeover gradually and observe your dog for any changes that would warrant a return to the old food.

FOOD AND EXERCISE

We have discussed only one aspect of keeping your dog happy and healthy, namely food. Proper exercise, another requirement for good health, is discussed elsewhere in this book. But timing of exercise and feeding should be addressed here. It is never a good idea to exercise heavily and be fed immediately afterwards. Conversely, it is also a bad idea to eat a big meal and then go out for exercise. Remember when you were a child, and you were warned not to go swimming immediately after lunch? The same admonishments are wise for dogs. Do you remember trying to run laps in gym class right after lunch? Do you remember how you felt and how you performed? Some studies have suggested that heavy exercise immediately preceding or following a meal may contribute to bloat, a life threatening gastric disorder. While there is no conclusive evidence to either prove or disprove this theory, waiting an hour before exercising after eating or before eating after exercise seems to be a wise practice. From my experience, the only exercise Penni wants after dinner is a quick trip to her toilet spot and a brisk trot to her bed or a jump up on my bed for a nap, and if I try to have her run an agility course shortly after eating, her speed and performance suffer.

CHOOSING WHAT'S BEST FOR YOUR DOG

We all want what is best for our dogs so that they can live long, happy, healthy lives. To achieve that end, we want to select the best food for them. In summary, here are suggestions on making the choice for a best food. Learn to read and interpret the label. Compare prices. Select a food that fits your dog's life style and life stage. Test the food. Does your dog like it and do her eyes, skin, coat, teeth, growth rate, energy level, and bowels indicate that she is receiving optimum nutrition (*Zezula* 5)? Keep up to date with the literature. Learn about trends. Learn to recognize a fad from an improvement. Finally, consult with your veterinarian. If you follow these guidelines, you can be assured that you are providing the best diet for your new best friend and that you and she will enjoy each other's company for years to come.

This chapter is written with the advice of CCI's Penni, CGC, NA, NJ, NGC, OAC, OAJ, therapy dog extraordinaire, 6 year old Pembroke Welsh corgi, as well as the assistance of Mom's Rocky Black Bandit (Rocky), 12 year old Labrador Retriever, and FS China Anniversary (Honey), 9 year old Golden Retriever.

Florence Scarinci's Penni

REFERENCES

AAFCO Definitions of Dog Food Ingredients. 1997-2001 6 Jan. 2002. http://www.mindspring.com/ ~woofsportsusa/aafco.htm

"AAFCO Statements Explained." *Food For Thought Technical Bulletin No. 50 R*. Iams Co. 2000. 17 Dec. 2001. http://www.iams.com/qanda/FFT/50raafco/50raafco.htm

Animal Protection Institute. *Selecting a Commercial Pet Food*. 2001. 18 Nov. 2001. http:// www.api4animals.org/doc.asp?ID=689

Animal Protection Institute. *What's Really in Pet Food*. 2001. 18 Nov. 2001. http:// www.api4animals.org/doc.asp?ID=79

"Answers to Common Questions About Feeding Dogs & Cats." *Food For Thought Technical Bulletin No. 56 R*. Iams Co. 2001. 17 Dec. 2001. http://www.iams.com/qanda/FFT/56ranswers/ 56ranswers.html

"Answers to Common Questions About Pet Food Ingredients." *Food For Thought Technical Bulletin No. 58R*. Iams Co. 2001 17 Dec. 2001. http://www.iams.com/qanda/FFT/58ranswersfood/ 58ranswersfood.html

Bren, Linda. "Choosing Pet Food By the Label." *Consumer Research Magazine*. June 2001: 22+ *Expanded Academic ASAP*. Infotrac. Nassau Community College Lib., Garden City, NY. 17 Jan. 2002 http://elt.x.../purl=re1_EAIM_0_A76697167&dyn=5!xrn_3_0_A76697167?sw_aep=suny-nassau

Cargill, John. "Decoding Pet Food Label Lingo." *Dog World* Nov. 1997: 26-32.

"Choosing Pet Food." *Questions and Answers*. Iams Co. 2000. 17 Dec. 2001. http:// www.iams.com/qanda/PetOwner/choosing/choosing.htm

Code of Federal Regulations. Title 51.

Cusick, William D. *Meeting the Nutritional Needs of Your Breed of Dog*. Wilsonville, OR.: Doral, 1997.

Dzanis, David A. "Interpreting Pet Food Labels-Part 1 General Rules." FDA Veterinarian Newsletter. September/October 1998. 7 Jan. 2002. http://www.fda.gov/cvm/index/fdavet/1998/ november.htm

Fogel, Bruce. *Natural Dog Care*. New York: DK, 1999.

"Feeding Dogs for Life Stages." *Nutrition*. Purina. 11 Jan. 2002. http://www.purina.com/Dogs/ nutrition.asp?article

Freeman, Lisa M. "Trick or Treat." *AKC Gazette*. 118 (Nov. 2001): 22.

"Frequently Asked Questions About Dog Nutrition." *FAQ: Dog Nutrition*. PETsMART.com 2001. 30 Dec. 2001. http://www.petsmart.com/articles/article_7768.shtml

Hansen, Russell S. *Feeding Adult Dogs*. 11 Jan. 2002. http://www.wpvq.com /wtipfeeddog.htm

How To Feed Your Dog. For Paws Corgi Rescue. 2000. 6 Jan. 2002. http://www.forpaws.org/articles/feeding.htm

Kerns, Nancy. "Top Ten Dry Dog Food." *Whole Dog Journal*. Feb. 2001: 3-8.

"Milk-Bone Calorie Information." *Calorie Information*. Milk-Bone. 11 Jan. 2002. http://www.milkbone.com/cal.html

Mindell, Earl. *Earl Mindell's Nutrition and Health for Dogs*. Rocklin, CA.: Prima, 1998.

Morn, September. "Before You Give That Dog a Bone." *DogFancy* Feb. 2002: 18.

National Research Council. *Nutrient Requirements of Dogs*. Washington, D.C.:National Academy Press, 1985.

Palika, Liz. *The Consumer's Guide to Dog Food*. New York: Howell, 1996.

"Pet Poison Prevention Tips." *APCC Toxicology Bulletins*. ASPCA 2002. 11 Jan. 2002. 16 Jan. 2002. http://www.aspca.org/site/News2?page=NewsArticle&id=6428

Pitcairn, Richard H. and Susan Hubble Pitcairn. *Dr. Pitcairn's Complete Guide to Natural Health for Dogs & Cats*. Emmaus, PA: Rodale, 1995.

"Rawhide Rules: Choosing Chewables for Your Dog." *PETsMART Staff Report*. PETsMART.com 16 Jan. 2002. http://www.petsmart.com/articles/articles_7shtml

Regulation of Pet Food. Uncle Ben's of Australia. 2001.6 Jan. 2002. http://www.speedyvet.com/ Learningcentre/course1/4_3AAFCO.htm

Rubin, Dawn. *Dietary Requirements in Dogs*. PetPlace.com. 2001. 11 Jan. 2002. http://www.petplace.com/Articles/artShow.asp?artID=3425

Rubin, Dawn. *When Do You Change from Puppy Food to Adult Food?* PetPlace.com. 20016 Jan. 2002. http://www.petplace.com/Articles/artShow.asp?ID=2994

Thompson, Mary. *Off to a Good Start, a Manual for Raising Your New Puppy*. Holbrook, MA: Adams Media, 2000.

"Understanding Ingredients." *Questions and Answers*. Iams Co. 2000. 17 Dec. 2001 http://www.iams.com/qanda/PetOwner/ingredients/ingredients.htm

Zezula, Jerilee A. *Doc Z's Canine Nutrition Primer*. Nashua, NH: PigDog, 1995.

TABLE 4. Dog Food Manufacturers

BRAND	MANUFACTURER	URL
Alpo	Nestle Purina Petcare Company Checkerboard Square St. Louis, Missouri 63164 800 778-7462	www.alpo.com
Annamaet	Annamaet Petfoods Box 151 Sillersville, PA 18960 215 453-0381	www.annamaet.com
APD Advanced Pet Diet	Breeder's Choice Pet Foods, Inc. P.O. Box 2005 Irwindale, California 91706 800 255-4286	www.breeders-choice.com
AvoActive	Breeder's Choice Pet Foods, Inc. P.O. Box 2005 Irwindale, California 91706 800 255-4286	www.breeders-choice.com
AvoDerm	Breeder's Choice Pet Foods, Inc. P.O. Box 2005 Irwindale, California 91706 800 255-4286	www.breeders-choice.com
Back to Basics	Beowulf Natural Feeds Inc. 801 E. Hiawatha Blvd. Syracuse, NY 13208 800 219-2558	backtobasicspetfood.com
Beneful	Nestle Purina Petcare Company Checkerboard Square St. Louis, Missouri 63164 800 778-7462	www.purina.com
Best In Show	Best In Show Foods Inc. P.O. Box 850 Jupiter, FL 33468-0850 800 364-3287	www.bestinshowpowerfood.com
Bil-Jac	Bil-Jac Foods 3457 Medina Rd Medina. Oh 44256 800 842-5098 330 722-7888	www.biljac.com

TABLE 4. Dog Food Manufacturers

California Natural	Natura Pet Products	www.naturapet.com
	1101 S. Winchester Blvd. San Jose, CA 95128-3919	
	800 398-1600 909 599-5190	
Canidae	Canidae Pet Foods	www.canidae.com
	San Luis Obispo, CA 93403-3610	
	800 398-1600 909 599-5190	
Come 'N Get It	Nestle Purina Petcare Company	www.comengetit.com
	Checkerboard Square St. Louis, Missouri 63164	
	800 778-7462	
Cycle	Heinz Pet Products	www.cycledog.com
	PO Box 57 Pittsburgh, PA 15230	
	800 469-7387	
Diamond	Schell & Kampeter	www.diamondpet.com
	PO Box 156 Meta, MO 65058	
	800 442-0402	
Dog Chow	Nestle Purina Petcare Company	www.purina.com
	Checkerboard Square St. Louis, Missouri 63164	
	800 778-7462	
Eagle Pack	Eagle Pet Products Inc.	www.eaglepack.com
	1011 W. 11th St. Mishawaka, IN 46544	
	800 255-5959	
Eukanuba	Iams	www.eukanuba.com
	7250 Poe Ave Dayton, OH 45414	
	800 525-4267	
Evolve	Triumph Pet Industries, Inc.	www.triumphpet.com
	7 Lake Station Rd. Warwick, NY 10990	
	800 331-5144	
Fit & Trim	Nestle Purina Petcare Company	www.purina.com
	Checkerboard Square St. Louis, Missouri 63164	
	800 778-7462	

TABLE 4. Dog Food Manufacturers

Flint River	Flint River Ranch 1243 Columbia Ave, B6 Riverside, CA 92507 909 682-5048	www.food4pets.com
Friskies	Nestle Purina Petcare Company Checkerboard Square St. Louis, Missouri 63164 800 778-7462	www.friskies.com
Fromm	Fromm Family Foods PO Box 365 Mequon, WI 53092 800 325-6331	www.frommfamily
Gravy Train	Heinz Pet Products PO Box 57 Pittsburgh, PA 15230 800 469-7387	www.gravytrain.com
Health Wise	Natura Pet Products 1101 S. Winchester Blvd. San Jose, CA 95128-3919 800 532-7261	www.naturapet.com
High Hopes	Life Works LLC 5942 N. Northwest Highway Chicago, IL 60631 877 467-1946	www.highhopes4pets.com
Hi-Tor	Triumph Pet Industries, Inc. 7 Lake Station Rd. Warwick, NY 10990 800 331-5144	www.triumphpet.com
Holistique Blendz	Solid Gold Health Products for Pets Inc. 1483 North Cuyamaca El Cajon, CA 92020 800 364-4863	www.solidgoldhealth.com
Hundchen Flocken	Solid Gold Health Products for Pets Inc. 1483 North Cuyamaca El Cajon, CA 92020 800 364-4863	www.solidgoldhealth.com
Hund-N-Flocken	Solid Gold Health Products for Pets Inc. 1483 North Cuyamaca El Cajon, CA 92020 800 364-4863	www.soldigoldhealth.com

TABLE 4. Dog Food Manufacturers

HyRation	Eagle Pack Products, Inc.	www.eaglepack.com
	1011 W. 11th St Mishawaka, IN 46544	
	800 255-5959	
Iams	Iams	www.iams.com
	7250 Poe Ave Dayton, OH 45414	
	800 675-3849	
Innova	Natura Pet Products	www.naturapet.com
	1101 S. Winchester Blvd. Ste J225 San Jose, CA 95128-3919	
	800 532-7261	
Kibbles N Bits	Heinz Pet Products	www.kibbles-n-bits.com
	PO Box 57 Pittsburgh, PA 15230	
	800 469-7387	
Lick Your Chops	Integrated Pet Foods	www.integratedpet.com
	610 Jeffers Circle Exton, PA 19341	
	800 LI CHOPS 800 542-4677	
Life Span	PetGuard Inc.	www.petguard.com
	PO Box 728 Orange Park, FL 32067-0728	
Mighty Dog	Nestle Purina Petcare Company	www.mightydog.com
	Checkerboard Square St. Louis, Missouri 63164	
	800 778-7462	
Mmillenia	Solid Gold Health Pet Products	www.solidgoldhealth.com
	1483 North Cuyamaca	
	El Cajon, CA 92020	
	800 364-4863	
Natural Balance	Dick Van Patten's Natural Balance Pet Foods Inc.	www.naturalbalanceinc.c om
	12924 Pierce St. Pacoima, CA 91331	
	800 829-4493	
Natural Blend	Royal Canin USA Inc.	www.naturalblend.com
	5600 Mexico Rd. Ste 2 St. Peter's, MO 63376	
	800 592-6687	

TABLE 4. Dog Food Manufacturers

Natural Life	Natural Life Pet Products 412 W. St. John St. Girard, KS 66743 620 724-8012	www.nlpp.com
Nature's Recipe	Heinz Pet Products PO Box 57 Pittsburgh, PA 15230 800 469-7387	www.naturesrecipe.com
Neura	Old Mother Hubbard 9 Alpha Rd. Chelmsford, MA 01924 800 225-0904 978 256-8121	www.oldmotherhubbard. com
Nutro	Nutro Products, Inc. 445 Wilson Way City of Industry, CA 91744 800 833-5330	www.nutroproducts.com
Pedigree	Waltham PO Box 58853 Vernon CA 90058 800 525-5273	www.pedigree.com
PHD Perfect Health Diet	PHD Products, Inc 404 Irvington Street Pleasantville, NY 10570 800 743-1502	www.phdproducts.com
Pinnacle	Breeder's Choice PO Box 2005 Irwindale, CA 91706 800 255-4286	www.breeders-choice.com
Prescription Diet	Hills PO Box 148 Topeka, KS 66601 800 445-5777	www.hillspet.com
Precise	Precise Pet Products PO Box 630009 Nacogdoches, TX 75963 800 446-7148	www.precisepet.com
Prism	Eagle Pet Products Inc. 1011 W. 11th St. Mishawaka, IN 46544 800 255-5959	www.eaglepack.com

TABLE 4. Dog Food Manufacturers

ProPlan	Nestle Purina Petcare Company Checkerboard Square St. Louis, Missouri 63164 800 778-7462	www.purina.com
Puppy Chow	Nestle Purina Petcare Company Checkerboard Square St. Louis, Missouri 63164 800 778-7462	www.purina.com
Purina HiPro	Nestle Purina Petcare Company Checkerboard Square St. Louis, Missouri 63164 800 778-7462	www.purina.com
Purina Moist & Meaty	Nestle Purina Petcare Company Checkerboard Square St. Louis, Missouri 63164 800 778-7462	www.purina.com
Purina O.N.E.	Nestle Purina Petcare Company Checkerboard Square St. Louis, Missouri 63164 800 778-7462	www.purina.com
Reward	Heinz Pet Products PO Box 57 Pittsburgh, PA 15230 800 469-7387	www.rewarddog.com
Science Diet	Hills PO Box 148 Topeka, KS 66601 800 445-5777	www.hillspet.com
Sensible Choice	Royal Canin USA Inc. 5600 Mexico Rd. Ste 2 St. Peter's, MO 63376 800 592-6687	www.naturalblend.com
Show Bound Naturals	Integrated Pet Foods, Inc. 610 Jeffers Circle Exton, PA 19341 800 542-4677	www.integratedpet.com
Skippy	Heinz Pet Products PO Box 57 Pittsburgh, PA 15230 800 469-7387	www.skippydog.com

TABLE 4. Dog Food Manufacturers

Solid Gold	Solid Gold Health Products for Pets Inc.	www.solidgoldhealth.com
	1483 North Cuyamaca El Cajon, CA 92020	
	800 364-4863	
Steve's Real Food	Flint River Ranch	www.food4pets.com
	1243 Columbia Ave, B6 Riverside, CA 92507	
	909 682-5048	
Triumph	Triumph Pet Industries, Inc.	www.triumphpet.com
	7 Lake Station Rd. Warwick, NY 10990	
	800 331-5144	
Waltham	Waltham	www.waltham.com
	PO Box 58853 Vernon, CA 90058	
	800 525-5273	
Wellness	Old Mother Hubbard	www.oldmotherhubbard. com
	9 Alpha Rd. Chelmsford, MA 01824	
	800 225-0904 978 256-8121	
Wysong	Wysong Corp.	www.wysong.net
	1880 N. Eastman Rd. Midland, MI 48642-7779	
	989 631-0009	

BARF: THE RAW FOOD DIET

by Joan Adams

Joan Adams shares her knowledge and experience with feeding corgis a raw food diet.

BARF is an acronym for Bones and Raw Food, or Biologically Appropriate Raw Food. The diet was developed by Dr. Ian Billinghurst, B.V.Sc.[Hons], B.Sc.Agr., Dip. Ed., a practicing veterinarian in New South Wales, Australia. After graduating from Sydney University with an honors degree in veterinary medicine, Dr. Billinghurst began a small animals practice. The question asked most frequently by his clients was "What should I feed my dog?" Contrary to his lifelong experience of feeding a raw diet and consistent with his professional training, he also had begun to feed his dogs a "scientifically balanced" commercial dog food. Over a period of time, his once healthy dogs became ill patients. Dr. Billinghurst began to question the diet change and started reading about "natural diets," which he learned were what he had always fed his dogs. The bulk of the diets was raw meaty bones and healthy table scraps, including vegetables and vegetable oils, fruits, small amounts of grain, and organ meat. He supplemented this with vitamins occasionally.

MY EXPERIENCES WITH BARF

When I became interested in showing and training dogs, I asked my vet the same question as had Dr. Billinghurst's clients, "What should I feed my dog?" Like most vets, mine advised me to feed a high quality kibble. I asked my dog friends, who said the same thing. From 1984 to 1998, I fed a "scientifically balanced" kibble and my companions looked fine. However, as I look back to those years, my animals were not fine. They had constant problems with runny eyes and noses, itchy skin, parasites, and continuous trips to the vet. They drank large quantities of water and were always scavenging for more food. The vets could only recommend anti-inflammatory and steroid medications to help. Because of the serious side effects of the medications, I changed their kibble, but the problems continued.

In 1998, my pride and joy, my corgi Lessa, changed my way of thinking. I raised and trained Lessa in the hope of competing with her in conformation and performance events. When she was almost four years old, I began to contemplate breeding her. Prior to her being bred, I had the necessary health and genetic testing done. Approximately two weeks after she had been anesthetized for her hip x-ray, Lessa began having Grand Mal seizures lasting from one to three minutes. I was terrified and immediately took her to my veterinarian. He ran several tests, but could not find anything physically wrong with her. She was diagnosed with epilepsy, but I disagreed with this diagnosis because I knew her parentage: I owned her sire, her dam, and one of her littermates. I contacted several doctors, including the veterinarian who had begun this particular line more than 30 years ago, and found that epilepsy was not considered a problem in this breed or line. Although my veterinarian and a holistic veterinarian had prescribed medications for Lessa's seizures, nothing worked. I decided to send her to the Louisiana State University Veterinarian School for another opinion. They performed numerous tests and made the determination it was either distemper or Granulomatous Meningo Encephalitis (GME). The doctors told me they could perform a spinal tap for a definite diagnosis. We had the spinal tap done and the results were positive for distemper. They told me there was nothing they could do.

A friend of mine had recently started feeding her dogs the BARF diet. Since the doctors couldn't do anything to help Lessa, I thought I would try changing her diet from a commercial dog food to a natural diet. During this time, Dr. Billinghurst was in the United States presenting a seminar. Because I wanted to learn more about BARF and was willing to do anything to help my girl, I went to the seminar. The seminar made a lot of sense to me, and I purchased the book *Give Your Dog A Bone*. After attending the seminar and reading the book, I decided to give the diet a try. With the assistance of the holistic veterinarian, I started changing Lessa's feedings and transferred her to the BARF diet within a week. She was on medication for her seizures, but it made her a zombie and did not stop the seizures. Once she had been on the diet for a few months, I noticed her seizures were declining; they eventually stopped. However, she was still like a zombie, and I could tell she was very unhappy and embarrassed because she couldn't control her body. She could not walk, run, or play.

Because she was so unhappy and I was not convinced it was the medication that had stopped her seizures, I consulted my veterinarian. We agreed to wean her off the medication, which I did over the next several weeks. Her seizures did not return, and Lessa once again was self-confident and happy. She was on the BARF diet and no medication. For more than six months, she remained seizure free.

In April 1999, I noticed a lump on her breast and immediately took her to my vet. He confirmed a mammary tumor and advised me that we needed to have it removed and tested. I was hesitant to do this, but needed to know if the tumor was benign or cancerous. I agreed to the operation. Lessa came through the surgery well. However, two weeks after being under anesthesia for the surgery, Lessa again started having seizures. She was immediately put back on medication, but the seizures did not stop and during one of them, her heart gave out. Because I did not believe the diagnosis of distemper, I had a necropsy done; the results were GME. I firmly believe the anesthesia was the culprit in Lessa's seizures returning, but I also believe the BARF diet was what helped her fight the encephalitis for so long.

During the same time Lessa was diagnosed with her tumor, her dam, Beryl, was also diagnosed with a mammary tumor. Beryl's pathology results confirmed cancer. Beryl

was spayed. My veterinarian believed he had removed all the cancerous tissue, but two to three weeks after Beryl's surgery, she had another tumor. I took her back to my vet and he determined that the cancer had spread to her stomach wall. He did not recommend further surgeries and expected her to live only a few months. Beryl, like Lessa and all my dogs, was on the BARF diet and did not act sick. She surprised everyone and lived seventeen months after her diagnosis. She was happy and eating her BARF diet until the end.

As people become more health conscious toward themselves, they also want their animal companions to live healthier and longer lives. Because our lifestyles have become more and more hectic, processed dog food for our animal companions is less time consuming, but is it healthy?

My personal experiences tell me that processed dog food is less healthy than a BARF diet. Lessa's and Beryl's illnesses convinced me that the diet improved their immune systems. I believe that if they had been eating processed dog food, they could not have fought the diseases as long as they did. Since putting my animal companions on the diet, I have seen tremendous changes: energy levels have increased, teeth have no tartar, eyes are bright and shiny, no allergies, coats gleam, and no parasites.

CHOOSING BARF FOR YOUR DOG

If you have been questioning the healthiness of your companions or their diet, you may want to begin reading about the raw diet. You can begin your research by reading *Give Your Dog a Bone* and *Grow Your Pup with Bones* by Ian Billinghurst, *Natural Nutrition for Dogs and Cats: The Ultimate Diet* by Kymythy Schultz, and *The Holistic Guide For a Healthy Dog* by Wendy Volhard and Kerry Brown, D.V.M. Of course, always consult your veterinarian about your companion's health and any questions or concerns you may have.

Once you have decided to try a raw diet, remember to keep it simple. BARF should consist of 60 percent raw meaty bones (RMB). The rest should be 40 percent food scraps and raw vegetables. A balanced diet should be achieved over time and not over night. Most dogs can be switched cold-turkey, but start with lean chicken or turkey necks for the first couple of days., and keep the meals small. When your dog becomes accustomed to the change, add some bland, pulped vegetables. You need to crush the vegetables in a blender, food processor, or juicer because dogs are unable to digest the cell walls of the plants. Remember that you are striving for vegetable matter consistent with the stomach contents of a prey animal.

Once your dog is used to the simple diet, you can start adding richer foods, such as fatter chicken, eggs, and liver. After a few weeks, you can think about adding supplements if you want. To give your dog time to develop a stronger digestive system, you may want to stay away from the harder and fatter bones for a few months. After a lifetime of eating processed dog food, older dogs, especially, need time to adjust their systems.

During the adjustment to the new diet, some dogs will go through a normal detoxification process. They are cleansing their systems of toxins and impurities they have acquired while eating a processed food diet. Diarrhea is the most common side effect of the detox. Pure pumpkin from a can is one of the best ways to stop the diarrhea. If you think your dog is reacting to a new food, begin an elimination diet by going back to feeding your dog one thing for a short period of time. Gradually, add items back one at a time. An elimination diet should be able to determine which food is causing the diarrhea. If you feel

there is something else causing the diarrhea, then drop off a stool sample with your veterinarian to check for another cause. During the course of the detox, keep the diet bland until the dog is feeling better and you can proceed without further problems.

A frequently asked question is "How much should I feed?" As previously stated, Billinghurst recommends 60 percent RMBs and 40 percent vegetables. Most people use the following formula to help determine how much to feed:

1. Multiply your dog's weight by sixteen to get the number of ounces he weighs.
2. Multiply the number of ounces by 2% (.02) of his body weight.
3. Multiply the total by 60% (.6) to give you the weight of RMBs.
4. Multiply 2% of his body weight by 40% (.4) to get the ounces of vegetables you feed.

This is only a guide. If your dog is overweight, reduce the RMBs and increase the vegetable mix. If your dog is too thin, increase the RMBs and decrease the vegetable mix. You know your dog and should be able to tell if he needs any adjustments in the diet. As I have said, keep the diet simple and use common sense.

DEVELOPING AN INDIVIDUAL DIET

Now that you have a guide for how much and what to feed, you can begin to develop your dog's individual diet. Raw chicken is considered the best to feed your dog. Chicken has the best essential fatty acid content of all bones. Because most of the chickens in butcher shops and supermarkets are very young, their bones are very soft and free of toxins and their bone to flesh ratios are extremely balanced. If you ever try to break a raw chicken bone, you will find it is almost impossible because it is so pliable. Once your dog has eaten through the flesh, the bones are safely pulverized. Wings are a good source of bone marrow, but you should also feed backs and necks. Because of the nutritional quality, chicken can comprise the majority of the RMBs fed to your dog. Raw chicken does carry bacteria, but a healthy dog normally has no problems with it. Use common sense, and after handling raw chicken or any raw meat, wash your hands, and sterilize all utensils and cutlery.

Even though you may feed mostly chicken, you will also want to feed beef and lamb bones for balance and variety. Lamb bones can have too much fat, and the excess should be cut off. Beef bones usually have less fat and flesh, but they can be older, harder, and have more toxins, so you should not give a lot of them. Many people also feed pork, fish and rabbit RMBs. Pork can be very rich and fatty. Rabbit is good but difficult to get. Venison is also good, but very lean and rich.

When you feed RMBs, make sure there is some meat with the bone. Don't feed just bones or just meat; RMB means a combination of the two. RMBs should be fed every day, preferably before other food. If you feed the bones after a meal, dogs are usually too full and won't eat them unless the meal was very small. Therefore, feed the RMBs in the morning and the vegetable mix in the evening.

The vegetable mix can consist of a variety of vegetables and fruits. Dogs are omnivores and should have a lot of green leafy vegetables in their diet. Vegetables provide many nutrients, including fiber, most of the vitamin B groups (except B-12), biotin, folacin, and large quantities of vitamin A, C, E, K, and carotenoid. Carotenoids have antioxidant and anti-aging properties. Antioxidant vitamins from green leafy vegetables are vitamins A, K, E, and C. Vitamin C is also an anti-stress vitamin. These vitamins are all essential for growth, reproduction, and prevention of disease, aging, and degeneration.

Give your dog whatever vegetables you have available. You can offer raw, crushed celery, carrots, pumpkin, spinach, lettuce leaves, bell peppers (red, green, or yellow), parsley, and so on. They are all nutritious. However, do not give large quantities of the cabbage family over a long period. The cabbages can depress the thyroid gland. Also, give raw beans and peas only in limited amounts.

Along with green leafy vegetables, raw fruits contain fiber, vitamins, antioxidants, enzymes, and carbohydrates. You can give dogs any fruit, but the tropical fruits are valuable because they have lots of antioxidants and enzymes. Fruit is especially important for older dogs. It is considered a youth food because of the low amounts of fat and protein. Fruit also helps keep the skin and body free of degeneration. Ripe and overripe fruit is the best, but do not feed rotten fruit because it may produce botulism in your dog. You will need to break down the cellulose cell walls in fruit as you do with the vegetables. Dried fruits are natural laxatives and excellent additions.

Besides feeding green leafy vegetables and fruits, you need to include raw meat in your dog's diet. Meat provides water, energy, and minerals. Meat is not a complete food and is deficient in some vitamins and minerals, so you should not feed a meat-only diet. Meat should be fed in large chunks so the dog can tear and chew. You can feed a variety of raw meat: beef, lamb pork, venison, and chicken.

You can also feed organ meats, but not in large quantities. Organ meats should make up only 10 to 15 percent of the diet for a dog that is not growing, reproducing, or working. If you have a hard-working dog such as a racing, herding, or field trial dog, the percentage of organ meat fed can be will be higher. Liver is the most popular organ meat, but kidneys, hearts and brains are excellent. Liver and kidneys have protein, iron, most B vitamins, and vitamins A, E, D, K and C. Hearts are an excellent source of B vitamins, iron and protein, but do not have vitamin A or many fatty acids. Brains provide good levels of vitamin C, some B vitamins and fatty acids. Brains do not have a lot of vitamin A and E. Other organ meats are tongue and tripe, but they are not as beneficial for your dog.

Many people also feed their dogs fish. However, Dr. Billinghurst recommends not feeding a lot of it. He does recommend feeding sardines, because sardines have part of the omega-3 group. Personally, I do feed my dogs sardines, mackerel, and canned tuna on occasion.

Although feeding a lot of cooked or canned food is not recommended, there are some foods you cannot find unprocessed or raw. Dairy products are an example. Unless you have or have access to a dairy farm or goats, it is difficult to find raw unpasteurized milk. Milk is not an essential part of the dog's diet, but raw milk does have benefits, providing calcium, water, sodium, magnesium, potassium, protein and some vitamins. However, if you can't get raw milk, there are other beneficial dairy products. Cheese provides protein and fat. It is a cooked food and not complete, but you can feed it in small amounts as part of your dog's varied diet. Cheese does have high protein, but is lacking in fatty acids. But cottage cheese is excellent for your dog. Cottage cheese has the amino acids leucine, isoleucine and valine, which help build up muscle and help heal wounds. Cottage cheese has high quality protein, but be aware of the sodium content. Another good dairy product is yogurt, which has friendly bacteria that help keep the bowels healthy. Yogurt is excellent when a dog has diarrhea, any time you think your dog's bacterial balance is upset, or when your dog is on antibiotics. The friendly bacteria, sometimes called probiotics, protect the bowel from the effects of antibiotics. Yogurt also provides calcium, vitamins, protein and enzymes.

The BARF diet also advocates feeding raw eggs. Eggs contain saturated and unsaturated fatty acids, enzymes, minerals, protein, and all the vitamins except C. The shell and yolk are an excellent source of calcium. Everyone has heard that eggs are harmful, but all the documentaries on wild canines show them eating eggs. Egg whites do have an enzyme inhibitor that can make them hard to digest for very young, sick, or old dogs, but usually there is no problem. Egg whites also contain avidin, which binds with biotin, making it unavailable to your dog. In contrast, the egg yolk contains biotin. Therefore, a biotin deficiency should not occur. If you experience problems with the egg whites, you can cook them but leave the yolk raw. Eggs are usually fed once or twice a week. If you want to feed the shell for the calcium content, you should crush it to make it more palatable. It has been my experience that the dogs do not like the hard shell, but crushing it alleviates this problem.

GOING FROM HERE

Now that you have a general idea of the BARF diet, you can decide if you think it is beneficial for your companions. Always remember to keep it simple and use common sense. The diet is always flexible. You are striving for balance over time and not during every meal.

Continue researching all the natural diets to find what is best for you and your companions. There is a wealth of information available from books, the Internet, and hundreds of people and veterinarians who advocate feeding naturally.

COOKIES! TREATS FOR YOUR CORGIS

by Emily (& Bailey) Calle

Yummy! Emily Calle has collected some terrific recipes to treat your corgi.

"Cookie!"

There are few more powerful words in a corgi's English vocabulary. Dog treats, cookies, brownies (you name it, they make it) are readily available at almost any pet supply store. But there's something a little more special, and often more economical, about making them yourself. And, when creating treats at home, you can be sure that your corgi's nutritional requirements are being met—or not met, depending on how indulgent you feel! So, collect up the ingredients, fire up the oven (or cool down the freezer) and get cooking! Your corgi will be thrilled, and you'll know exactly what he's getting.

"Bone" appetit!

Note: All temperatures are in Fahrenheit degrees.

BISCUITS, BROWNIES, & COOKIES

Biscuit Recipe

Ingredients:

1 c. flour
½ c. whole wheat flour
½ c. oats, 2 tbsp. wheat germ
1 tbsp. brown sugar,
½ - ¾ c. hot water with bouillon cube,
3 tbsp. oil

Form in a ball and knead about 1/2 minute. Roll out dough onto lightly floured surface about 3/8 inch thick. Cut with cookie cutters or just into shapes. Bake at 375 for 15-20 minutes until slightly brown and firm. Note: For variety, liver powder, dried vegetable flakes or mashed cooked green vegetables or carrots may be added. Adjust water accordingly.

Zephyr's Chicken Brownies[1]

Ingredients:

12.5 oz. canned chicken
1 ½ c. warm water
2-3 cloves fresh garlic
2 eggs
2 ¼ c. whole wheat flour
1 ¾ c. wheat bran

Put canned chicken, warm water, garlic & eggs into blender and blend until smooth. Set aside. In a bowl, mix whole wheat flour, wheat bran & previously blended ingredients. It should be the consistency of brownie dough; add more bran if too wet or more water if too dry. Spread into a 9"x12" greased cake pan. Cook at 350 for about 35-40 min. It should be dry on top and edges slightly pulled away from sides. Cool and cut into 2"x3" pieces. (A pizza cutter works best.) Freeze portions in zip lock bags. Defrost as needed. These make great training treats or Kong stuffing. If your dog can have corn, it can be made with cornmeal instead of bran, or I am sure oat bran would work too. Just remember to use it within 1 day of defrosting as it contains no preservatives.

Chicken Jerky

Ingredients:

1 lb. ground chicken or turkey
3 tsp. low sodium teriyaki
sprinkle of garlic powder (not garlic salt) or 1 garlic clove
¼ tsp. ground ginger

Mix all ingredients together and spread out very thin on a cookie sheet (very flat). Bake at 150 for 2 hours (prop the oven door open a crack). Turn over and slice into strips like jerky. Bake at 150 for another 2 hours. Cool, put into baggie, and freeze.

Lamb and Rice Biscuits

Ingredients:

1 ½ c. cooked brown rice
½ c. uncooked brown rice, 2 c. rice flour
1 lb. lamb shank
1 egg
2 tbsp. vegetable oil
½ c. lamb broth
½ tsp. salt
1 heaping tbsp. chopped garlic
1 heaping tbsp. dried parsley

NOTE: White rice can be substituted for brown. Rice flour is made by grinding rice in a food processor until it is a fine powder. Lamb broth can be taken from cooked lamb shank.

Boil lamb shank in 4 c. water until thoroughly cooked. Drain and save broth. Cut meat from shank and grind very fine in a food processor. This should yield about 1 cup of lamb meat. Preheat oven to 350. Combine rice flour, cooked rice, uncooked rice, lamb meat, and salt in a large bowl, mix. Add in egg, oil, and broth and mix thoroughly. Roll dough out onto lightly floured surface (preferably rice flour) to about a ½" thickness. Cut out biscuits with a cookie cutter (preferably a dog bone shape). Transfer biscuits to an ungreased baking sheet. Bake for 5–15 minutes for small (1") or 30-35 minutes for large (3") biscuits. Transfer to rack to cool. Store in an airtight container and refrigerate.

Santa Fe Liver Cookies[2]

Ingredients:

1 lb. beef liver with juice
2 eggs with shells,
2 tbsp. garlic powder
1 grated carrot
1 tbsp. wheat germ

1 tbsp. brewer's yeast
1 tbsp. plain low-fat yogurt

1 tbsp. K-Zyme powder
1 small can V-8 juice
cornmeal as needed

Put liver, eggs and garlic powder in food processor and blend until smooth. Add the other ingredients. Add cornmeal as needed until mixture peaks. Spread on a greased cookie sheet evenly and bake for 1 hour at 250 until almost firm to the touch. Cut while warm and freeze for future use. Makes lots of cookies that can be broken and will not gum up your pockets or hands!

Liver Cookies

Ingredients:

1 lb. liver
3 eggs
garlic powder as flavor
1 c. flour
1 c. cornmeal

Blend liver and eggs in blender. Add remaining ingredients. Mix well. Pour on edged cookie sheet, greased with vegetable oil spray. Cook at 350 for about 20 minutes. Makes a fairly solid sheet, which can be cut in squares and frozen individually. Does not crumble.

Sunshine Liver Brownies[3]

Ingredients:

1 lb. calf liver
1 c. flour
½ c. corn meal
3 tbsp. garlic powder or fresh garlic

Puree all the ingredients in a food processor. Pour onto a cookie sheet lined with greased aluminum foil. Mixture will be thick. Press flat and even. Bake at 350 for 20 minutes. Brownies are done when the pink is gone. Do not over bake or the brownies will crumble.

Beef Biscuits

Ingredients:

1 c. whole wheat flour
1 c. cornmeal
½ c. wheat germ
½ c. cooked ground beef
½ c. beef broth
½ c. vegetable oil
1 egg
½ tsp. salt
1 heaping tbsp. chopped garlic

Preheat oven to 350. Combine cornmeal, wheat germ, flour, cooked ground beef, and salt in a large bowl. Mix. Add in egg, oil, and broth and mix thoroughly. Roll dough out onto lightly floured surface to about ½" thickness. Cut out biscuits with a cookie cutter (preferably a dog bone shape). Transfer biscuits to an ungreased baking sheet. Bake for 5-15 minutes for small (1") or 30-35 minutes for large (3") biscuits. Transfer to rack to cool. Store in an airtight container and refrigerate.

Note: Turkey, chicken or any meat of your choice may be substituted for the beef.

Tuna Biscuits

Ingredients:

8 oz. can of tuna in oil
2 c. cornmeal
2 ¾ c. flour
¾ c. water
2/3 c. vegetable oil
½ tsp. salt

Preheat oven to 350. Drain oil from tuna in can. Combine cornmeal, flour, and salt in a large bowl. Mix. Add in drained tuna, water and oil and mix thoroughly. Roll dough out onto lightly floured surface to about ½ inch thickness. Cut out biscuits with a cookie cutter (preferably a fish shape). Transfer biscuits to an ungreased baking sheet. Bake for 5-15 minutes for

small (1") or 30-35 minutes for large (3") biscuits. Transfer to rack to cool. Store in an airtight container and refrigerate.

Cheese Sticks

Ingredients:

2 c. whole wheat flour
1 ½ c. cornmeal
1 c. grated cheddar cheese
1 c. grated Swiss cheese
1 egg
1 c. milk,
¼ c. vegetable oil
½ tsp. salt

NOTE: other cheeses can be substituted for cheddar and/or Swiss

Preheat oven to 350. Combine flour, cornmeal, cheeses, and salt in a large bowl. Mix. Add in egg, oil, and milk and mix thoroughly. Roll dough out onto lightly floured surface to about ½" thickness. Cut in strips, ½"x3", and roll strip to make round. Take two strips and intertwine them, pinch ends together. Transfer intertwined strips to an ungreased baking sheet. Bake for 30-35 minutes. Transfer to rack to cool. Store in an airtight container and refrigerate.

Peanut Butter Biscuits

Ingredients:

2 c. whole wheat flour
1 c. wheat germ
1 c. peanut butter
1 egg
¼ c. vegetable oil
½ c. water
½ tsp. salt

Preheat oven to 350. Combine flour, wheat germ, and salt in a large bowl. Mix in peanut butter, egg and water. Roll dough out onto lightly floured surface to about ½" thickness. Cut out biscuits with a cookie cutter (preferably a dog bone shape). Transfer biscuits to an ungreased baking sheet. Bake for 5-15 minutes for small (1") or 30-35 minutes for large (3") biscuits. Transfer to rack to cool. Store in an airtight container and refrigerate.

Peanut Butter Training Treats (or hollow bone stuffing)

Ingredients:

1 c. chunky all natural peanut butter
1 c. skim milk
½ c. wheat flour
½ c. white flour
1 tbsp. baking powder

Preheat oven to 350 (for treats) or 325 (for stuffed bone). Combine the milk and peanut butter in a blender, food processor or large bowl with hand mixer and mix until smooth.

Add the baking powder and wheat flour. Combine until well blended. Slowly add the white flour in a tablespoon at a time, until a thick dough ball forms.

Set the dough aside.

To stuff a bone: Purchase an empty, hollow shinbone (sterilized) from your local pet store. Using a pastry bag (or a Ziploc bag with one corner cut off) fill the bone. 1" should be left on either side for filling expansion. Bake at 325 for about 90 minutes, or until a **long** toothpick (or knife, or bamboo skewer) inserted into the filling comes out clean. Filling should have baked into a hard, crunchy mass. Let cool for about 2 hours, then give to your dog.

To make training treats: Spray a baking sheet with nonstick cooking spray. Make tiny balls out of the dough (about ½ the size of the size treat you want, as the dough expands) and set 1" apart on the cookie sheet. Bake at 350 for 5-9 minutes,

depending on size. They are done when they are hard and crunchy (like kibble) but not burned.

Oatmeal Biscuits

Ingredients:

1 ½ c. uncooked oatmeal
1 c. flour
1 c. cornmeal
1 egg
½ c. vegetable oil
½ c. water
½ tsp. salt

Preheat oven to 350. Combine oatmeal, flour, cornmeal, and salt in a large bowl and mix. Add in egg, oil, and water and mix thoroughly. Roll dough out onto lightly floured surface to about ½" thickness. Cut out biscuits with a cookie cutter (preferably a dog bone shape). Transfer biscuits to an ungreased baking sheet. Bake for 5-15 minutes for small (1") or 30-35 minutes for large (3") biscuits. Transfer to rack to cool. Store in an airtight container and refrigerate.

Pumpkin Doggie Cookies

Ingredients:

15 oz. can mashed pumpkin (not spiced pie filling)
¾ c. Cream of Wheat or wheat germ
½ c. dry powdered milk

NOTE: rice cereal can be substituted for wheat germ if dog is wheat sensitive.

Preheat oven to 300. In a bowl, combine the mashed pumpkin, cream of wheat or wheat germ and powdered milk. Mix until the consistency is even. Drop cookie sized spoonfuls onto a lightly greased cookie sheet and bake for 15-20 minutes.

Low-fat Biscuits

Ingredients:

2 c. whole wheat flour
½ c. rye or buckwheat flour
½ c. brewer's yeast
1 c. bulgur
½ c. cornmeal
¼ c. parsley flakes
¼ c. dry milk
¼ c. warm water
1 c. chicken broth
1 egg beaten with 1 tbsp. milk (for glaze)

NOTE: vegetable broth can be substituted for chicken broth

Combine flours, brewer's yeast, bulgur, cornmeal, parsley flakes and dry milk in a large bowl. In a small bowl, combine dry yeast and warm water. Stir until yeast is dissolved. Add chicken broth. Stir liquid into dry ingredients, mixing well with hands. Dough will be very stiff. If necessary, add a little more water or broth. On a well-floured surface, roll out dough to ¼" thickness. Cut with knife or cookie cutter into desired shapes. Transfer biscuits to cookie sheets and brush lightly with egg glaze. Bake at 300 for 45 minutes. Turn off heat and let biscuits dry out in oven overnight.

Low-fat Wheat or Rye Crisps

Ingredients:

1 c. whole wheat or rye flour
¼ c. soy flour
1/3 c. water
½ tsp. bone meal
3 tbsp. oil or shortening

Mix flours. Mix oil or shortening with water. Add liquid to flour and mix well. Roll out on cookie sheet and bake until golden brown at 350. Break into bite-size chunks (or precut with cookie cutter before baking).

Low-fat Dog Biscuits Deluxe

Ingredients:

2 c. whole wheat flour
¼ c. cornmeal
½ c. soy flour
1 tsp. bone meal
1 tsp. sea salt
¼ c. sunflower or pumpkin seeds
2 tbsp. oil
melted butter or fat
¼ c. unsulfured molasses
2 eggs mixed with ¼ c. milk

Mix dry ingredients and seeds together. Add oil, molasses, and all but 1 tbsp. of egg/milk mixture. Add more milk if needed to make firm dough. Knead a few minutes, let dough rest ½ hour or more. Roll out to ½". Cut into shapes and brush with the rest of the egg/milk mixture. Bake on cookie sheets at 350 for 30 minutes or until lightly toasted. To make biscuits harder, leave them in the oven with the heat turned off for an hour or more.

Nice-Breath Biscuits

Ingredients:

2 c. whole-wheat flour
½ c. cornmeal
1/3 c. chopped fresh mint or 1 tbsp. dried mint
½ c. chopped parsley
6 tbsp. safflower oil
¾ c. water

Combine flour, cornmeal, mint and parsley in large bowl. Add oil and water. Mix thoroughly. Roll out to ¼" thickness on floured surface and cut into desired shapes with cookie cutters. Bake at 350 for 40 minutes, or until lightly browned. Let biscuits dry in oven several hours. Store in airtight container in refrigerator.

FROZEN TREATS

Frosty Paws

Ingredients:

32 oz. container of plain, nonfat yogurt
1 large mashed banana
¾ c. cold water

Mix all ingredients in a bowl. Put into small containers or an ice-cube tray and freeze.

Variation on Frosty Paws recipe

Ingredients:

1 ripe banana
4 oz. fat free yogurt (vanilla or banana flavor works best)
2 oz. water
3 T peanut butter

Mix all ingredients together in blender. Pour into Frosty Paws sized cups (a cut down Dixie cup or similar small container) and freeze.

Carob Variation on Frosty Paws[4]

Ingredients:

¼ c. carob kisses for dogs
8 oz. plain yogurt
1 large banana, water as needed

Grind kisses in processor to fine power, add the rest of the ingredients and process, put into ice cube trays and freeze.

Frozen Pumpkin Treats

Ingredients:

1 pie pumpkin

Cut the top off of the pumpkin, clean it out and cut either in half or in manageable pieces. Roast skin down in a hot oven at 400 - 450, until soft, then skin and puree in a food processor, hand blender or even a potato ricer. Freeze in ice cube trays.

More Frozen Treat Ideas
- Chicken/beef broth frozen into ice cube trays (low salt)
- Frozen Jell-O Jigglers

SPECIAL DIETS

As we all know, corgis are renowned for their ability to get a little hefty on even a modest amount of food. When they do get a little rotund, and lose their lovely figure, it's often quite a chore to withstand the sad eyes and the pitiful noises at dinner time that come when the ration is simply reduced.

However, there is hope. The trick is to implement the Green Bean Diet or the Pumpkin Diet. The idea is to replace half the dog's ration with either rinsed, unsalted green beans (canned or fresh), or canned, no sugar added pumpkin (not spiced pie filling). The results are impressive, and your corgi will think he's being given a special meal, not a special diet.

CREDITS

Most of these recipes are folklore, handed down and reprinted in many places. Exceptions are listed below. Thanks to the authors!

1. Posted to Corgi-L by Judy Neuhaus, 3/16/01, reprinted with permission.

2. Posted to Corgi-L by Pat Nolan, 4/17/96, original credit given to Sherry Thommen, reprinted with permission

3. Posted to Corgi-L by Kay Jackson, 2/15/97, original credit given to "Flash-paws," reprinted with permission.

4. Posted to Corgi-L by Steve Siemens, 6/5/99, reprinted with permission.

Emily Calle and Bailey

THE SPIFFY CORGI

by Nancy Matzke Moncrieff

This low-maintenance breed can be kept healthy and clean by following the basic care guidelines Nancy Moncrieff outlines in this article.

The practical herding dog doesn't require a lot of care; corgis need minimal grooming. Here is a compendium of grooming advice gleaned from the archives of Corgi-L, articles from breeders, and basic dog care knowledge. If you spend some time grooming your dog at least once a week, you will have a happy, healthy, and spiffy pet.

TEETH

Dogs' teeth and gums are subject to decay and disease just as humans' are. One of the most common problems in senior dogs is infections and loss of tooth. This can lead to malnutrition and disease.

Brush your dog's teeth using a doggy toothpaste and a brush or washcloth. Don't use human toothpaste; it is bad for dogs, and dogs don't like it. Get that yummy liver-flavored stuff. Some recommend that you clean the teeth daily; most say once a week.

You can get teeth cleaned at your vet's; however, the vet will probably have to put your dog under anesthesia to do the deep cleaning. This is a costly and risky procedure, although sometimes necessary.

FACE

Banshee, my rescue Cardigan, has a congenital tear duct problem that causes her eyes to discharge. I use a washcloth and gently wash her face daily. She not only loves it; she demands it by pushing her head under my hand until I comply. This means, of course, that her mix-breed buddy Pixel thinks it is a good idea too. She rubs her face with her paw when she wants a wash! You probably don't have to do this routinely, but I included it because my gals think this is fun. My guys don't, and don't usually need it.

EARS

Prick-eared dogs don't generally have a lot of ear problems, but you should ensure that ears are bright, clean-smelling, and healthy. You can cleanse them with a cotton ball or washcloth moistened with a little mineral oil or pet ear cleaner. Only clean the external portion of the ear.

In our household, the corgis wash each other's ears. From what I've read, this is a common corgi trait.

Should your dogs ears smell foul, become red and inflamed, or if you see a large build up of dark brown wax, see your vet. Your dog may have an infection or something in the ear, such as a foxtail or mites.

COAT

Corgis have a double coat that enables them to be outdoors in rough weather. This firm coat does not need a lot of care, but you need to ensure the dog is free from any mats, and the skin is clean.

Brushing

To keep the coat shiny and clear from mats or tangles, comb or brush your dog at least once a week. You can use combs: a coarse one at first, then a finer one to finish the coat. Many folks recommend a Zoom Groom, which is a rubber brush with pointed "bristles" that removes loose hair. Don't use a "slicker" brush, as this may pull out too much healthy hair.

Have an extra brushing session if your dog gets wet through the undercoat. Combing will keep the coat from matting.

When your dog sheds his coat (that's called "blowing" the coat), brush him daily. You'll get enough hair to make another corgi, but it is in one place, rather than scattered throughout your house! Many use an undercoat rake to help the dog blow the coat. Misting the coat first can help the hair from flying around.

Bathing

You don't need to bath your dog often; too much bathing can dry out the skin and cause more problems than it fixes. When your dog gets that "doggy" smell, or investigates that really neat stagnant pond, give her a bath using a very mild premium pet shampoo. Never use human shampoo; it's too hard to rinse out, and residual shampoo can cause skin irritation. Dilute most doggy shampoos before you apply them; you only need enough shampoo to get the skin clean. Big foamy bubbles, while cute, can leave residual soap on the skin. Rinse your dog thoroughly until the water runs clear. Then comb your dog to remove any tangles and excess hair. If you don't blow dry your dog, keep her someplace where she can't immediately replace the smell of that bath with something she finds more appealing, such as bird droppings or a compost heap!

ANAL GLANDS

If your dog is doing the "butt-scoot" boogie, he may have clogged anal glands. These glands are located beneath the tail. To express them, locate the "lumps" beneath and on either side of the anus, and squeeze gently using an upwards motion. Be aware that a really clogged gland can expel quite a bit of matter; do this over a towel or sink and stand to the side, not directly behind the dog.

Some recommend this be done routinely, whether or not the dog has problems. Others say that frequently expressing the glands actually causes the need. As this is not one of my favorite things to do, I wait until needed! Only one of my dogs needs it done now and then.

If you cannot get anything out, or if the butt-scooting continues, see your vet. The gland could be very impacted or another problem could be causing the discomfort.

TOES

Long nails can cause foot deformities and difficulty walking. Your dog should have relatively straight nails that do not extend far beyond the end of the paw. If your dog plays or walks a lot on cement, this may happen naturally. Most dogs need to have their nails trimmed anywhere from weekly to monthly. If you don't want to do it yourself, take the dog to a groomer or a vet to have it done.

You can trim the nails using a commercial dog nail clipper. This has the advantage of being quick—but watch out for that quick! If you go too deep, you can cause pain and bleeding. Be sure to have some syptic powder nearby to stop the bleeding should you accidently go too far.

Many prefer to grind their dog's nails using a battery-operated nail grinder, such as a Dremel. Don't get a high-powered commercial grinder that goes too fast, though.

If your dog and you disagree on the need for nail trimming, try using a bit of peanut butter in a kong or on your fingers to keep him distracted.

PROBLEMS

Skunk

If your dog meets with the wrong end of a skunk, I recommend a commercial skunk scent remover. As we live in the country, I've had way too much of this experience! I use Skunk-Off™, and keep it handy at all times. I think it is worth the money. I also add some to the wash to deskunk the clothes I was wearing when I bathed the dog. There are other commercial products.

If you want a home remedy, one groomer recommends you warm up some vegetable oil, let it sit on your dog for 20 minutes, then bathe in Dawn (a dish detergent that removes oil), followed by a normal bath. Here is another solution that I found works:

1 quart 3% hydrogen peroxide
1/4 cup baking soda
1 teaspoon of liquid soap (Dawn is best)

I've never had much luck with vinegar or tomato juice, but others swear by it. If your dog was heavily sprayed, you may need to rebathe your dog several times during the course of a week.

Fleas

If you live in an area prone to fleas, no matter how well you groom your dog, she is subject to carrying the little pests. Fleas will find her even if all she sees of the great outdoors is a short walk or two. Use a good flea prevention medicine, such as Advantage™. Most people feel, and I agree, that flea collars are useless.

Don't wait to see the fleas. They are small and often embedded deep in the under-coat. If your dog is scratching excessively, or shows signs of dermatitis such as flakes of skin, use an extra-fine, or flea, comb, and see if you dig up any adult fleas. If your dog is at the point where you see the fleas jumping on the skin, he is badly infested.

Should your dog get fleas, shampoo with a flea killer, then use a preventative that kills adult fleas, not just the eggs. Also be sure to bomb (or use some other equally effective means that gets into the crevices and carpets) your home once to kill the fleas, then, a few days later, again to kill the larvae as they hatch.

CONCLUSION

That covers the corgi from head to toe. At first grooming may seem like a chore, but if you make it a fun time for yourself and your pet, you can turn it into an opportunity to get close to your buddy while keeping him happy and clean.

For those of you who have met me and my menagerie rolling in the dust, please stop laughing. You may think that reading my advice on grooming is like reading Oscar Madison's advice on housecleaning. Most of what you read here isn't my personal expertise, but advice I've collected over the years and in researching this article. I confess to being a bit lax sometimes, but I'm convinced that the basic grooming advice I've collected in this article is practical, and I try, really, I try. I hope you will too!

FIRST AID AND PREVENTING ACCIDENTS

by Maenad Widdershins

Maenad Widdershins provides a concise reference to common medical problems that can affect your corgi.

Bliss '02

It is my fervent wish that you and your corgi never require any of the information in this chapter. It is, however, not a perfect world, and having some knowledge of rudimentary first aid will be helpful if your corgi needs your help one day.

If you are interested in learning CPR for your pet and other resuscitation techniques, which are beyond the scope of this small guide, some Red Cross chapters are now offering first aid classes for pet owners.

These tips are for educational purposes only and do not replace professional veterinary care; always consult your veterinarian.

FINDING HELP IN AN EMERGENCY

Do you know if your vet is available 24 hours a day? Many veterinarians no longer provide 24-hour emergency service to their clients but, instead, refer you to an area emergency clinic. Do you know where it is and how to get there? Keep the number near the phone along with your regular vet's phone number, and make sure you know how to get to the emergency clinic. In larger metropolitan areas, it may be wise to know where the two closest clinics to you are, in case traffic becomes an issue. Try to make a point of driving by the emergency clinic sometime when you are out running errands. Then, when you need to find it in a hurry, you won't be trying to navigate to an unfamiliar place in the dark or during rush hour.

FIRST AID KIT

Many dog supply catalogs carry versions of a good basic first aid kit. Make sure that yours includes, in addition to the traditional bandages, the following: tweezers, blunt-tipped scissors, liquid antihistamine (i.e. Benadryl), hydrogen peroxide (replace frequently, as this breaks down over time), eye wash, syringe (without needle, for dosing medication), antibiotic ointment, and hydrocortisone cream. These are basic items; you can always add things. Also make sure that you have a muzzle, or a bandage long enough to wrap around your dog's muzzle and then back around the neck. I have even used a dog leash to muzzle a dog that was hit by a car.

ALLERGIC REACTIONS

If your dog begins to swell up rapidly and have trouble breathing, he may have been stung by an insect or ingested something to which he is allergic. Some dogs will break out all over in hives as well. Antihistamine dosage is typically 3 milligrams per pound (please check with your veterinarian for the proper dosage for your corgi). If you will be outside with your dog and going a long distance from your car, be sure to carry some Benadryl with you, as you will want to administer it as soon as possible after you notice the reaction occur.

BLEEDING

Use a clean dry cloth, towel, or bandage, and apply firm pressure to the wound. This will usually slow the bleeding. Do not remove the cloth, as you will disturb the clot that has begun to form. If the bleeding is on the limbs, you can apply pressure to the artery supplying that limb. Pressure should be applied to the upper inside of the leg. For those corgis with tails, you can apply pressure to the underside of the tail to help slow blood loss. The use of tourniquets is not recommended, as cutting off all blood supply to the limb will also cut off the oxygen supply to the tissues, and the limb will begin to die.

Once the bleeding has slowed, you can trim the hair away from the wound. Apply KY jelly around the wound before trimming will trap loose hairs in the ointment and prevent the hair from falling into the wound and causing infection. Flush the wound for five minutes with warm water and apply an antibiotic ointment. Wrap with gauze. You want the gauze snug, but not so tight you cut off the circulation. If the injury is on a paw, try using a clean sock to protect it.

Unexplained bleeding, or excessive bleeding from the gums, could indicate a serious problem and you should seek veterinary help as soon as possible.

BITES

Dog Bites

The biggest problem from bites is usually infection. If there is a lot of bleeding, treat as you would for a bleeding wound and seek veterinary attention. Please remember not to use your hand or leg to break up a dogfight, or there will just be one more patient!

Snake Bites

These often happen out of your view. Dogs will swell up and may have difficulty breathing and become lethargic. If you managed to kill the snake that bit your dog, bring it with you to help identify the kind of venom to which your dog has been exposed, but be careful handling the snake's head. Some snakes' fangs will remain venomous for up to 24 hours after death. Keep the dog as quiet as possible. Carry the dog to the car, and crate them for the trip to the vet, or have someone help

you restrain them in the vehicle. Seek veterinary attention immediately!

Insect Bites

If your dog has an allergic reaction, administer antihistamines. (Less than 30 lbs., dose with 10 mg of diphenhydramine, and 25 mg if they weigh between 30 and 50 lbs.) Only administer medication if your dog is conscious, alert and not vomiting. If they have been stung, try to locate the stinger and remove with tweezers, or you may be able to scrape the stinger off with a credit card. Most dogs are stung on the face or mouth. If minor swelling occurs, an ice pack may provide some relief.

Porcupine Quills

Not really a bite, but still quite painful. These can be removed with pliers, but this is best done by your veterinarian, after your dog has been sedated.

CHECKING FOR SHOCK

Capillary refill is useful for ascertaining whether your dog is in shock. Lift up your dog's lips and press a finger on the gums, then remove your finger and time how long it takes for the gums to return to their normal pink color. Normal capillary refill time is 1 – 2 seconds. If it takes longer than 2 seconds for normal gum color to return, this could indicate shock; you should get to a veterinarian immediately. If capillary refill time is less than 1 second, your dog should also be checked by your veterinarian.

CHOKING

Have someone help you restrain the dog while you check inside the mouth. If there is something caught between the back teeth, you may be able to remove it with blunt tweezers or pliers. If the dog is choking on something and his airway is completely obstructed, it is probably safer, as hard as it might be, to wait until he loses consciousness before clearing the obstruction. If the dog is still conscious when you try to clear his airway you will only get bitten, resulting in two patients instead of one.

Although related to suffocation not choking, be sure that you keep food bags out of reach and dispose of them in a trash can where your corgi cannot get to them. It is not unheard of for a corgi to meet a tragic and untimely end when trying to get those last bits out of the bottom of the potato chip bag. If they are unable to back out of the bag or get it off their head, they can suffocate.

DEHYDRATION

Check for dehydration by pinching (not hard) a fold of skin between your fingers and pulling it gently away from the body. If it returns quickly to normal, your dog is probably adequately hydrated. If the fold stays, then your dog is dehydrated. If the dehydration is due to other complications such as illness, see your vet, as IV fluids may be required. The fold test is not as accurate with elderly dogs, as their skin loses its elasticity. Checking the mucous membranes for moisture may be helpful, but if you have any doubt, seek veterinary assistance.

DISC PROBLEMS

If your corgi suddenly starts limping and gets steadily worse quickly, starts dragging a foot, or worse yet, cannot support his weight on his back legs, get him to the veterinarian immediately. Other signs of disc problems include crying out with pain without being touched, standing with the back arched, or losing control of the bladder or bowels. Immediate veterinary care could make the difference between a full recovery and a paralyzed dog.

DIARRHEA

This symptom has many causes. It is possible that your corgi has ingested something that upset her digestive system. Some dogs are more sensitive to this than others. It could also be parasites. If your dog is mature (older than 1 year), or not terribly aged, diarrhea is not severe, and your dog shows no other symptoms of illness (i.e. no temperature), you can try resting the digestive tract. Pull all food for 24 hours, but continue to provide fresh water. After 24 hours, start with a bland diet such as rice and lean ground turkey (cooked).

Be aware that using some over the counter anti-diarrhea medications can make matters worse if you are dealing with an intestinal parasite. Many of these medications work by slowing the gut down, so if you are dealing with a bug like Giardia, you would only be giving the beasties time to multiply, eventually making your dog sicker. (Keep in mind if you go hiking: your dog shouldn't be drinking from the stream anymore than you should!) Some medications such as Pepto-Bismol can actually mask symptoms such as blood in the stool and could delay diagnosis of a serious condition.

If the diarrhea doesn't improve when you pull food, or your dog exhibits other symptoms such as lethargy, fever, or vomiting, please check with your veterinarian. (In my experience, diarrhea that has not been helped by resting the tummy has required veterinary intervention, so I have never used any of the over-the-counter medications).

To cut down on the icky factor, it's helpful to have some no-rinse shampoo around the house. Those fuzzy bunny butts are cute, but when they're not feeling well, it's best to have something to clean up with before letting them back on your carpet!

FEVER

Normal temperature for a dog is 100.2 - 102.8° Fahrenheit. You can take your dog's temperature rectally, with a mercury or digital thermometer. K-Y jelly may help make it a little more comfortable for your dog; a little dab on the end of the thermometer helps it to slip in. If your dog has a fever, you should consult your veterinarian. Temperatures under 100° and over 104° Fahrenheit are considered emergencies.

FOREIGN BODY INGESTION

As careful as we all try to be, our dogs sometimes eat things that aren't meant to be eaten. If you know that your dog has eaten something that just wasn't meant to be digestible, check with your veterinarian and then induce vomiting. Use 1 teaspoon of 3% hydrogen peroxide administered by syringe. The biggest danger with large objects is their ability to block the digestive tract. If your dog is vomiting, especially after eating, and doesn't appear to be having bowel movements, you need to see your veterinarian.

As a precaution, don't give your corgi chewy toys that he can consume too quickly. Some corgis are so greedy they will eat things whole that were meant to be chewed and eaten in small pieces. This includes rawhides and other treats that can be swallowed in large pieces. I once had to make one of my dogs vomit back up a hair scrunchy that was swallowed in the excitement of playing with the neighborhood kids. If you see it go down, it's better to get it back up quickly than have to go through surgery later. Do not induce vomiting if your dog has swallowed a sharp object. If they should eat something sharp like a Christmas tree ornament, feed them cotton balls soaked in milk and see your veterinarian.

HOT WEATHER CONCERNS

Always be sure your dog has plenty of water available in the hotter months, and **never** leave your dog in your car in warm weather. They just don't have our ability to cool the body down by sweating profusely. It doesn't take long for your car to become much warmer than the outside air, and once body temperature starts to rise, damage can occur very quickly. Fluffies may be more comfortable in the hotter months if you shave them down a bit.

When the weather heats up in your area, cut back on your dog's activity and slowly work them back up to their previous level. Cut down the duration of exercise sessions, as well, until your dog is acclimated to the heat.

If your dog does collapse in the heat, get him into a shaded area, and wrap him with wet towels. In particular, apply wet towels to your dog's undercarriage where the fur is less dense, especially the armpits and groin area, and you can bring the body temperature down more effectively. Do not soak their foot pads, as these need to stay dry to help them sweat through the pads. Seek veterinary attention immediately.

POISONING

Curious corgis can really get themselves into a lot of trouble in this area. But you have a wonderful tool in case your corgi ingests something that is toxic: the ASPCA has an Animal Poison Control Center, with the phone number 1-888-4 ANI-HELP. **POST THIS NUMBER NEAR YOUR PHONE**. They work on a case-by-case basis, and there is a fee for their services (as of January 2002 it is $45.00). However, veterinarians specifically trained to deal with poisoning staff the hot line 24/7. Try to reach your veterinarian for advice first; she may advise you to call the Poison Control Center. Also be sure to let your vet know if you have already spoken with the Center, so they can work together to save your corgi.

There are foods we enjoy as humans that are toxic to our dogs. These include onions, onion powder, alcoholic beverages, yeast dough, coffee (caffeine overdose), tea (caffeine), large quantities of grapes and raisins, and moldy foods, especially cheese. Chocolate poisoning can occur more quickly than you might realize. I walked out of the shower one morning to find my two-year-old child sharing a Costco-sized bag of semi-sweet chocolate chips with a more than willing corgi accomplice. Fortunately, I take quick showers, but I was surprised to discover how close we came to a toxic dose. Chocolate has a substance called theobromine in it. Theobromine's half-life in the body is 17.5 hours, and the toxic dose is 100-150 mg/kg of dog. That means a 25-pound corgi could receive a toxic dose of chocolate with only a little more than 3 oz. of baking chocolate. Baking chocolate is the purest form of chocolate we usually have around our homes, but a dedicated corgi could still poison himself on other types of chocolate if he managed to ingest enough of it. Levels of theobromine in different formulations of chocolate are; milk chocolate: 44 mg/oz., semisweet: 150 mg/oz. and baking chocolate: 390 mg/oz.

Always keep all medications out of the reach of your corgi. Make sure all bottles are stored out of reach, and take your pills over the sink, or somewhere else where they won't drop on the floor where an ever-alert corgi could snatch them up. Tube medications also pose a risk, as some topical ointments can be quite poisonous when ingested.

Houseplants can also be a problem. It is impossible to list here all of the plants which are problematic; however, they include azalea, oleander, castor bean, and sago palm. If you place houseplants within reach, check their toxicity. (The University of Illinois currently maintains a toxicology home page at www.library.uiuc.edu/vex/vetdocs/toxic.htm).

Outdoor plants can also be a problem if your corgi is apt to bother them, but more important than the plants themselves may be the fertilizers and treatments you use in your yard. Here in the northwest, slug bait is very toxic to dogs, and unfortunately the formulations used by the manufacturer make them quite attractive to the dogs. Even placing the bait in special containers is no guarantee; a woman at a nursery tried to sell me dog-proof slug bait containers, until she found out I had a corgi. Corgis have proved themselves more than a match for this kind of thing in the past. Consider gardening organically, and if you do choose to use something containing toxins, confine your dogs in the house during use, and keep them out of that area of the yard until it is safe. Read the label before you purchase, and consider organic alternatives that will be safer for your pet—and the planet as well! Also be alert for mushrooms in your yard. It is probably safest to remove all mushrooms before your dog can ingest them, as it takes an expert to distinguish what is safe from what is not, and there are some tragically lethal fungi out there.

Pest control poisons, such as mouse or rat poisons, can be deadly to your pet. If you must put out bait for rodents, place it out of your dog's reach and keep track to be sure they are all removed when no longer needed. Record what type of bait was used and write on the calendar when you put them out, so you can let your veterinarian know if the worst happens.

Household chemicals can also be harmful. Keep mothballs, potpourri oils, coffee grounds, homemade play dough, detergents, and cleaners out of your dog's reach. There are many safety latches available for cupboards if you have a dog that is able to open cupboard doors.

Automobile supplies include one of the most deadly toxins to our dogs, antifreeze. For your own cars, try to use one of the safer antifreezes that have been developed to be less toxic to pets. Try to watch your corgi in parking lots where someone else's radiator may have leaked. Strange as it may seem, antifreeze tastes quite sweet, and about 3 tablespoons is enough to end a 30-pound dog's life.

If you know your dog has ingested something, you can induce vomiting if the substance is not caustic. If you're not sure, contact your vet or the poison control center. If they advise you to induce vomiting, use 3% hydrogen peroxide administered with a syringe. Use 3 teaspoons per 10 pounds of body weight. Repeat up to three times about every 15-20 minutes. The vomit will be rather foamy, and your dog will glare at you. Do NOT induce vomiting if your dog has ingested a sharp object, if

the poison is caustic or petroleum based, if his heart rate has slowed, if he is having difficulty breathing, or if he is behaving depressed or, alternately, is very hyper, or if the container specifically states not to induce vomiting.

VOMITING

Like diarrhea, vomiting can have many causes. It is a good idea to check and see what your dog has vomited to make sure no foreign substances have been ingested. Some dogs will vomit after ingesting some toxins, so check around to see if your dog could have ingested anything. If your dog is behaving strangely, then call your veterinarian. Check for fever and make sure the dog doesn't become dehydrated. If vomiting continues and resting the stomach doesn't help, then please see your veterinarian.

A FINAL WORD

This is by no means meant to be a comprehensive guide to caring for your pet. I hope that I have included most of the situations that you might encounter. I wish you and your corgi and long, happy and healthy life.

Maenad Widdershins' Tarzan

TABOO: TOXIC AND POISONOUS SUBSTANCES

by Marilee Woodrow

You'd be amazed at what is toxic to a corgi! This guide helps us learn what to watch out for to keep our pets safe from accidental poisonings.

Here are some general guidelines to protect your corgis and other pets:

Pet-proof your home and yard the same way you would child-proof your home for a 2-year-old. Numerous household products such as hand soaps, detergents, mothballs, polishes, bleaches, turpentine, boric acid, lighter fluid, many paint removers, and even health and beauty products, can be toxic if ingested in large enough amounts.

Different poisons act in different ways and require different treatments. If you suspect your corgi has ingested something toxic, your best success will come from trying to determine what was ingested and how much. Then call your veterinarian immediately!

If your vet is not available, call the nearest veterinary emergency clinic or a Poison Control Center. Be sure to indicate your corgi's age, any medical conditions, and regular medications to whomever you speak with.

Keep these numbers handy:

- National Poison Control Center numbers: (900) 680-0000: a charge will be applied to your home phone bill.
- ASPCA Animal Poison Control Hotline: (800) 548-2423 or (888) 426-4435 are credit card only numbers.

To be effective, any first aid treatment (such as inducing vomiting, the administering of milk or cooking/mineral oil or following any product label information in case of accidental ingestion) must be administered before the poison is absorbed into the GI tract and is only intended to minimize the effects. Receiving immediate veterinary treatment increases the chances for a better or complete recovery.

COMMON TOXIC PLANTS AND SUBSTANCES

The following is a compiled list of some common plants/substances that can be toxic to your pets if ingested. We have tried to include as many as possible, but we know no list can be absolutely complete.

Poisonous Plants (* indicates this substance is known to be *extremely* toxic):

- Amaryllis: Bulbs
- Azalea: Entire Plant
- Bittersweet: Bark, Leaves, Seeds
- Black Locust: Bark, Leaves, Berries
- Boxwood: Bark, Leaves
- Buckeye/Horse Chestnut: Sprouts, Nuts, Leaves
- Buttercup: Bark, Leaves
- Caladium: Entire Plant
- *Castor Bean: Entire Plant
- Chinaberry Tree: Bark, Berries
- Chrysanthemum: Entire Plant
- Cocklebur: Entire Plant
- Crocus: Entire Plant
- Daffodil: Bulbs
- Daphne: Bark, Leaves, Flowers
- Dumb Cane/Diffenbachia: Entire Plant
- *Easter Lily: Entire Plant
- Elderberry
- Foxglove: Leaves
- Fruits Seed Pits of Almonds, Apples, Apricots, Avocado, Cherry, Peach, Pear, Plum
- *Hemlock: Entire Plant
- Holly: Leaves, Berries
- Hyacinth: Entire Plant
- Hydrangea: Entire Plant
- Iris: Bulbs
- Ivy, English and Baltic: Leaves, Berries
- Japanese or Chinese Tallow Tree: Bark

- *Jerusalem Cherry: Entire Plant
- *Jimson Weed/Thorn Apple: Entire Plant (Extremely Dangerous)
- Lantana: Entire Plant
- Larkspur/Delphinium: Leaves, Seeds, Young Plants
- *Lily of the Valley: Leaves, Flowers
- Ligustra/Privet: Leaves, Berries
- Marigold: Entire Plant
- Marijuana: Residual Substance
- Mistletoe: Entire plant, but the berries are the most toxic
- Monkshood: Entire Plant
- Morning Glory: Seeds, Roots
- Mountain Laurel: Entire Plant
- Nightshade: Entire Plant
- *Oleander: Entire Plant (Extremely Dangerous)
- Philodendron: Entire Plant
- Poinsettia: Entire Plant
- Poison Ivy, Oak, and Sumac: Entire Plant
- Pokeberry: Entire Plant
- Potato: Unripe (green) Tubers, Sprouts
- Rhododendron: Entire Plant
- Rhubarb: Leaves
- *Rosary Pea: Entire Plant
- Tobacco: Entire Plant
- Tomato: Plant greens, vines
- Walnut: Green Shells
- Wild Mushrooms/Toadstools:

  The Amanita species are the most common severely toxic species found in the United States.

- Wisteria: Entire Plant
- *Yew: Entire Plant
- Youpon Tree

OTHER TOXIC/POISONOUS SUBSTANCES

Onions: any form—raw, cooked, dehydrated, powder—can cause Heinz body (hemolytic) anemia (even worse for cats)

Chocolate: caused by Theobromine, a naturally occurring compound in chocolate. The toxic dose of theobromine is about 100 –150 mg/1 kg of body weight. Toxic dosages include 1 ounce of Milk Chocolate per pound (Milk chocolate contains 6 mg. of theobromine per ounce); 1 ounce of semi-sweet chocolate per 3 pounds (Semi-sweet chocolate contains 22 mg. of theobromine per ounce); 1 ounce of baking chocolate per 9 pounds (Baking chocolate contains 35-45 mg of theobromine per ounce). Toxic signs may occur at lower dosages. Theobromine can also be found in cocoa mulch that is marketed for use in your gardens.

Naphthalene/Moth Balls

Antifreeze: (containing ethylene glycol) 1 teaspoonful can kill a 7 pound animal.

Insecticides: most unless specifically delineated "animal/pet friendly"

Metaldehyde: found in most snail and slug baits

Marilee Woodrow with Tinker Bell and Cisco

WARNING!
IT SHOULDN'T HAPPEN TO A DOG
by Jamie L. Longstreth

Every day we are bombarded with warnings of potential dangers to our children, our pets, and ourselves. We all know that chocolate is poison to dogs. We know the dangers of certain types of houseplants. We know that a dog unattended on a leash can choke himself. We know, for the most part, how to react to crises and avoid a tragedy. I would like to tell you a story that may help save a life someday.

Seven years ago, I adopted a beautiful Pembroke Welsh corgi named Max. Max was the light of my life. He was so much more to me than a pet. He filled my days with his sweet presence, kept me on my toes, and taught me the meaning of love. I was a self-defined "cat person" my entire life, until my daughters asked for a puppy. I agreed with the usual codicils, you must walk it, clean up after it, brush it, care for it, and so on, with the full realization that where children are concerned, I would most likely end up doing the bulk of the work myself. I had experience with dogs, being "sister" to my mother's three. So the search for the perfect dog began.

We lived in a small rented house with an unfenced yard. I knew that I wanted a small dog with high intelligence, and due to my work schedule, one that would train easily and was not "hard-headed." I did not want a terrier, a beagle, or a toy dog of any kind. Herding dogs are the most intelligent and easiest to train, but most herding dogs are rather large. So, my research led me to the corgi, and I decided on a Pembroke, for both the slightly smaller size and the greater availability. The local Kennel Club put me in touch with breeders, and soon, a suitable puppy appeared.

Max came to us from a good breeder who was selling him as a pet. He was perfectly standard in appearance, but his personality led the breeder to feel he would do better with a family than being subject to the travails of the show circuit. We went to meet him, his mother, and his siblings. It was love at first sight. We arranged to come back in two weeks and take him home. Max was five months old, with knobby knees, a pink spot on his nose, and adoring eyes. The pink spot faded in time, and despite the fact that my daughters had wanted a dog, Max was completely mine. His loyalty was to me. He went everywhere possible with me. He loved me above all others. I came to feel the same way. I loved him more than I had loved most people.

Max lived with us for seven years. He saw me through huge emotional, physical, and career upheavals. He traveled with me, comforted me, and kept me alive by giving me a reason to live. He was the darling of my circle of friends. He received much attention and love at picnics, parties, and other gatherings. He was a mascot of sorts, and his antics led him to have his own stories circulated among the groups and communities with which I associated. He was welcome everywhere.

One morning, I woke up to our kitten Greebo licking my face, pawing at me, and doing everything possible to rouse me. I noticed that Max was no longer in his customary spot at the bottom of the bed, and thought he had awakened earlier and gone upstairs to sleep with one of the girls. I went upstairs and found him lying on the living room floor, suffocated, with his head in a snack bag. His love for treats had led him to search for crumbs in the bottom of a bag either left out or fished out of the trash. My world crumbled as I realized what had happened.

I had many conversations with Max's spirit over the next days and weeks. I felt that I had neglected him by allowing this to happen. He assured me that it was an accident, but that I could help other dog lovers by warning them of this seemingly innocent hazard. And so, the Silver Hammer Foundation was born.

Please, dog owners and dog lovers, cut any bag in half before discarding it. Grocery bags, snack bags, bags that have contained animal food, meats, or birdseed. Simply cut it in half, and prevent this happening to any other dog. Even if you don't have a dog, even if you have your trash receptacle locked away or out of reach, another animal could get into it later and suffocate. Like the old six-pack rings, the simple action of cutting it into harmless pieces could save a life. Just do it. It shouldn't happen to a dog.

For more information on the Silver Hammer Foundation, e-mail MorganLFy@aol.com, or write to:

Silver Hammer Foundation
564 Lougeay Road
Pittsburgh PA, 15235

Brochures are available at no charge for display and distribution for vet clinics, humane foundations, shelters, rescue organization, breeders, and individuals. Contributions to defray printing and mailing costs are graciously accepted, and may be sent to the address above.

In Memory of Leaning Oaks Conan Maxwell Silver
Hammer
"Max"
1995-2002

BASIC OBEDIENCE TRAINING FOR YOUR CORGI

by Arleen Rooney

Sit! Read! Learn!

I love my dog, and I feel my dog loves me, so why doesn't he behave in the way I want? That question has confronted just about every dog owner since the canine became a companion family member and our best friend.

All puppies come into the world with a clean slate. Keeping that in mind, as they grow up, their behavior reflects their life experiences. But undesirable behavior can be rechanneled into desirable behavior. It's more of a challenge, but it can be accomplished if we employ patience, consistency, and positive, reward-based training.

STARTING WITH PUPPIES

Socializing a puppy is very important in the first eight weeks of its life, and proper socialization is one of the benefits of getting a corgi from a responsible breeder. The unsocialized dog is timid and can act aggressive when it becomes fearful. It's just trying to protect itself and discourage interaction—"I want you to go away and leave me alone."

Dogs, including puppies, are opportunistic and will do things that work for them. Using that as a base to launch any training program will bring good results, provided the dog owner practices on a daily basis.

A dog trainer will show an owner how to train her dog, but, like any form of schooling, there is homework involved. Three short five-minute sessions per day are suitable for a puppy from three months old up to a year of age. Puppies and young adolescent dogs have a shorter attention span and thus are more easily distracted. To keep their interest alive, a play period after each short training session can be a positive reward and motivator.

A dog is considered a teenager from one year up until two or three years of age, depending on the breed. Some breeds mature faster then others. Like the human teenager, the canine teenager may act like doggie Einstein one day and totally ignore anything learned the next. He is "tuning you out." Be patient, he hasn't forgotten, he is just preoccupied with his youth and the new-found freedoms of maturing and gaining confidence.

The best time to start training a puppy, whether in formal obedience or simply in desirable manners, is at three months of age, so most group classes list their minimum age as three months.

ATTITUDES THAT WORK

Rather then setting up your corgi to fail, set her up to succeed. Don't overdo or jump ahead of your training program, and don't show off. You may have to take several steps backwards if you do.

As an accredited dog trainer, I have found that working and herding dogs seem to be quick to catch on but can also be stubborn. If your corgi is having a "I'm tuning you out day" or is just not with it, do not get frustrated and nag the her. End the training practice doing something you know the dog will do well and reinforce the good performance by a lot of verbal praise in an enthusiastic, happy voice.

The old method of using choke chains and prong collars is going out of fashion, as the new positive reward method of training is taking hold. Dogs will work for food, and thus the use of treats to lure them into a desired behavior is a strong motivator. There are also the positive rewards of a favorite toy, a walk, a car ride, a play session, and—most important—verbal and physical praise.

A puppy or dog needs to understand the action desired before the word used for that action has any meaning. Although we may think a dog knows its name, it doesn't identify its name as we do ourselves. A dog responds to its name in a positive way when it is called by its name and it brings a good experience. **Never** use your dog's name in connection with a negative—no, bad, or whatever—use it **only** in a positive way.

FINDING A TRAINING CLASS

You can call your local park and recreation department, PetsMart, or Petco chain store, or check with local dog clubs for some leads on a good training class for your dog. The park and recreation group classes are often the most economical, although they may have a larger group and your dog won't get as much individual attention. However, if you are highly motivated, you and your dog will do well in a large group class.

For those that want smaller classes, local obedience clubs, dog clubs, and pet store chains have limited enrollment in their classes. They will be a bit more expensive but still affordable.

Most group classes run from six to eight weeks.

There are trainers who do in-home training; the benefit of this is that you and your dog receive individual attention. In group classes, if you miss a class, it's hard to catch up, and there are dropouts mid way through. In-home training is a bonus, as you just pick up where you left off and continue practicing what you've learned until the next session. You can check with local canine rescue groups or with your vet or groomer for trainers who do in-home training. The prices can vary, so shop around and find one that is realistic for you. Feel free to ask for references from these trainers and check them out.

Group classes don't always address issues such as housetraining, socialization,

aggressive behavior, and other issues such as barking, digging, chewing, and jumping. This is where individual training may really help turn your incorrigible dog into a canine good citizen.

BASIC TRAINING

To get you started here are some basic training exercises.

To teach your dog SIT

Take a treat between thumb and index finger with palm up, bring your hand to the dog's nose, let the dog sniff the treat but do not give it to the dog. Take your hand with palm up and bring it over the dog's head; as you do so, the dog's body will follow gravity and sit down. As soon as your dog's butt hits the ground, use your positive marker word (letting the dog know he has done what you wanted) "**yes**," give the dog the treat, and release the dog from the exercise by saying "**okay**."

To teach your dog DOWN

When down, a dog is lying comfortably on its hip in a reclining position. First put your dog into a sit as above, but this time do not give the dog the treat or say yes when it sits. After the dog sits, take your hand palm down with the treat, and bring it to the ground by the dog's front paws and around towards the back of the dog. When the dog goes down, say your positive marker word "**yes**," give the dog the treat, and release the dog from the exercise by saying "**okay**."

To teach your dog STAY

Put your dog in a sit (later you can do it from a down position), take your hand palm facing the dog, and say "**stay**." Stand directly in front of your dog, say "**yes**" if the dog doesn't get out of position, give the dog a treat, and say "**okay**" to release it from the exercise. Later you can extend the duration the dog "stays" in the sit/down position by walking to the end of the leash, to the left and right side of the dog, and around the dog.

To teach your dog to COME

Have a friend or family member hold the dog on the leash; you walk up to the dog, let it sniff the treat in your hand. Walk a good distance away and in an animated, happy voice call your dog by name and say "**come**." Have the handler run with the dog on leash to you. Take the dog by the collar and say "**gotcha**," "**yes**," and give it a treat.

"Come" is the most important word your dog can learn. It means to come to you directly, like Lassie came to Timmy. It doesn't mean to tarry or veer off course; it means come to you directly and swiftly. Come can save your dog's life in a dangerous situation. Don't overuse the word, or it will lose its effectiveness. Only use it when you mean "come to me and stay with me."

To teach your dog WAIT

Wait is similar to STAY but for a different use. WAIT means do not move and is useful to teach dogs to wait when you open a car door or open your front or backyard door. It will teach dogs not to bolt or dash out from cars or doorways. Put your dog in a sit or down position. Take your hand and swing it like a pendulum in front of your dog, say "**wait**," stand in front of your dog. If your dog doesn't move, say "**yes**," give the dog a treat, and say "**okay**" to release it from the exercise. You will extend the WAIT as you do the stay as you progress. Start with five seconds, building up to a full minute. Don't see how long your dog

will stay, take it slow, and set your dog up to succeed.

To teach your dog to SETTLE

Settle is similar to down but for a different use. "Settle" means chill out, lie down quietly and stay put, park it, go to your place. This is useful when you want to enjoy the presence of your dog without having to entertain the dog or have the dog act pushy for attention or be in your face. You can enjoy watching TV, having company, talking on the phone, working on the computer or in the garden, or whatever, and the dog will lie quietly in its place. Using a mat, rug, or old towel is good, as you can move it from place to place. Put the dog in a sit, then a down. Instead of giving the dog a treat when it goes down, squat down yourself and hold the treat down for a count of a few seconds, then say "**yes**," give the dog the treat, and say "**okay**" to release the dog from the exercise. You extend the duration as you continue to practice. The second step is to attempt to stand up without giving the dog the treat and see if the dog remains "down or settled" as you get up. If he does, then you say "**yes**," give the dog the treat, and release it from the exercise by saying "**okay**."

LEARNING GOOD MANNERS

There are many other things besides basic obedience your dog should learn. These include sitting to be greeted by a person; standing for examination by a trainer, vet or groomer; being comfortable with brushing or having its paws and body handled; learning to have a gentle mouth and discourage puppy nipping and chewing on you or your personal belongings; and walking on a loose leash without pulling. There are too many things to cover in one short chapter, but any good dog trainer should be able to guide you and your dog to graduation with honors at the end of a training course. But you have to do your part: practice and be consistent.

Most dogs that wind up at animal shelters or are given away are those who have not been given the opportunity to be taught the proper way to behave and so have behav-ioral problems. However, these dogs are very trainable and just need the patience, consistency and love of their human(s) to bring out the best in them. Working with your dog in training helps build the ani-mal-human bond. It's fun, and the rewards are tremendous.

Arleen Rooney training a corgi to stay

TALES OF THE URBAN COWDOG: RAISING A CORGI IN THE BIG CITY

by Daphna Straus

You can take a corgi off the farm, and he'll show up the city slickers! Daphna Straus tells how well corgis adapt to city living.

Welsh corgis, both Pembroke and Cardigan, possess a unique adaptability that allows them to live happily in a variety of settings. Unlike other intelligent herding breeds that require a great deal of space and outdoor freedom to thrive, many corgis are quite happy living in urban settings. What are the rewards and challenges city dwellers face when sharing their lives with corgis?

The corgi's size makes it the ideal choice for the urban fancier who prizes the personality and intelligence of a herding dog. Though somewhat small in stature, few corgis seem to think of themselves as "little dogs." They romp and play as easily with Golden Retrievers as they do with dachshunds. A food-motivated corgi (of which there are many) rarely shrinks from a dispute over a fallen treat, no matter what sort of dog may challenge him. Napoleonic complexes aside, corgis do not suffer when their living quarters are less ample than those of their country cousins. Of course, most dogs would relish a sprawling home and fenced yard in which to roam, but most corgis adapt very well to life in an apartment. Many corgi owners agree that their dog would be more content to curl up with them in a telephone booth than be left alone in a mansion. As an apartment dweller myself, I never stop appreciating the fact that I have a big dog in a small package.

Despite their adaptability to relatively small living quarters, no corgi should be deprived of exercise and the opportunity to socialize with others. The corgi's outgoing personality is often enhanced by urban life, where every outing is a chance to meet new dogs and their owners. Because few city dwellers have "doggie doors" and backyards, the opportunities to meet and greet on walks are many and are an important part of an urban corgi's daily life. My own Pembroke, quite the little ham in public, seems to appreciate that he can try out his clownish antics on a new audience every day.

It is quite common to witness looks of surprise from people who are unfamiliar with the corgi's athleticism. I often hear remarks like "He sure can run with those little legs!" My usual reply is "This dog can outrun me!" The fact that corgis are short legged and relatively small belies their agility and their need for exercise. A city person who does not have access to a nearby park—preferably one with an off leash area—should consider some other type of pet. Too many corgis are obese, a condition that is particularly dangerous considering the physical structure of these dogs. As they are not high-strung or hyperactive dogs, many corgis can become couch potatoes if given the chance. To allow this to happen is to deprive these bright, active dogs of their potential.

Ironically, the herding instinct is another quality that makes corgis well suited to city living. The corgi's inherent desire to keep close to his flock (or his loyalty to his master) often means that he will be content to walk alongside, behind, or in close proximity to his owner. While some curious scent hound breeds cannot be safely allowed to wander off leash, well trained adult corgis can usually be trusted off leash on supervised walks, provided no vehicles are present. Many cities, including New York City, have adapted off-leash policies in parks at specific hours, such as between 9 p.m. and 9 a.m. Urban corgis and their owners can safely take advantage of vehicle-free, untethered exercise experiences in places like Riverside Park and Central Park (automobile-free on weekends only) in Manhattan, Redwood Regional Park in Oakland, California, and San Francisco's Crissy Field.

The corgi's lowness to the ground may add to his talent for tracking, but for the urban corgi owner, this trait poses something of a challenge. The scents and objects on city streets can be irresistible to curious corgis, especially those who like to taste-test whatever they find. Corgis who must be exercised in urban settings often require extra vigilance from their owners. A reliable "leave it!" is a must, especially before taking advantage of off-leash areas.

While it would be foolish to suggest that a corgi (or any dog) would be better off in a city than in a suburb, the opportunities for socialization and the corgi's adaptable disposition mean that corgis can and do lead happy lives in places like New York, San Francisco, and Boston. As long as a corgi is given ample exercise and playtime with his "person," geography becomes a secondary consideration. So next time you and your corgi are visiting the Big City, hop into a cab, explore the urban oasis of a public park, and hit some outdoor cafes. Your corgi just may help you make some new friends!

Daphna Straus and Zabar unpack after moving to the Big City

"COME GROW OLD WITH ME…" LIVING WITH SENIOR CORGIS

by Lynda McKee

Lynda McKee offers sound advice on dealing with the problems of senior corgis.

When your first corgi puppy finally arrived at your home, the last thing on your mind was where you would be some 12, 14, or even 16 years later. You ticked off your puppy's many "firsts," but all too soon you will be sadly ticking off the "lasts." The intervening years will go by very fast. You took many puppy pictures. Please take many senior photos too.

This article is not meant to replace your veterinarian's advice and experience. It is intended to give you an idea of some of the things you and your senior corgis may encounter.

CONTRIBUTORS TO LONGEVITY

It probably never occurred to you to ask about the longevity of the bloodlines from which your puppy comes. It certainly is fun seeing mom, grandmom, and great-grandmom when you visit litters. It gives you an idea of what your puppy will look like, but more importantly, it will give you an idea of your pup's life span. You will most likely never see an obese senior corgi. Keeping your corgi's weight down throughout its life will contribute significantly to a long, happy, and healthy life. Good veterinary care is essential. Good care on your part is critical.

ROUTINE CARE

No later than age ten (but ask your own veterinarian) your corgi should have a complete geriatric work-up with blood work, urinalysis, and possibly x-rays. These results will serve as a baseline for future comparisons. A yearly geriatric exam will work for another year or two. You may then want to go to one every six months. Remember that the first year of a dog's life is comparable to about 16 human years. After that, one human year is about four years for a dog. A 10-year-old dog is comparable to a 52-year-old person; a 14-year-old dog is comparable to 68 years. This baseline can help identify kidney problems, for example. When things develop quickly, remember it is quickly for us. If your vet says your corgi has about 6 months to live, that is comparable to two years for a person. Things that you might let go for a day or two such as not eating, coughing, or diarrhea, may develop into something critical quickly in a senior dog.

Consider making a 3-minute exam a daily event. Take the time to observe your corgi doing the following things: get up from lying down, sit, stand, stretch, shake, lay down, trot, poop, pee, eat, and drink. Know the normal smells of their ears, breath, and skin. Just by these routine observations, you will know when something isn't quite right. Become the kind of owner who can say to their vet, "She just doesn't look right." And the vet will know that something is amiss.

Routine grooming should continue. Your corgi may develop clumps of hair under her throat, almost like a mat. Be sure to comb out the coat thoroughly. Check mammary glands and testicles for lumps and bumps. Note the location of growths and monitor the size and color. Should either change, a trip to the vet is warranted. Your corgi may develop "skin tags" on the muzzle or legs. Spayed bitches may carry more and more coat as they age, and may not go through the massive sheds of their youth. Be careful when bathing a senior corgi. They may have difficulty standing for an extended time. Also be more aware of the weather, as a senior can chill easily.

Toenails seem to grow overnight. Long nails can adversely affect your corgi's mobility. The nails may change shape, and become thicker, more brittle, and yellow in color. Dental care needs to continue, but tooth cleaning will no longer be so routine. The bacteria released during the cleaning can find their way into the bloodstream and set up an infection that can lead to dire consequences. Kidney and heart problems can follow such an infection. Your vet may put your corgi on antibiotics prior to cleaning teeth for that reason.

Thoughts are changing with respect to vaccinations. Yearly rabies shots are still needed due to state law, but ask your vet about "routine" vaccinations. The latest thinking seems to be to vaccinate every three years, if that frequently. Consider titers rather than shots. Consider no shots at all.

What food to feed seems to be a never-ending point of discussion. There are many "senior" foods, but some veterinarians question their worth. If your corgi has ongoing medical problems, such as heart, liver or kidney disease, then a prescription diet may be needed. B/D is a new food manufactured by Hills that shows some promise for seniors in that its claims are supported by evidence from feeding studies. It is meant for dogs with some symptoms of senility, but it shows promise as a good all-round senior food. It is not uncommon for dogs to become stool-eaters in their senior years. A multi-vitamin/mineral supplement may be needed. Watch your dog eat at least one meal every day. Monitor the amount of water she drinks. Changes in eating or drinking patterns will warrant to trip to the vet's office as will a sudden loss or gain in weight.

SENIOR PROBLEMS

We are fortunate in that our breed tends to be long-lived, with no major health issues. While 13 to 14 years old seems to be the normal lifespan, it is not uncommon for corgis to live far longer. Arthritis is common in aging joints. Treatments may include buffered aspirin, Rimadyl, Adequan, or Etogesic. As with every drug, possible side effects must be weighed against the benefits. Many older dogs find relief from alternative treatments such as acupuncture, chiropractic, and veterinary orthopedic massage. The latter can best be described as a combination of massage and acupressure. Being kept warm and having a soft bed in which to cuddle will help the arthritic patient. Exercise is still needed but not the frantic exercise of youth. Gentle strolls and swimming are great for both dog and owner. Many dogs benefit from receiving daily doses of a glucosamine supplement, such as Cosequin DS, ArEncaps, or Arthramine. Always ask for your veterinarian's advice regarding exercise and supplements. Keep her informed of what you are giving your senior citizen.

Many Pembrokes unfortunately seem to "lose their rear end." There are many possible causes; the question remains "why?" Your corgi may start losing muscle mass in the rear legs. You may feel or even see tremors in the front and rear legs. Feet that used to revert back to normal position when flipped over no long revert. Your corgi may be standing on his rear toes or on the tops of his feet. She may stand "up under herself" in an attempt to relieve pressure on aging hips. A veterinary examination is definitely needed. Spinal tumors, compressed discs, nerve damage, or degenerative myelopathy are some possible causes. Tests such as a complete set of x-rays, MRI, spinal tap, and blood work may be suggested in searching for the cause. There is inherent risk in some of the tests, so the possible benefits need to be weighed. Corgis can and will adapt to the use of a cart, but are known for their stubbornness and are not noted for the ease with which they adapt to a cart. Keeping your corgi's weight down, as well as exercise, is vital for helping your dog maintain a quality life. Your corgi may no longer tolerate being crated because of the stiffness that can result.

It is not uncommon for spayed bitches to have incontinence problems. PPA and DES can be used to treat the condition, but again ask your vet. A doggy door may help with getting the seniors out on their schedule rather than interrupting your sleep. Do not withhold water when your dog has kidney disease. Your dog is not breaking its housetraining, so please do not punish her. She needs more frequent trips outside.

Vision and hearing may deteriorate as your corgi ages. We know the breed is famous for its "selective hearing" in its youth, but your older corgi actually may not hear or see a car coming. He may be reluctant to go out at night. She may be hesitant to go up and down steps. Be careful when you waken a sleeping old dog. He may snap at your simply because you startled him. They will sleep through all sorts of things—doorbells, car horns, people coming and going—and never know it. They may not be there at the door to greet you because they didn't hear the car drive up. A veterinary ophthalmologist can determine whether cataracts are affecting your corgi's vision. A blind dog can do very well in familiar surroundings. Lights and vibrations can be used to get the attention of a deaf dog. Dogs adapt well to their disabilities; we are the ones that have trouble.

Dogs do not suffer from strokes in the same way people do. They can have transitory ischemic attacks (TIAs) in which they have a spaced out look on their face: a look of confusion. You may never see your corgi have such an attack, or he may have them several times a day and you aren't there to witness them. Old dogs can suffer from Cognitive Disorder Syndrome (CDS). It is something like old-age senility. Some dogs improve on the drug Anipryl.

Cancer remains a concern. Monitor the size and color of any growths you find during your grooming or tummy-rubbing sessions. An increase in size or change in color warrants a trip to the vet. A bitch that is spayed before her first season has an almost zero chance of developing breast cancer.

Some old dogs will have a seizure or two and then never have another one. The cause could be one of many things, but going too long between meals is an easy one to fix. You may want to put your corgi back on the three small meals a day that he ate as a puppy, or offer a bedtime biscuit or three.

You may come home one day to find your corgi walking like a drunken sailor. One possible cause is vestibular syndrome. It greatly affects their balance, causing them to be nauseous. It comes on suddenly and may be gone in a week or linger for several months. Good supportive nursing care is needed. Once recovered, she may never have another episode, or episodes may recur every several months.

To learn more about taking care of senior dogs, consult your veterinarian, friends and books. One of my favorites, though no longer in print, is *Active Years for Your Aging Dog*.

Other good sources include *Old Dogs, Old Friends* and *Dog Owner's Home Veterinary Handbook*. Of course there are a myriad of internet sites. My personal favorites are:

- The Senior Dog Project (www.srdogs.com),
- AltVetMed: Complementary Alternative Veterinary Medicine (www.altvetmed.com),
- Holistic Veterinary Medicine Sites (www.petsnergy.com/holistic.html).

These sites contain a wealth of information and links for just about every conceivable condition.

ADAPTATIONS FOR THE SENIOR CORGI

Your corgi wants most his dignity and sense of self-worth. She wants to get around on her own and participate in the activities she has enjoyed throughout her lifetime. You want your senior citizens to remain an integral part of family life. Some adaptations for both of you may be needed.

Washable throw rugs may be needed to help weak limbs stand on slippery surfaces. Easily washable bedding may be needed for corgis that are having bladder problems. A doggy door may be needed to allow ready access to the outdoors. Pet cleaning supplies and paper towels may become part of your weekly shopping list as you clean up the accidents. A flashlight by the door serves to signal your deaf companion that it is time to come in or to locate a senior who has become lost in the yard. Thin pads may need to replace those thick cushy beds. The thick beds may be too difficult for your corgi to negotiate when going to and from bed.

Ramps can be purchased or made that will allow your senior citizen access to her favorite couch, chair, or bed. Deck steps can be replaced with ramps. A ramp may be needed to get in and out of the car and house. Wooden steps may need to be carpeted to provide better traction for weaker joints.

It is hard for a retired show dog to watch the youngsters come and go while the senior remains at home. Your older corgi may enjoy going along for the ride to shows. They will still enjoy "shopping" among the vendors, and who can resist the expressive eyes of a senior pleading for a piece of liver at a show? The senior may not be able to keep up with the speed of the youngsters on walks, so take the time to walk with your seniors and leave the youngsters at home. You will enjoy the stroll and will sadly realize that you can now, at last, outrun them should the need arise.

Corgis that were notorious ball freaks and Frisbee catchers will need to have their activities reshaped. You may be rolling the ball short distances rather than throwing it long. The Frisbees may be chewed, rather than chased. Dogs that enjoyed chewing rawhides and Nylabones may have to have other more easily chewed items. Retired agility dogs can still do tunnels and pretend to jump bars laid on the ground. What your corgi wants most is your attention and cookies (or vice versa!). They want to continue to be the integral part of your life that they were in their youth. They deserve special moments of the day: sleeping on the bed, sharing your breakfast, just being with you outside. You will come to cherish the dignity and serenity of your senior citizen.

Whether to bring a young puppy into a senior household will depend upon the circumstances. For some seniors, the presence of a puppy is rejuvenating. Others cannot tolerate the puppy's antics. Dogs with mobility issues do not need a rambunctious youngster knocking them over. It is the senior's right to discipline young upstarts. Some dogs will relish the role; others will detest it. Remember your senior will require more and more care and has earned the right to your attentions. If you cannot devote time to both the old and the young, then wait for a youngster.

KNOWING WHEN IT'S TIME

Your corgi will continue to slow down. Your heart will become aware of a ticking of a clock. A time is approaching that you never dreamed of some 13 or more years ago when that first corgi puppy entered your life. Or you may have already traveled this road...you know what's ahead. For those who have yet to travel it, it is not an easy journey, and does not have a happy ending. Old dogs often do not go quietly in their sleep. They rely upon you to help them make a transition to a different life. You may have criticized others for having dogs that should have been put to sleep months ago, but you may now find yourself in their shoes. Unfortunately, sometimes family circumstances and finances factor heavily into a decision.

How will you know when it is time? List three things that your corgi enjoys doing. When she can no longer participate and have joy in the activity, in even a scaled-down version, it is time to start thinking. A medical condition may be un-fixable. Much as we want it, no vet has found a way to make a dog younger. Often we will go to heroic efforts to buy our beloved corgis another month, another week, even another day. Quality of their life becomes an issue. Dignity becomes a priority. Yes you will wonder whether you let him go too soon. You will berate yourself for letting her go on too long. It is not an easy decision. You may cry for years afterwards.

You can ask for advice, but only you can make the decision. Your corgi will actually help you, if you listen to him and his wants. He will let you know that he is tired and ready to move on. He will be there for you later on, waiting to be reunited with you. I tell people to listen to your heart. Your heart will know. Your corgi's heart will know. When you listen to your heart, you can never go wrong. Stay with your beloved friend. Kiss him on the head and let him go. He will always be with you, in your heart, forever.

With heartfelt thanks and tears to Tiffy (1968-1982), Callie (1983-1997), and McKinley (1982-1999) and the kitties Nikki (1972-1990), Ditto (1981-1996), and Rascal (1980-1998). They taught me as much in their deaths as they did in their lives. I miss you all…. Cori and Bickley, both whelped in May of 1988, are adding to my experiences with living with corgis.

Lynda McKee and 16 year old McKinley showing in the Veteran's Class

INTERLUDE

RILEY

I get up on Saturday morning and read my e-mails. Hmmh. The performance corgi list is having an anniversary contest and one of the categories is "funniest performance story." Too bad, neither of my guys has ever done anything amusing in the ring. Well, I think to myself, time to get off the computer and head out to the big dog show at the Expo center. So, off we go, me and my two CD boys. Riley is in Novice B today. I go and check out the rings. They're great, curtains around all sides, fully matted. Really nice. My hopes for placing rise—today will be our day!

The steward calls "Number 37," and we proudly trot into the ring. I seem to have Riley's attention. The judge says "Forward," and off we go. But wait: the leash is heavy now…it feels as though I'm dragging dead weight…a quick glance down reveals the problem…my dog's nose is **inhaling** the ring mats. Not just sniffing, **inhaling**. As I continue to drag him down the heeling pattern, I cannot get him focused. I ask the judge if we may move on. As we move to the figure 8, he begins to respond to me. Now we're back on track. I begin to do the outside loop of the figure 8. Uh oh. Leash is heavy again. Really heavy. And twitching.

I look. Riley is now laying on his back, four stubby legs straight up in the air, and squirming with a huge smile on his face. Hmmh. I try to pick him up but am unsuccessful. The crowd is laughing.

The judge allows us to continue. At heel free, I take five steps forward, but Riley is still sitting at the starting line. I call him. He takes two steps, then drops onto the floor, on his back, wiggling all over. Again, the crowd laughs as I attempt to scoop him up.

Soon, it is time for stays. Well, at least this is one exercise he can do. He's never broken his sit-stay. I leave him and walk across the ring. So far, so good. 30 seconds into it, he begins to lean. Tip over, really. He's trying to sit, but it's hard to sit when you are also trying to inhale the mats. He finally falls onto his side, facing me and all the other exhibitors, spectators,

131

stewards and the judge. This is horrifying, because, after he has fallen over, I realize that his, hmmh, his, well, his, "winky" is hanging out for the whole world to see (note: he is a neutered dog). Oh my God.

The judge dismisses us from doing the down-stays. "Thank you," I reply.

They can't take away your CD, can they? ~*Kristine Gunter*

HAYLEY

The following is a true story that happened to me in our backyard on October 9, 2001. My corgi Paris's sister, Hayley (AM/CAN. CH. Kallista Dangerous to Kiss, CGC, PHC), who belongs to Millie Williams, was visiting us from Michigan following her "honeymoon" with a nearby corgi here in Tennessee.

This is hawk migrating season. They follow the air currents along the top of Clinch Mountain as they head south. Thousands of them pass through every year, and occasionally one gets lost and ends up in our neighborhood. We used to have them all year flying above the school playground at the elementary school where I worked last year. They'd play in the air currents and coast and zoom around. The kids thought they were eagles, and we'd watch them during playtime. They were also out at a corgi breeder friend's house the other day when we were playing with her puppies. She said that's why her dogs (especially the pups) are never out alone.

This particular morning, after we got home from our walk in the park, we had breakfast, did obedience homework, and I was letting the furry ones out one more time for a minute to tinkle and sniff before I came in to start housework. For some reason, I was bringing each dog out one at a time and playing with them. Hayley was last. She said I saved the best for last! She ran around the yard, and then she wanted me to rub her belly. I was bending over, giving her tummy rubs and telling her about the beautiful puppies she's making, when all of a sudden she looked up and let out a loud, blood curdling "YIP!" I wondered if I'd touched a sore spot or something. She hopped up, moved over about 4 feet, rolled over, and motioned with her head for me to come over there and rub her belly again. Then it happened. This humongous dead bird fell from the sky right where I had been standing. It like to have scared me to death! Lawsy! If I'd been standing there, it would have knocked me out. It sounded like a tree limb hitting the ground.

The birds in the neighborhood had been having fits all morning. This bird fell from way up above tree top height. Hayley must have seen it get killed and start falling. That's when she yipped, and then she was smart enough to lure me away from where it fell so I wouldn't get hit either. This bird must have weighed 10 lbs. or so, and it was dead long before it hit the ground. There were puncture wounds on its back. I don't know if this dead one was a large pigeon, an owl, or a small hawk. When my husband went out to "play bird undertaker," the hawk had already swooped down into our yard, picked up its breakfast, and carried it away.

Today's Kallista corgi commercial: Have a problem getting bonked on the head by dead birds? Is the sky falling at your house? Get the new Kallista early warning system, guaranteed to save your life!

And not only did Hayley save my life, at the end of November, she gave birth to 9 healthy corgi puppies back at her home in Michigan.
~*Susie Noel*

ELVIS AND MURPHY

Elvis was such a character. He was addicted to fetching. One time a friend brought her six-month-old daughter to visit. Kimberly was laying on the ottoman. I was talking to her mom, so Elvis wasn't getting much attention. He decided he wanted to play fetch and that Kimberly was the one who was available to play with him. So he jumped onto the ottoman and put a tennis ball in her tiny hand. Then he sat with his head cocked looking at her and waiting for her to throw it.

Elvis had an uncanny sense that children were delicate creatures. He never showed any aggression toward a human, and, in particular, he was gentle with children. One time we were at a very crowded food and wine festival. We ran into a small child who was eating animal crackers. The boy took an animal cracker and held it up to Elvis's mouth. With all of us watching intently, Elvis gently took the cookie in his mouth. At which point—I'm sure to the chagrin of his mom—the little boy took it back out of Elvis' mouth and took a big bite of it for himself! Elvis made no attempt to reclaim his snack.

Elvis hated the rain. Whenever it was pouring outside, he would do what he could not to have to go out and do his business. One night I knew he needed to go, as he had been holding it pretty much the whole day. I opened the door and sternly said, "Elvis, go pee pee outside." He looked up at me as if to say, "you first," and didn't budge. Once again I said, "Elvis, go pee pee outside."   He took a

step toward the door and stopped.   So the third time I yelled, "**outside**." He walked toward the door, very slowly. As soon as his front paws were outside, he stopped. I looked in amazement and realized that he considered himself to be outside and was about to pee on my door frame.

I was working long hours and worried about poor Elvis sitting home alone too much. So I decided to get another corgi to keep him company. I did not think I had the time to put in for housebreaking and bonding that a small puppy would need, so I went in search of a corgi between 1-2 years who was already housebroken. After calling around to a few breeders, I came across Murphy. Murphy was 18 months old and recovering from quite an ordeal. She came from the finest line of corgis; anyone in the show ring would recognize her grandfather, one of the all time champions. Murphy was co-owned by two breeders, who had high expectations of her offspring. Alas, her first delivery was a disaster. One of the puppies got stuck, and she ended up getting spayed. Following that trauma, a massive infection almost killed her. She wasn't even allowed to go near her puppies due to the infection.

When I took Elvis to meet her, she was only 17 pounds, missing a lot of coat, and afraid of the world. I decided that it was okay if she shied away from me as long as she got along with Elvis. She immediately took to him, and that was all I needed. I put her in the car for the 90 minute journey home. She was in the front seat of the car, and Elvis was in the back. About five minutes into the journey, she suddenly began to shake. For a split second, I wondered if I had made the right decision. As I was driving, I longed to hold her and tell her everything was going to be okay. Elvis must have realized her fear. He jumped into the front seat with her, put his paw on her back, and put his head down across her shoulders. It was all I could do to keep driving. He held her the whole drive home.

Murphy grew from the shyest dog in the world to a pet therapy dog. Once a month or so, we make a visit to the hospital to see the patients. The only part of this process she doesn't enjoy is the required bath. One day the nurse said she had a special patient for us to see. She took us to a room where I saw a woman who was restrained to the rails of the bed with leather cuffs. The nurse undid the restraints and explained that, although this woman was in her early 40s, she had the mind of a 2 year old. We put Murphy on the bed close to her. She seemed a little afraid. The nurse sat her up and held her hand and together they petted Murphy. I wasn't sure if we were getting through to her. She did not say a word and, after several minutes, she seemed to lose interest. So I took Murphy's paw, waved it to her, and said "bye bye." As I was taking Murphy out of the room, we heard this little voice say "bye bye," and I turned to see the woman waving back to Murphy. We could hear her repeating it as we went down the hall.~ *Jean Gordon*

MERRY AND PIPPIN

When Emma went looking for Merry (PWC) to flea spray her, she looked all over the house without success. Finally she noticed that the bed had an unusual lump under the spread. She looked closer, and there was a brown eye peeking at her from a small hole chewed in the spread.

Another time, Pippin (also a PWC) had been scolded about going through a hole in the fence and into the vegetable garden to pick and eat tomatoes. The next day Emma went into yard, Pippin was not in sight. Emma checked the vegetable garden, and there was a fluffy butt sticking out from under a zucchini leaf.

When out on a walk, Pippin was excited at seeing a squirrel run across the street and up a tree. She followed the squirrel's progress up the tree and parallel the street on an electrical wire. As Pippin walked along with her eyes glued to the squirrel, she did not notice that she was getting close to the curb until she suddenly fell into the street. She got up, looking very sheepish and I began chanting, "Cats and birds and squirrels, oh my!" a la *The Wizard of Oz*.
~*Jean Gordon*

WHAT CORGIS DO

CSV 2002

PERFORMANCE EVENTS: WHERE THE ACTION IS!

by Lynda McKee

Jobs for corgis! Lynda McKee, whose versatile corgis do so many things, tells you how to get your pet and you started in athletic activities.

GETTING STARTED

Corgis were developed to be the all-round farm dog, capable of performing a myriad of tasks, with an easy-to-care-for coat and needing minimal amounts of food to boot (despite what they would like us to believe!). As such, the breeds are well suited for performing the full range of AKC activities open to them: obedience, tracking, herding, and agility. **We** know they would also do retriever work, lure course, go-to-ground, and so on, but the AKC restricts those activities to the breeds that were historically developed to do them. That does not exclude other non-AKC activities, such as Frisbee catching and flyball, and we all know that a Pembroke or a Cardigan can be the world's best therapist. And of course there are the conformation and junior showmanship rings for corgis and their owners who are so inclined.

BASICS

Your corgi, Pembroke or Cardigan, needs to be in good condition to successfully compete in performance activities. Take a critical look at weight (many corgis are just too fat) and nail length and get to work on both early on. Remember that your vet is used to seeing dogs that are overweight, so don't take his or her word that yours is just fine. A corgi can weigh 25 pounds and be fat!

Your corgi needs to be well socialized, as it will encounter all types of dogs, people, and conditions as you travel and participate in classes, matches, trials, and tests. It goes without saying your dog should be up-to-date on all necessary vaccinations; heartworm and flea preventatives and worm checks should be routine. A neutered corgi will solve some of the problems associated with being in heat at the wrong time (both males and females!) Horsemen

use a "fitness for use" exam, and you may want to consider whether your corgi is structurally suited for a particular activity, but give them all a try first and let your corgi help you decide.

All corgis need a reliable come off leash, sit/stay, down/stay, and a "wait" command to be a pleasure around the house, along with walking on a loose leash and paying attention to you. They also need these basic skills in the various performance areas, although some areas demand a more polished version. It is very frustrating to deal with a dog that won't come to you when you are trying to herd sheep or go on to the next agility obstacle.

Next let's consider you, the handler. Consider your physical condition and limitations as well, although many agility, obedience, and tracking classes are really aerobics in disguise. You may need to trim up as your dog tones up! AKC is most encouraging of disabled handlers. You will see people in wheelchairs and on crutches doing obedience, agility, and tracking. You should also consider whether **your** shots are up-to-date and get a tetanus booster if you will be around livestock or wire fences.

WHERE TO BEGIN

A quality obedience class might be the best place to start, so that you and your corgi can acquire those basics skills previously mentioned. Many training groups also offer a Canine Good Citizenship (CGC) test as a graduation ceremony. While a CGC is not an official AKC title, you can list your dog's name in its CGC Archives, and you will receive a nice certificate to frame or put in a scrapbook. Some pet visitation groups have CGC certification as one of several requirements for membership.

You will next need to find a class or private trainer or mentor to help you to your goals.

Many people have trained dogs to titles solely from a book, but a class or the cost of private lessons will generally prod you into doing the suggested training. There are also practical considerations. For herding, you will need livestock, and for agility, you will need a lot of equipment. People will attend classes solely for those reasons, as most of us do not have livestock nor do we have the space for all the agility obstacles. (Many people will go on and at least acquire some of the items needed; one friend bought a small farm so she could have livestock!)

Attend a dog show, agility trial, obedience trial, or match and watch the performances of the dogs and handlers. When you see something that you like, once the team is done showing, ask for suggestions for classes. Keep in mind where you live and your weekly schedule. Some people drive two or more hours each way to attend a class, but a newcomer is not likely to devote that much energy. You will probably get several suggestions. Go watch a class or two and decide if the setting is right for you and your dog. You may be better off with private lessons at first before going into a group class. Again, time and economics will be major factors. Also remember that you get what you pay for. If several people recommend the same instructors to you, those people might be better choices than a class just down the street from you. For herding and tracking, you may need to rely on the grapevine. You can ask those same people at the shows who tracks or herds and get references that way.

SELECTING YOUR ACTIVITIES

Many people and their dogs can handle training multiple activities, but others can only do one thing at a time. Your first goal might be a Companion Dog (CD) title in obedience, but you also work in agility at the same time. You might be really interested in herding, but the practicality of driving a long distance to work your dog who will tire very quickly in those initial stages of training may make you put herding aside for the time being.

People who tell you that you can't do (fill in the activity) because it will ruin your dog for (fill in another activity) have never done what they are telling you that you and your corgi can't do. Don't believe such naysayers for even one second! When you are training certain very selective exercises, or are getting ready to compete with your corgi for a title, you may, however, need to be careful. For example, tracking involves encouraging the dog to work well away from you. Fine for agility but not a good idea to start at the time you are getting ready to show in obedience, where the dog has been taught to watch you for directions. You can give multiple commands in herding, tracking, and agility, but not in obedience, where a second "come" command will result in a non-qualifying score. Dogs are situational and they respond to the situation as well as the command, but that is after you and your dog are somewhat experienced. Your dog may sit on the agility pause table but won't sit on command in an obedience class!

You might try attending a "fun day" or clinic and try the activity. Your corgi (or you) may fall in love with the activity and be a natural. Other times your corgi may need repeated exposures to the activity to learn that it is okay, especially herding. Just because your corgi doesn't turn on to sheep the first time it sees them does not mean that it is a dud in herding. If you have multiple dogs, ask for help in selecting the one that might be the easiest to train in the activity you want to pursue. If you and your corgi quickly progress in an activity, you will be more likely to continue with it than if you are dealing with a difficult to train dog.

MY STORY

I acquired my first Pembroke, Tiffy (the Tiff in Tifflyn), in 1968. Eight months after her death in early 1982, I acquired my first show dog. McKinley and I went from Novice A to the coveted CH UDT title. He taught me more than I ever taught him. He made me become a better trainer and the successes of my later dogs are due to him. Callie came about a year and a half after McKinley and made me famous. Callie is the breed's first Versatile Corgi Excellent (VCX) and I was thrilled to have her included in *The New Complete Pembroke Welsh Corgi*. Her grandson Cruiser gave me not only another breed first but an AKC first as well when he became the first breed champion of any breed to be a Champion Tracker (CT). Cruiser is featured in *About Turn: The 1997 Obedience Year in Review*, was honored on the front cover of the *Pembroke Welsh Corgi Club of America Newsletter* (June 1998 issue), and is the featured corgi tracking on the PWCCA Performance Page on its Web site. Yes I work full time too; I teach high school mathematics. My performance articles are dedicated to those who have taught me best, my Pembroke Welsh corgis:

- Ch. BluJor McKinley of Tifflyn UD TD HC VC (5-14-82 to 2-15-99)

- Ch. BluJor Sio Calako Kachina CDX TDX HT Can. CD VCX (11-10-83 to 9-6-97)

- Ch. Tifflyn Encore Encore CDX TD AX HC VC (working on her TDX)

- Tifflyn Replay By Bickley CDX TD NA HC (currently the cheerleader of the house)

- CT & Ch. Tifflyn The Funseeker CD TDX VST AX NAJ HC VCX (currently working on his MX, OAJ and readying for his CDX this summer)

- Sua Mah Tifflyn Artistic TD OA NAJ (currently working on her AX and OAJ)

- "Tiffy" the one who started it all (5-10-68 to 1-9-82)

NEXT STEPS

A journey of a thousand miles begins with a single step. It's up to you to take that first step. Who knows? In a couple years, you may be receiving **your** Versatile Corgi certificate at the Pembroke Welsh Corgi Club of America annual banquet!

Linda McKee with Callie, the first Pembroke Versatile Corgi Excellent

PERFORMING WELL IN THE CONFORMATION RING

by Patti Kleven

Patti Kleven, an experienced handler, explains how to succeed in the show ring.

Mary Elizabeth Simpson with Ch. Windcrest Grant A Wish

Some dog handlers are born, some dog handlers are made. I was born to be a dog person, but it would be many years before I was to become a dog handler. My parents were German shepherd dog exhibitors when I was young. Somewhere after their third child was born, they lost their desire to participate in the dog show game. I never did. As a kid I remember putting on dog shows in the back yard with all the neighborhood dogs. Of course, we always watched the Westminster dog show on television. I would dream of competing at that show. Thirty years later, after marriage and a family, I finally did compete at that show with the show dog of my dreams.

My first Pembroke Welsh corgi brought me back to the dog show world. She was bought for my daughter, but she was the show dog I had waited for all my life. She taught me many of the things that I have noted below, and she introduced me to some of the closest friends I have today. I was a novice and I made mistakes, but we both survived and she went on to greatness in spite of me. The day we walked onto the green carpet at Westminster, I was very nervous. I had dreamed of this since I was a child. Somehow we made it around the ring. The judge pointed to us and the dream became real: an Award of Merit at Westminster. It was the happy ending that I had wished for since I was a child.

I hope these tips help all of you find happy endings to your dreams. They are lovingly dedicated to Am/Can/Int/BIS CH M-Candol's Lacey Britches, HT, ROM: "Lacey B."

Good conformation dog handling looks very simple. The handler trots the dog around the ring, stands it for the judge, and runs around again to gain the 1st place ribbon. To the novice, it looks so easy, but good handlers put a great deal of work into that "easy" performance in the ring. The following is an outline for achieving that "easy" performance.

Get Your Dog in Shape

A dog with excellent conformation and breed type will usually be noticed in the ring by the judge. Why is it that some of these dogs are not in the ribbons? Conditioning is a big part of the total picture. Most breed standards specify that the dog be in working condition. A dog that "rolls" while it is moving is very obviously not able to do the job it was bred to do. A dog that looks or feels overweight is not in show condition. Take the dog home and work on conditioning with exercise and controlled diet before approaching the conformation ring.

Practice Makes Perfect

Any performance requires practice, and conformation showing is a performance. You and the dog must become a team to show the dog to its best potential. Practice gaiting the dog to determine how fast or slow the dog should be moving. Have a friend videotape the dog moving at different speeds to determine what speed makes the dog look the best. Practice stacking the dog, and videotape how the dog is set-up to be certain that the dog is presented to the judge properly. Think of an outline of your breed of dog. Your dog should be stacked so that the judge can view the dog's outline to compare it to the breed standard.

Go To School

Conformation classes can be very helpful if they are used correctly. Good trainers can help you identify problems and give suggestions on how to solve them. Bad trainers can ruin a dog's attitude toward dog showing. Remember that there are many different ways to teach a dog to be happy and attentive in the ring. Try out suggestions, and if they are not comfortable for you or your dog, seek out other trainers for other suggestions. Dog shows are noisy, unnatural situations for many dogs. Classes can expose your dog to ring-like situations to take away some of the fear of the unknown. On the other hand, too much or too serious a class can take away some of the enjoyment of the ring for a dog. Short working class situations with positive reinforcements for the dog are usually the most successful.

A Little Grooming Goes a Long Way

Never take a dirty dog to be shown at a dog show. It is disrespectful to the judge to bring a dirty dog to be evaluated. If you are paying for a judge's opinion of your dog, make the dog look and feel like it belongs at the show and not out on the farm. Brush out dead coat and trim up feet as needed to make the dog look its best. Remember that many grooming aids, if left in a dog's coat, are illegal at AKC events. Chalk, powder, mousse, and sprays are used all the time at dog shows, but moderation and an understanding of how these products work on your dog's coat are necessary before using them. Remember that most judges are very knowledgeable of how to groom a dog, and if you are using aids to artificially enhance your dog, they will be able to see or feel it. They are within their right to excuse you from the ring if they feel these aids are excessive.

Pay Attention

Judges are given two minutes per dog to evaluate, place, hand out ribbons, and take pictures. This does not leave much extra time. Handlers need to have their dogs ready to walk into the ring when the steward calls you. Judges do not have time to wait while the handler finds his bait, does that final comb out, or whatever else the handler does to keep a judge waiting. Pay attention to the pattern of judging. Most judges will use the same pattern all day. Watch the breed before you to see what pattern the judge instructs the handlers

and dogs to use. Most likely, this will be the pattern you will be called upon to use when your breed is being judged. Pay attention while you are in the ring to what your dog is doing with one eye, and to what the judge is doing with the other eye. Remember that you have only about two minutes to make an impression on the judge with your dog. There is no extra time to visit with your friends, let your dog sleep or bother other the other dogs, or do anything else that is not directly concerned with exhibiting your dog.

Dress for Success

Be professional in the way you exhibit your dog and in your style of dress when you are in the ring. Dress as though you are going to work in a downtown office. Conservative clothing that is comfortable for you and accentuates the dog is the best style to choose. Ladies look nice in dresses, suits, or pantsuits of a solid color that are flattering to the color of the dog. Choose a color that allows the outline of the dog to be seen from a distance; for example, don't choose a black outfit for showing a black dog. Men should try for a suit and tie of a conservative color that, again, accentuates the dog. Remember that the idea is to show off the dog, not the handler. A truly great handler becomes almost invisible in the ring.

Have Fun

Conformation dog show exhibiting is a hobby for the vast majority of handlers. Most of the time spent at the show is not spent in the ring. Get to the show early enough to scope out the surroundings, find a grooming spot, and get the dog and yourself ready to show. Talk with other exhibitors, not only those in your own breed. Go to a ring where other breeds are being shown, and you may also meet some new friends. Dog shows are great venues to talk with other people who love dogs. As time goes by, the reasons you have for attending a dog show may include enjoying the friends that you have met along the way.

Just Do It

At some point you need to jump in and just start showing your dog. You won't be perfect at first, no matter how hard you try. You'll learn more by being out in the ring than any book or class can ever teach you. Pop a breath mint in your mouth and your dog won't know how nervous you are. Take a deep breath and put on a smile. You will probably lose more often than you will win. But if you believe in yourself and your dog, the judge may just believe in you as well. And if he doesn't point to you and give you the blue ribbon, there is always another dog show!

Patti Kleven and Lacey B

"GET OUT" AND ENJOY AGILITY
by Robin Early

Robin Early introduces you to agility and offers advice on getting started.

As I started to write this article, I thought, who am I to be writing about corgis doing agility? I'm just an average person with average dogs, who perform pretty well at agility trials. But then I thought, well, most of the folks who read this will be pretty much just like me.

So, how did I get started in agility? I got my first corgi almost eight years ago. Simon was also my first dog (not counting those my family had). All I wanted was a companion, but one who would come when called, sit and lie down and stay on command, and walk nicely on a leash. Having never trained a dog before, off I went to obedience school. One class and I was hooked! After taking several obedience classes, someone suggested agility class, which sounded like fun to me, and that was the beginning.

What Is Agility?

Agility, developed in England in the late 1970s, was based on the equestrian sport of stadium jumping. Unlike horses who carry their riders over a series of jumps, our canine friends perform the obstacles on their own, with only verbal and body language guidance from us. Unencumbered by a rider, our dogs are able to negotiate a variety of obstacles, such as Weave Poles, A-Frame, Teeter-Totter, Dog Walk, Tire, Tunnel, and Table. Although there are several different organizations that sponsor agility trials, with rules that vary from organization to organization, the game is basically the same. The dogs must perform correctly over a series of obstacles (12-20) in a predetermined order in a certain amount of time. In most cases, the dog with the fastest time and the cleanest performance is the winner.

The organizations all have set jump heights. What height your dog jumps is generally determined by your dog's height at its withers (shoulders). Again depending on the organization, the jump heights vary from dog to dog. For AKC (American Kennel Club) agility, corgis that measure 10" or under at the withers jump 8". Dogs measuring over 10" but no more than 14" jump 12". The majority of corgis end up in the 12" AKC class.

In addition to the different jump heights, all associations have different levels, which basically are beginner, intermediate and advanced, although they are called things like "novice," "open," and "excellent." In order to move from one level to another, generally you must have three qualifying scores at the lower level. For example, to move from novice to open, you would have to qualify three times in novice. The associations have different scoring methods, although they are fairly similar. Using AKC as an example, at the novice level you can have two off courses (dog takes the wrong obstacle before successfully completing the correct obstacle), two refusals (generally the dog runs by, or breaks the plane of an obstacle before completing it successfully), table faults, and time faults. A perfect score is 100, and you can qualify with a score of 85 or better. You generally lose 5 points for each fault. Table faults are 2 points and time faults are 1 point per second over the standard course time (at the novice level). However, there are nasty things called "non-qualifying" faults. Although in most cases you can complete the course, if your dog knocks a bar, has an unsafe execution of the teeter-totter (a "fly-off"), or misses the contact zone on the downside of a contact obstacle, you will receive a non-qualifying score. The courses increase in difficulty and number of obstacles, and the time you have to complete them decreases as you move from level to level. When you reach AKC's top level, the Excellent B class, you cannot make any errors!

AGILITY CLASSES

Different associations also vary in the "classes," or categories, in which you can compete. NADAC and USDAA trials, for example, generally offer three or four runs per day, including two standard runs and two "game" runs. NADAC has several different games, including Jumpers, Gamblers, and Tunnelers. You can earn titles in all of these events. AKC offers two classes: Standard, which includes, jumps, tunnels, weave poles, contact obstacles and the

Robin Early's Belle winding through the weave poles

table. They also offer Jumpers with Weaves, which is generally just jumps and weave poles. AKC's agility titles are as follows: NA and NAJ (Novice Agility, Novice Agility Jumper); OA and OAJ (Open Agility, Open Agility Jumper); EA and EAJ (Excellent Agility, Excellent Agility Jumper); MA and MAJ (Master Agility, Master Agility Jumper); and the coveted MACH (Master Agility Champion).

There are several corgis who have achieved not only the coveted MACH title, but who are now working towards a double or triple MACH. My own little Belle is trying her best to earn a MACH. I figure if she stays sound and we are both having fun, it will probably take us two more years!

DIET AND EXERCISE

Although it is always important to keep your corgi lean and fit, it is crucial if you plan on participating in the sport of agility. If you presently own a corgi (or are owned by one), you know that they are "easy keepers" and love to eat, so it is a challenge to keep your corgi's weight down. Although it is important for all dogs to be kept lean, it cannot be stressed enough that if you are asking your corgi to jump, he must not be overweight. No matter what kind of diet you feed your dog, you should know how much you are feeding and should adjust the size of the meal based on activity. If you and your corgi go on a long hike one day, feed him a little more. On the other hand, if you can't exercise your dog, or if you've attended a training class and used lots of treats, cut back on his portion. You should easily be able to feel your corgi's ribs (no digging to feel them).

Keeping your corgi fit is very important. Walking, hiking, swimming, and retrieving are all wonderful forms of exercise. If you are lucky enough to have access to water where you can let your dog swim, you can't get much better exercise. Retrieving is wonderful too; teach your dog to retrieve a ball or Frisbee. A word of warning: keep your throws low; you don't want your corgi leaping into the air to catch. Use common sense when exercising your dog. Make sure he gets time off. With puppies, do not overdo exercise. Basically, let your puppy tell you how much she can do.

And speaking of diet and fitness, although most anyone can do agility, remember that it is a sport where you are basically sprinting for 30-45 seconds, so it makes it more enjoyable if the human half of the team is also fit. I know lots of folks who started out in agility overweight and out of shape, and decided after a few agility trials that perhaps it was time to get a little more exercise themselves!

Basic Training

Generally speaking, before you even begin taking agility classes, your corgi should have a solid sit, down, stay, and—very important—a recall. There are many different opinions on when to start a dog in agility. As a rule of thumb, no jumping or full height A-Frames should be undertaken until all growth plates have closed. So be sure to check with your veterinarian before you undertake any jumping with your corgi. Does this mean you have to wait until your dog is fully grown before beginning agility? No, you can actually begin with puppies, introducing them to tunnels,

Lynda McKee's Shanay in a tunnel

letting them walking over boards on the ground, and so on. But keep in mind that you need to let your puppy be a puppy. So, although obstacle familiarization with a puppy is not a bad idea, that is pretty much all it should be.

You can generally find an agility instructor in your area by checking with your local dog club or going online. Before enrolling your corgi, try to watch a class. Make sure the instructor has experience with various breeds of dogs. It is also important to make sure that your instructor uses only positive training methods when teaching agility. The strongest correction I give my dogs is either "oops, wrong," or, if Simon is, for example, tunnel happy and playing the game without me, he might get a "time-out." Agility is no place for harsh corrections.

Agility Trial Time

What can you expect at your first agility trial? You'll have to fill out a form to enter. Most likely your instructor will help you with this and tell you when she thinks you and your dog are ready. Once you have entered, you will generally receive a confirmation of your entry about a week before the trial. The confirmation will give you directions to the trial site and tell you what time the classes start and how many dogs are in each class. Don't be surprised when you arrive at your first trial and it looks like tent city. Though not a requirement, lots of agility folks purchase tents or sun shades to keep themselves and their dogs out of the weather. But I competed for three years before I finally bought a shade myself, so don't worry about running out and getting one right away. Depending on where you live, trials are often held in fields on mowed grass, or in covered horse arenas. Footing can vary from padded matting, to grass, to dirt or sand. All footing has its advantages and disadvantages.

Do the Dogs like It?

Agility is for anyone who wants to have fun with their dog. Not only is it fun for the humans, but most of the dogs love it too. I don't think I've ever seen a corgi running agility who wasn't wearing a big ole happy corgi grin! There are folks of all ages with all different breeds participating in the sport of agility and having a great time. Personally, my corgis love agility. Of course, they pretty much love all the "games" that Mom invents. Agility trials are just plain fun.

Creative Corgis

Agility is a team sport: the dog performs the obstacles, but relies on the handler to tell him the obstacles. Or at least that's what we humans think. Sometimes, however, our clever little furry friends want to play the game their way and prove to us that we really should just wait outside the ring, let them loose, and watch them run. My Simon, like many other corgis, has an affinity for the tunnel, so it is often a challenge to get him to perform the correct obstacle. What do I do when Simon gets it into his head that he really doesn't need my help? The game ends, and we go home and practice more.

One thing I cannot stress enough: Do not ever get mad at your dog when doing agility! If he doesn't get it right, whose fault is it? Ummm, think about that. Who, after all, trained him? The name of the game in agility is **fun**! Keep that in mind at all times.

For more detailed information on the sport of agility, you can check out the following Web sites:

- **www.akc.com**. This is the American Kennel Club site. You can click on their agility link for more specific information about AKC agility.
- **www.nadac.com**. This is the North American Dog Agility Club's Web site.
- **www.usdaa.com**. This site belongs to the U.S. Dog Agility Association.
- **www.dogpatch.org**. This is a wonderful site, with all sorts of doggie information. If you click on the agility link, you will get links to all sorts of agility information, including how to get started, course information, the history of agility, and on and on.
- **www.cleanrun.com**. Another excellent agility resource site, with lots of information, a calendar of events, and a store.

Robin Early's Belle doing an agility jump

Jumping Belle

CORGIS AND OBEDIENCE, BOTH FORMAL AND INFORMAL

by Linda Kerr

Linda Kerr offers good advice on where to begin in competitive obedience.

No, the title of this chapter is **not** an oxymoron. Corgis and obedience go very well together. In fact, obedience training with a corgi is almost required. Corgis are a very intelligent but independent breed. After all, weren't they bred to drive cattle to market? And didn't they do that by being independent and intelligent? Some less positive people might even refer to them as stubborn. I prefer independent, but then they don't call me Pollyanna for nothing.

As most corgi owners will tell you, these dogs have a way of wiggling into your heart and getting you to devote your whole life to spoiling them and catering to their every whim. Watch out: you could be sorry if you end up with a problem on your hands in the form of a very smart, overbearing, overweight, overindulged, cute little wiggling bunny-butt who thinks that he or she rules the dog pack in your house. Sound familiar? By the way, you Cardigan owners will pardon my reference to "bunny-butt" in this chapter. I happen to be owned by two Pembrokes right now. From what I hear from the Cardi people, their corgis are very similar to Pems in terms of obedience training, so I hope you will read on and benefit from this chapter as a corgi person.

Obedience doesn't mean that you have to enter obedience trials, although they are lots of fun. Obedience just means that your dog will do what you ask him to do when you ask him to do it. What a novel idea! It could even save his life someday. Imagine what a strong "Come" command could do if your dog is headed for that squirrel across the street and a car is coming. It also comes in handy when you go to the vet and that little squirmy body is bouncing all over the office. You can enforce a sit-stay on the scales, or a stand-stay while the vet is examining your dog.

One thing I have discovered in working with corgis is that they will always present you with a challenge, sometimes when you least expect it, and you have to be on your toes to stay ahead of them. I love their enthusiasm and their intelligent way of solving problems. It keeps me at my best in training and also ensures that we both have lots of fun along the way. I have a feeling that if we didn't keep it fun, there wouldn't be much training going on at our house.

BASIC TRAINING

You don't have to send the little dear off to Boot Camp, although there are some that would certainly learn from it! At the very least, I recommend the American Kennel Club's CGC (Canine Good Citizen) training for your dog. It is available at many training facilities that also provide the evaluation at the end of the classes. The CGC consists of 10 steps that prove that your dog can be a good citizen in society and that you are a responsible dog owner. If you do not have a CGC class available to you, you can watch your local paper to see if any kennel clubs or obedience groups are offering the test to the public. The AKC is currently working to provide more emphasis on the CGC requirements and have just updated the CGC Evaluators Guide to make the evaluations more uniform across the country. For more information, access the AKC web site at www.akc.org or e-mail cgc@akc.org. If you do not have a facility near you that offers CGC, I would recommend that you take a Basic Obedience course, and order the CGC brochure from the AKC that outlines the 10 steps to see what is required. Basic Obedience classes should include the behaviors required for CGC, and more.

There are many training facilities around the country. You should check out your local options carefully before paying money and then finding out that you do not feel comfortable with their methods of teaching. It's a good practice to visit the training facility and observe a class or two before signing up. You want to ask questions about the trainer's credentials and experience. Perhaps you could even talk with some of the students after class to see what they think about it. Most instructors are in favor of positive training methods these days, although few still resort to the old "yank and jerk" practice of using choke chains and jerking to make corrections before the dog even has the opportunity to understand what the command means. Sometimes it is worth driving a little further or paying a little more money for a class if it provides what you are looking for. A smaller class size is also preferable, as the instructor would be able to provide you with more one-on-one attention, and you would be able to do more in a shorter amount of time with your dog.

Some breed clubs and kennel clubs in your area may offer classes. Most kennel club classes are good, because they are usually taught by people with experience in the show ring and years of experience with obedience training.

TRAINING CORGIS

When I got my first corgi, my past 10 years of obedience training experience had been with German shepherds. The shepherds are also intelligent and fun to train but are usually more serious and focused on the task. It is as if they are saying, "Give me a job to do and I will do it." The corgis, on the other hand, seem to be saying, "Give me a job to do and make it fun and I might do it, but where is the cookie?" Another analogy might be this scenario:

German Shepherd: You throw the dumbbell over the high jump and command the German shepherd to get it. The shepherd looks at you and thinks, "Okay, you threw it and gave me a command to bring it back to you. Never fear, I will get it for you, but don't talk to strangers while I am gone."

Corgi: You throw the dumbbell over the high jump and command the corgi to get it. The corgi looks at you and thinks, "Well, if you wanted it, why did you throw it over that tall thing that I have to jump over, can't you see I have short legs? Well, I will go get it but you better have that cookie ready when I get back. Oh, did you see that cute little Cardi over there, maybe I should go over and say hi… Mom, why are you frowning at me?"

Corgis are different from some other dogs to train, and most of them will require a firm hand but not hard corrections. This is a fine line to walk, and you know your dog better than anyone else. You will know

just how, and how much, to correct your dog. Usually a firm "Uh-Uh" and a stern look will do with my corgis. It gets their attention, and they know they need to try again to earn that cookie or praise from me. I never say "No" to them during training because I know they are trying, and I just need to get the message across to them of what I want. The more physical correction I use, the more independent they get. They are so much fun to train, because they seem to enjoy learning new things constantly and get bored with a lot of repetition. If the exercise is boring to them, such as heeling, I break it up with play or a more active exercise that they enjoy.

COMPETITION OBEDIENCE: GETTING STARTED

For anyone who desires to compete in obedience trials with their corgi, I would say, "Go for it!" It is a great hobby, and the time you spend training and practicing with your dog will enhance your bond together. Where else can you pay entry fees, drive 300 miles round trip, pay for a hotel room, gas, and meals, and come home with a 35 cent ribbon (or nothing) to show for it? But, best of all, where else can you and your beloved canine companion have so much fun and camaraderie with people that share the love of dogs and of the sport of obedience.

My first obedience dog was a German shepherd, and I followed that with another shepherd, and then another. I still have all three shepherds now, by the way, and they get along just fine with the two corgis. I was fortunate to have mentors who gave me encouragement and training, not to mention confidence to walk into the obedience ring for the first time. Again, the best place for support like that will come from a breed club, such as a local or regional corgi club or a local kennel club. It helps to have other people who are training for the same purpose. You can even meet together and work your dogs, taking turns playing "judge," and so on. Without the help from my German shepherd friends and my obedience instructors, I would never have had the nerve to walk into that ring for the first time. Most obedience people are glad to help newcomers to the sport.

CONTACTS AND INFORMATION

A good way to start is to find out where shows are going to be held in your area and go to watch obedience competitions. Most dog show superintendents have Web sites that will list the shows they are superintending in your area. Not all dog shows will offer obedience, so you will have to be sure to check to see if it is included at a particular show. A local kennel club, obedience club, or breed club will be holding the event, but most will hire a superintendent (unless it is an obedience-only trial) to send out premium lists, take entries and fees, send out judging schedules, prepare the catalog for the event, and set up all the rings and equipment.

Table 5, "Superintendents," on page 156 lists some of the superintendents and their locations around the country.

I have listed the states in which these superintendents have their home office, but the shows that they put on can be in many different states. Most of them stay within an area surrounding their office. For example, if you live in Texas, Oklahoma, or Arkansas, it is possible that Onofrio would be the superintendent for a show in your area and have information that could help you locate an obedience trial to observe. Onofrio also superintends shows in other states, such as Florida.

TABLE 5. Superintendents

Name	Location	Web site, e-mail, phone
Jack Bradshaw	CA	mail@bradshaw.com
Brown Dog Show Organization	WA	bdogshows@aol.com
Thomas Crowe (Moss-Bow)	Large organization that covers most of the Eastern Seaboard and beyond	www.infodog.com mbf@infodog.com
Eileen McNulty	NY	emcnulty@mcnulty-dogshows.com
Jane Garvin	OR	jane@garvinshowser-vices.com
Nancy Matthews	OR	(503) 253-9367
Jack Onofrio	OK	www.onofrio.com
Bob Peters Dog Shows	NC	www.bpdsonline.com
James A Rau, Jr.	PA	raudog@epix.net
Kevin B. Rogers	MS	Krdogshows@aol.com
Kenneth A. Sleeper	IN	rjdogshows@ctinet.com
Nancy Wilson	AZ	nancronw@aol.com

COMPETITION TRAINING

Ask your local training facility if they teach "competition" obedience. If they do not, they should be able to recommend a place that will teach the level you would like. Before entering into the competition obedience world, I would recommend a class on the basics first. These would include most of what is in the CGC training; coming when called, sit, sit-stay, down, down-stay, walking on a loose leash (and not pulling you down the street), meeting other dogs and people in a polite manner, and accepting grooming and petting from a stranger. Many facilities require that you obtain your CGC training or Basic Obedience Training before entering a competitive level class.

Competition obedience includes different levels of obedience required from the dog. The first step is called **Novice** and results in your dog earning a CD (Companion Dog) title. The next level is called **Open** (CDX title) and then **Utility** (UD Title). You can go from there to earn UDX and OTCH, Utility Dog Excellent, and Obedience Trial Champion titles. As you can imagine, the higher up in obedience competition you go, the more difficult and demanding the exercises become. For example, Novice consists of the following exercises: heeling in a pattern called out by the judge on leash, heeling in a figure eight pattern on leash, heeling off leash, stand for exam (the dog must remain standing still while judge examines him), recall (coming when called), a "finish," which means the dog returns to heel position by your left side when commanded to do so following the recall, and, lastly, the sit-stay for one minute and the down-stay for three minutes while your dog is laying in a line with other dogs while you stand across the ring.

I won't go into the exercises required for Open or Utility, but they can be found in the AKC Obedience Regulations book, which can be ordered from the AKC, or you can read it online at www.akc.org To obtain your copy, write or call The American Kennel Club order desk at 5580 Centerview Drive, Raleigh, NC 27606, Tel: (919) 233-9767, e-mail: orderdesk@akc.org. The first copy is free but if you wish more than one copy they are $2.00 each.

Everyone showing in the obedience ring should read this booklet thoroughly. I recently attended an AKC Obedience Regulations Seminar, and even though I have read the book many times and shown for 10 years, I learned even more from this seminar. The Regulations book will also explain the scoring used by the judges. When you walk into the ring with your dog, you start out with 200 points. For every mistake you make as a handler (Yes, we can goof up too!), such as giving a second command, and for every error your dog makes (Surely not **my** dog!), such as not sitting straight at your side or coming in straight to you when you call him, the judge will deduct points. There are minor and substantial deductions, which are listed in the AKC Rules book. There are also things you can do that will result in a NQ, or Non-Qualifying Score. If you end up the exercises with 170 or better score, you will have "qualified." You must do this three times before three different judges in order to earn your title. This is true for all levels of competition.

The Open and Utility exercises build on these Novice exercises, but involve other tasks and are more challenging to both you and your dog. However, it is these exercises that can bring the most enjoyment to both of you. Remember, though, that you are doing this to **have fun**! If you reach the point when it is not fun for you or your dog, it is time to quit and do something else for awhile.

READY TO SHOW?

Many people ask the question, "How will I know when I am ready to go into the ring?" You will know when the time is right. Ask yourself these questions:

Have we proofed all exercises for all imaginable distractions that could happen at a dog show?

Noises from chairs being dropped, children hanging over the gate with hot dogs, popcorn, and balloons, and so on.

Have you practiced in different locations, or have you only worked out in the training facility?

It is helpful to practice at your local Pets-Mart, in schoolyards and church yards, and at the shopping mall parking lot (on leash, of course). This could prepare your dog for distractions and get him used to working for you in different environments.

Have you shown in some practice matches?

Most clubs hold Fun Matches or Show & Gos, in which you can pay a nominal fee, usually around $5 or so, to get some "ring time" and take your dog into a dog show environment with other dogs around. If it is a Fun Match or a Show & Go, you can use corrections in the ring on your dog. If it is a Sanctioned AKC Match, you are encouraged to treat it as if you were really showing and are not supposed to correct your dog in the ring. The more you can practice at Fun Matches and/or Show & Gos, the better it is for both of you. It will simulate a **real** show environment and serve as a useful training tool.

These are just some suggestions to think about before you actually enter a show. Your instructor will have more and will be able to help you to know when the time is right.

DON'T HURRY — GETTING THERE IS HALF THE FUN

I remember well when I couldn't wait to get my first little corgi into the Novice ring for the first time. She was only 14 months old, and I just knew she was ready! Ha! Did she show me! My instructor told me she didn't think my dog was ready, but I entered anyway. When we got to the heeling off leash part, I heeled perfectly to the judge's directions. I thought my dog was with me. I glanced down at my left side where she was supposed to be, but there was no dog! I turned around, and there she was in the middle of the ring, smiling that little corgi smile with that "catch me if you can" look. Remember what I said about a reliable "come" command? Well, we didn't have it! She proceeded to run around the ring as only a little bunny-butt can do, with me, two stewards, and a judge chasing her, making us look like fools—all except the judge of course. Needless to say, we didn't qualify that day! I have had non-qualifying days before, but this was the first time that the judge has ever **excused** me from the ring. I promised myself it would also be the last time.

We spent the next six months working on off leash work and coming when called. I used a light line on her, and we worked everywhere I could think of. We didn't go back into the ring again until we had this perfected and she was more mature. She earned her CD title in three shows with excellent scores, but she did it when we were ready, not when I pushed us to be ready just to make a show. It is so nice to hear comments from the judge like, "nice corgi," "good working dog," and "I like the way she works," as opposed to "catch your dog if you can and you are excused from the ring." No comparison! It is also good to know that you are setting a good example of what a corgi can do in the ring. There will always be dog shows to enter. Wait until you **both** are ready and enjoy the trip, not just the destination of the show ring. The most important thing is that you and your dog are building on your relationship during training in a positive manner.

RECOMMENDED READING

For corgi owners, I highly recommend the book by Barbara Cecil & Gerianne Darnell entitled *Competitive Obedience Training for the Small Dog*. It helped me make the transition from German shepherds, whose heads are always up right by your left side, to the "vertically challenged" corgi view. You use different training techniques for the smaller dogs. For example, Abbey, my oldest corgi, would find it difficult to look up at me during heeling. I knew that I had her attention but when she kept her head held high for a long period of time, she would start "reverse sneezing." After reading this book, I started putting some white tape on my pant leg near my knee in an "X" pattern. I encouraged her to focus on this spot and treated her a lot in the beginning to teach her this new technique. This gave her an area to look at and a way to focus her attention on me without looking in my face all the time, Border Collie style. Of course, you do get strange looks when you forget the tape is there and walk into Kroger's with this big white X on your jeans.

Other good training books on my shelf include *Purely Positive Training* by Sheila Booth, *Culture Clash* by Jean Donaldson, *Expert Obedience Training for Dogs* by Winifred G. Strickland, and *Beyond Basic Training* by Diane Bauman.

I also recommend any dog training book written by Carol Lea Benjamin. She has one also for rescue dog owners, entitled *Second Hand Dog*. I find her books very easy for anyone to understand, and her drawings are not only cute but helpful. There are also many books on the market about clicker training. One of the most recognized authors on clicker training is Karen Pryor, author of *Don't Shoot the Dog*. The basic concept of clicker training is that you use a clicker to "mark" the desired behavior with a clicking sound, and reward with a treat, the millisecond the dog performs the desired behavior. This provides instant positive reinforcement and works for many areas of training. It has been used successfully for years in training marine animals, such as dolphins.

As you can see from this abbreviated discussion, there are many paths you could take in training your dog, just as there are many kinds of classes and instructors out there. My advice is to listen to people that have done obedience (other corgi people are invaluable resources), read books, go to classes, watch obedience being done in the ring, and ask questions. Then take all this good advice and only use what you know will work with **your** dog; file the rest of it away for the next dog. Dogs are all different, and what works for one person and one dog may not be the best thing for you right now. You know your dog better than anyone, so if someone suggests a training method that you feel uncomfortable with, don't do it. Get another opinion. No matter how long you are in obedience, you are constantly learning from your dog, other people, books, articles and, most of all, experience—the best teacher of them all.

Linda Kerr and Abbey (Sandfox's Midnight Dancer, CD, CGC, TDI)

GETTING STARTED IN TRACKING

by Lynda McKee

Many corgis make excellent trackers. Lynda McKee tells you how to team up with your dog and enjoy tracking.

Tracking is an activity that comes easily to Welsh corgis, and it has nothing to do with their lowness to the ground. The breed's natural inquisitiveness and desire to be doing things, along with their love of toys and food, make it very easy to train in this most natural of all dog activities. Pembroke Welsh corgis always rank among the leading breeds in tracking when the end-of-the-year tallies are done. The breed is currently among the leaders for holders of the challenging Champion Tracker (CT) title. But even the most proficient CT corgis started their tracking careers along the lines that will be outlined below.

BASICS FOR A TRACKING DOG TITLE

To earn a Tracking Dog (TD) title, your corgi must follow the scent of a stranger over a course of 440 to 500 yards and find the glove or wallet that has been left at the end. Your corgi must also first be certified by a licensed tracking judge as being ready to enter a test. The certification track is like a real test track. The track will be 30 minutes to 2 hours in age and will have 3 to 5 turns, with the certification track being 30 minutes old. Most test tracks are between 30 and 45 minutes old. It will be in an open field (think "pasture") and will stay only in this open field. There will be neither obstacles like fences or woods, nor any drastic changes of cover. There will be two flags 30 yards apart indicating the direction in which the tracklayer walked. You must be 20 feet behind your dog when it is in motion. Once you pass the second flag, the two of you are on your own. It is up to the teamwork that you and your corgi have established. There are few more exciting thrills than to find the glove at the end of the track.

Tracking is pass/fail. There are no scores, no one to "beat." Passing teams earn their title, but those who are not successful will try again at another test. Even these teams are not failures, for the bonds that are established as you and your corgi work in tracking are unlike any other. There is mutual respect and trust in each other. A dog and person who have established such bonds can never be deemed failures.

EQUIPMENT

Obtain a set of the AKC rules for tracking tests and read them. You will need a buckle collar and six-foot lead (preferably leather), the dog's favorite food or toy, two flags (surveyor's flags work fine—or those flags the gas company uses to mark gas lines work just as well or even two bicycle flags or bent coat hangers with a piece of surveyor's tape attached), a glove, and about 15 minutes of time. That is all that is needed to get started. Later you will need a non-restrictive tracking harness, a line 20 to 40 feet with an identifying marker at the 20-foot point, water and a bowl, more flags and gloves (dogs like to chew them up!), a notebook and pen, rain suit, boots, lip balm in the winter and sunblock in the summer, clothing appropriate for the weather, a *Rand McNally Road Atlas* (to find the places tests are held), and a watch.

GETTING STARTED ON THAT TD TITLE

It is helpful to have someone assist you the first few times you go tracking. Your tracking buddy will put a flag in the ground. You will stand with your corgi at this flag. Your partner will tease your corgi with your chosen item (toy or food) and the glove. When the corgi is very interested, your partner will turn, walk in a straight line about ten steps, turn and face you waving the glove, place the glove and item on the ground at the base of a second flag, and then return to you on the exact same path. Once your partner faces you, point to the ground, give your tracking command (I use "Where's your ball? Find it!" or "Where's the glovie? Find the glovie!" or "Where are the cookies? Find the cookies!") in an excited tone of voice, and keep your dog on the same path your buddy just walked—that's the purpose of the two flags. Your corgi will probably visually mark the glove and run out to it without tracking a step. That's okay—you make the biggest fuss you can possibly make over what your corgi has just done—effusive praise, let your dog play tug-of-war with the glove after it eats the cookies. Really whoop it up.

Your partner repeats the procedure as before, proceeding from the second flag, but this time goes about 20 steps. If I am food training a dog to track (which is how I teach puppies), I assess the dog on this track. If he does not at some point drop his nose, then I change the procedure slightly on the third track. The third track will be 30 steps in length. I will rub a piece of food on the sole of one shoe to encourage the dog to drop his nose. I will also put a few tiny pieces of food along the track (think a slice of hot dog that has then been quartered). Dogs are generally catching on to the idea on the third track and will be highly motivated. You will most likely be too, but stop. If you track your dog again, do it later on in the day, but it is better to do the next series on another day.

Your next training session will start with a 15-step track (half the distance of the last track done at the first session). This session will go 15-30-50, then 20-40-60, then 30-60-80, etc. Each series indicates the steps walked and each series is done on separate days. Should the dog at any time have trouble, you will do one more track at half the distance as the troublesome one and then quit. You and your dog should be ending each session with a "More! More!" attitude. You want to build on success.

For the first two weeks or so, if you can get out three or four times, that would be great. If your only available time is on the weekends, that's fine too. Your first job at this point is to convince the dog that the item is always there, and he must have his nose down and pull you along to it. Your other job is to keep the dog on a straight line between the two flags and not let him deviate from the track. I work my beginning dogs on a 15-foot lead knotted halfway. I do not go past the knot for these beginning tracks. The saying is that the dog must "earn line"; that is the purpose for suggesting that you start your dog on a 6-foot leather leash. Your dog will not be able to go more than 6 feet off the track and the leather will be easy on your hands.

These beginning tracks are double-laid, which means that your tracking partner walks out and back. When your dog can do about a 100-yard track in this manner, then you will drop back to a 50 yard, single-laid track, which means the tracklayer does not return along the same line. At this point, you will be using a lot of space since the tracklayer needs to continue past the glove about 10 yards and then turn and walk about 30 yards then turn again and walk the same distance back as the track went out. By this point, you have most likely scouted out promising training areas.

When your dog can successfully do 150 yards or so as a single-laid track, you will drop back to a 50-yard track once again. This track will be the first one your dog does not see being laid. Let it age 5 minutes and then go get the dog. He should be able to successfully run this track. You again work back up to the long tracks, single-laid but now keep careful track of the time. You can jump the age up in 5 minute-increments as you up the length of the track, keeping in mind that each track is about twice the length of the previous one and that each new session begins at half the length of the last track.

When the tracks are about 15 minutes in age, you can again drop the length and now introduce turns. You begin by working first right (or left) turns, then the other turn, then put two turns together to make a U, then add a third turn, and so on. Once your dog can do both a right and a left turn on the same track, it is ready to go on to multiple turns. You gradually increase the overall length of the track, the number of turns, and the age. Once the dog is introduced to turns, he runs two tracks a session. Once he is up to 3 turns, he runs one track during a training session. I am omitting many details, of course, but I hope you are getting the general idea.

The critical part of tracking is your ability to read your dog. You must be able to read what he is doing in all types of weather and in all sorts of fields. A tracking test may be suspended during a torrential downpour and stopped for lightning, but otherwise it will go on. That means you need to train in all types of weather: wind, rain, sun, heat, that white stuff we don't get too frequently in Atlanta. It means in tall cover (which, for a corgi, means knee high on you! But you may have cover up to your waist too!), short cover, wet grass, dry grass, all sorts of weeds. You must be able to read your dog's body language and indications of losing and re-finding the scent. This part of tracking is where the trust and teamwork come into play.

How long does it take to earn a TD title? Practically speaking, it depends upon you and your dog! It takes a motivated person training their first dog about four months to become certified to enter a test. I have had a dog get certified its eighth time out—exceptional corgi with an experienced handler! A friend had her springer out a total of 26 training sessions, including the test they failed and the test they passed. It will also depend upon whether you run into any unusual training problems. I have encountered none with the corgis I have worked with, but I did train a most unusual English springer spaniel for a

friend. Corgis are born to track, so don't expect any unusual things from them.

When you think you are ready to be certified, you contact a licensed judge. A regulation track will be laid for you. Should the judge pass you on the track, you will receive four certificates good for one year saying that your dog is ready to enter a test. You must include an original certification each time you enter a TD test. Once you pass a test, you may continue to enter tests, if you wish, and you no longer need a certification to do so.

WHAT'S NEXT?

The American Kennel Club offers two more tracking titles: Tracking Dog Excellent (TDX) and Variable Surface Tracker (VST). Both require a TD for entry. There currently are no rules regarding certification for either advanced title. It is very difficult to even get into one of these tests and the pass rates are very low. The pass rate in TDX is about 15% and has been that way for years. The pass rate for VST is even lower. These titles take dedicated dogs and handlers and many many miles of training tracks. Dogs that earn all three tracking titles are awarded a Champion Tracker (CT) title as well. The CT title is a prefix to the dog's registered name. Corgis always are near the top for titles earned in tracking—don't discount an advanced title until you give it a try!

I started tracking in 1984 and earned my first TD in 1985. Since then I have earned 10 TDs, 3 TDXs, and 1 VST (giving that dog a CT) as well as helping other people earn tracking titles on various breeds. In 2001, I became a provisional Tracking Dog judge. I believe the biggest thrills I have had in showing dogs were that first TD, each TDX, and the biggest one of all—that VST that gave Cruiser his CT.

Suggested Readings

- *Tracking Dog: Theory and Method* by Glenn Johnson. The "bible" of tracking.

- *Tracking From the Ground Up* by Sandy Ganz and Susan Boyd. A more "doable" version of Glenn Johnson's classic methods.

- *AKC Tracking Rules and Regulations* by the American Kennel Club (available free from AKC or at most education booths at the larger dog shows)

Cruiser, Ch. Tifflyn The Funseeker CDX, MX, AXJ, PHC, VCX, with Lynda McKee

Cruiser is the first Pembroke Variable Surface Tracker and the first of any breed to achieve Champion Tracker

Lynda McKee's Cori at the end of her TDX track

FLYBALL FUN
by Linda Kriete

If you want to know more about a terrific team sport, Linda Kriete tells you how to enjoy flyball.

WHAT IS FLYBALL?

Flyball is a team sport for dogs that was invented in California in the late 1970s. Legend has it that Herbert Wagner first showed it on the Johnny Carson Show to millions of Americans. Soon afterwards, dog trainers and dog clubs were making and using Flyball boxes. In the early 1980s, the sport became so popular that the North American Flyball Association (NAFA) was formed and became the worldwide authority for Flyball.

Flyball is a relay race with four dogs on a team. The course consists of a starting line, four hurdles spaced 10 feet apart, and a box. The first hurdle is 6 feet from the start line and the box is 15 feet from the last hurdle, for a 51 foot overall length. The first dog jumps the hurdles and steps on a spring-loaded box that shoots out a tennis ball. The dog catches the tennis ball and then runs back over the four hurdles. When the dog crosses the starting line, the next dog goes. The first team to have all four dogs run without errors wins the heat. Tournaments are usually organized in either a double elimination or round robin format. Double elimination is usually best of 3 or best of 5. Round robin is usually best 3 out of 5 and the first team to win 3 heats receives 1 point towards their standing in the tournament. The hurdles' heights are dependent on the height of the dogs in the team, 4" below the shoulder height of the shortest dog; 8" is the minimum height, and 16" is the maximum height.

TITLES

The dogs earn points towards Flyball titles based on the teams' time:

- Less than 32 sec.: Each dog earns 1 point
- Less than 28 sec.: Each dog earns 5 points
- Less than 24 sec.: Each dog earns 25 points

Titles earned are:

- FD - Flyball Dog (20 pts.)
- FDX - Flyball Dog Excellent (100 pts.)
- FDCh - Flyball Dog Champion (500 pts.)
- FM - Flyball Master (5,000 pts.)
- FMX - Flyball Master Excellent (10,000 pts.)
- FMCh - Flyball Master Champion (15,000 pts.)
- ONYX - ONYX Award (20,000 pts.)

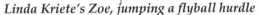

Linda Kriete's Zoe, jumping a flyball hurdle

• FGDCh - Flyball Grand Champion (30,000 pts.)

CAN I DO FLYBALL WITH MY CORGI?

Of course! Corgis make a great height dog and many have come to love this sport. There are currently 103 PWCs and 19 CWCs registered with NAFA (January 2002)

HOW DO I GET STARTED?

Find a training club that teaches flyball or contact an existing team in your area. You can find a list of teams on the Flyball Home Page (see Web site listing below).

BASIC TRAINING

While you do not need formal obedience training to do flyball, it is very important to have a good recall with your dog before you begin this sport. There are lots of loose dogs and distractions, and you need to be able to have your dog come to you when you call. Luckily you can use just about any motivator to get your dog's attention: food, toys, loud sounds.

At flyball classes, your dog will be taught how to jump over the four flyball jumps, catch the ball out of the box, and race with the other dogs. It helps a great deal if your dog can already retrieve a tennis ball to your hand.

Dogs cannot compete in flyball until they are a year of age. Training can be started before they are a year old, but should be kept to a minimum and carefully supervised until they are fully developed. Do not be in a hurry to train your dog too quickly; take the time to make sure they are trained correctly to compete in this sport to minimize any risk of injury.

DIET AND EXERCISE

It is extremely important to keep your corgi lean and fit if you plan on participating in the sport of flyball. While it is beneficial for all dogs to be kept in good condition, it cannot be stressed enough that if you are asking your corgi to jump and push on the flyball box, he must not be overweight. Running your hands over your dogs sides, you should easily be able to feel your corgi's ribs (no digging to feel them).

Conditioning your dog is also very important. Walking, hiking, swimming, and retrieving are all wonderful forms of exercise. At a flyball tournament your dog could do as many as 45 races over the weekend. This is a lot for a little dog to run and they need to be in good physical condition.

MY EXPERIENCE

Six years ago I overheard someone at the training club I belong to mention flyball. I had no idea what that was, but when I asked, she suggested that I come to a practice and find out. So I took my ball-crazy PWC, Zoe, to a class and we were hooked. However, all the training doesn't fully prepare you for what your first tournament will be like. The excitement, the sounds, the noise, the thrills. And, of course, you never know what your dog will do on their first time out. While our first venture was far from stellar, our teammates gave us much support, and Zoe soon learned that the racing was the same at a tournament as at practice. She got so excited waiting for her turn to run. Zoe raced for several years, earning her Flyball Master title (5,000 points). She suffered a minor shoulder injury while running around the yard at home, and at age 10 is starting to get arthritis. Therefore, she only plays flyball occasionally these days, but she still loves the game.

When I introduced my second corgi, Tab, to this sport, he caught on very quickly. He is not a ball- or toy-driven dog and didn't see much point to this game—that is, until I introduced special treats to the game. Being the food hound that he is, when he discovered that really good treats came with this game, he was all for it. Now he also enjoys barking and racing with his teammates, and being cheered on and praised; the food is just the icing on the cake. Tab just became the first PWC to earn the ONYX title (20,000 points) and is the #1 PWC registered (103 PWCs and 79 CWC's registered) with the North American Flyball Association (NAFA). He loves this sport and is going strong.

LINKS

- http://www.flyballdogs.com/
- http://www.flyball.org/
- http://www.i-flyball.com/
- http://www.flyball.com/

BOOKS

- *Flyball Racing: The Dog Sport for Everyone* by Lonnie Olson. Hungry Minds, Inc. 1997.

  Book Description: Flyball, a ball catching race for dogs, has tremendous spectator appeal. The fast-paced action, as well as limitless possibilities for comedic performances by the canine athletes, are just two reasons why Flyball has such international interest. Special features of the book include construction plans for all jumps as well as the Flyball box, the F.A.T. (Flyball Aptitude Test), and training methods based on positive reinforcement. Lonnie Olson is President of the National Association of Dog Obedience Instructors, and is an Obedience and Flyball judge.

- *Flying High: The Complete Book of Flyball* by Joan Payne. KDB Publishing Company. 1996.

  Book Description: A book for beginners, teachers, and competitors, takes you from the beginnings of flyball to current day competition. You will find step by step procedures for skill development, problem solving techniques, a conditioning program for flyball, equipment selection and sources, ring and course diagrams, and where and how to begin. The author does an especially good job of transmitting her excitement with the sport and as part of a dog/handler team! You'll want to go right out and get started!

Linda Kriete's Tab

Tab is the first PWC to earn the ONYX title (20,000 points) and the number one PWC registered with the North American Flyball Association

Linda Kriete's Zoe hits the flyball box

HERDING WITH CORGIS

by Elizabeth Trail

What could be more natural for a corgi than to herd? Elizabeth Trail explains how corgis help out around her small sheep farm.

People who doubt the historical appropriateness of competitive herding with corgis maintain that corgis traditionally worked only as the most rudimentary drovers. I think that this is a misinterpretation of what corgis actually did. There would be no reason to create a specialized breed to "follow a cow up the lane." Cattle are creatures of habit and will come to the barn for feeding or milking just fine on their own. It is when cows are being asked to do something outside of their normal routine, or something that they don't want to do, that a dog is needed, and then the dog needs real herding skills!

Of course droving, or moving stock to market, is actually fairly complicated—cattle must be gathered and made to leave their familiar farm, herds fan out in all directions at a crossroad or want to linger by a stream, strange dogs rush out of farm entrances and scatter the cattle, another herd is encountered going in the opposite direction in a narrow lane. A drover's ability to handle these situations competently would come out of daily herding and working experience around the farm.

We have a small farm, probably similar to the sort of small holdings corgis came from in Wales—fencing somewhere between bad and nonexistent, hodgepodge of pens around the barns that grew up without a lot of planning over past years, steep rocky pasture, and animals of the "a few of these and a few of those" variety—ducks, geese, chickens, sheep, and ponies. No cattle yet. Rats in the barn, foxes on the prowl. Oh, and neighbors whose livestock—cattle, pig, ducks—wander over frequently.

Daily usefulness around a small farm requires versatility. Having a dog with only driving skills would be like having a car with only forward gears! In daily life on a farm, you often find yourself on one side of the flock and the dog on the other, with the dog bringing the animals along between you, which is called a "wear." Or you may be needing to send the dog around to the far side of the stock and have him bring animals toward you, which is called a "gather." The day's work may call for bringing animals between two gates along a line parallel to you, which is called a "cross-drive," putting animals through a gate or into a barn, which is called a "pen," or separating out the animals you want to keep in the barn from the ones who are going out in the field, which is called a "shed." And right there are most of the skills in an advanced herding course.

Picture yourself trying to get reluctant sheep out of the field and into the paddock for the night. Since it is silly for both you and the dog to climb that hill, you tell your dog to go get the sheep. If you're lucky, he will run wide around the edge of the field so he can come in at the sheep from behind (the "outrun"), get them moving without alarming or scattering them (the "lift") and bring them down the hill to you (the "fetch"). You are standing there holding the gate, ready to slam it shut and tie it as soon as the flock is in. So the dog works the back side of the sheep, covering them so they can't turn and run, and putting on the pressure so that the sheep decide that going through the gate is better than dealing with the dog. On the farm, you can tie the gate and go in the house for dinner! At a herding trial, you just got your "pen"!

On my little farm, the hay man will be here in a few minutes with a new round-bale for my sheep. A corgi will go through the gate ahead of me, drive the sheep into a corner and hold them while Jimmy and I roll the heavy bale into the center of the paddock.

This afternoon my son and his corgi will be sent to put the sheep out into the pasture for a few hours. She will have to get the sheep away from that new bale of hay, bunch them up and put them through the gate, and then chase them up the hill into the field.

This evening I'll send my Border Collie to the top of the field to bring the sheep down, because of the long outrun, but a corgi will step in to help put them back through our too-narrow gate into the paddock. Tomorrow, my corgis may let me know that the neighbor's pig or steer is in the yard again, and I will turn a couple of them out to drive the wayward animal home.

In a month we'll be doing shots and shearing, and a corgi will bring the flock into the paddock and then help us corner and catch each new sheep to work on, and put each finished one back out the gate.

And in the meantime, there are rats in the barn to be chased, cats and children to be kept in line, foxes and night intruders to be warned, and visitors to be greeted: all jobs that our versatile little corgis excel at!

How do I know that these are natural jobs for corgis? Because genes don't lie! When you start using your corgis on stock around a farm and watch how simply and naturally they figure out these tasks on their own, you know their ancestors are whispering in their ears!

My corgis aren't highly trained obedience dogs—they started out as conformation dogs and knew how to come when called, stand on a table, and put their ears up for cookies. Watching a four year old show bitch on her first exposure to stock move around the imaginary clock face and balance exactly opposite her handler, or a five-month-old puppy size up the situation at a gate and move to the back of the stock to put them through, is a revelation!

Sue Mesa, a Cardi breeder who was my first herding trainer, said that she had never seen a corgi who did not naturally

gather (bring the stock toward the handler), often in preference to driving (moving the stock away from the handler). These genes would not be here in this advanced form unless they had been selected for and used over past centuries!

I will readily concede that cattle are more natural to corgis than sheep, and my corgis show a marked preference for bigger stock. I wish that there were more cattle trials available for corgis. But whether a farm has a few sheep or a few cattle, many of the daily realities are the same. Animals go out to pasture and come back to the barn. They need to be kept from crowding or escaping during feeding. They get docked or castrated or need their feet trimmed. They get sick and need medication. These are universal daily happenings on any small farm, and a useful dog can save a thousand steps and hours of frustration.

So let's not sell our corgis short! They are truly versatile little farm dogs with very useful herding skills and a range of inborn natural talents.

Corgis are not Border Collies. They bark more, and tend to nip at heels. They prefer to work in close and excel at paddock jobs. They aren't as fast or as wide on long outruns, and they aren't built for hours of long sweeping flanks and gathers, so I tend to send my BC out for this type of work.

But my corgis are better than the BC at driving my neighbor's animals home, whereas the BC wants to gather them up and bring them to me. And the BC doesn't even DO pigs, who smell funny and are totally unimpressed by "eye," whereas the corgis rely on mouth and momentum to send that porker bolting for his own yard.

All in all, the modifications needed to work sheep instead of cattle are more in style and details than in the overall picture. Sheep require a little more delicate handling, a bit more finesse. This is where some of us feel that we have to stretch our corgis' natural abilities beyond what they were bred for in order to trial. But as far as proving a corgi's ability to manage stock in a useful way, I see no real discrepancy between the sport of herding and the inborn herding and stock-management abilities my corgis show me naturally every day around the farm.

THE MAGICAL MEDICINE OF THERAPY DOGS

by Linda Kerr

A visit from a corgi can provide therapy for many. Linda Kerr shares her experiences with many different types of therapy work, and offers a guide for getting started.

First of all, I should explain that I am fairly new to the wonderful world of corgis, or corgwyn, as some would have it. My main dog experiences, for more than 20 years, have been with German shepherds. I have trained and shown in obedience with them, but when our youngest German shepherd became ill with epilepsy, we had to quit training for open obedience, because she couldn't navigate the jumps while on the anti-seizure medications. Just when we were considering another dog so I would have one to work with, my husband was diagnosed with lung cancer. He was one of the lucky ones, and in the year following his surgery to remove part of his lung and a few lymph nodes, he went through both radiation and chemotherapy like a real trooper. During this time, we concentrated only on his recovery and my dog training activities were put on the shelf.

When he was well enough for us to consider another dog, we decided that another German shepherd was out of the question. We still had three in the household, one with epilepsy and two older ones, so a fourth large dog just wouldn't work. I had seen corgis in a herding class I was taking with one of the shepherds and also in obedience work. We started looking for a corgi and were blessed with our Abbey. She is a tri-color Pembroke Welsh corgi and the queen of the house. She loves everyone, especially children and all other dogs. She was my first real "Certified Therapy Dog."

My husband's illness brought me in contact with many people that were ill, and we spent a lot of time in the hospital. I knew that I wanted to become involved with therapy dogs. Then Abbey opened my eyes one day, and it all fell into place.

THERAPY PUPPY

One weekend when Abbey was only 10 months old, we were attending a dog show in a large arena; the floor was crowded with people and dogs. It was one of those shows where you had to make your way precariously around all the handlers and their prized canines. I noticed that Abbey had locked onto someone and was pulling me through the crowd. I assumed that she saw someone that we knew and was trying to get to them, but when I looked up, I realized that she was making a beeline for a little girl in a wheelchair. Abbey's little long body just wiggled all over, and she couldn't get to the little girl fast enough. It was as if the little girl was her long lost buddy, and she wanted to give her a welcoming hug.

As we approached the wheelchair, I could see that the little girl was paralyzed and unable to talk. I asked her parents if Abbey could "say hello" to her. They were thrilled that we wanted to visit and gave us permission. As I held Abbey up so that the little girl could touch her, Abbey just beamed as if to say, "See Mom, I just knew I had to get here." Tiny, drawn hands that could barely move tried to stroke Abbey's soft black coat and managed to touch her carefully. Abbey's ears went back and a smile came across her little muzzle. The little girl smiled in return, and I knew that we needed to do. We needed to get into therapy work; it was Abbey's mission in life.

BECOMING AN OFFICIAL THERAPY DOG

The first thing we had to do in order to be accepted as a therapy dog was to pass the AKC Canine Good Citizen Test (CGC). We worked on the exercises, and Abbey passed with flying colors. The AKC CGC Program includes all the good things that a dog should know in order to be a good citizen. It stresses coming when called, sit and down on command, and stays. It also includes sitting quietly for petting, which is a big plus for a therapy dog—we can't have them jumping up unexpectedly on people or being wild. In other words, they must be "Good Citizens." More information about the CGC Program can be located at the AKC Web site at www.akc.org.

One organization that offers therapy dog training information and certification is Therapy Dog International. Therapy Dogs International, Inc., (TDI) is a volunteer group organized to provide qualified handlers and their therapy dogs for visits to places where they are needed. The primary objective of the TDI dog and handler is to provide comfort and companionship by sharing the dog with the patients in hospitals, nursing homes, and other institutions, as well as other places a therapy dog could help. This is done in a way that increases emotional well-being, promotes healing, and improves the quality of life for the people being visited and the staff that cares for these people. Information on this program can be found at www.tdi-dog.org

Another therapy organization is the Delta Society, with its Pet Partners program. This is similar to the TDI program and also requires testing and certification of the dog and handler. There can be two levels of therapy work. One, called *Animal Assisted Activities*, involves casual visits where residents of a care facility can pet the animals or enjoy a demonstration of their special training, such as obedience and agility. Another deeper level is the *Animal Assisted Therapies*, which are employed by health and/or human services professionals as part of their practice or specialty. These activities are used to facilitate specific therapeutic objectives for each patient, and progress is closely monitored by the health professional. More information regarding the Delta Society can be found at www.deltasociety.org

Abbey (Sandfox's Midnight Dancer, CD, CGC, TDI) is also an obedience dog and we are currently training for Open obedience, which is the second level of AKC obedience competition. Our new puppy Sofie (Edenfaire April Angel, CGC) is training

for Novice, which is the first level. You don't have to train for formal obedience to be a therapy dog, but the training you receive for the CGC and therapy dog certification is similar.

OUR VISITS TO THE NURSING HOME

We started our therapy work by joining nursing home visits with a group of other therapy dogs: a German shepherd, a standard poodle, and an English setter. Needless to say, Abbey was the smallest dog in the group and was very popular. She was the only dog that residents could hold in their lap and cuddle. Abbey has learned to stay outside the room and wait her turn to visit. We use this time to practice on our obedience commands, such as heel, sit/down, stay, and attention. When I say "OK," she knows it is time for her to visit with the next person. She sometimes gets up on her hind legs so the resident can pet

her head, or she waits until I lift her up onto the bed or into a lap. She has learned the "Say Hello" command and will walk up and nuzzle the person, waiting to be petted. She also gives "corgi kisses" upon command and only if the patient wants them. The favorite is "Shake a Paw," when Abbey holds up her paw for a shake. Now we are learning some new entertaining tricks.

One day we were visiting a lady who had suffered a stroke. As I held Abbey up on her lap, she stroked Abbey and mumbled a few words. The Activities Director who was accompanying our visit whispered to me, "Very good, that is good." Since Abbey was fairly new to therapy work at the time, I thought she was talking to Abbey and praising her for being so quiet. When we left the room, she said to me, "That was wonderful. I have not seen that much response from the patient before." It is times like this that make the therapy work even more rewarding.

We also regularly visit with a lady who used to have a corgi. She looks forward to our visits each month. The first time we met her was in the Activity Room. As soon as we entered the doorway, she had trouble communicating but I could see that reminiscent smile on her face. I recognized that far-away look and knew that I had brought her a special visitor. Her friend explained to us that she knew that the lady used to have a corgi.

On a recent visit, we had a very special corgi moment. We had just started our rounds, and as we came down the hall there was a gentleman in a wheelchair in the middle of the aisle. He was looking right past the English setter, the German shepherd and the standard poodle, all Therapy Dogs. I was the farthest away from him, but I could hear him saying something over and over again. As I got closer to him, I could hear him saying, "Welsh corgi, Welsh corgi." He was focused on Abbey and Sofie and didn't even look at the other dogs who were standing right next to his wheelchair. As I approached him that is all he said, "Welsh corgi." I held each of the corgis up for him, and, as he stroked their soft fur, he repeated it over and over again: "Welsh corgi." I could tell that even though that is all he could say to us, he had a love for the breed and must have had a special corgi in his life at sometime. It is times like this that make therapy work so special.

THERAPY DOG IN TRAINING

Our puppy Sofie is a very special "fluffy" corgi. She loves to snuggle and cuddle, and I am positive she will make a great therapy dog. I have already taken her on a couple of visits, and at 8 months of age she already seems to know that these people need special attention and love. She will lay quietly in their laps and let them pet her. We are on the road to therapy dog certification with Sofie, and she will then be making regular calls with us also.

THERAPY BEGINS AT HOME

Corgi owners were among those doing therapy work at Ground Zero after 9/11. My personal therapy began at home that day. I was supposed to go to work at a part-time job that morning. As I watched the TV in horror, I called in and told them I would be in later. When I finally went in to work, I took Abbey with me. I share a small office with only one other woman. She met me outside the office, and while we hugged, cried and consoled each other, she said to me, "I am **so** glad you brought Abbey today, we need her." The rest of the employees proceeded to love and pet Abbey, and she took it all in with her usual loving self, not realizing the comfort she was bringing to everyone.

In the days following the tragedy, the corgis made me laugh and remember what I have to be thankful about. They were so comforting, and demonstrated to me that life had to go on even in the face of terror.

ON THE ROAD

I take the corgis with me everywhere. Last October, my 85 year-old mother had heart surgery, and we made the trip from North Carolina to Indiana. Now, you should understand that my mother is **not** that fond of dogs. However, when she met the corgis, especially Abbey, who is older and more trained than the puppy, she fell in love with them. When she came home from the hospital, I stayed around for a few days to help out. One day I needed to leave to run an errand for her, and she wanted me to leave Abbey with her. Well, this was unheard of! Her answer when I questioned her about it was, "Well, Abbey is a therapy dog isn't she, and I need therapy." Right!

I also took Abbey to a convalescent home nearby, where my step-father was recovering from surgery. I went into the office of the Director and showed him our credentials first, to make sure that we would be welcome. As I walked down the hall with her to my step-father's room, I was stopped every step of the way by people with walkers, in wheelchairs, and with nurses, all who wanted to visit with Abbey. It took me a long time to get to his room, because Abbey was in her glory "saying hello" to everyone on the way. She wiggled and visited all the way down the hallway. I could tell by the residents' responses that they did not have therapy dogs at this facility. When we return to Indiana for a visit, I plan to take Abbey back to see them, even though my step-father is at home now.

SCHOOL VISITS

The AKC has a great educational package that is available for schools. It contains coloring book pages that explain what to do when you meet a stray dog, and so on. I have visited two schools with Abbey and used this information to teach several rules that children should understand when meeting a dog, whether it is with its owner or alone. I take Abbey's brush along and let the children take turns grooming her. I talk with them about the responsibility of owning a pet, and Abbey shows off her

obedience "tricks" to them and shakes their "paws."

PLANS FOR THE FUTURE

There is a program in some schools called R.E.A.D, *Reading Education Assistance Dogs*, which assists children with reading difficulties. The goal of the R.E.A.D. program is to demonstrate how registered therapy dogs and their handlers can be instrumental in improving the literacy skills of children in an effective, unique and, most importantly, fun manner. Literacy specialists acknowledge that children who are below their peers in reading skills are often intimidated by reading aloud in a group, often have lower self-esteem, and view reading as a chore. For more information on this program go to www.therapyanimals.org and click on R.E.A.D.

I have been asked by another person locally to help get this program started in our area. Abbey and Sofie would be great for this, since they already have had practice. They love to lie on the bed when my granddaughter visits and we read *Harry Potter* together. They wanted to go with us to see the movie but I had to draw the line there. I think they just wanted the popcorn!

REWARDING EXPERIENCE

Therapy work is very rewarding, and I highly recommend it. It is not to be entered into lightly, and you should definitely go through the certification processes I have mentioned above. Not only will you have a better trained dog to facilitate your visits, but the certifying organizations also provide insurance should any aspect of your visit go wrong. Once you have a certified dog, you will probably meet other people that do therapy work. There may even be a therapy club near you.

I would recommend that you start out small and only plan one visit per month. Once you make the initial contact with a facility, you will want to take your credentials and a plan to show what you intend to accomplish, and you should work with the facility to establish a visiting schedule agreeable to both parties. They can then post your visit on their monthly calendar, which will allow them to be prepared for you and to notify the residents of your visit ahead of time.

Remember, not everyone loves dogs as we do, and some people just want to be left alone. We must respect their wishes. But I am sure there will be plenty of people that **do** want to visit, and it will be a rewarding experience for them, you, and your dog that you will all look forward to each month. Many assisted living nursing home residents used to have dogs and have treasured pictures of them on the walls in their rooms. When you leave after visiting, the smiles on the residents' faces stay with you, and you can hear their "Thank you for coming and bringing the dogs" all the way home.

Linda Kerr's Abbey makes a nursing home visit

A NOBLE PROFESSION: CORGIS AS SERVICE DOGS

by Florence Scarinci

Through her interviews with five people who use corgis to aid them in everyday life, Florence Scarinci shows us how the corgi's natural intelligence and personality allow many of them to work as eyes, ears, alerters, special friends, and many others means of service to humans.

The corgi was bred for work. There is no denying that their high intelligence and willingness to work as a team made them excellent herding dogs. Now that the need for their herding instincts has diminished, their abilities have been put to use in assisting humans in other ways as service dogs.

I interviewed five people who use corgis or corgi mixes to give them a greater measure of independence and to assist in life skills. Their stories will amaze you. Pat Griesmeyer is paired with hearing dog Pedro, a six year old Pembroke Welsh corgi. Sidney Wiseberg calls hearing dog Tommy, a six year old, tricolor Pembroke, his best buddy. Both Pedro and Tommy were specifically bred and professionally trained by Canine Companions for Independence to be hearing dogs and were acquired free of charge from that organization. Robin Walloch's self-trained red brindle Cardigan Welsh corgi, Brinn Brin, is 13 years old and still working hard. Eleanor Britton purchased Meg from a Pembroke breeder to be "an intuitive companion for a special child." Ida Duplechin rescued corgi mix Lily four years ago and discovered her talents for service dog work quite by accident.

These corgis' "jobs" are varied, as are the jobs of their owners. Pat Griesmeyer has an important position as a fashion consultant. When Pat is not wearing her hearing aids, she relies on Pedro, a handsome tricolor

Pat Griesmeyer's hearing dog, Pedro

PWC to alert her to important sounds. She removes her hearing aids when she goes to

bed and needs Pedro to tell her to get up in the morning so that she is not late for work. Before Pedro's arrival, Pat never slept through the night. Pat says, "I had never been able to use an alarm clock until Pedro came. Now as soon as the 'Big Ben' goes off, he starts to paw me ever so gently. If I don't respond fast enough, the alert gets more intense until he is jumping on me full force. Then, when he is satisfied that I am getting up, he lays down next to me and proceeds to give me my morning kisses. This is how I wake up every day. How lucky can you get?"

Corgis are independent thinkers. Once taught a few sounds to which they must alert, hearing dogs often expand their repertoire to sounds that only their person needs to know about. For instance, Pat tells us that Pedro has learned that there are times when Pat needs help with the laundry. "As every woman knows, sometimes the washing machine becomes unbalanced. One day I was doing the wash and the unbalanced machine had 'walked' and was shooting water all over the floor. Using an alert different from his jumping and poking alert, he led me to the offending machine. Now as soon as he hears that bumping sound, he becomes frantic and uses that same alert until I understand that I must check the machine."

Now retired, Sid Wiseberg previously owned a service business in New York City. He worked from his home and had one phone for personal calls and one for business calls. Sid gradually began to lose his hearing and also began to realize that his 38% hearing loss was making it difficult, if not impossible, to hear his business phone ringing. "It was vital that I not miss these calls. I could lose a valued customer and a good part of my income," Sid lamented. The people who serviced Sid's hearing aids told him about the Canine Companions for Independence hearing dog training program. After a two and one half year wait, Sid was paired with Tommy, who would alert Sid to his business phone ringing but would not alert to the ringing of the house phone, since most of those calls were directed to Sid's wife. Tommy alerts to the doorbell ringing, the microwave timer going off, and other sounds that Tommy thinks Sid should know about by jumping on Sid's knee. Sid then asks Tommy, "What?" and Tommy runs to the source of the sound and lies down in front of it. Now that Sid is retired, Tommy has taken on two additional

Sid Wiseberg and Tommy, his hearing dog

"retirement jobs." One is keeping Sid healthy by making him take long walks every day. The other job is serving as a therapy dog. He and Sid visit New York Presbyterian Hospital's pediatric cancer and neurological wards and a school for autistic children. Tommy's loving, outgoing personality brighten the day for these children.

Brinn Brin performs many tasks for Robin Walloch, who has a variety of challenges including juvenile rheumatoid arthritis, reflex sympathetic dystrophy, and heart problems. He attended college with Robin, carried her books and picked up dropped items such as pencils and notebooks from the floor. If a degree could be awarded to a dog, Brinn would certainly be a candidate

since he had perfect attendance and impeccable behavior in college. Robin tells us, "I went to take a final exam one day and the professor noticed Brinn and told me he could not come in. I informed him that the dog had attended every class and had slept under the seat during the lectures. Everyone in the class verified this. The professor had never noticed him." Perhaps Brinn's most important function is as a cardiac alert dog. Robin says that he behaves in a certain way when her heart is about to "act up." At 13+, Brinn is helping to train a young dog to be his successor. When his working days are over, Brinn Brin will continue to be Robin's best friend.

Robin Walloch's service dog Brinn Brin

Just two years old, and living with the Brittons only 17 months, red-headed tricolor Meg, who chose Eleanor and her son Kenneth, is helping Kenneth who has autism, learn appropriate social skills. Nine-year-old Kenneth is tall and strong, but with Meg he is learning to be gentle and kind. Eleanor says that Meg is a patient teacher and understands that Kenneth is trying to learn these skills. Meg is well rewarded for her job as teacher. She enjoys the chew strips that Kenneth gives her every day as a "peace offering."

Ida Duplechin, a self described "take charge" businesswoman, gradually lost her vision and hearing and with that, her job, her health insurance, her marriage, and her identity. Ida adopted corgi mix Lily from rescuer Dixie Davis, because Lily was a "happy puppy" at a time when Ida desperately needed some happiness in her life. She was not looking for a service dog, just a dog to fill the emptiness she was experiencing after the loss of her heart dog, Shorty, who had recently died. What she got was her lifeline.

Corgi puppy Meg chooses her special boy, Kenneth Britton

"Adjusting to blindness and my hearing loss has been gut-wrenching," said Ida. "Lily was there for me. She reminded me to get up out of bed. She reminded me that she was hungry and thirsty. She reminded me when she needed to go outside. She pulled me out of myself everyday. I could still care for my animals; I began to care for myself again. As I learned to walk with my cane, frustration set in. My hearing loss disqualified me from any of the dog guide school considerations. I had my cane to feel my way through the world. It wasn't enough. I couldn't find my way home from the bus stop. One day, Lily and I were taking a walk. I had my cane and I ended up following her as she wound her way around garbage cans, trash and abandoned cars. We made it to the bus stop. I was shocked. I began to teach Lily the routes to various locations. She showed complete concentration on her job. Once she traveled to a site, there was no problem in returning home or re-visiting the site."

Ida Dupelchin's service dog Lily

Ida goes on, "Lily has continued to develop her abilities to care for me. She reminds me when it is time for my medicine and warns me of visitors if I don't hear the doorbell. She also sleeps with me and has awakened me from apnea episodes. She has another sense of determining if someone has evil in his or her heart. Two sharp barks warn me of something or someone she perceives as a threat. I have never been afraid when Lily I with me. I know she is watching out for me. We are a great team. She has kept the world open to me. In my darkest moments, she has been there to love me. In my most professional moments, she has been there as my silent partner."

People who have corgis as service dogs agree that their personalities are ideal for working with them. Pat says that they are "very attuned." They are always watching your body language to see what you are doing." They seem to reason; "You can actually watch them figuring out a situation, sizing it up and deciding what to do about it." Robin feels that "they have great empathy and form a real bond." Eleanor calls them "intuitive." Ida concurs, when she says that Lily can read her mind. Sid adds that corgis can be gentle, eager to please, and excellent with children. Ida says that Lily has a good work ethic, and Pat agrees, adding that they also have a great sense of fun and know when to play.

Pat, Sid, Robin, Eleanor, and Ida all agree that their dogs have changed their lives for the better. Perhaps Ida summed up all their feelings when she said, "I cannot imagine what life would have been without Lily." To which Pat replies, "Pedro is my sense of peace."

INTERLUDE

CRUMPET

They should give herding certificates for particular, specific, demonstrated skills—like herding cats. My PWC Crumpet would have qualified. (Actually, she did qualify the "real" way, too, at a herding trial later on. By then, I wasn't surprised.)

One Saturday, we were busy cleaning the house. At the time, we had three indoor cats, who all basically hated each other. After a while that day, it slowly dawned on me that I hadn't seen any cats for a long time. That was odd. Usually on cleaning day, we'd have cats darting from room to room to avoid both the cleaning implements and each other, but there was no sign of them. Hmmm.

Puzzled, I went on a room-by-room search, curious where they could be. I was just about to panic, thinking that someone might have left an outside door open, when in passing the bathroom and giving it a quick glance, I did a double-take, then burst into side-splitting laughter. There, on the clothes hamper, sitting elegantly side by side, were all three cats—with a corgi below, giving them "the eye."

It seems that Crumpet had silently gathered and herded them all to their "perch" and was firmly **keeping** them there. Now, up to that point these cats would not tolerate even being in the same room together without fur flying. I'd have said it would have been impossible for the three of them to sit side by side without one or more meeting a sorrowful end. I am quite certain that this was not their idea.

I'll never know how Crumpet did it, but from that moment on, I gained a new respect for the corgi herding instincts. ~*Nancy Boyd*

PENNI

Penni was bred by Canine Companions for Independence to be a hearing dog, and I was her puppy-raiser. She was released from advanced training because she had excessive energy and was easily distractible, so I adopted her. We channeled that energy and took up agility. Today she is competing on the open level in AKC and the elite level in NADAC.

But what is most gratifying is her work as a therapy dog. When I was puppy-raising her, she was certified as a therapy dog and began visiting a nursing home as part of her socialization. She was a great favorite at the home, because she is extremely affectionate, small enough to sit on laps, and loves petting, brushing, and, of course, treats. After I adopted her, she went right back to being a therapy dog, adding another nursing home and a school for deaf children to her visits. I could write pages on her successes as a therapy dog. There are people who never smile until she comes to sit on their lap. There are stroke victims whose therapy is to pet her. There was one woman, an Alzheimer's patient, who rarely talked but told me her dog was also named Penni.

She loves to visit the children at the special education class in the school for the deaf. These children have learning and emotional disabilities in addition to their deafness. Some are on medication. Some need to learn proper social interaction. We do different activities each time we visit. One time I brought some agility equipment. The students had to design and set up a proper course and run Penni through it. They practiced reading and following directions, measuring distances, taking turns, encouraging each other, and having patience with themselves and Penni when she didn't perform correctly.

Another time one young man who was on Ritalin had just had an emotional outburst and had put himself in a voluntary "time out" in another room. The teacher thought a visit from Penni would be a stress reliever. So we went to the room. There was the student in fetal position on the floor in a darkened room (this was a position he chose; no one had imposed it on him). Penni is very empathetic. She senses and responds to people's emotions. She snuggled next to the boy in the curve of his body and licked his face. He sat up and smiled and his anger dissipated.

Penni has introduced these kids to the wonderful world of dogs. She had a tooth pulled recently so they learned about brushing dogs' teeth and hygiene in general. They have bathed her and brushed her. We are going to the Westminster Kennel Club show in February. To raise money for the event, the students baked and sold dog biscuits, another lesson in following directions and measuring and figuring out expenses and profits and in working for what you want. In planning the trip we have located a deaf woman who is a breeder of corgis and she is coming to the school to talk to the students about careers with dogs.

All of these wonderful things—bringing happiness, relief from tedium and stress, teaching life skills—took place because of Penni. Because of her, I am even studying American Sign Language. I had hoped when I was puppy raising her for CCI that she would change one life. Even though she is, as they say, COC, "change of career" she touches many lives. *~Florence Scarinci*

KEN'S CORGI ACRES

It all started about five years ago, when I (Steve) thought that Ken needed a pal. So we went to the local shelter, and, lo and behold, there was a pup there that totally attached herself to Ken. She had weird legs and the cutest smile, and all she wanted to do was give kisses. We paid for her, but in two days they called and she had distemper. We found a vet and saved her from death, since they killed 75 pups at the shelter that week. She became Dutchess, the queen of the acres.

Next was Boyer, who was cast off by a lady who "didn't have time for him" and returned him to his breeder. We got him from the breeder, as she didn't have room for him and he was getting too old. He became the major couch potato at the acres,

Then came Duke, the Cardi. After they'd had him a year, he was taken to the vet by his first owners, who wanted to put him down for growling. Well, we now know he does the Cardi growl when he is happy! A foster person said he bit them (which we found out later he didn't), so with much ado, he came here to become Duke Doo, the King of the pack.

Dusty and Bubba are a father and son who we got from a lady who thought she could raise corgis but found out that males fight when a female is in season. She called me and said, "Either take them or they will be put down." We got them.

Finally, Miss Lady Blue was found wandering the streets of an Ohio city and was almost put down until someone realized what she was. With help from her foster mom and dad, she became the wonderful Miss Lady Blue.

We have also had a few fosters here (Missy, Dylan, Lady Sadie, and Chance); all but Chance have gone to happy corgi homes. That is the condensed version of the story of an independent rescue house for corgis of both breeds and also for corgi mixes. I hope that someone may read this and be inspired that, just because you may not be rich (we are by no means wealthy), that doesn't mean you can't either foster, give a home to, or at least help in the rescue of a pup in need. If it had not been for us, I can truly say that at least four of the pups that live here, and at least three of the ones we helped, would have been put down for reasons that are not the best in the world. *~Steve Siemens*

MAGGIE MAY

Maggie May is our first corgi, and hopefully not our last. She adopted us when she was three months old, and just now turned 10 months. Whenever I call to my husband in the other room to let me know that a meal is ready, Maggie runs to me and lets out a few choice barks, bouncing all the way. She then takes off like a shot to whatever room my husband is in, and barks and barks until he gets moving to the kitchen. She herds him all the way. We've never seen anything like her antics, and she does nothing short of keeping us totally entertained. *~Lynne Brady*

CORGI FUN, MYTH, AND MAGIC

CORGI GAMES AND PICNIC FUN

by Kat Connor-Litchman

Corgis are not party poopers! Kat Connor-Litchman offers tips for planning a gathering for corgis and their people, including a great list of fun races and other games you can organize with a group of corgis.

Corgi gatherings can be a great way to meet new people and their dogs. Some of the regional gatherings have been quite successful and grown throughout the years. There are many ways to ensure that your corgi picnic is a success—here are just a few.

Often people set up e-mail lists or Web sites to help in planning the gathering. Make sure the rules are known to all up front. The dogs that attend should be up to date on all vaccinations. Will dogs other than corgis be allowed to attend? Think about setting a minimum age for dogs attending. Very young pups may not be suited to a rambunctious gathering. The pups may not have had all their shots, may get easily tired, and may pick up something that is harmful to them. Yes, they need socialization, but they need to do it safely.

Think about having a sign in sheet for the guests' names, addresses, and e-mail addresses, as well as their dogs' names. This can come in handy when planning for the next year's gathering.

It is nice if you have someone to host the picnic who has a fenced-in area for the dogs. If not, see if you can borrow snow fencing from a local contractor to set up as a temporary barrier in case a dog strays from its owner. Tables and seating should be available. If not already at the site, remind people to bring their own. If there are neighbors nearby, clear it with them first as corgis and kids, when excited, can make a lot of noise! Parking should be plentiful and nearby.

Crates or X-pens can be a good way for a tired or wound-up dogs to get a rest without being bothered by any of the other picnicers. Encourage people to bring one for their dogs. This will enable them to continue to enjoy the picnic, while their dog takes a rest. Keep a watch, and be prepared to separate dogs if needed. Have small trash bags and pooper-scoopers handy to pick up after the dogs. Large trash bags will be needed to pick up the regular trash items. Water bowls, with plenty of water for refills, is also a necessity.

If you think you may have people traveling a distance to attend the party, find out what local accommodations are available that will accept a corgi-sized dog. Gather together a list of local attractions and eating establishments to hand out to long distance travelers if needed.

Have people bring portable sunshades to set up to provide shade for food, people, and dogs.   Cameras should be handy to record the events of the day.

If the meal is to be potluck, have everyone RSVP with his or her food dish so you can keep an eye on what is being signed up for and perhaps direct others who ask towards items that are needed. Ask everyone to bring a desert to share. If it is a smaller gathering, with someone manning the grill, ask for donations at the door to defray the costs of the hot dogs and burgers. If it is to be a bring your own food and drink picnic, make that clear from the start.

If the gathering will be large enough, think about having a silent auction to benefit CorgiAid. Have everyone bring an item or two to donate for the auction. You can leave the auction items on display throughout the day and have people bid for them as the picnic goes on. You can also think about contacting dog food companies and local pet store retailers about donating items.

If you can, have one person coordinate each aspect of the picnic—site selection, games, auction, food, prizes—but have all of them report to one person. In this way, no one person will responsible for all aspects of the picnic, and if an emergency occurs, that person's duties can be quickly picked up.

Prizes can be as simple as a little treat after the contest for the dog, little ribbons that can be purchased at local craft or award stores, or small dog toys. You can let your imagination run wild here. Remember though, that too much food might not be good for many of the dogs. Prizes can also be chits that may be used towards a raffle at the end of the day. Judges may be as generous as they like!

CONTESTS FOR "THE BEST"

These contests can be run in several ways. The first is simply to have the dogs enter and award a small prize or ribbon to the winner of the contest. The second is to charge a small entry fee of twenty-five or fifty cents to each entrant. The fee money goes to a charity of choice, such as Corgi-Aid. Some contest favorites are:

- Best Trick
- Most Tricks
- Longest Tail
- Shortest Tail
- Largest Ears
- Smallest Ears
- Biggest Smile
- Loudest Bark
- Quietest Bark
- Fastest Male
- Fastest Female
- Slowest Male
- Slowest Female
- Best Costume
- The Most Fluff
- The Least Fluff
- The Longest
- The Shortest
- The Lowest to the Ground
- The Highest
- Oldest Corgi
- Youngest Corgi
- The Most Corgis From One Family
- The Corgi that Traveled the Farthest to Attend
- The Corgi with the Closest Birthday to the date of the picnic
- The Corgi with the Farthest Birthday to the date of the picnic
- The Heaviest Corgi
- The Lightest Corgi
- Best Pants on a dog
- Best Skirts on a bitch
- Reddest Dog
- Blackest Dog
- Whitest Dog
- Best Kisser

RELAY GAMES

There are literally hundreds of variations to the relay theme. Here are a few to get you started.

Hedgie Relay

In this spirited game, Hedgies are attached to wooden dowels with a stout cord. Two teams line up at a start line. With your Hedgie dangling in front of your corgi's nose, you lead your dog to a finish line, touch the line, and then make your way back to the start. You can add a variation on this theme by having the contestants eat something, both dog and handler, before proceeding back to the start line to tag the next team in your line. The team with all the dogs back at the finish line first wins the relay race.

Owner/Dog Hot Dog Relay Race

For this race, use a length of rope to mark the starting line and the finish line about 30 or 50 feet apart. Have the teams of owner and dog line up for the race. Make sure there are a few feet separating the teams. You may have to run this race in several heats. On the count of three, those at the line toss out the hot dogs over the finish line, and then go running after it with their dog on lead. The object is to retrieve the hot dog, and run back to the start line with as much of the hot dog intact as possible. The corgis are supposed to be the ones carrying the hot dog back over the finish line. Once back at the start, after the race, the owner has to grab the hot dog, saliva and all, and hold on to it until all the heats are done. Then, if further heats are needed, the same hot dog is used in run off heats and the one with the most hot dog left over, wins. You have to be careful to toss the hotdogs far away from each other so fights don't erupt over dogs claiming other's hot dogs as their own.

Running Relay Race

Have the dogs and owners divide up into two teams for this relay race. You will need two long handled spoons or ladles. You will fill the ladles with water. Have a small can or bucket at the finish line. The object is to have the owner hold the leash in the same hand as the ladle, fill it with water, keep the ladle in the leash hand, and run to the other end and fill the bucket with the water. The team then races back to the start to pass the ladle off to the next member of the team. The winning team is the one to first fill the bucket with the water. The trick is in keeping the water in the ladle! You can substitute dried beans for water if you like.

A variation on this race is putting a potato in the spoon at the start line, having the owner/dog team run to a flag or cone, and then back to the start line without dropping the potato. The fastest time wins. If the potato is dropped, it must be scooped before the team can continue with the race.

The Gobble and Go Relay Race

This is a fun race and the dogs love it as they get to eat their prize as they go! Have participants line up in two or three teams, depending on the number of corgis. Cut up hot dogs into one-inch pieces. Get two or three people to replace the hot dog pieces on paper plates after each dog has had his turn. Have them stand directly opposite the dogs, about 30 feet away. You will need to have one hot dog replacer to each team of owner/corgis. The dogs are on leashes. On the go, the teams race to the paper plates. The dog must chew and swallow the hot dog pieces before being allowed to race back to the team and tag the next set of racers. The entire team must then sit so the judges can determine the winning team!

Kibble Relay Race

For this game, make as many relay teams as you want, with at least four corgi/owner pairs per team. Line up at the start. The teams are each given a spoon with kibble on it. The human part of the team holds the spoon while walking to an assigned end-point (cone, chair, rock), circling around and heading back to pass of the spoon to the next team in their line. If a piece of kibble should fall from the spoon, the handler has to pick it up and put it back on the spoon. If the dog should eat the fallen kibble, then another member of the team has to replace it before the team can proceed. Whichever team gets through all the pairs in their team first, wins.

Watermelon Relay

This race can be both fun and refreshing for corgi and owner alike! Set up two teams of corgi/owners in lines. Have two large bowls with watermelon slices that you and your corgi will run to. Both you and your corgi will have to eat a slice of watermelon before you can go back and tag the next member of your team.

Recall Race

In this race a holder holds the dog, a timer watches, and the owner calls the dog to him from a prescribed distance. It is helpful if the timer has someone to scribe the results for him. The fastest recall wins.

The Leave-It Recall

This is a fun race, and often comes out with a dark horse winner! Have the dogs lined up in a row, separated from their owners by about 25 feet. Each dog should be directly across from its owner. Have a plate with a hot dog morsel on it placed midway between each dog and owner. The object is to have the dogs run to their owners when called, ignoring the hot dog along the way. The first dog to its owner is the winner. It can be amusing to see who is able to pass up the tasty treat!

MUSICAL CHAIRS/SITS

There are a few variations on this children's game, which you can tailor to the dogs that are attending the picnic. You need a tape player and some fun music. Doggy-themed music, like "Bad Bad Leroy Brown," "How Much Is That Doggy in the Window," and "Who Let The Dogs Out," works well with this.

For the first version, you will need circles of cardboard or posterboard, cut about two to three feet wide. Make one for every dog team that will be in the contest. You could also use hula hoops, as they are more durable. If you have a large group, you might want to do this in several heats, with the top one or two winners from each heat in the final competition. One person will run the tape player and another will remove a circle after each round of play. The dogs should be on lead when walking around the circles while the music plays. When the music stops the dog must claim a circle and go into a sit. The owner does not have to be on the circle. It is nice to give the dogs that did not get a circle a bone or small treat on their way out of the game. The winner is the last pair left standing on a circle. If two dogs claim a spot at the same time, the dog to sit first gets the spot.

In the second variation of this game, chairs are used for the owners. When the music stops, the dog must sit before the owner can pick a chair. If the dog gets up, the owner has to give up the chair while trying to get the dog to sit again.

The third variation is simply musical chairs played with chairs for the humans. The dogs are simply an accessory as the humans try to win the chairs. The dogs are on lead for this one as well.

THE 7-LEGGED RACE

For this race you use two humans and one corgi for each team. Tie together the inside legs of the humans and have the corgi on a lead. Mark a start and finish line with some rope. On the go, each team tries to get from the start to the finish in the fastest time. It can get fun as the dogs start to run around the humans, further tying them up!

HOT DOG FETCH

For this game, the dogs are off leash, sitting next to their owners widely spaced from one another. The owner tosses out a hot dog and tells the dog to "fetch." The winner is the dog that brings the whole hot dog back first. This can be funny with corgis, who have their own idea of what to do with the hot dogs!

LAZY SUSAN DOGS

This is a fun game for a smaller crowd. The corgi that eats the most in a timed segment wins both the cookies and a small prize. You will need a sturdy Lazy Susan that spins well, some small dog bones or treats, and peanut butter. Raise the Lazy Susan a few inches off the ground with a couple of bricks, or something sturdy. This will save your back! Put a small bit of peanut butter on the bottom of each biscuit and affix it to the Lazy Susan, like the numbers of a clock. Use the same number of biscuits for each dog, about six or eight. Sit in front of the Lazy Susan and slowly spin it. Have someone time the dogs for whatever time is agreed upon, anywhere from ten to thirty seconds. If a dog takes a biscuit off and drops it, then goes for another, then count it as eaten. The goal is to get the biscuits off the Lazy Susan.

BOBBING FOR HOT DOGS

This is just a fun game for the dogs, and a way for some of them to cool down on a hot day. Partially fill a small children's wading pool with water. Cut hot dogs in thirds and float them in the water. Then give each dog an allotted amount of time to bob for the dogs. This game can be turned into a contest by filling a dishpan with water, and placing smaller slices of hot dog on the bottom. Give each corgi 30 seconds to gobble up as much as they can.

OBSTACLE COURSE

You can set up a fun obstacle course for dogs to try out at their own speed, on their own time. Things you might want to try using include children's play tunnels and poles set in the ground to weave through. Set up very low hurdles for the dogs to jump over. Try walking the dogs over bubble wrap, or oddly textured surfaces. Make a bone box by filling a box with shredded paper. Put a bone in the bottom of the box. The dog then has to sniff out his treat. You can have the dogs go through tires, or hula-hoops. Set up a walk board that is only a couple of inches off the ground so as to avoid injury. Make it at least 10 inches wide. Have the dogs walk over the board. Large cardboard tubes to make tunnels with can be found at building supply stores. If someone in your group does agility with their dogs, try asking them to do some informal try out sessions for dogs that may never have tried agility before. You can have the obstacle course set up just to try for fun, or turn it into an event by timing the dogs as they go through.

CORGI LIMBO

Set up a corgi limbo by using a long pole held in place on top of a stack of bricks. Remove a brick from each side as the dogs go through to make the limbo stick lower. You can also use jump poles from agility to set the limbo stick, or a couple of volunteers sitting in a chair. This can get hard on the back!

SCAVENGER HUNT

To play this scavenger hunt, you have to first mark off an area that will be off limits to the dogs prior to the game being played. Gather together a variety of little dog treats and larger biscuits. You can add toys too, if your budget allows. Get a volunteer to hide all the goodies. For the hunt itself, the dogs must be on lead. The owners are responsible for keeping peace between the dogs. It might be suggested that very food aggressive dogs sit this one out. Whatever is found by the dogs, they keep! It might be a nice idea to set up a smaller section for seniors or puppies that might not be able to keep up with the crowd. You can vary this game by hiding doggy toys with bits of smelly sausage like kielbasa to scent the items. Another version of this is to do a real scavenger hunt, perhaps while lunch is being prepared. Give the participants a list of things to find around the area. You can pre-hide items, or use local flora and fauna. One Corgi-L list member said she does this and always includes a one-pound rock to be found. She said it is amazing how far off the mark most people are at judging what a pound is!

TOSS AND CATCH

Use small slices of hot dog or other soft food. The owner stands opposite the dog, with someone holding the dog's leash for safety. The owner then tosses the dog a treat and if the dog is successful catching it in his mouth, the owner moves back a step. The winner is the person who is able to move the furthest back from their dog. You can also vary this by awarding prizes for three in a row, and so on.

QUICKEST VEGETABLE EATER

Select the vegetable to be eaten, usually a carrot. Have them all about the same size. The pre-peeled, little ones in the bag are

ideal for this game. Line the dogs up, and on the go have the owners hand the carrot to their dog. The first dog finished wins!

TALENT SHOW

This can be a fun event to watch. Each owner/corgi team performs their favorite trick, or series of tricks. The applause can signal the winner, or a blind count of hands can be done by having everyone close their eyes, then vote by a show of hands. This way no one's feelings are hurt!

CROSS-DRESSING CORGIS

This is a dress up game for both the corgis and the humans. The object is to be the fastest to get themselves and their corgis dressed and back across the finish line. You will need a large amount of various clothing items. Try getting donations from people cleaning out their closets or visit second hand clothing stores or yard sales for XL and larger clothing sizes. The larger sizes make it easier to get the clothing on and off, especially on a hot day. The clothes have to go over whatever clothing you are already wearing. Get hats, shoes, boots, bras, girdles, pants, skirts, shirts, and so on. You then line up the clothes in piles. Have a pile of hats, a pile of top clothes, a pile of bottom clothes, and so on. Try to get at least six piles of clothes for the contestants. Next you need 2 piles of toddler size 4-5T tee shirts and bandanas. You can have each participant bring a set of clothing. Just specify what each should bring so it will be even. Once you have the clothing, it can be used again year after year.

Each contestant and his or her corgi have to run past the piles of clothing and grab one item from each pile. They also have to grab a shirt and bandana for their corgi. They then run to an area marked off for dressing. This should be a good bit away from the clothing piles. The contestants then put on each article of clothing and then dress their dogs. The clothes can be put on anyway they like. Bras and buttons and zippers do not have to be fastened. The bras and girdles often end up on the outside of the shirts. After the clothing is on, run for the finish line! The first contestant across the finish line with all clothing in place on themselves and their corgi is the winner. This game is a must for the cameras!

Kat Connor-Litchman with Wendy and Rylie

CREATIVE CORGIS: BOOKS, MOVIES, AND VIDEOS

by Raelene Gorlinsky

Raelene Gorlinsky has compiled a great reference list of published media involving corgis—fact or fiction.

Although corgis are not the most common pets included in modern stories, there are quite a few books out there with corgi characters, ranging from children's picture books, to story books for older children, to adult mysteries and fantasies. There are also all the non-fiction books about raising and training your corgi. To be complete, we've also included a list of movies and videos.

The books and videos that are currently in print can be ordered through most bookstores or at an online bookstore such as Amazon.com (www.amazon.com) or Barnes & Noble (www.bn.com). Many of the books listed are out of print (marked OOP). They can be difficult to find and often command collectible prices as much as $100. They occasionally appear at online auction sites such as eBay (www.ebay.com) or Amazon Auctions (auctions.amazon.com/). They may also be available from used book dealers. Several online sites provide searches through large groups of online used book dealers. Try ABE Books (www.abe.com/) or AddALL Used and Out of Print Book Search (www.add-all.com/used/).

CHILDREN'S BOOKS

Ace the Very Important Pig by Dick King-Smith, illustrated by Lynette Hemmant. 1990; Alfred A. Knopf, Inc.; paperback. The story of the great-grandson of the famous herding pig Babe. Megan is the snobby corgi pet of the farmer.

*Beanie the Corgi Goes to Washington,*1998; paperback. Coloring book from the Parks and History Association. Beanie the tour dog shows children the famous monuments and buildings in Washington, DC. 16 pages. Available at 1-800-990-PARK or www.parksandhistory.org.

Corgiville Fair by Tasha Tudor. 1971; Little, Brown and Company; paperback or hardcover. Corgiville is a village inhabited by corgis, cats, rabbits, and boggarts. The corgis are clever and brave, and Tasha Tudor's illustrations are sweet and entertaining.

A Dog for Richard by Essex Hope, illustrated by Faith Jacques; 1960 (OOP); University of London Press Ltd.; paperback. This is about Bob, a Pembroke Welsh corgi pup given to Richard for his birthday. When Richard grows up, he wants to have no kids and 16 dogs, who will all be allowed to sleep on the bed. Bob runs away in terror during a fireworks display and the story follows his adventures to a happy ending.

Dogzilla by Dav Pilkey.1993; Harcourt Brace & Co.; hardcover. The book is labeled "EG: This book has been rated Extremely Goofy. Some material may be too goofy for grown-ups." The irresistible scent of the smoke from the grills at the Mousopolis Annual Barbecue Cook-Off awakens the dreaded Dogzilla (a Cardigan Welsh corgi) from her sleep inside the extinct volcano. The mouse army is unable to drive off the monstrous mutt, but the Big Cheese saves the city from the colossal canine with a fiendish plan.

A Giftdog's Gift to Santa by Denny Kodner, illustrated by Art Smith.1992 (OOP); Harris Publications; hardcover. This is the story of Santa's flight to deliver gift pets on Christmas Eve. The sleigh crashes and the dogs have to dig Santa out of the snow, plus find their way back to the North Pole to let them know help is needed. The mischievous corgi pup makes friends with a wolf pack, who guide and help the pet dogs. Proceeds from the sale of this book were contributed to the Morris Animal Foundation and the Dog Museum.

Gladwyn Goes to Town by Paul Callan, illustrated by John Battaglia.1977 (OOP); Hodder and Stoughton Ltd.; hardcover. Gladwyn the corgi lives in the Welsh countryside, but decides to make a visit to his royal relations at Buckingham Palace. He has many adventures on his first visit to London, but finally gets to see his "cousins" and is treated to an excellent meal before being driven back to his home by Prince Charles himself.

The Great Corgiville Kidnapping by Tasha Tudor. 1997; Little, Brown and Company; paperback or hardcover. Caleb Corgi notices a worrisome increase in the number of raccoons in Corgiville, some of who seem to be discussing how to stuff and roast a fowl. Babe the prize rooster is suddenly kidnapped and Caleb must find and rescue him.

Just Call Me Jones by Dora Cox. 1976 (OOP); Carlton Press Inc.; hardcover. Ms. Cox's delightful biography of her corgi, Jones, as he himself might have written it.

Keeping Up With Jones by Dora Cox. 1979 (OOP). The continuing adventures of Jones, the Pembroke Welsh corgi.

Little Dog Lost by Rene Guillot, illustrated by Wallace Tripp. 1970 (OOP); Lothrop, Lee & Shepard Co.; hardcover. A corgi puppy who gets lost in the woods and is adopted by a mother fox. He learns to survive in the wild as a fox, but is found at Christmas by humans and adopted by a little girl. The corgi later goes back to the woods to help his injured fox mother, who eventually comes to live at the farm woodshed under the care of the corgi's human family.

Little Golden Book of Dogs by Nita Jonas, illustrated by Tibor Gergely. 1952 (OOP); Simon and Schuster; hardcover. There are short poems and simple drawings of 20 breeds. Here is the poem, The Corgi:
The Welsh corgi is brown with four little white socks.
He's a very good watchdog and looks like a fox;
With his tiny stub tail and his sharp little face

He seems quite at home almost any old place."

Megan a Welsh Corgi by Margaret S. Johnson. 1957 (OOP); William Morrow & Co.; hardcover. Megan is a British farm corgi, learning to herd from her mother. Then Mrs. Gray shows up and convinces the farmer to sell her the puppy so she can take her back to America to compete in dog shows. Megan does not like living in a tiny apartment and having to always be quiet and calm. Mrs. Gray doesn't understand why her dog wants to chase animals in the park. Megan luckily meets up with an old dog friend and his rancher owner. Mrs. Gray finally accepts that Megan is not happy living in a city and being in dog shows, and lets the rancher take her off to herd cows on the ranch with her border collie friend.

The Money Tree by Sarah Stewart, illustrated by David Small. 1991; Farrar Straus Giroux; paperback. No actual mention is made in the story of corgis, but the illustrations throughout the book show the woman with her three pet dogs, one of who is a red and white Pembroke.

Profile of Glindy, A Welsh Corgi by Esther Elias. 1976 (OOP); Christopher Publishing House; hardcover. The true story of the author's 14-year relationship with her corgi, Glindy. It is a light-hearted collection of anecdotes and incidents.

Queening of Ceridwen by Esther Elias. 1982 (OOP); Christopher Publishing House; hardcover. Sequel to *Profile of Glindy,* this is the story of Glindy's mate, Ceridwen.

The Queen's Holiday by Margaret Wild, illustrated by Sue O'Loughlin. 1992 (OOP); Orchard Books; hardcover. A very Victoria-like Queen decides to go to the seashore. With her go her page boy, lady-in-waiting, bodyguard, groom, doctor, palace guard, maids, footman, and butler. And of course, her five corgis. "But it was a long, long walk to the seaside, and on the way everyone got rather hot and silly." The cartoon drawings of the corgis running in terror from an alley cat, fainting, and begging the butler for help are just hysterical! The Queen sternly calls everyone to order, sets things straight, rescues the corgis, and marches everyone down to the seashore for a marvelous day.

Rex Q.C. by Dorothea King, illustrated by Nicola Smee. 1984 (OOP); Little, Brown and Company; hardcover. "Q.C." is Queen's corgi. This is a short picture book of a typical day in the palace from a dog's-eye view. Rex is not at all in awe of his royal owners—he notices when the Queen oversleeps (she stayed up too late watching TV) and the Duke puts on two different colored socks (he was in a hurry because the Royal Garden Party ran late).

Shorty by Arthur D. Smith. 1985 (OOP); AKA Publishers Intl.; hardcover. These are the adventures of Jase Miller and his corgi, growing up on a farm during the 40s. At Shorty's death (of old age), Jase says "I stood there in the morning light and thanked the little dog with the too-short legs. I thanked him for his courage and for what he had given to me. He came to me when I was a boy, and he helped me grow to be a man."

Slop! A Welsh Folktale retold by Margaret Read MacDonald, illustrated by Yvonne LeBrun Davis. 1997; Fulcrum Publishing; hardcover. The corgi companion is included in the vivid illustrations of this folk story about an elderly couple and their "wee folk" neighbors.

Zelda and the Corgis by Diana Avebury, illustrated by Hugh Casson. 1984 (OOP); Piccadilly Press; hardcover. Zelda the papillon and her three dog friends have many adventures in London—including returning a lost corgi to Buckingham Palace and then discovering that he is NOT one of the royal corgis.

TASHA TUDOR BOOKS

Tasha Tudor is a revered and respected author, illustrator, and corgi owner. She has written and/or illustrated more than 80 books, most intended for children. Only a few of the books are specifically about corgis (the two Corgiville books are included in the list above), but Ms. Tudor incorporates her beloved corgis into the illustrations of almost all her books. Many of her books are now out of print. Here are some of the best-known and most beloved books by or about Ms. Tudor:

The Art of Tasha Tudor by Harry Davis, illustrated by Tasha Tudor. 2000; Little Brown & Co.; hardcover.

A Child's Garden of Verses by Robert Louis Stevenson, illustrated by Tasha Tudor. Simon & Schuster; hardcover or paperback

The Night Before Christmas by Clement Clarke Moore, illustrated by Tasha Tudor. 1975; Simon & Schuster; hardcover or paperback. The traditional holiday poem is cleverly illustrated by Ms. Tudor, and the corgis are on hand to greet and assist Santa when he comes down the chimney.

The Private World of Tasha Tudor by Tasha Tudor and Richard W. Brown. 1992; Little Brown & Co.; hardcover.

A Time To Keep by Tasha Tudor. 1977; Simon & Schuster; hardcover. A sweet children's book about all the favorite annual holidays, with corgis participating in the celebrations.

ADULT FICTION

The Accidental Tourist by Anne Tyler. 1985; Knopf; hardcover / Berkley Publishing; paperback. Macon Leafy is a travel-hating writer of travel books who avoids adventure. Then he meets the astonishing

Muriel, who is trying to train his unmanageable Cardigan Welsh corgi, Edward. Anne Tyler's most famous best-seller.

Diamond In the Ruff by Emily Carmichael. 2001; Bantam Books; paperback. This is the sequel to *Finding Mr. Right*, in which we met Lydia, a gorgeous woman who had been reincarnated as a Pembroke Welsh corgi named Miss Piggy. She was sent back to Earth (from the Afterlife) to help her old friend Amy find true love. Miss Piggy's owner, Amy, is now on vacation with her new husband, so Amy's friend Joey is caring for her corgis. Joey is not a romantic person; as a wedding planner, she sees everything possible that can go wrong with people's love lives. But Miss Piggy, in her role of Cupid in corgi costume, has her own ideas about Joey's future.

Dog & Pony Show by Pam Bliss (cartoon stories). 2001; Paradise Valley Comics; paperback. These are illustrated comic stories that include several Cardigans.

Dr. Nightingale Follows a Canine Clue by Lydia Adamson. 2001; Signet; paperback. Part of the Dr. Nightingale mystery series. Dr. Nightingale is a country veterinarian, and in this one the corgi pet of a friend leads her to the woman's body.

A Feral Darkness by Doranna Durgin. 2001; Baen Publishing; paperback. The very realistic and wonderful Cardigan "Druid" appears in the life of pet groomer and dog rescuer Brenna Fallon, and helps her save her home, uncover an unsavory use of local dogs, and investigate a new strain of rabies.

Finding Mr. Right by Emily Carmichael. 1998; Bantam Books; paperback. A romance novel that features a woman reincarnated as a Pembroke Welsh corgi, and given the job of matchmaker among humans. Lydia is recently deceased; unfortunately, her death occurred while she was carrying on a hot affair with the husband of her best friend Amy Cameron. David,

the straying husband, died too. Amy is a nice woman who has two champion corgis and is active in corgi rescue. So the beings in charge of the Afterlife decide that Lydia must redeem herself by returning to earth and finding Amy a new husband. But they don't make this easy for Lydia—the formerly gorgeous and sexy human Lydia is reincarnated as an overweight, scarred, flea-infested, stray corgi named Miss Piggy.

Off the Leash, Memoirs of a Royal Corgi by Matthew Sturgis. 1995 (OOP); Hodder & Stoughton; hardcover. Quoting from the back cover: "At last, the real Royal lowdown: a carpet level view of the House of Windsor. One of the Queen's corgis has been persuaded to set the record straight. Here is a full and frank account of the personalities, peccadillos and power struggles of the Royal Household. A fascinating firsthand account of the British Royal Family at work, at play, at home, at each other's throats—told with all the biting honesty for which corgis are justly famous."

Tails of Love (anthology) Bliss/Griffin/Koehly/Sattler. 2001; Barbour Publishing, Inc.; paperback. In these four inspirational (religious) short stories, pet dogs play matchmaker for their owners. In "Dog Park," great Dane owner Matt blames Bamboo for biting his dog, even though Lynne insists her little corgi did no such thing.

Rita Mae Brown mystery series

The series features corgi Tee Tucker and cat Mrs. Murphy assisting their owner, the local postmistress, in solving mysteries in their small Virginia town. The animals "talk" in the books, but only to other animals—humans are a little slow on the uptake and just don't understand when clearly spoken to.

- ***Wish You Were Here*** (1990)
- ***Rest In Pieces*** (1992)

- *Murder at Monticello* (1994)
- *Pay Dirt* (1995)
- *Murder, She Meowed* (1996)
- *Murder On the Prowl* (1998)
- *Cat On the Scent* (1999)
- *Pawing Through the Past* (2000
- *Claws and Effect* (2001)
- *Catch as Cat Can* (2002)

C.C. Benison's mystery series

Corgis are not active characters in the books, but are seen in the royal household. It is mentioned that the main job of the palace footmen is to care for the royal corgis.

- *Death at Buckingham Palace* (1996)
- *Death at Sandringham House* (1997)
- *Death at Windsor Castle* (1998)

COOKBOOKS

In the Kitchen With Corgis. 2000; Columbia River Pembroke Welsh Corgi Club; spiral-bound (still available: http://www.oregoncorgis.org)

25th Anniversary Cookbook. 1994 (OOP); Lakeshore Pembroke Welsh Corgi Club; comb-bound

BREED BOOKS

Cardigan Welsh Corgis by Mrs. Henning Nelms & Mrs. Michael Pym. 1990 (OOP); T.F.H. Publications; hardcover

The Cardiganshire Corgi by Clifford Hubbard. 1952 (OOP); hardcover

The Guide to Owning a Pembroke Welsh Corgi by Sheila Webster Boneham. 2001; T.F.H. Publications; paperback

The Illustrated Standard of the Cardigan Welsh Corgi. 1995; Cardigan Welsh Corgi Club of America

The New Complete Pembroke Welsh Corgi by Deborah S. Harper. 1994; MacMillan Publishing Company; hardcover. Previous edition was *The Complete Pembroke Welsh Corgi* by Mary Gay Sargent and Deborah S. Harper.

The New Illustrated Study of the Pembroke Welsh Corgi Standard. 2000; Pembroke Welsh Corgi Club of America

Our Friend the Welsh Corgi edited by Rowland Johns. 1951 (OOP); hardcover

The Pembroke Welsh Corgi by Deborah S. Harper. 1998; Hungry Minds Inc.; hardcover

The Pembroke Welsh Corgi, Family Friend and Farmhand by Susan M. Ewing. 2000; Hungry Minds Inc.; hardcover.

Pembroke Welsh Corgis by Ria Niccoli. 1995; T.F.H. Publications; hardcover.

Puppy Kisses are Good for the Soul by Howard Weinstein. 2001; Toad Hall Press; paperback. Two sections. "The Amazing Life & Times of Mail Order Annie" covers the life of the author's Pembroke Welsh corgi, and includes tips and information on selecting and raising a pet. "Teach Your Puppy Well" has more detail on how to raise and train a dog.

The Welsh Corgi by Charles Lister-Kaye. 1965 (OOP); Popular Dogs; hardcover

Welsh Corgis by E. Forsyth-Forrest. 1955 (OOP); hardcover

Welsh Corgis: Pembroke and Cardigan by Richard G. Beauchamp.1999; Barrons Educational Series; paperback

Your Welsh Corgi, Cardigan - Pembroke by Robert J. Berndt. 1978 (OOP); Denliger's; hardcover

VIDEOS & MOVIES

Fiction

The Accidental Tourist. Based on the book by Anne Tyler.

Murder She Purred from Disney (1998). Based on the books by Rita Mae Brown.

Cowboy Bebop (with Ein the corgi), Japanese anime, 13 volumes. This is a series of Japanese anime cartoons about Spike, a bounty hunter in the future. Ein the corgi shows up starting in episode 2. Spike is tracking down a dog stolen from a lab where it was the subject of secret experiments that turned it into a super-intelligent "data dog". The cartoon corgi is cuter and smarter than all the human characters. He escapes from the various groups chasing after him, but finally decides on life on Spike's spaceship, where he can be spoiled and admired by Spike's partners. Each episode is about 20 minutes long; the shows are two episodes per tape. They are available in Japanese or dubbed English. *WARNING: Like many Japanese anime, these "cartoons" are not for children—they are filled with extreme violence, bad language, criminal activity, and other dubious items.*

Little Dog Lost. Based on the book by Rene Guillot.

The Corgi Conspiracy. This is a funny mock documentary about a supposed WWII Nazi plot to take over Great Britain by having rabid commando corgis kill the Royal Family.

Non-fiction

AKC Pembroke Welsh Corgi Standard

AKC Cardigan Welsh Corgi Standard

Take Peace – Corgi Cottage Christmas (Tasha Tudor)

Take Joy – The Magical World of Tasha Tudor

Raelene Gorlinsky's son, Jonathan, with Phantom, Foxy, and Phoenix

A DICTIONARY FOR CORGIS

compiled by Jean Macak and the members of Corgi-L

Special dogs deserve a language to match. Jean Macak and others of Corgi-L, a mailing list for all things corgi, share the vocabulary that has developed over the years to describe corgi behavior and activities.

Aaarrrooooo: Characteristic sound, similar to a warbling howl, made by the corgi when happy, excited, or just waking up.

Bath: A process by which the humans drench the floor, walls, and themselves. You can help by shaking vigorously and frequently. Often followed by the opportunity to wrestle towels and get a treat.

Bicycles: Two-wheeled exercise machines, invented for dogs to control body fat. To get maximum aerobic benefit, you must hide behind a bush and dash out, bark loudly, and run alongside for a few yards; the person then swerves and falls into the bushes, and you prance away.

Bump: The best way to get your human's attention when they are drinking a fresh cup of coffee or tea.

Bunny Butt: The affectionate term used by humans to describe the view as your Pembroke Welsh corgi leaves the room.

A Bunny Butt

Butt Wiggle: What you do when you see people and/or dogs which you would like to **frap** with.

Corgese: The language used by Cardigan and Pembroke Welsh corgis, and the special words for items belonging in their wonderful world.

Corgi Drumstick: Also called the corgi chop or corgi prosciutto—the lovely ham hock that a well muscled corgi has. It includes the hind leg, up onto the rump.

Corgwyn: The Welsh plural for corgi.

Dead Bug: Lying on back with all four feet in the air, sleeping.

A Dead Bug

Dead Cow: Lying on side, with all four feet sticking straight out, the legs on the bottom, lying on the floor, the legs on the top, sticking out into air (too short to lie on the floor as well!)

Deafness: A malady that affects a corgi when its person wants it in and the corgi wants to stay out. Symptoms include staring blankly at the person, running in the opposite direction, or lying down.

Dog Bed: Any soft, clean surface, such as the white bedspread in the guest room or the newly upholstered couch in the living room.

Doing Nails: The periodic attempt by humans to remove your toes using primitive instruments of torture. All physical and vocal forms of protest are allowed.

Drool: What to do when your person has food and you don't. To do this properly you must sit as close as you can and look sad and let the drool fall to the floor or, better yet, on their laps.

Faerie Saddle: The ridge of differently textured and colored fur right behind the shoulders, made by the magical saddle of the wee folk.

Faerie Steed: The nickname given to corgis based on their role in folklore as the steed of the faerie folk.

Faerie Kiss: A small white spot seen on the forehead of corgi pups, said to have come from the kiss of a faerie. This usually fades as the pup grows

Fluff: A corgi coat type where the hair is very long and fluffy. Considered a fault based on the dog standard—but don't let the corgis know!

A Fluffy with a Hedgie

Flying Corgi: That wonderful position, belly flat on the ground, with legs splayed straight out the

back. Also known as Flying Frog and Frog-Dog.

Frap (**F**rantic or **F**requent **R**unning **A**nd **P**laying): The corgi behavior of happily running about at full tilt, which seems to occur for reasons unknown to humans. Also, what you do in the obedience ring when you are tired of heeling. Includes running wildly around the ring with a big corgi smile on your face, so everyone will know you are enjoying it.

Garbage Can: A container designed to test your ingenuity. You must stand on your hind legs and try to push the lid off with your nose. If you do it right you are rewarded with margarine wrappers to shred, beef bones to consume, and moldy crusts of bread.

Hedgie: The favorite stuffed prey of many corgis, usually in imminent danger of losing its inner fluff

Lean: Every good dog's response to the command "sit!"—especially if your person is dressed for work or an evening out. This is especially effective before black-tie events.

Leash: A strap that attaches to your collar, enabling you to lead your person where you want him/her to go.

Love: A feeling of intense affection, given freely and without restriction. To show your love, wiggle your nubbin or wag your tail and gaze adoringly. If you're lucky, a human will love you in return

Neck Roll: What corgis do when they see anything dead or smelly, including dried up nightcrawlers on the driveway. You just put your neck down and follow with rest of your body, then roll back and forth on top of the deceased "matter" with all four little legs in the air. This is especially effective when you have just had a bath.

Nose Art: The beautiful designs you make on mom's van window with your nose when she lets you ride in the front seat. May also be made on sliding glass doors, storm doors, and bay windows. Also known as nose painting and pupkus.

Nubbin: Small stump of a tail in the Pembroke Welsh corgi that wiggles vigorously when excited or stands upright when inquisitive.

Power of da Fluff: Pembroke Welsh corgis are said to posses this when they are born with an unusually long and fluffy coat.

Scootching: The strange act of bunching up dog beds, pillows, or rugs with the front paws and "jet propelling" them backwards.

Scritches: As in belly scratches, or tummy scritches.

Shed: What corgis do twice a year, January through June, and July through December.

Sniff: A social custom to use when you greet other dogs. Place your nose as close as you can to the other dog's rear end and inhale deeply. Repeat several times, or until your person makes you stop.

Sofas: These are to dogs like napkins are to people. After eating it is polite to run up and down the front of the sofa and wipe your whiskers clean.

Squinchy: A facial expression mastered by corgis to convey cuteness.

Thunder: A signal that the world is coming to an end (similar to the Vacuum Cleaner). Humans remain amazingly calm during thunderstorms, so it is necessary to warn them of the danger by trembling uncontrollably, panting, rolling your eyes wildly, and following at their heels.

Vacuum Cleaner: A loud dangerous machine that humans use for unknown reasons to remove evidence of beautiful corgi fur. Only two responses permitted: frantic barking, accompanied by an attempt to herd, or cowering behind the toilet.

Wastebasket: A dog toy filled with used tissues, paper, envelopes, and old candy wrappers. When you get bored, turn over the basket and strew the papers all over the house until your person comes home.

Jean Macak's Scout, Betsy, and Albert

THE STORY OF THE RAINBOW BRIDGE

(author unknown)

A story loved by all dog owners.

Just this side of heaven is a place called the Rainbow Bridge. When an animal dies that has been especially close to someone here, that pet goes to the Rainbow Bridge. There are meadows and hills for all of our special friends, so they can run and play together. There is plenty of food, water, and sunshine, and our friends are warm and comfortable. All the animals who had been ill and old are restored to health and vigor. Those who were hurt or maimed are made whole and strong again, just as we remember them in our dreams of days and times gone by. The animals are happy and content, except for one small thing: they each miss someone very special to them, who had to be left behind.

They all run and play together, but the day comes when one suddenly stops and looks into the distance. His bright eyes are intent. His eager body quivers. Suddenly he begins to run from the group, flying over the green grass, his legs carrying him faster and faster. You have been spotted, and when you and your special friend finally meet, you cling together in joyous reunion, never to be parted again. The happy kisses rain upon your face; your hands again caress the beloved head, and you look once more into the trusting eyes of your pet, so long gone.

Then you cross Rainbow Bridge together…

AFTER THE FINAL TRIP

by John M. Klaus

Humans live longer than corgis, longer than most animals. Knowing this, we nonetheless bring companion animals into our lives with great joy, and the miraculous symbiotic relationship between very different species provides us with endless wonder and pleasure.

All too often, as our time with a companion animal draws inevitably to a close, we are faced with an awful decision. Our dear and loving companion is ill. There is no hope of recovery, let alone of a normal life. Our friend is suffering, and, as has always been the case throughout our time together, turns to us for help and comfort.

It is as difficult a task as we can face. Do we take heroic measures and perhaps prolong misery? Or do we make a decision only a human can make, and put an end to pain?

Look into your friend's eyes and speak gently. The answer will be there.

Do not despair, my dearest friend.
That final office you performed
Could not extinguish this bright flame,
My fiercely burning, loving soul.

Yours was the power. You used it well.
An instant. Then the pain was gone.
Oh, dearest friend, my soul stayed there.
I heard your gentle words of love.

Do not grieve overmuch, my friend.
If bitter tears should dim your eyes,
I'll help to wipe that dew away,
I'll help replace it with a smile.

An ancient English legend tells
That animals, on Christmas Eve,
Precisely at the stroke of twelve,
Can speak as humans, and converse

Amongst themselves, or with mankind.
So, were it now that magic hour,
And I could speak my heart to you,
I'd give you this to understand:

The flesh you knew, it is no more.
My spirit, though, lives on in you.
If you should sense me close at hand,
Then you must know that I am there.

If, not rememb'ing I am gone,
You stretch your hand to stroke my head,
Then I am where I've always been,
Beside you, if not there in flesh.

And, should you see my lonely bed
Now empty, as it's never been
Through all the time I've spent with you,
Or come upon my well-used lead,

Or find my now-dry water bowl,
Or see the dish from which I ate,
And weep because my form is gone,
I am there, too, though I'm unseen.

I am not dead. My spirit lives
So long as you remember me.
Throughout your life I'll stay with you
As close as thought, or breath, or smile.

My most important job in life
Was giving you my deepest love.
That task is more important now.
I'm with you always, now as then.

Nor, when you, too, shall leave the earth,
Will I leave you alone in death.
My love transcends this mortal sphere,
And, when you die, we'll meet once more.

My spirit now is free to roam
Throughout the earth, the skies, the stars,
But I prefer to stay by you,
To live deep in your heart and mind.

My earthly body, true, is gone,
Returned to earth, from whence it came.
But my eternal body lives,
And loves, and waits for your embrace.

With all grief past, my dearest friend,
When we shall meet on distant shore,
We two, transfigured, young again,
Will cross the Rainbow Bridge to heaven.

So don't despair, my dearest friend!
Grieve briefly, and then live your life
Aware, and fully, to the end.
My life has surely showed you how.

Your ev'ry moment is a gift.
Take full advantage of each hour.
Yes! Live! Love! Share your many gifts!
And that, my friend, I learned from you!

Then, when you lay your burden down,
And when we two meet face-to-face,
Eternity we'll have to share!
My soul lives in your heart'til then.

I've given all my heart to you,
My dearest friend. It's all I have.
Oh! Treat it gently! Hold it close!
And some day bring it back to me!

John Klaus and Crew

John with his daughter Elizabeth, son Benjamin, and (left to right) Foxworth (rescue PWC), Samantha (PWC), Hedydd (rescue CWC), Shadow (rescue Keeshond), Welly (PWC), Logan (rescue Great Pyrenees), and Amy (rescue PWC).

THE TELLING: HOW THE CORGI GOT A FAERY SADDLE

by Peggy Neumeier

In which the newest generation of puppies learns an important story.

It's almost time...

As Hayley busied herself around the grounds of the castle, her litter of puppies followed her with great curiosity. They had heard the rumors spreading like wild fire—a trip was being planned!

"Please, mama, when are we leaving?" the little spotted pup asked. Hayley always took extra time answering this one's questions. Hayley knew from the time Miss Barney Anne was born that she was very special. It was touch and go for a long time, but with all the special attention she received from Milliemom, she finally caught up with the rest of her rowdy littermates and was well on her way to being grown.

"Very soon now, Cookie, it's almost May Day." Barney Anne didn't quite know what this "May Day" was, but oh how she loved it when her mama called her Cookie. From the minute she was born she looked different from her brothers and sisters. She was what they called a "whitely"—mostly white, with little tan and cocoa colored spots making her look like one of those famous Spotted Corgi Cookies she had heard so much about. And since she was just so sweet, Hayley took to calling her Cookie.

Each pupster and adult alike had their own little backpack, and each was allowed only three things inside. A twig from the castle grounds, a special collar or bandana, or toy to have for comfort, and an offering of f-o-o-d. Milliemom always said it just wasn't polite to go visiting without bringing a homemade morsel from the chef.

Over the last few weeks, the puppies had all heard bits and snatches from hushed conversations about The Telling. From what they could gather, once every generation, the eldest and most wise from all of Corgidom would pass on the story of the Fairy people to the youngsters. Corgis from all over the world would soon be gathering near the house of Lucy May in Or-E-gone. There were the Mish-E-gan corgis, well-represented by Hayley and her little family. The "Boyz from Long-eye-land" were coming to serve as the Sergeants at Arms for the ceremony.

There were corgis from O-hi-O, corgis from Floor-a-duh, and Lone Star corgis, too. Why even the corgis from Ten-ah-see-ya would be there. President Barney, Paris Lynn, and her new brother Chester were all wearing matching bandanas from their Angelic sister, Silver. But no corgi could have guessed that the Boss Hisself was letting Angelic Silver and Sweet George come to the gathering as a special favor to St. Frank. With two loving angel corgis there, every corgi who was with da Boss could see and hear The Telling, too. How exciting it was! This was Cookie's first trip, and it was going to be a doozy.

∞∞∞∞

Lucy May knew she was the wisest of all corgwyn and it was up to her to pass The Telling to all the young ones. She had done her research and gotten all her facts just so. She even jotted her thoughts down on little pieces of white bark from the tree in the back yard. Lucy smiled to herself every time she noticed a piece of the white tree lying nearby. "Bark," that's the silliest name for a piece of tree that only makes the slightest "woosh" as it falls to the ground. Now BARK was one of her favorite words; B-A-R-K was the deep, robust chant she made every time one of those pesky squirrels dared to invade her space.

Next to BARKing, her favorite thing was F-O-O-D! and if anyone knew how to put out a spread, it was a corgi. Lucy trotted down the path, dragging her favorite blanket with her to the special place she had picked for all the corgis to meet. Off she went, out past the white tree, through the little space she created in the privet hedge, away from the house, to the farthest corner of her property where the old willow stood.

Each corgi has her own magical spot for meditation and this was Lucy's: a huge old willow tree, gnarled and bending with one large broken branch hanging from the last winter storm. Lucy worried about her old friend that winter, but the flush of pale green growth signaled that life was returning again to the willow, and the glen. In these last few days of April, crocuses and snowdrops opened here and there in the glen. The wildflowers crowded in among the shoots from the bulbs her mama planted for her to enjoy. Rolling and scootching and coming in full of yellow dandelion stains and pussytoe fluff was her favorite spring ritual. And this spring was so special! It was her 17th spring, and her turn to spin and weave the story of the enchanted little steeds whom the fairies loved so.

Lucy had gathered up spare twigs from around the willow tree and set them in a pile for the bonfire. As each corgi guest arrived, they would take their twigs from their own backpacks and add them to the ever growing pile.

This was the first step in a chain of events that brought the corgi community together for the first time in a decade.

ooooo

"We've got to leave…we'll never get all the way to Or-E-gone in time" was all Hayley could say. Today was the day they were waiting for. You could feel the electricity in the air!   Some of the older corgis who had been present at the last Telling were staying home so that Milliemom and the chef wouldn't become too suspicious. But Hayley had her family in tow, and off they went to join the caravan of corgwyn who were headed West.

All the corgis from the Southern states traveled up the coast highway and joined up with the New England corgis. At the very tip of the Everglades, a truck driver named Brucedad helped load the back of his big rig with backpacks and luggage of all shapes and sizes. As he drove north, he would stop along the way and pick up any hitchhiking corgis he saw. He always stopped at road side cafes and eateries, for, as everyone knows, where there's food, there's corgis!

When the sixteen wheeler arrived in New England, the Long-eye-land boyz took over driving, so poor Brucedad could get some sleep. "Besides," Dickens said, "I know this U-nighted States like the back of my paw." The little red and white driver had just pulled into a rest stop in Mish-E-gan, when a familiar voice was heard over the loud speaker.

"Will the driver of this big ole rig please stop blocking the exit ramp?" It was Hayley, giving her friends a hard time. Butt wiggles and ear kisses were exchanged all around as Brucedad helped each corgi pup into the back of the rig. "We still have McCabe in In-dye-anna and corgis in Ill-i-noise to pick up before night fall," Hayley yipped.

"Let's get this truck a truckin," was Brucedad's favorite saying, but the corgis just looked at each other with that tolerant look they saved for humans and off they went.

ooooo

Lucy couldn't remember ever being this excited. It was such an honor to be chosen for The Telling. Everything was ready out in the glen. Each of her most precious blankets were carefully placed here and there for her guests. She had no idea how many corgis would come, but every corgi who was any corgi would be there.

Lucy settled herself on her mama's feet to listen to the TV, hoping to catch the weather forecast for tomorrow. Tomorrow was the big day! And as she slipped into slumber, the weatherman announced tomorrow would be a lovely day.

Lucy awoke at the crack of noon, as was her usual custom, and already there were drips and drabs of corgis arriving at her house. "Lucy May," her mama called, "you have company!"

Being the superior hostess that she was, Lucy invited all her friends to follow back to the glen. Each corgi brought their twigs to place on the bonfire pile, and each had something delicious to share. Cheese steak sandwiches, home made biscuits, peanut butter treats in all shapes and sizes were scattered about on the little low table Lucy had prepared.

As the day progressed, the bonfire stack became huge, the treat table was full, and there were more corgis than anyone had ever seen before. There was every color corgi imaginable in the little glen: red and white, tris, merles, brindles, Pems and Cardis. Every size, every shape, but they all had one thing in common. They were all excited to hear the story that Lucy had been preparing to tell.

All the corgis struck up friendships over the buffet table. The puppies ran and played creating a game area where they all tried the "Alpha roll" on each other. The boy corgis were busy with tug-o-war, while the little girl corgis traded bandanas and whispered stories of this weeks "big crush."

Woe unto the adult who wandered into the play area, for they were set upon by a pack of yipping, growling youngsters. Even Teddy and Dickens, the Sgt. at Arms, played a little rough and tumble, letting a few of the young ones drive them from the top of a nearby compost pile, while winking to each other as the boys raised their fur and bragged to the girls just how fierce they had become.

By night fall everyone was ready to start, and Lucy called upon their President Barney to light the bonfire.

"It is my great honor, as your President, to begin the ceremony!" And with that, Barney pulled a roman candle out of his very deep pocket and set the wood pile ablaze.

All the corgis ooohed and aaahed as the kindling ignited. There was a round of applause and "speech, speech" was heard through the crowd. Always the diplomat, Barney was prepared to say a few words.

"Gather round, young and old alike, for tonight is a special night. Tonight the history of our people will be told for all the new generations to hear. Come and sit close by the bonfire that unites us. We have each brought to The Telling a branch from our own yard. And each branch represents each clan that has traveled here tonight. Joining all our families in the bonfire that unites us in spirit, as we are united tonight."

The crowd roared with approval, as Barney turned to Lucy to give her the floor.

"Dear friends, tonight it is my honor as the oldest amongst us to pass on the story of how we corgwyn came to live with humans." The older corgis smiled and looked down at the children who surrounded Miss Lucy. All their little tails and bunny butts wriggling with anticipation. Heads cocked to one side, eyes wide with wonder, waiting like little sponges to absorb the ancient knowledge.

High in a branch in the old willow, Silver and George also looked down upon the scene. The two corgi angels sat watching and listening so that all the others who had already gone to be with Da Boss could see with their eyes and hear with their ears, the wonderful story, just one more time.

Miss Lucy cleared her throat and began.

Long ago, high in the rolling Welsh countryside, three children, a pair of sisters and their brother, watched over the family cattle. As the cattle grazed, the children played hide and seek in and out among the rocks and boulders that dotted the landscape.

Meagan, being the most curious of the three, found a cave that they had never seen before. The sun shone brightly that day, and something from deep inside that cave reflected the sunlight back into the eyes of the child.

"Tay, Dylan," she called. "Come and see what I've found!" All three danced back and forth with excitement at the opening of the cave. "Go see what it is," called Dylan. "You go first," cried Meagan. But it was Tay, the oldest (if only by a few minutes) and bravest of the little group who entered. As soon as the sun was blocked out by the depth of the passage, Tay felt the damp and coolness inside. She loved the earthy smell of the moss that clung to the walls. It was mixed with the scent of heather that was carried in by the breeze.

"Hurry!" Meg's voice echoed off the walls of the cave. But Tay didn't answer. Her eyes, becoming accustomed to the darkness, filled with the most wonderful sight she'd ever seen.

As big brother to the girls, Dylan knew his Da would have his hide should anything happen to one of his sisters when they were supposed to be tending to the cows. "Tay come out now!" he said. And his words bounced from wall to wall and deep into the cave where his sister now stood.

"NO…come in and help me, both of you!" was her reply.

The sparkling object that first caught the little girl's eye still shone brightly in the cave. She finally got close enough to see

that it was a tiny buckle, and gasped. There on the floor of the cave lay a tiny, broken harness, its buckles made from pure gold. The leather straps were jewel-covered. When the other two children finally stopped their chiding and taunts of "scaredy cat" and "You first" and met their sister inside, their gaze fell upon the lovely tack.

"It looks just like the harness Da puts on Willy when she pulls the cart to town," Meagan spoke up. "Ay, but it's too small and too dear for the likes of our pony" was Dylan's reply. As the curly haired little girl bent over to pick up her find, she heard the tiniest moan come from further into the cave.

"Who's there?" came to her lips. Another moan brought all three children closer to the origin of the sound. "Tis just me, children—don't be afraid," and out of the darkness a tiny iridescent figure hovered just above the cave floor. Being the brave children that they were, fear was the last thing that sprung into their minds.

"My name is Isobelle, and I have a favor to

ask of you all. I have been waiting a long time for you to come close enough to see my broken harness. You see, only children and the pure of heart can see me! I'm afraid while riding up and down these mountains my fairy steed spooked and bolted into this cave, breaking her harness and throwing me to the ground."

"We will help you!" cried all three children, "but where is your pony?"

The shimmer of the little fairy brightened at the innocence of the child's question. "Oh, child, it's not a pony I've been riding, but my fairy steed—my corgi!" The children looked at each other in total confusion for they had never seen nor heard of a "corgi" before this day.

At just that very moment, a wee black button nose peeked its way out from a mossy blanket not three feet from where the children stood. The fairy made a clucking sound and out came two more little faces.

"They're puppies!" All three children cried in unison. The children had never seen puppies so soft with bright black eyes, red and white fur and stubby legs. "They have no tails!" Dylan shouted gleefully as the pups bounded out from their hiding spot and covered the children with warm, wet kisses.

Now, every fairy knows that they can not care for more than one corgi, for each pup needs his own master to love and obey and devote their life to. Next to the fairy stood a larger version of the three pups, their mother. She watched her babies bounce and jump and roll and play with the three wide eyed humans. Isobelle looked at the mother dog and she nodded her head.

"I have a favor to ask of you now and if you can do it, your reward will be priceless." "Anything!" came the giggling reply. "If you can mend this harness for me, I shall be forever in your debt." The children looked at each other without saying a word and left the cave.

"Well my girl," Isobelle said, "it looks like we will have to wait a while longer." No more than an hour had passed when the three children came bursting into the cave, each with a small box in one tiny hand.

"I've been watching Ma when she mends the holes in our socks, and I think I can fix your harness" said Tay, barely able to get the words out before catching her breath.

"And I've brought the pot of dye that our Da rubs into Willy's saddle to make it soft and shiny. Once it's sewn, I'll stain the thread to match the harness so it will look like new again," Dylan spoke up, still clutching the small tin of dye.

And the third child had wrapped in her kerchief a few biscuits, fresh from the window sill where her mother placed them to cool just a few minutes before. "I know Ma wouldn't mind if we shared these with you," Meagan said, speaking to the fairy but secretly hoping there was enough for the puppies, too.

So while one child sewed, and one child polished, they all enjoyed the biscuits Meagan brought.

Quicker than you can "Fairy Dust," the harness was good as new and ready to be placed on the back of the mother dog.

The sun was getting low in the sky and it was past time for the children to drive the cows home. "We have to leave right now or we'll never get the cows home in time for their evening milking," said Dylan, although in his heart of hearts he longed to play with the funny little red dogs some more.

"Yes children, it's time for all of us to be on our way." Isobelle started to saddle the mother dog. "You have all been so kind to me I must repay you." And with that, Isobelle touched each puppy on the shoulders with the tiniest amount of dust from her magic bag. The dust made the fur over the puppies shoulders just a wee bit darker than the rest of the dog, like a shadow.

"I want each of you children to take your puppy home and love them and care for them as you have cared for me today. The shape of my saddle on your puppies' shoulders will always remind you of the day you fixed my broken harness and shared your heart with the Queen of the Fairies and her fairy steed."

With that, each child collapsed to their knees, hugging and kissing the three wee puppies. "Thank you so much…" But before they could finish their sentence Isobelle was atop her fairy steed and gone from the cave.

The three children began to drive the cows home, and the red and white pups fell in behind them like it was the most natural thing in the world.

And of course, it was.

∞∞∞∞∞

The bonfire burnt back to nearly nothing, but the glow from the last few embers warmed the little spotted pup. Now she knew, and the story would burn in her heart forever. And someday, all the corgis would be making the trip to Mish-E-gan, and it would be her turn for The Telling.

It was long past midnight when Isobelle, the Fairy Queen, first appeared. Tiny, shimmering silhouettes dotted the glen and stood near each sleeping corgi.

"Dust each steed as they sleep, so when they awake, they'll each be back home, safe and sound," Isobelle instructed her fairy subjects. She then set about her work and one by one the corgis disappeared, until as the first golden ray of dawn crept into the glen, only one corgi remained asleep on her blanket, under the old willow tree.

Isobelle stroked this one's fur and spoke softly, "there are special plans for you, my girl."

Lucy awoke with that first ray of light and looked around. "But, they've all gone," she woofed softly. Like the tinkling of a bell, a little voice popped into Lucy's head.

"Not quite all!" and as Lucy gazed up into the willow for the first time, she saw her old friends, Silver and George.

"This story ends and a new adventure begins," said George. "Da Boss has sent us for you Lucy, but don't worry, you can keep an eye on your special place, just like I help Paris Lynn and Barney whenever they need me," yipped Silver.

"And I watch over all my family at Narnia," said George.

And with the soft whisper of wings, the threesome were on their way Home.

In loving memory of Lucy May Bananabrain (1984-2002) and all our beloved furkids, waiting at the Rainbow Bridge.

Peggy Neumeier and McCabe

A MAGIC NIGHT IN THE MAGIC KINGDOM

by Cindy Read

In the summer of 2001, a large group of corgis from the Corgi-L and Corgese-L lists ran away together and went on a fantasy trip to Dizzy World. Here is one story from that adventure.

It was late in the evening at Dizzy World, and all the corgis were strolling back to Cindy Reller's palace after the fireworks display, which they agreed was beautiful but a bit too noisy. Some of their friends had already gone home, and the rest of them knew that vacation would soon be over; so they were feeling tired and happy but also a bit wistful.

"It seems like a lot of corgis and not-a-corgis and c*ts have gone to the Rainbow Bridge lately," said Blue sadly. "They'll live in our hearts forever, but sometimes I just wish could see them here on earth again." Banjo and Brenna sniffed in agreement. Da President Barney said, "Angel Silver whispers in my ear sometimes, but it's just not the same," and Paris Lynn nodded.

Betony piped up, "If this was **really** a Magic Kingdom, we could see our friends at the Rainbow Bridge and I could meet my great great great aunt Crumpet. The moms have her picture in our living room and sometimes they say I look a bit like her, 'cepting I'm more athletic."

"Yes, yes," Riley chimed in. "And maybe I could meet that famous wise old Sir Guy that I've heard so much about. He's supposed to tell wonderful stories."

All the other corgis started to call out the names of their special friends and relatives who were at the Rainbow Bridge. But although they'd explored Dizzy World really thoroughly, no one could remember seeing any signs that said "Entrance to Rainbow Bridge, this way." Besides, they didn't want to go the Bridge themselves yet, not even for a visit.

Suddenly Betony (who loved to listen to music) yipped excitedly. "I have an idea, I have an idea, I have an idea! Remember that song 'When You Wish Upon A Star'? Maybe if we all sang it together and wished real hard…" The next thing anyone knew, a blurry furry pack, led by the Corgi

Constellation of Sundance, Moonshine, and Stardust, took off at high speed for Cindy Reller's palace and raced up the winding stairs to the very very top of the highest tower and out onto the roof, which was surrounded by a stone parapet. Under the direction of Princess Cheveau, they formed a circle, raised their noses to the dark sky, and began to sing:

When you wish upon a star
Makes no difference who you are
Anything your heart desires
Will come to you.

If your heart is in your dream
No request is too extreme
When you wish upon a star
As dreamers do.

Like a bolt out of the blue
Fate steps in and sees you through
When you wish upon a star
Your dreams come true.

Most of them had their eyes skrunched tight shut, they were wishing so hard, but when they got to the end of the song, Kristie, Brassy, and Jesse had started to peek.

There was a long moment of deep stillness—"Keep wishing," whispered Rosie,—and then, softly at first, a breeze came up carrying the sounds of harp music. The light all around them shimmered and got brighter and, as their eyes all popped open, red-orange-yellow-green-blue-purple a rainbow arch appeared in the sky and one end descended like a ramp, all the way down to the roof of Cindy Reller's palace. The sound of joyful barking and mewing and singing and squeaking all mixed together burst from the sky and grew louder and louder as a host of Bridge Angels raced down.

What a reunion and meeting it was! Everywhere you looked there were fraps and ear-licking and aroooooos. Barney and Silver rolled and kissed each other. "Hello,

Paris," said Silver to the beautiful little black-headed tri by Barney's side. "You're a lucky girl to have found that special family. Take good care of Susiemom and Waynedad for me" Betony bounded up to an elegant-looking red-headed tri and shyly (at least shyly for her) said, "You must be Crumpet." "Yes, my dear. I see from the Bridge that you're a good sweet girl, but sometimes you're too hard on that Evancat. I taught her to play when she was just a kitten, so you be nice to her. And good luck with that agility." Meanwhile, Sir Guy gathered quite a crowd of young-uns around him, Riley front and center, and began telling them tales of the Faerie Folk.

The party went on into the night, although Liddle Silber and some of the puppies got so exhausted that they just konked out in flying corgi position or on their backs with all four feet in the air, right in the middle of everything. Finally, though, Sir Guy (who was still Wise About All Things), said "Come, come, my Angel Friends. Soon the Magic will fade with the Coming of Dawn, and we must return to the other end of the Rainbow Bridge to await the Full Reunion in the Ripeness of Time." And, like the good dogs they still were, the angel corgis quickly obeyed the request to "Come," followed close behind by all the others who had come down from the Bridge with them.

The Dizzy World adventurers watched quietly, some with tears in their eyes, as inch by inch the Rainbow Bridge faded slowly into the darkness after the last angel passed over it. They were too tired even to return to their rooms in the palace, and, sprawled out or snuggled together, they all feel asleep on the roof, as the magic night in the Magic Kingdom faded and the pink light of dawn began to show in the east.

Cindy Read and Betony

BLUEBONNET JILLIE

by Walt Boyes

Once upon a time, the Fabulous Jilliedog was snoozing on the deck in the back yard of the house she shared with Laddybuck, and her girl Andrea, in the land of Texas. It was not such a faraway time, nor a terribly faraway place, either.

She was having a comfortable snooze. She was dreaming dreams full of sheep and cows and running after them. She was making little barking noises under her breath, and her feet were jerking a little, as if she were running while she was lying down.

She was dreaming of these things because she was a Corgi, and those are some of a Corgi's favorite things. Corgis love to run after sheep and cows and make them go where they are supposed to go.

If you have been paying attention so far, you know that Corgis come from the land of Wales. That's why they are called Welsh Corgis. In Wales, Corgi dogs are used to herd cows and sheep by the people who live there. Sometimes Corgis also get used as magical riding animals by the residents of the land of Faery. Faery is a land that is east of the Sun and West of the Moon, and is hard to find. One of the ways to get there is from the land of Wales.

It might have been that Jillie was dreaming about herding regular sheep. It could also have been that she was dreaming about herding magical sheep for her Faery friends. You see, although Jillie lived in the land of Texas with her girl Andrea, the magic was strong in her, and she often had adventures.

Suddenly, Jillie sat up straight, wide-awake.

Her ears twitched back and forth like radar. Her nose sniffed the wind. Something was strange. She looked at the sky, but she could see nothing strange. It was a nice, clear day. The sky was high and blue, with just a few raggedy white clouds. The sun was warm, and she was just thinking about circling around three times, nose to tailbone, and curling up again to sleep when she sensed it again.

Something was wrong in the field behind the house. Something was very wrong.

Jillie sat very still and then slowly looked around.

Laddybuck didn't even twitch. He was so sound asleep he wasn't moving much, except to breathe. He had been chasing the water coming out of the lawn sprinkler all morning and he had run about a hundred miles in a big circle, barking and biting at the water as it squirted and squirted. Everything normal there.

Andrea was swinging on her swingset in the other corner of the back yard. Up, squeak. Down, squeak. Up. Down. Nothing wrong there.

Jillie stood up. She shook herself. She started at her nose, and the shake moved up her head to her neck, down her back and finally her back end where her tail wasn't moved back and forth and back and forth. Then the shake moved back toward her head, and finished at her nose again. Gingerly, Jillie moved down the steps of the deck to the lawn. She slowly paced over the lawn to the diggy hole.

Now, you've heard of diggy holes. All dogs have them. Jillie's was a way for her to get under the fence and out of the yard whenever she wanted to. Andrea's Daddy kept filling in Jillie's diggy hole, and this time he'd put a couple of big rocks on top of the dirt in front of the fence. Jillie knew exactly what to do. She put her nose between the rocks and pushed. The rocks rolled apart enough for her to get her paw between them. She dragged the rocks away from her diggy hole, went back, and began to dig.

Jillie didn't have to dig very much, because she was a magic dog, like all Corgis, and could make herself very small and thin when she wanted to, like going through doors and under fences. This was also useful for hiding behind the couch if she had done something bad. Jillie smiled to herself as she remembered the time she had stolen the whole package of hamburger out of the shopping bag, and hidden and eaten it all.

In just a couple of seconds, and so quietly that Andrea never noticed, and Laddy didn't wake, Jillie was under the fence, and trotting down the sidewalk to the end of the street.

Jillie nodded to the neighbors as she passed them on the sidewalk. There was Guitar Man, who lived next door and the Gardening Lady, at the corner house, who had ten green thumbs. And there was the nice lady whose daughter was Andrea's best friend. They all smiled and waved, and Jillie smiled back, tongue lolling out of her mouth a little as she trotted toward the field.

As soon as she passed Gardening Lady's house, Jillie stepped off the sidewalk into the field. The field was high with weeds and flowers. It was colorful and beautiful. It was springtime. In Texas, springtime means wildflowers. There are hundreds of kinds and colors. And there are bluebonnets. In Texas, the bluebonnets are beautiful and important, because they signal the coming of spring. In addition, in Texas, bluebonnets grow everywhere.

They were especially lovely in the field behind Jillie's house. There were whole patches of nothing but bluebonnets. Andrea's Mommy and Daddy would dress her in a very pretty dress and plop her down in the middle of the biggest bluebonnet patch they could find and take pictures of her every year. Sometimes they made Jillie lie down in the bluebonnet patch and take pictures of her, too.

Jillie stopped and nosed the bluebonnet patch, warily. No, the problem wasn't on the bluebonnets.

Whatever she was feeling, it wasn't them.

Jillie moved quickly and quietly through the field. She went wide around one patch of very thick weeds, because she knew that was where the rattlesnake lived. She went around another patch because she had gotten in trouble just the other day for trying to chase Mrs. Bunny and her babies, who lived in the weeds in the middle of the field. Jillie grinned to herself. She just loved bunny. But Mrs. Bunny was big, and she had big back feet with big sharp claws on them, and she had told Jillie she was welcome to try to eat her babies, and just see what she'd get. Jillie told herself she was never going to get that hungry. Besides, Andrea liked bunnies, too. Just not to eat. She liked to cuddle them and pet them, and coo to them and do all the things to them that she should only do to Jillie. And sometimes to Laddybuck. Oh, well, Jillie told herself, better to just avoid the subject of bunnies altogether.

Then she saw it. It looked like a dog but wasn't. It was long and skinny, and had very long legs and a low, bushy tail. Its face was sharp, and so were its fangs. It was gray, and the air around it was shimmery, like a rainbow. One minute it wasn't there, and the next it was, and it was growling and snarling right at Jillie!

Jillie backed away, a low rumble in her throat. She barked her low raspy bark, and the not-dog looked sharply at her. As it turned, she recognized it. It was a coyote. Since it had appeared by magic, it must be a magic coyote. Jillie had heard about the magical coyotes of the Native Americans, but she had never seen one. She must be close to the Double File Trail, she thought to herself.

What was the Double File Trail, you ask? Well, long before the settlers from the south and the east moved into the land of Texas, many other people had lived there, in their turns. There was an old trail, just wide enough for two people to walk side by side, that ran from the south of the land of Texas to the North, and it was called the Double File Trail.

Long ago, Jillie had discovered that the Double File Trail was a way into the land of Faery. Over the years, she had visited the land of Faery many times, and had some strange adventures there. However, she had never visited the part of Faery where the magical creatures of the Native Americans lived.

The coyote stopped growling. He wagged his long, bushy tail. He smiled sort of a sharp, toothy smile. He moved a step toward Jillie. She stopped backing away. She smiled also a sharp, toothy smile. She wanted him to know that she was a tough and magical Corgi. She loved to keep not-dogs like him away from sheep and small girls and the other members of her flock.

Slowly, Jillie and the coyote came closer to each other. Finally, they touched noses, tall nose to short one. They sniffed. They sniffed down each other's flank, and sniffed each other's rears, like dogs and wolves and coyotes do. They made friends.

The coyote made a movement that told Jillie he wanted her to follow him. He turned around and stepped onto a path that hadn't been there a moment before. He trotted up the path a short way, turned, and looked at Jillie. He panted a little, to show he was waiting. She made up her mind, and trotted up the path after him. In the field behind her, the path disappeared. They trotted side-by-side through a field full of bluebonnets, Indian Paintbrush, Mexican Hats, and the other spring wildflowers of Texas. Jillie could hear the birds, and here and there a cicada chirping. Coyote set a fast pace, and Jillie found herself working hard to keep up with him, since his legs were so much longer than hers.

Every few hundred yards, there was a big oak tree, all by itself, with a few cactus plants around under its drip line. Coyote excused himself politely, once, and went and did his business under one of the oaks. Jillie waited, and when he came back, they went on up the trail again. Coyote seemed to know where he was going. Jillie thought she would just tag along and see what happened. He seemed nice enough, for a magical coyote.

Wondering what was going to happen, Jillie trotted alongside Coyote, up the trail. They trotted together, silently, for a long time. It got later and later, and finally Coyote let her know that they were going to find a place to sleep. Soon, a branch path joined the Double File Trail. Coyote turned down it, and they came quickly to a place where there was a small camp with a tipi. Coyote came to the edge of the clearing around the camp and barked once, then sat. Jillie sat too. The camp was very quiet.

Coyote barked again. A woman came out of the tipi and looked at him. Then she waved. She motioned them to come closer. First Coyote and then Jillie walked closer, closer, and then up to the woman. She had her black hair parted in the middle of her head, and done in long heavy braids. She was wearing a leather dress and heavy leather moccasins. She said something to Coyote, which Jillie did not understand, and he sat. So Jillie sat too. The woman came out of the tipi again with a very tightly woven basket. It had food in it. She put it in front of Coyote. He sniffed it. He ate a bite of it. Then he backed away and he let Jillie know that she could go first.

Jillie found that she was very hungry. She ate slowly, though, and didn't eat it all. When she had eaten about half, she decided to stop, even though she didn't want to. Coyote moved back to the basket, and finished the food. He sat, and smiled at the woman. She smiled back, first at Coyote, then at Jillie. She picked up the basket, and went back into the tipi. Coyote circled around behind the tipi. Jillie excused herself, and went behind the oak tree. When she was finished, she found Coyote behind the tipi. He was curled up in the shadows. She curled up next to him, and before she knew it, they were both asleep.

The next morning, Jillie and Coyote ate again from the woman's basket, did their business behind the oak tree, and went back up the branch trail to the Double File Trail. Coyote turned up the trail, and Jillie followed. They trotted together silently again for a long time.

Finally, Jillie and Coyote came to a river. There were bluffs overlooking the river, and the path curved around the bluffs and down to the river edge. At first, Jillie thought they were going to swim across the river, but Coyote found a small cave in the bluffs at the very edge of the river. He hesitated for a moment, and then he went inside the cave. Jillie followed. Inside the cave, it was dim, but not dark. Light filtered down from above somewhere. Coyote padded toward the back of the cave, and again Jillie followed. The cave narrowed until it became a passageway. It never got completely dark, but there were times when Jillie kept moving forward because she could smell Coyote in front of her better than she could see him.

Suddenly, he stopped so suddenly that his big bushy tail slapped Jillie in the face. She yelped quietly. She moved forward so she was standing next to Coyote. They were at the end of the passage. In front of them was a large cavern. It was big enough to have its own clouds, and it had trees and plants and lots of people, all huddled together. There were some very strange looking creatures moving around in the corners of the cavern. The people were obviously afraid of them. The creatures were snarling, snapping, and trying to grab the people. Some of the people had sticks and were using them to hit the creatures.

Jillie knew what to do. There were people in her flock. These were people. So they must be in her flock too. She was a brave Corgi, and she wasn't going to let any nasty creatures get her people. She charged between the people and the creatures, barking and snapping. Her eyes flashed. Her bunny butt hugged the ground as she sprang at the creatures. They backed up, startled.

The people shouted. Behind Jillie, Coyote had started to change his form. His outline shimmered, and flowed into the shape of a human woman. His shape grew until he had become a very big woman, able to touch the roof of the cavern. She punched her hand into the roof of the cavern and made a hole large enough for her to continue to grow bigger. She enlarged the hole. Then she reached down, and picked up one of the people and carried it up out of the cave. The creatures became very angry when they saw this. Jillie understood that it was going to be her job to keep the creatures away from the people while the Changing Woman, who used to be Coyote, carried them out of the cave. The Changing Woman kept carrying the people up out of the cave. Jillie kept charging and snapping at the nasty creatures.

She dodged their claws as they tried to grab her. Not one of them laid a paw on her. She dodged, ducked, and turned, just like she would do if she were herding sheep in Wales. Finally, all the people were out of the cave, and the Changing Woman reached down and picked up Jillie in her huge hand. She raised her hand until Jillie, too, was out of the cave. The shape of the Changing Woman flowed upward too, and with a last wave of her hand, she sealed the entrance to the cavern below. As the cavern sealed, the Changing Woman changed back into Jillie's friend Coyote.

They were very far from Texas, Jillie saw. They were in a place where it was very dry. The sun was hot, and there were very tall mountains in the distance with snow on them. Jillie knew that there were no mountains like that in the land of Texas. She knew snow when she saw it, though, because once it had snowed at Andrea's house, and for a few hours the back yard was covered with cold icky white stuff. Laddy, of course, had loved it, and kept yapping and running and jumping in it.

There were some very tall bluffs across the valley from where they stood, and the people pointed to the cave openings they could see. Jillie could still not understand what they were saying, but it was clear that the people thought they would have a safe new home here.

Coyote looked at the people, and then he looked at Jillie. Silently, they backed away from the people, and trotted off down the path they found leading off the mesa. They trotted side-by-side, big Coyote and short Jillie, for a while. It wasn't long, though, before the trail started to look a lot like Texas. Coyote seemed to know where he was going. After a while, Jillie thought she knew where she was going too.

Soon, the field that the trail ran through looked a lot like the field behind Andrea's house. Coyote stopped at a branch path. He nudged Jillie with his muzzle. He licked the side of her face. Then he turned and ran up the trail without stopping and without looking back. Jillie stood watching him until she couldn't see him any more. Then she headed down the branch trail into the field behind Andrea's house.

She was far off in the field. She was on the other side of the creek, and she could just barely see Andrea's street and the houses in the gaps in the trees that lined the bed of the creek. She headed toward the wooden footbridge over the creek. She was suddenly very tired.

Just then, the brush in front of Jillie rustled and a bedraggled looking duck emerged, squawking violently at Jillie. Jillie could see that the duck had been hurt. One of her wings was very badly hurt. Jillie sat. The duck stopped squawking. The duck looked at Jillie. Jillie just sat. The duck quacked once. The duck quacked again. Then the duck flopped down at Jillie's feet, its chest heaving. Behind the duck, Jillie could see that she had almost come upon the duck's nest. It was a Mother Duck and it had a nest full of eggs that looked like they would hatch any minute. Carefully, Jillie picked up the Mother Duck in her mouth, and holding her tenderly, put her back in the nest with the eggs. Then Jillie curled up around the Mother Duck and the eggs until the Mother Duck came to. The eggs were starting to hatch, now, and between the two of them, the Mother Duck and the Mother Corgi, they got the ducklings out of their shells and prepared for life.

Jillie decided she needed to take the Mother Duck and the ducklings home. She barked until she got them all in a line, behind her. First came the Mother Duck, and then each duckling. She started them off behind her, and she came out of the field, onto the sidewalk in front of Gardening Lady's house. They marched like a little parade around the corner of the block and down the sidewalk to Andrea's house. Jillie marched them right up to the fence, and dug at the diggy hole until the hole was big enough for the Mother Duck and the ducklings to waddle through into the back yard. She led them through the back yard and up onto the deck.

Laddy woke up, and looked at the Mother Duck and the ducklings. He was a little wild eyed. He started to bark and bark. Jillie barked and barked. Andrea stopped swinging and came running to see what Jillie had. She stopped at the steps to the deck, stunned. For there on the deck were Laddy and Jillie, and the Mother Duck and six brand new ducklings.

"Mom, Mom!" Andrea shouted, "You'll never guess what Jillie found!"

THE DOG SHOW (FROM THE CORGI'S PERSPECTIVE)

by Millie Williams

A look at the show ring from the other end of the leash.

When the class was over, the Pembroke Welsh corgi sat in her crate, wiggled her toes, and began to count them. She knew it was very, very close. One toe, add four toes, add one toe, add four toes and again, four toes from today. Two toes left over, take away one. She sat there, thinking.

"Hey, Mr. Labrador!" she called out to the dog in the crate below her.

"Aah, yep, Honey Dog?" said the Lab back in his very slow and casual way of speaking.

"How many toes ya got?" she asked.

The lab considered this for a moment. "I have four on each foot and I have four foots…," he said.

Tierre was a little worried. What if she had figured wrong? What if the Labrador didn't understand math? She ventured, "Can you help me count my points? To make sure they are right?"

There was a brief pause, then the lab said, "Well, I wasn't very good at math. I know what a triple is in field work, and sometimes I get lost after that. But I will try to help you."

Tierre explained that she was trying to keep an accurate count of her points and how she did it. She explained once, twice, then three times. The lab thought he understood. But it was in a different way.

"Okey dokey, Honey Dog. Look at it this way. I have four foots and four toes on each foot." Tierre nodded. It sounded like he was getting it. "Now you have three wins of four points each." Tierre sighed. This could take a while. She tried to listen and not get confused with what he was saying.

"That takes up three foots and leaves you with one foot. On the one last foot, you have two single points. So that's two toes

counted. Now that leaves you with two toes. Then you take away one toe because it isn't needed. That leaves you with one toe that doesn't have a point. So you just need one point to finish your championship."

Oh! The lab had gotten it! And in a way that Tierre had not thought about! She wiggled with delight.

"Mr. Labrador, thank you, thank you!" she called out.

"Okey, dokey, Honey Dog," he called. "I'm glad you are almost there."

Tierre pushed her blanket about to make it more comfortable. She fished out the chewie that the Human had left behind for her.

"Hey, Mr. Labrador. Want to share a chewie?"

"Thanks, little one, but I got a good one down here right now. You go ahead and enjoy that one." This was accompanied by a furious wagging of his tail, and Tierre grabbed the bars of her crate, as she was sure it was going to wiggle and crash down with her inside of it. Too late, she remembered the advice that it was not a good thing to please a Labrador too much. They could be deadly, even though they didn't mean to be. She had heard stories of Labradors accidentally whacking corgis in the face with their killer tails. Finally, the small earthquake stopped as the Lab dug out his chewie and began to smack on it.

Tierre also settled down with her chewie. She wondered what was going on at home. Soon, she tired of chewing and closed her eyes for a bit. She could hardly wait to see what tomorrow at the show would bring.

The next day, there was much tension in the air. A famous handler and his famous dog were in Tierre's class. Tierre felt confident, even a little bit cocky, and marched into the ring like she owned it. She was getting the hang of this dog show stuff pretty good. She was glad that she had such a long lineage of show dogs behind her, each passing on tidbits of information that helped her do well in the show.

The famous judge walked up and down and looked at each girl. With measured deliberateness, she examined each corgi for outstanding features and flaws. Tierre was reminded of a poem that the Human liked to say at ringside:

Standing tall the judge looks and looks,
And tries to recall the standard book.

There was more, but she could not think about that now. She watched the Human and did all that was asked. Finally, after what seemed to be a very long time, the judge turned and pointed to a beautiful tricolor girl and told her she was the Winner's Bitch. Tierre blinked, not understanding. She looked to the Human for guidance. The Human's face told her all that she needed to know. She had not earned the last point for her championship. She felt tears coming and quickly turned away and rubbed her eyes with a beautiful white paw, then whirled around and stacked herself again. There was always the Reserve Winner's Bitch award, and she wasn't going to go home with nothing for the Human! Straight and tall she stood, making her mind empty so that she could concentrate. The famous judge approached and handed the Human a ribbon that was half purple and half white. Tierre wondered if she could cut the ribbon in half and glue two purple halves together to make a whole purple one.

They came out of the ring and made their way back to the grooming area. As she was lifted into the crate, she felt the tears coming. She had tried so hard! Her Human had groomed and showed her to perfection! What had happened?

"Honey Dog, how did you do today?" came a slow, deep voice. Tierre quickly rubbed her face on her fleece rug.

"Um, well, I guess I lost." A small silence followed.

"Did you try your best?" asked Mr. Labrador.

"Oh, yes!" she said and began to cry again.

"There, there, little one," the Labrador's soothing, deep voice said. "It all depends upon how you look at it. Remember when you were explaining how to count up on your toes and I showed you another way to do it?" He listened to the sniffling and continued. "There are many ways of looking at things. Were you last in your class?"

"Nooooo…" wailed Tierre. "I tried my hardest."

The Labrador interrupted the conversation by taking a long scratch at his neck, forcing Tierre to hold on for her life, and, for the moment, she forgot about crying and her worries.

"Well," said the lab, "let's look at it this way. What did you win?"

"A purple and white ribbon."

The lab thought hard. "That's a reserve ribbon. And the major held in points?"

"Yes," said Tierre, interested now in where this was going to go.

"Well, little one, this is a good thing! You tried your hardest. You are pretty and well mannered and well bred. You won a reserve to a major. Didn't you tell me this had happened to you before?"

"Oh, yes," she replied, "twice before. And my mother, Hayley, has lots of major reserves."

"And do you think less of your mother because of that?"

"Oh, no…" she trailed off. She could see where this was going. "Um. Mr. Labrador?"

"Yes, Honey Dog?"

"I won a reserve! To a major! I was one dog away from finishing my championship! I beat all the other dogs who were entered. That's not a bad thing, is it?"

Suddenly the earthquake struck again and she flung herself to the floor of the crate to hang on for dear life. She had managed to make that Labrador happy again, and his tail was wagging.

"Honey Dog, I think now you understand. It's not that you win, although that is a wonderful thing. If you cannot be in first place, then you must make the dog ahead of you break the record by being right on his tail. Do you see now?"

Tierre was a little uncertain about the tail part but she said, "Thank you for explaining it to me."

The next weekend, Tierre yawned as she watched the Human roll out of bed. It was late, much later than they normally arose. But it had been nice to just sleep in, without the hustle and bustle usually associated with the household waking up. The corgi liked sleeping in the same room as the Human. She thought that the motel was the strangest house she had ever seen. It was like upstairs in the house: a bathroom, and a bedroom with a TV, and a window that was useless, because she could not see out of it like she could the sliding glass door in the Human's bedroom. There was no kitchen here, nor a computer room, nor a living room.

After a while, the Human was ready and gave Tierre and Duncan, her uncle, some cookies to eat to settle their stomachs. This was a routine on a show day, and Tierre did miss her big breakfast that the Human usually gave her. But she knew she would be fed later on, and before that, there would be chicken to nibble on in the ring. It was her favorite part of showing. All she had to do was stand there and hold position and the Human would give her bits of chicken. It was a snap to do!

They went for a quick walk, and then the two corgis were settled in the back seat of the car while the Human packed up all their worldly goods. Then they went to the Restaurant of the Clown, where the Human ordered breakfast for herself. It smelled so good! Tierre tried hard to think of other things as they drove along.

Soon, they were at the show grounds and found a parking spot. The Human pulled something out of the bag. It was a hash-brown thing. Now, one thing all the corgis loved is a hash-brown thing. Mostly, the Human did not eat them, but shared them with the corgis that were with her. But sometimes she ate them herself, although the corgis had seen this occur more when she went into the Restaurant of the Clown than when she was driving along. The Human had been walking a lot and drinking water and taking vitamins and doing what she called "healthy things," so the corgis hoped that the delicious, greasy, wonderful smelling, calorie laden, crispy, hot, hash-brown thing would come their way.

And it did! Carefully the Human tore it into two equal pieces and gave half to each corgi. Uncle Duncan could hardly control his drool. This was a treat, indeed! After they had all finished their breakfasts, the Human got out of the car and spread a shade tarp over it. The day promised to be sunny, and she did not want her corgis to get too warm. There was a tree there, but she worried that the sun would move the shade. Then she went off to see the lay of the land.

While she was gone, Tierre had many things to think about. First, she reviewed all the points that a show dog must remember when it goes into the ring. Head up, look proud, and prance happily. Then she thought about her coat, and her enthusiasm wilted. There just wasn't any coat. It was all gone. It had been coming out in handfuls for weeks and weeks, and there were about a hundred hairs on her whole body. She sighed, deeply. What could she do?

Sensing her unhappiness, Duncan asked her what the trouble was. Carefully, she explained to him and was amazed when he laughed. He quickly explained that the lack of a coat was not to be penalized very much. It was the dog underneath that counted. Did she have perfect white teeth? Yes. Did she have correct conformation? Yes. Did she know her routine? Yes. Did she have pride in being fortunate enough to be born a corgi? Yes. Duncan explained that these were the qualities a judge would look for. If the judge felt that her coat was the only important thing, the judge wasn't knowledgeable enough, and she should not take it personally. Tierre brightened a bit at this.

When the Human came back, she set up the grooming table and went to work. Both corgis were brushed and combed and fluffed and shined up to within an inch of their lives. Both corgis enjoyed this part so much. It was the corgi equivalent of being at a spa. It was invigorating and they were charged up and ready to go.

After the Human picked up the armbands, the steward called Duncan into the ring. Now, Duncan had just decided that he was in love. There was a scrumptious smell just outside the entrance to the ring. He danced. He pranced. He flirted with the judge. He looked about, here and there for the beautiful girl that must have left such an incredible smell. Alas, he could not find her. The Human tried to smile gratefully at the judge for giving her any ribbon at all,

after that performance, and resolved to look up Uncle Bill, who was Duncan's sometime handler. She was getting tired of boys in love.

Next, it was Tierre's turn. "Go get'm, kid!" Duncan called out, as he turned round and round, trying to find the source of the heavenly smell again. Tierre's mouth was dry as she entered the ring. She found herself towards the end of the line of girls and this was fortunate, as it gave her a minute or two to think about what she had to do.

Up and down, round and round, this one put here, that one put there. The judge scrutinized the girls carefully and poked and prodded all of them, then rearranged them again. Finally, Tierre was at the head of the line. "Take them around again," called the judge, and Tierre knew she had to try her hardest to stay in the number one place. With every bit of grace she could muster, she flew around the ring and was overjoyed when the judge pointed at them. It was a point! It was the last toe! She bounced and wiggled and the Human picked her up and hugged and kissed her hard.

Then, they had to do it all over again! It was the Best of Breed competition, and Tierre's adrenaline level was still high. And she won this class, too!

Afterwards, walking through the crowd, she spotted her old friend, Mr. Labrador.

"Oh! Mr. Labrador!" Tierre waved hard and then pulled the Human as hard as she could over to where the lab was standing.

"Honey Dog! How are you? Oh, I have wondered how you were doing this weekend. Have you been in the ring, yet?"

Tierre explained that she had won, and won big. She was so proud to tell her friend all about it. The Human stood there with a perplexed look on her face, wondering why her small red corgi was making such a big deal over this sweet old Labrador.

"I am so very proud of you, Honey Dog. I'm sure your Human is, too. Now you go on your way with her and we'll talk another time. I expect that I'll see you again at the shows?" he said in his sweet and slow way.

Tierre reached up and gave him a big kiss right on his nose! The Labrador blushed slightly and wagged his tail. The Human really thought this was too much, to be so familiar with a strange dog. She turned and pulled Tierre along with her.

"Goodbye! Good Luck!" called Tierre, and the Labrador smiled in return.

Soon, they were all packed up and ready to go. The Human said goodbye to her friends, and Tierre and Duncan settled down for the long ride home. The air conditioner was on high, and they had worked hard all morning. It was time for a long nap. They turned this way and that, to get comfortable, and soon the only sound coming from the back seat was gentle snoring.

THE TALE OF THE OWL WHO WHO'S AT NOON

by Joe Novak, as told by Maggie

Joe Novak and Friar Tuck

The sun stood high in South Worcester County. Nay a breeze, nay a wisp of movement among the forest primeval. The silence hung heavy as da 'n me sat in our wooded acre.

"It's been one year to day," sez da wid a sadness about him. "One year ago from this date—on the second of August—Sir Guy of the Glen traveled over Bifrost Bridge—the Rainbow! And I miss him so!"

A call sounded out 'o the bog 'o our wooded acre, clear in the hazy, summer's day. "**Whhooooooo!**" Deep 'n booming it was as it carried through the hot 'n sweltering August air. "Whoo-hoo-hoo!" it continued one more time. Then quiet descended once again upon our wooded acre—a silence as loud as the call that had preceded it!

Dear ould da was startled from his reverie. "Bejabbers! What was that?" sez he, "An owl? From the sound 'o it: a Great Gray."

I recognized the cry; 'twas nay from an owl, Great Gray or otherwise. 'Twas a call from the maidenly Clotho, the spinner, one of the fate sisters who spins the threads of life. She resides in the land 'o the Fay wid her two sisters.

A flashing glimmer 'o light began to wink above the ould bog. A wee will-o-wisp floated toward da 'n me, then halted at the copse 'o aspen. A sound commenced from the bog. A buzzing like the static moan of a universe remembering its origins—microwaves left over from the big bang! The sound 'o a warding spell.

The will-o-wisp grew, 'n suddenly, there stood Gitchie Manitou. Upon one shoulder perched Clotho weaving a warding spell. But—wonders 'o wonder—by their side stood a corgi, alert, eyes bright and his fur the color 'o spun gold. A magnificent male in his prime.

"Sir Guy!" I gasped, "Sir Guy is that you?"

Guy looked up to the great Manitou who gave a nod. Wid a bark 'o joy, Guy bounded across the pasture, in full frap mode he cantered about us, his beautiful face reflecting the noonday sun.

Dear ould da was sleeping, affected by the warding spell, wid his closed eyes remming in dreamscape 'n a huge smile creasing his ould face. Da is transported to a field 'o clover, wid the sweetness 'o a summer's day. Sunlight silvers the lilac-shadowed stone wall; its light turns the purple lilac blossoms blue. A gentle breeze caress the lilacs and waves across the field 'o clover as though over an enchanted sea. 'N da fraps an enchanted frap wid a ghostly Guy among a field 'o gold.

'N da dances his ghostly dance wid the beautiful ghost he knew as a west wind moved across a field 'o barley. Da forgot the sun in his jealous sky as Guy frapped in fields 'o gold!

Wid a start, da woke from the land 'o dreams. "**Wow**! What a beautiful dream I had," he sez wid a smile in his voice.

"**Whoa**! What is **that**?" sez da. Music floats down from our house. It emanates from da's office. Tom T. Hall is singing—can that be? Yes! Its "Old Dogs and Children and Watermelon Wine."

We ran to da's office, but the music fades to silence, and da wonders if he is still in dreamscape. I detect a faint scent 'o ozone—is that pixie dust on da's CD player? Tom T. Hall's CD lies on da's desk in its flat, hinged container; a pixie-dusted paw print outlined in blue is shimmering on the cover.

We walk back outside and dream our dreams of peaceful sleep in shady summertime. Of old dogs and children and watermelon wine.

'TWAS THE NIGHT BEFORE CHRISTMAS– CORGI VERSION

by JoAnn Schmidt

(With apologies to Clement C. Moore)

drawing by
TASHA TUDOR

'Twas the night before Christmas, all was quiet as could be,
Not a creature was stirring, not even a flea;
All stockings were hung by the chimney with care,
Hoping that Santa Claus soon would be there;
Our Corgis were nestled all snug in their beds
With visions of chew toys dancing 'round in their heads;
The Missus in her nightgown and I in B.V.D's
Were counting our champions and arranging pedigrees,
When out in the driveway I heard a faint sound,
"It's nothing," I thought, "just a cat hanging 'round."

But I listened again, and I heard the word "SIT,"
Had I too much egg nog?–was I having a fit?
I sprang to our window, and through eyes bloodshot red,
Thought I glimpsed eight wee Corgis who were pulling a sled!?!?!?*
With a short little driver so lively and quick,
I couldn't be seeing a CORGI St. Nick!!!
He bounced from the sleigh with a leap of great zest,
And whistled and barked that his team take a rest.

"Heel, Rover! Down, Fido! Down, Bootsy! Sit Sable!
Down, Reddy! Down, Foxy! Stay, Shorty! Wait, Mable!
He gave praise and a treat as each dog did obey,'
Then prepared to leave them with the firm command: "STAY!"

As when the ideal dog performs in the ring,
Santa's team scored 200 — doing not one wrong thing!
Then up the front sidewalk, he labored with glee,
Pulled a bag full of dog toys much much bigger than he.

"This isn't for real–you're a dolt, you're a goof!"
I was telling myself, "next he'll be on your roof"
Then, overhead, sure enough, was a scuffling sound,
And down the chimney Corgi St. Nick came with a bound.

He WAS dressed in red fur from his head to white paws,
But some soot here and there tarnished K-9 Mr. Claus;
A bundle of toys was near crushing his back,
And he looked quite relieved to be lightening his pack.
His hazel eyes twinkled! His ears lay back with joy
As he carefully selected each Corgi's dog toy!
His droll little mouth was drawn up in that smile.
With which only a Corgi can bewitch and beguile!

The stump of this tail, he wagged with such glee,
That his whole body shook quite enthusiastically.
He had a fox face and a long, but round bod,
That wriggled with pleasure as he worked at his job.
He was spritely and gay - a real canine elf,
And I laughed when I saw him, in spite of myself.

But I blinked both my eyes, and I scratched at my chin,
Still wondering if this was some dream I was in.

He gave not a bark nor a yip nor a giggle,
But, with all stocking filled, he turned with a wiggle,
And, scampering to my feet, put his paws on my knees,
Gave my hand a quick lick and was off with the breeze.
He sprang to his sleigh, to his team gave a "BARK",
And away they all sped though the depths of the dark;
But I heard him exclaim, ere he drove out of view:
'MERRY CHRISTMAS TO YOU–AND TO ALL CORGIS TOO!"

COPYRIGHTS AND CREDITS

ARTICLES

Performance Events: Where the Action Is! Copyright 2002 by Lynda McKee. A previous version of this article appears on the Web site of the Pembroke Welsh Corgi Club of Greater Atlanta.

Herding With Corgis. Copyright 2001 by Elizabeth Trail. This article was originally posted on ShowPem-L and Corgi-L and various versions have since been used with permission in several Corgi newsletters in the US, Canada, and Australia. Excerpts appeared in the PWCCA Newsletter.

Getting Started in Tracking. Copyright 2002 by Lynda McKee. Parts of this article are adaptations from an invited article that I wrote for the Mayflower Pembroke Welsh Corgi Club *Corgi Cryer* in 1989, entitled An Introduction to Tracking. That article has been reprinted in the *First Ten Years of the Corgi Cryer* as well as in the *Pembroke Welsh Corgi Club of America Handbook.*

Warning! Copyright 2002 by Jamie L Longstreth.

Greta and Max. Copyright 1998 by Jamie L Longstreth

Bluebonnet Jillie. Copyright 1998 by Walt Boyes.

'Twas the Night Before Christmas–Corgi Version. Copyright 1974 by JoAnn Schmidt. First printed in the TIDE, December 1974.

"When You Wish upon a Star," lyrics by Ned Washington. Copyright 1940 by Walt Disney Productions.

ILLUSTRATIONS

The table of contents page 1, book pages 10, 18, 36, 114, 119, 120, 136, 152, 160, 172, 175, 200, 209 (dead bug): graphics courtesy of Andrea Adams

Pages 21, 49, 98, 113, 123, 124 : graphics courtesy of Pam Bliss

Page 230: graphic courtesy of Walt Boyes

Corgi lines on the title page, section dividers, introduction, and interlude pages, and margin pictures on left-hand interlude pages: graphics courtesy of Susan Brogan

Pages 209 (bunny butt), 210 (love), 217, 218, 222, 223: graphics courtesy of Debbi Hopkins

Table of contents page 2, the corgis in the introduction and right-page interlude margins, the corgis on top of each book page, illustrations on pages 19, 79 86, 138, 146, 166, 171, 176, 178, 182, 192, 210 (frog and fluff), 212, 226: graphics courtesy of Karena Kliefoth

The end page graphic courtesy of Keith Kirkpatrick

Page 3: graphic courtesy of Cathy Santarsiero

The cover, pages 9, 41, 94, 137, 191: graphics courtesy of Chris Vrba

Page 244: graphic courtesy of JoAnn Schmidt

PHOTOS

Page 185: Photo of Meg and Kenneth courtesy of Eleanor Britton

Pages 42, 48: photos courtesy of Barbara Bronczyk

Page 93: photo courtesy of Emily Calle

Page 185: photo of Lily courtesy of Ida Duplechin

Pages 148, 150, 151: photos courtesy of Robin Early

Page 207: photo courtesy of Raelene Gorlinsky

Page 183: photo of Pedro courtesy of Pat Griesmeyer

Pages 159, 181: photos courtesy of Linda Kerr

Page 216: photo courtesy of John Klaus

Page 145: photo courtesy of Patti Kleven

Pages 167, 170: photos courtesy of Linda Kriete

Page 199: photo courtesy of Kat Connor Lichtman

Page 112: photo courtesy of Jamie Longstreth

Page 211: photo courtesy of Jean Macak

Pages 8: photo courtesy of Nancy Matzke Moncrieff

Pages 141, 149, 164, 165: photos courtesy of Lynda McKee

Pages 225: photo courtesy of Peggy Neumeier

Page 20: photo courtesy of Cindy Nicotera

Page 242: photo courtesy of Joe Novak

Page 35: photo courtesy of Pat Pearce

Pages 229: photo courtesy of Cindy Read

Page 24, 118: photos courtesy of Arleen Rooney

Pages 69: photo courtesy of Florence Scarinci

Page 142: photo courtesy of Mary Elizabeth Simpson

Page 122: photo courtesy of Daphna Straus

Page 23: photo courtesy of Chris Vrba

Page 184: photo of Brinn Brin courtesy of Robin Walloch

Page 105: photo courtesy of Maenad Widdershin

Page 17: photo courtesy of Millie Williams

Page 184: photo of Sid and Tommy courtesy of Sid Wiseberg

Page 109: photo courtesy of Marilee Woodrow

A WARM AROOOOO OF THANKS FROM CORGIAID TO ALL WHO HAVE CONTRIBUTED TO THIS BOOK.

**Financial Support for Cardigan and
Pembroke Welsh Corgi Rescue**